KILLERS
NEVER SLEEP

KILLERS NEVER SLEEP

❧ A BUCK TRAMMEL WESTERN ❧

WILLIAM W. JOHNSTONE
AND J.A. JOHNSTONE

PINNACLE BOOKS
Kensington Publishing Corp.

www.kensingtonbooks.com

PINNACLE BOOKS are published by

Kensington Publishing Corp.
119 West 40th Street
New York, NY 10018

PUBLISHER'S NOTE: Following the death of William W. Johnstone, the Johnstone family is working with a carefully selected writer to organize and complete Mr. Johnstone's outlines and many unfinished manuscripts to create additional novels in all of his series like The Last Gunfighter, Mountain Man, and Eagles, among others. This novel was inspired by Mr. Johnstone's superb storytelling.

First Printing: January 2024
ISBN-13: 978-0-7860-4972-1
ISBN-13: 978-0-7860-4976-9 (eBook)

10 9 8 7 6 5 4 3 2 1

Printed in the United States of America

CHAPTER 1

Sheriff Trammel loaded his Winchester while Constable Merle Peyton of Woodbine Township repeated his story to the deputies.

"It's him, boys," the volunteer lawman told them. "It's Ben Washington himself. Don't let these old eyes fool you. I saw him as clear as I'm seeing each of you right now. He rode right past my store as bold as brass in broad daylight and looked me over as if I were nothing to nobody. And me knowing him since before he took his first steps, too." The old man rubbed his arms for warmth. "Never saw such a cold look in a man's eyes, at least not while he was still breathing."

Deputy Sherwood Blake and Deputy John "Hawkeye" Hauk had been in Trammel's office when the constable had first rushed to town to tell them the outlaw was in the county.

Hawkeye's question was for the benefit of the rest of the deputies listening. "Why did you come here instead of Cheyenne? It's the same distance between Woodbine and here. The warrant on Washington is federal and they've got deputy U.S. Marshals there."

"On account of Lefty Rollins being the only one in the

capital," Peyton explained. "His men are spread out all over the territory serving warrants or bringing men in for trial. Lefty was good in his day, but those days are long gone."

Hawkeye asked another question. "You're sure it was Ben Washington?"

"I had the displeasure of watching him grow up," Peyton said. "That was a long time ago, but he's the image of his old man now. Short and scrawny with a mess of wild hair that not even a good dunking in a barrel of rainwater could tame. He's got his father's look about him, too. That same arrogant swagger, even on horseback. I saw him stop by the Watering Hole Saloon first before he rode past my store on his way to his folk's old spread at the edge of town."

The constable pawed at his long white beard as he continued to tell them what he had seen. "I know Ben's a wanted man, Sheriff, and I'll admit I was trying to get up enough courage to arrest him as soon as he came out of the saloon. But when he did, I couldn't bring myself to do it. I couldn't even move out of my own doorway. I just stood there like an old scarecrow in a field. He's killed better men than me. Younger men, too. I . . ."

"Knock it off." Trammel had always liked Merle Peyton and did not want to see him needlessly punish himself. "Washington would've killed you if you'd gone anywhere near him. You did the right thing by coming straight here as soon as you could. You said you think he was visiting his folks?"

"No. I said he was going out to their old spread," Peyton clarified. "The bank here in Laramie threw his folks off their land a few years ago, long after Ben became an outlaw. His family had fallen behind on their payments to the bank."

Peyton's eyes got that far away look again. "I'd warned Ben's father not to buy that land. I've lost count of how many men have tried to make something out of that place and failed over the years. But being a Washington, he was always too stubborn and proud to listen. Some folks in those parts think the land is cursed and given the way Ben Washington turned out, I'm inclined to agree with them. That boy's always had something of the devil about him, even when he was just learning how to walk."

Trammel did not know much about Ben Washington except by his reputation. He and his gang were the most wanted bunch west of the Mississippi. They had raided wagon trains, stagecoach lines, and railroad strong boxes for years. There was hardly a bank in the Wyoming Territory that they had not robbed yet, but Laramie's bank was one of them.

Trammel did not know much about Woodbine Township, either, except that it was a tiny settlement on the outskirts of the county in the opposite direction of Blackstone. Peyton's general store, the Watering Hole Saloon, and a blacksmith were the only businesses that met the immediate needs of the few farms and ranches scattered around it. He knew they always came to Laramie for their more important needs and large orders each season but preferred to keep to themselves.

Deputy Blake finished checking his pistol and holstered it. "You think Ben Washington came to town looking for his folks, Merle?"

"I don't think so," the constable said. "I heard his folks died soon after they lost the place. First his mother, then his father. I think he might be looking for some kind of revenge."

"Any idea on where he is now?" Deputy Gary Bush asked.

Peyton did. "I might've been frozen stiff when Ben fixed me with a stare, but I followed him a good ways to see where he was heading. I watched him run down Lou Finney while he was working one of his horses in the corral, then herded Lou and his children back into the house. They're the people who took over the old Washington spread. Lou's wife had been putting clothes out on the line to dry at the time, and Ben got hold of her, too."

Trammel finished loading the last round into his rifle. "How many kids does Finney have and how old are they?"

"A boy and a girl around six or seven. The mother, Mary, looked like she might be working on their third, but I can't say for certain."

Trammel knew the presence of women and children in the house would make getting Ben Washington out of there tricky, assuming he was still there. "Do you think he might've left by now?"

Merle Peyton's hands began to shake. "If he hasn't already killed them and moved on, he'll be there. I stopped by the Watering Hole and asked the bartender what Washington did while he was there. He told me Ben was asking questions about who had moved into his family's place and the drunks were foolish enough to tell him. I guess he's blaming the Finneys for moving onto his parents' land, not that it was their fault. If anyone was to blame for them losing it, it was the bank here in Laramie, not the Finneys."

Deputy Blake folded his arms and asked Trammel, "How do you want us to handle this, Buck?"

Trammel knew there was only one way available to them. He looked out the window at the darkening sky. "Woodbine's a little over an hour's ride from here. It'll be dark by the time we get there, which is good for us."

He looked at his deputies. All of them knew how dangerous Ben Washington was, yet each man was eager to play a part in bringing him in. But Trammel had to consider Laramie's safety first. No one man was more important than an entire town.

"I wish I could take all of you with me, but with Hagen's Cattleman's Association convention going on over at The Laramie Grand right now, I need most of you to stay here in case things get out of hand."

He nodded toward Hawkeye, the youngest deputy in his office, who had also been his partner during his days as the town marshal in Blackstone. Despite his tender years, he had proven himself to be a good deputy. "You'll be in charge while I'm gone. Make sure those cattlemen don't have too much of a fun time at the town's expense. Keep them in the hotel if you have to. Blake and I will ride back to Woodbine with Merle to bring Washington here where he belongs. We'll hold him downstairs until his trial."

He saw the men trade curious glances amongst themselves. He knew they might not agree with his decision to leave Hawkeye in charge while he was gone, but they did not have to like it. "You boys better get out there and make sure you're visible. Don't tell anyone about Washington being around or we're liable to have a lot of scared citizens on our hands. Blake and I will be back as soon as we can."

Hawkeye spoke up as he led his fellow deputies out of the office. "Let's head over to Hagen's place and spread out from there. Those cattlemen will have a snoot full of liquor in them by now and we'll want them to know we're around."

Trammel waited until Blake was the last man in his office before he told the constable, "I know you're nervous, Merle. All you have to do is lead us there. Blake and me will take care of the rest."

Peyton continued to flatten his beard as he stood. "Woodbine's not much of a town, sheriff, but it's mine. I buckled under Ben Washington once, but I won't do it again. You can count on me. I'll go get my horse."

Trammel began to follow the constable when Blake held him back. "A quick word, Sheriff?"

Trammel let Merle Peyton go ahead. "Make it quick. The Finneys don't have much time."

Blake checked to make sure Peyton was out of earshot before saying, "Putting Hawkeye in charge of the men was a mistake. Charlie Root's next in line. It should've been him."

Trammel and Blake had not always agreed on what was best for the town, but he was disappointed that he had brought it up at such a delicate time. "Root might be the senior man, but Adam Hagen is throwing a big party for his cattleman buddies over at his saloon tonight. You know how he likes to cause trouble and Hawkeye's the only one he'll listen to besides me."

"And if Hagen breaks the law, he ought to pay for it," Blake said. "Make an example of him. I thought we're supposed to enforce the law, even with our friends."

Trammel was in no mood to explain himself, not even to his senior deputy. "We're paid to keep the peace, Blake. We have a better chance of doing that if Hagen listens to reason." He took his Winchester from his desk and beckoned Blake to move. "Now, if there are no further objections, I'd like to grab Ben Washington before he gets around to killing that family."

Adam Hagen did not even pretend to follow the conversation as the cattlemen discussed their business. He had not invited them to hold their annual meeting at The Laramie Grand because he wanted to become a rancher. He had invited them here so he could begin to reacquire power throughout the Wyoming Territory. Power on his terms.

Just about the only thing Hagen liked better than showing off was showing off in style. And as the owner of The Laramie Grand, he could finally do what he loved most.

The suite where he now entertained cattlemen from across the territory and beyond was the jewel in his tarnished crown. He had survived many lean years since leaving the army. Scrounging to make a living on the riverboats that paddled their way up and down the mighty Mississippi River. Scaring up card games wherever he could in cow towns like Abilene and Dodge City. He had been forced to return to Wyoming when his luck ran out in Kansas, and he had hoped to take his birthright from his father up in Blackstone. He had not been expecting his family to rob him of the fortune he had long schemed to control one day.

But Laramie had made him a new man. He not only controlled all the biggest saloons in town, but now, the hotel that had once been known as The Tinder Box Saloon had risen from the ashes of his ambition to become the very embodiment of his dreams. Hagen had succeeded in rebuilding his life and mortgaged everything he owned into making The Laramie Grand an oasis of opulence in the Wyoming Territory.

Everything in the hotel had been crafted to his exact specifications. Here in his suite and throughout the hotel, fine drapery and ornate furnishings gave the place a warm, inviting feeling that spoke of great luxury. The gaming floor had been modeled after some of the finest gambling dens he had visited during his time in New Orleans and was designed to attract a similar, well-heeled clientele.

Here in his office suite, he held court. The furniture was heavy, and the fabric on the cushions expensive. Even his oaken desk sported intricate carvings of Greek gods holding up the tabletop. The liquor the cattlemen drank had come all the way from Scotland. The lobsters and crab had been brought by train from Boston. And the women on each man's arm had been brought to Laramie from the finest houses in New Orleans at considerable expense.

Hagen was pleased to see his guests had been suitably impressed by his efforts, which was why Hagen had brought them here. He had not invited them to The Laramie Grand simply because he wanted to host a party or spread word about his new hotel. Bringing the leading cattlemen from across the territory was an investment in Hagen's future standing. His reputation had suffered a great deal after his family had turned their backs on him. Events like these could help him regain the influence he had lost.

Hagen looked beyond his current cluster of new acquaintances and noticed two men who had taken a particular interest in his safe. Unlike most businessmen, he had chosen to not hide it and made it the centerpiece of the room. He had taken considerable pride in designing the iron monster with the expectation that a few select guests would not only see it but marvel at it. At six feet in height and almost as wide as a grown man, the safe was as imposing as it was formidable. He wanted these men to see that any attempts to open it would be pointless. And that any money they decided to invest in his hotel would be well guarded.

Hagen had long grown bored with the conversation around him and begged their pardon as he walked over to the two men eyeing the monstrosity. He remembered he had greeted them when they had first arrived at the hotel but could not remember their names.

"I can see you gentlemen appreciate fine art when you see it," Hagen told them as he gestured with his glass toward the safe. "She's a beauty, isn't she?"

"I'll say." The taller of the two men sported a wide, drooping moustache. "Special construction from the looks of it."

Hagen was curious. "You know about safes, Mister . . . ?"

"Carter," the man shook Hagen's hand. "Wayne Carter. Got a nice spread of our own up north of here." He nodded at the man with him. "This is my brother Burt. And as for safes, I wouldn't say I'm an expert, but I can tell you didn't order this out of a catalogue."

Hagen could not remember inviting anyone by the name of Carter to attend the cattlemen's convention. He would be sure to have his man, Rube Miller, look into them later.

"That's because the only catalogue I consulted was right here." Hagen tapped his temple. "It's entirely of my own design. I sketched out how I wanted it to look, what I wanted it to be, and the ironsmiths in Cincinnati did the rest. I told them to make her impregnable, and they did." He knocked on the door and remarked on the lack of an echo. "Solid iron and the door is grooved so it's nearly impossible to pry open. The locking mechanism is an innovative design from the Yale Lock Company in New England. The combination lock has a timer on it so not even I can open it except during specific times."

Burt Carter cut loose with a low whistle. "I imagine a custom piece like this must've set you back quite a ways."

Hagen caught a hint of a familiar accent when the brothers spoke. A laziness about the way they pronounced their *t*'s. "I hear you two have spent some time in New Orleans."

Wayne did a better job of hiding his surprise than his brother. "Where'd you hear that?"

"From you just now," Hagen said. "The Cajun inflections are subtle but there if you know what to listen for. I spent a considerable amount of time in New Orleans on the riverboats of the Mississippi, so I'm more aware of it than most. I hope I didn't offend you by pointing it out."

Burt looked relieved. "No offense at all, Mr. Hagen. It's just that we're ranchers now and we want these folks to take us seriously. New Orleans isn't exactly a cow town."

Hagen could appreciate a man wanting to change his past but imagined there was more to the Carter boys than that. He decided there was nothing to be gained at the moment by dwelling on it. "I'm sure you'll fit in just fine, as long as your money's real and your credit is good." He returned his attention to the safe. "That's why I put so much effort into building this masterpiece. Sometimes, a man has to be willing to spend money if he hopes to make it. And I plan on keeping this baby well fed with cash from my gaming floor downstairs. And seeing as how you two are from New Orleans, I'm sure you found the surroundings familiar."

"I thought it reminded me of The Beau Soleil," Burt confessed. "Now I know why."

Hagen knew the gambling den well. "I hope it brought back fond memories."

Wayne laughed. "Some of the best times I can't remember were in The Beau Soleil."

"A toast, then." Hagen raised his glass. "Here's hoping The Laramie Grand can offer you a time you won't soon forget."

The men drank and Hagen decided to take the conversation in a new direction. "What did you say the name of your ranch was up north?"

"The Bar C," Wayne said as his brother hesitated. "We've only been at it for a year or so, but it's already showing great promise. Got ourselves a couple of prized bulls all the way from Texas we think will help us build a fine herd in a few years."

Hagen had heard of most of the ranches worth knowing in the territory, but the Bar C sounded like a small concern. If it was real. He gestured toward the other guests who were occupied with pretty women who forced themselves to laugh at unfunny jokes that were in poor taste. "You should have no trouble making some new friends here, that is if you can pry them away from the bar and the gambling tables long enough. You'll find they're a good bunch on the whole and not above willing to help when they can. Provided there's something in it for them, of course."

"Of course," Wayne said, "thought I must admit that Burt and I aren't used to this kind of soiree. You grew up around people like this, what with you being King Charles's son and all."

Hagen tried not to think much of Charles Hagen these days. He had learned too late that the man had only been an uncle, not his real father. Charles had raised him but had spent the rest of his life making Adam pay dearly for his illegitimacy. "I may have been to the manor born, but I made my own way in life. Hence my time down in New Orleans."

Burt raised his glass. "To self-made men."

Hagen was glad to drink to that. "I'm sure I've occupied far too much of your time, gentlemen. Move around a bit. Make some friends and not just of the feminine persuasion. I think you'll find it rewarding."

Wayne said, "We wouldn't be here if we didn't think we could get something out of it."

Hagen bid them goodbye and began to move around the room. He caught the eye of Rube Miller, the man he had hired on to keep an eye on his gaming floor and beckoned him to follow him to a quieter corner of the suite.

Miller had made the unfortunate choice to comb forward what little hair he had left into something of a pomade. He sported a waxed moustache that curled at the ends and preferred to wear coats with obscenely wide lapels.

But what Miller may have lacked in sartorial elegance, he more than made up for in his supervision of the gaming floor. Like Hagen, he was an old card sharp who had worked the riverboat circuit for years. He could spot a cheat from halfway across the room.

"Fine party, Mr. Hagen," Miller said when he joined him. "I'm sure you must be pleased."

"Concerned is more like it." He kept his back to the Carter boys. "What do you make of those two characters standing over by the safe?"

Miller casually glanced around the suite. "They say they're the Carter boys out of the Bar C. They say it's a small outfit north from here."

"I know, but I sense there's something more Cajun than cattlemen about them. They told me as much just now. Wayne covers his accent better than his brother, but Burt has the Delta written all over him."

"I caught that, too." Miller raised an eyebrow. "Guess

that's why he always kept quiet the few times I've spoken to them."

"Are they staying in the hotel?"

Miller nodded. "I helped them check in the day before yesterday. They brought their four brothers with them, but they came later, and I haven't seen them since. They've got a line of connecting suites on the fourth floor. I'm surprised the others aren't here."

Hagen was more troubled than surprised. "Have some of our boys keep an eye on them. And get some of our belles to pay them particular attention. I don't want them followed but keep track of where they go and what they do while they're here. They were a little too interested in my safe for my liking."

"Done."

"And send a wire down to our people in New Orleans. See if they know of any Carter boys. I'll be shocked if they do. Include a description of Wayne. Something tells me 'Carter' isn't their real last name."

Miller set his glass on a table. "I'll do it right now."

After his pit boss left, Hagen began to check on his guests and noticed the Carter boys were nowhere in sight. An interesting turn of events, especially for a couple of cattlemen looking to get their start in the enterprise.

CHAPTER 2

Night had already fallen on Woodbine as Trammel, Blake, and Constable Peyton reached the Finney spread. It was a clear evening, and the moon hung high overhead. A lone horse in the corral lifted its head as it caught their scent, but quickly went back to nosing the dirt at its hooves.

The three lawmen climbed down from their horses and tethered the animals to the branches of a tree.

Merle Peyton squinted at the log cabin in the distance. "I can see lights from inside. I sure hope that's a good sign the family's still alive."

Trammel pulled his rifle from the saddle scabbard and Blake did the same.

Trammel asked Peyton, "You ever go inside the house?"

"Plenty of times," the constable told him. "There's two ways in. The front door and a side door to the left. Mary uses that to hang wash and tend to a small garden she has out back. Both doors have thick beams that keep them locked, but I don't know if they've used them now."

Trammel had to think that Ben Washington had probably slid them in place as soon as he moved the family inside. He would not want to risk one of his captives making a break for it.

Since Blake had been quiet since their brief argument in his office, Trammel decided to ask his deputy, "How do you think we should do this?"

He was not surprised that Blake already had an idea. "One of us hits the front door while the other hits the side. We leave Merle out here to keep an eye on things and call out if Washington gets past us."

Peyton took down his double-barreled shotgun from his saddle. "It'll be that outlaw who calls out if he steps one foot outside. I'll give him a belly full of lead for his trouble."

Trammel was glad to see some fight had returned to the old constable. "We'll creep up together nice and slow. Merle, you'll crouch behind the corral there and stand watch. Blake, you take the side door while I take the front. When you're ready, give a low whistle, and we'll try both doors at the same time. We'll do it easy at first, so we don't make any noise before we go in. If your door is barred, come back front to me. We'll see if we can get a shot at him through one of the windows."

Blake levered a round into the chamber of his Winchester. "Got it."

Trammel was not through. "Washington's liable to grab the woman once we bust in there, so don't rush the shot. Aim careful and only shoot if you think you can take him. I'll do the same."

The three men spread out along the path as they silently made their way toward the rough-hewn cabin. Trammel kept his eyes moving constantly in the darkness. The horse in the corral trotted to the far side of the enclosure as they approached but did not make a sound.

Peyton remained behind Trammel as Blake broke off from the group toward the side door of the cabin.

Then, a dog began to bark from somewhere behind the house.

Trammel stopped moving and whispered back at Peyton. "You didn't tell me they had a dog."

"That's because I didn't know they did," Peyton whispered back. "Washington must've put it outside to keep from getting bit."

Trammel cursed under his breath as he began to move quicker toward the cabin. When he got to the edge of the corral, he gestured for Peyton to remain there while he continued on in a crouch. He kept his eyes on the windows and saw someone pass in front of the light, casting a shadow on the glass.

From inside, he heard a man say, "What's that mutt barking about?"

"Probably caught scent of a wolf or a coyote," a woman said. Her voice was hoarse and strained as if she had been crying. "He's good at that. It's why we keep him around. He's not used to spending so much time outside. He usually spends the night in here with us."

At six foot five inches tall and over two hundred and thirty pounds, Trammel had never been light on his feet, but moved as gingerly as he could onto the front porch of the cabin and approached the door as the dog continued to bark.

"Find a way to shut him up," he heard Washington say, "or I'll shut him up for good."

Mary said, "How do you expect us to do that if you have us cooped up in here with a gun to our heads?"

"Better a gun to your head," Washington shouted, "than a bullet in your brain. Now figure out how you get that mutt quiet before I do it my way!"

Trammel gripped his rifle tightly as he tried the door. It gave a little but not enough to open. Washington must have put the bar across it. He hoped Blake had better luck on his side of the cabin.

Trammel moved to the window and took a quick look inside. He saw a man he took to be Lou Finney on the floor in front of the fireplace. His head was bandaged. His hands were tied behind his back. A boy and a girl were bound and gagged beside him. Tear streaks stained their cheeks.

Mary Finney was between them, stroking her children's hair while they quietly wept against her.

Trammel felt his temper begin to build.

Ben Washington loomed over them with a Navy Colt in his hand. Merle's description of the outlaw had been right. He was probably about forty or so but looked much older. He had the long, gaunt look of a man who had not had a decent meal or a night's sleep in days.

The dog out back began to bark and whine even louder now as Blake had undoubtedly reached the side door. Trammel strained to listen for his deputy's whistle, but the dog was making too much noise for him to hear clearly.

Washington brought his free hand up to his eyes and cried out, "I've had it with that mutt. If he wants to bark, I'll give him something to bark about."

Trammel heard Mary and the children cry out as Washington stormed toward the side door.

The outlaw turned and waved his pistol in their direction. "And if one of you makes a sound, I'll come back in here and do the same to you."

Trammel could hear Washington was close to losing control of himself. And when the outlaw moved toward the side door, Trammel knew it was time to move.

He rocked to the edge of the small porch and threw all of his considerable bulk against the door.

The nails of the braces holding the bar across the door creaked and gave way as the door burst inward and Trammel stumbled inside.

Mary and the children screamed as Trammel brought his rifle up to his shoulder and aimed it at Washington.

Trammel saw the outlaw drop to a knee just before Trammel fired. His bullet went wide and struck the table in the kitchen.

Washington snapped off a shot that hit the open door instead of Trammel, before he launched himself at Trammel's midsection.

The impact carried both men backward and out onto the porch, where they tumbled to the ground.

Washington was much lighter and first on his feet as he began to aim his Navy Colt down at Trammel just as the sheriff kicked out with his boot and knocked it away.

Trammel rammed the butt of his Winchester hard into Washington's chest. He stumbled backward but remained on his feet as Trammel got to a knee and tried another thrust at the outlaw. But the wiry man dodged it and fired a roundhouse right that struck the sheriff flush on the temple.

The impact knocked Trammel to the side, causing him to drop his rifle as he tried to keep his balance.

Washington dove for his Colt, which had landed nearby, but Trammel blindly stabbed out and grabbed the man's right wrist, pinning it to the ground.

The desperate outlaw began to pummel him with his free hand, firing elbows down on the back of his head.

Trammel brought his head up quickly, connecting with

the base of Washington's jaw as he wrenched the pistol from his hand.

And as Trammel rose to his feet, he backhanded Washington with his own pistol, dropped it, and delivered a crushing right hand of his own that connected flush with the outlaw's nose.

Washington fell to the ground unconscious.

Blake and Merle Peyton rushed to Trammel's side as he stood over the bleeding outlaw.

"Well, I'll be," the constable said. "I never saw a man get hit that hard in my whole life. I figure he's dead."

"I didn't hit him hard enough to kill him." Trammel flexed his right hand. He did not think he had broken any bones, but it hurt something fierce. "Tie him up and get him on his horse. You have a place where we can keep him locked up for the night?"

Washington yelped as Peyton pulled his arms behind him and tied them with a length of rope he had brought. "We've never had call for a formal jail, but I've got a room in back of my store that ought to suit him."

From behind him, Blake said to Trammel, "Didn't you hear me whistling? The back door wasn't locked. I was planning on taking him from there."

"That dog was making too much noise for me to hear you," Trammel said. "What do you think about the idea of using Merle's storeroom for the night?"

"Not much," Blake said. "Washington's never been known to ride alone. He didn't just come here by accident, either. He's liable to be meeting some men here or nearby. Cheyenne is a bit tricky to find in the dark. I say we ought to bring him back to Laramie tonight where we know he'll be safe."

That was Trammel's thinking, too, as he watched the old constable struggle to pull the outlaw to his feet.

Washington complained as Merle kept hold of him. "My nose is busted. It's bleeding something awful."

Even in the weak lamplight that spilled out from the cabin, Trammel saw the amount of blood on the ground where Washington had fallen. "Keep a civil tongue in your head and I won't break your jaw."

Washington cursed and tried to spit at him. Trammel sidestepped it and landed a hard left jab flush against his temple, causing his knees to buckle. Blake helped Peyton keep the outlaw upright.

Trammel said, "Merle, you'd best fetch his horse. We'll drape him over the saddle and tie him in place for the ride back to Laramie. Blake here will keep an eye on him for you."

"Sheriff Trammel," Mary Finney called to him from the porch. "My family and I can't thank you enough for saving us like that. That animal would've killed us. I could feel it in my bones."

Trammel left Washington with Blake as he walked toward the frightened woman. "It wasn't just me, Mrs. Finney. You ought to thank Constable Peyton for riding to Laramie to get us and Deputy Blake here for coming up with the plan. If I hadn't gotten Washington, he would've." He remembered how her family had been tied up near the fireplace. He looked inside and saw the two children were tending to their father. "Looks like your husband had a pretty bad time of it."

Mary's eyes narrowed as she looked past Trammel at Washington. "That man over there beat him senseless as soon as he got us inside." She brought a hand to her left cheek and Trammel saw it was beginning to bruise. "He hit me, too, when I tried to stop him. But my husband is tough, sheriff. He'll be better in a few days."

"I'm glad to hear it." Trammel wished he could do more to help her, but she seemed to have everything in the cabin well in hand. "I'll see to it that he's charged for what he did to you today, but it'll be at the end of a pretty lengthy list. He's wanted in three territories, so I imagine Marshal Rollins will send a man to Laramie to take him into custody in a couple of days."

He watched the young Finney girl soak a rag in a bucket and hold it against a cut on her father's head. He was sad the children had to see their father in such condition. "I wish I could promise you he'll pay for this, but we can only hang him once."

Mary Finney's expression soured as she watched Merle Peyton bring Washington's horse from the barn. "Hanging's too good for a man like him."

Trammel did not know how to answer that, so he went to help the others put Washington on his horse.

CHAPTER 3

Back at The Laramie Grand Hotel, Adam Hagen strained to hear what young Hawkeye was trying to tell him, but the cattlemen he was hosting were enjoying the free women, liquor, and cigars he had provided them. He beckoned the deputy to follow him through the lobby and outside where they would not have to shout at each other.

When they reached the thoroughfare, Hagen placed his hands on his knees and coughed. "I think you just saved my life, Hawkeye. I love a good cigar as much as the next man, but it's worse than a chimney in there."

Hawkeye rubbed his eyes. "It sure was smokey. I haven't been inside the place since you finished working on it. It sure is a far cry from when it used to be called The Tinder Box."

"I'm glad you like it." Hagen had long admired the boy's grit, even back in Blackstone. He had proven his mettle a few months before when he helped bring the escaped Lucien Clay and his cohorts to justice. "Now, what is it you were trying to tell me in there?"

"I was telling you that Buck wants you to do your best to keep the party inside. He knows these cattlemen can get pretty wild, so he thinks it's best if they stay in one place. We wouldn't want any of your guests spending a night in jail."

Hagen never ceased to be surprised—and slightly disappointed—by how limited Trammel's grasp of a situation could be. "I'm not giving them free liquor and companionship because I like them. I'm doing it because I want them to spend money at my gambling tables. I want to keep them here more than Trammel." But he was curious. "Buck usually likes to stride in and threaten me in person. Why'd he send you instead?"

Hawkeye placed his hands on his hips as he looked away. "Afraid I can't tell you that."

Now Hagen was more than merely curious. "It's me, Hawkeye, not some town gossip. I've ridden with him longer than you have. He's not in trouble again, is he?"

"Probably not." Hawkeye's face reddened. "Me and my big mouth. I'm always saying too much at the wrong time."

Hagen knew the boy would only grow quiet if he pushed him for information, so he took a softer approach. "You haven't said anything yet, but if he needs my help, I'd want to be able to offer it."

"I guess you've got a point." He watched Hawkeye close his eyes as he wrestled with his conscience. "If I tell you, you can't breathe a word of it to anyone, at least not for a while. The sheriff would skin me alive if he found out."

Hawkeye, for all his youth, knew Hagen well. "I'll be as silent as the tomb. What's going on?"

The deputy looked around to make sure no one was listening before saying, "Merle Peyton told us Ben Washington's holed up over in Woodbine. Took a family captive. The sheriff and Sherwood Blake went over to get him about an hour ago. I expect they've made it there by now."

"Ben Washington?" Hagen thought it was almost too good to be true. "Here in Laramie? Why?"

"Merle didn't know that much," Hawkeye told him, "but he saw him buffalo a family that moved into his father's old ranch. Blake and the sheriff went over there to save them."

Hagen knew Merle. The man had been old when Hagen was still a boy. He had always been a bit touched in the head, but he was no fool. If he said he saw Ben Washington, it was true, but it did not make any sense. "Washington's never been the careless kind. He would've known someone in Woodbine was bound to recognize him. He's always been too smart to put himself against the likes of Buck. That's why he's managed to stay free for as long as he has."

"I can't speak for Washington's reasons," Hawkeye admitted, "but I imagine we'll know more by the morning. The sheriff and Blake ought to be back in town by then, that is if Washington doesn't get past them."

Hagen did not know Washington, but he knew Buck Trammel. He doubted the outlaw had ever gone up against the likes of him. Washington may have taken a family captive, which would have given him an advantage against another lawman. But as many had learned before him, it was better to stay as far away from Trammel as possible.

Hagen felt the spark of an idea form in his stomach. Yes, he might know what Trammel could do, but not everyone was so well informed. Especially not his cattlemen guests. Trammel had built a solid reputation for law and order, but Washington had a much larger reputation for being a dangerous menace to society.

Perhaps there was some money to be made from the cattlemen's ignorance. He had already sunk every cent he could beg, borrow, and steal into making The Laramie

Grand a success. If he played this right, he might just get his investment to pay off quicker than he had hoped.

"Uh-oh," Hawkeye said, breaking Hagen's concentration. "I've seen that look in your eye before. Never saw any good come from it."

But Hagen was too taken with his idea to allow the young deputy to ruin it for him. "You can tell your men I promise to keep my guests in my hotel, Hawkeye, on the condition that each of them feels free to stop in for a drink and a meal come suppertime. Anything they want. On me. I insist. Now, if you'll excuse me, I have guests to tend to." He patted Hawkeye on the shoulder as he hurried back inside.

Hawkeye called after him, "You'll remember to keep what I told you between us, won't you, Mr. Hagen?"

Hagen turned and threw open his hands as he backed into his hotel. "Remember it? I plan to profit handsomely from it."

He enjoyed the look of confusion on Hawkeye's face. He knew the boy would be disappointed in him for what he was about to do, but he would be sure to make it up to him. If his seedling of an idea flowered, there would be plenty of money in it for everyone.

Hagen ignored the questions from his staff at the front desk as he walked through the marble lobby and entered the gaming area to the left. The hotel had already been open a month, so the clerks knew how he liked to run things. It was high time for them to start making some decisions on their own.

He spotted Janine, the lovely hostess who had brought her troupe of dancing girls all the way from New Orleans, as she helped one of the cattlemen lose at the dice table. He caught her eye and gestured for her to join him.

She often affected a French accent when she was keeping the customers company but dropped the act whenever they were alone. Laramie was the farthest she had been from Louisiana in her life.

"Your timing's lousy," she said through a smile. "That idiot back there is about to lose a fortune."

"We stand to make a great deal more," he told her as he watched the crowd. "Where's Rube? I need to speak to him."

"He's in the back room dealing faro to a bunch of high rollers," Janine said. "They asked for him personally. He left Oren to mind the store."

Hagen had greater concerns than a single faro game. "Go get him for me, will you? And be quick about it. It's important."

As he watched Janine glide through the crowd of gamblers to tell Rube he wanted to see him, he took a measure of pride in how the place had turned out. There was no hint of the old bucket of blood it had once been. He had only bought the former Tinder Box Saloon for its location in the heart of Laramie.

He had spent every cent he had and every bit of credit the bank offered him to make this place the finest hotel in the territory. He had tripled the size of the old place and gave it a European flair. Brass fixtures, oil paintings, and rich, padded maroon wallpaper gave it class with a slightly decadent aura.

An ornate wooden bar was at the very heart of the building. The left side of it catered to the gamblers while the right side served as a formal salon for hotel guests who preferred to not partake in games of chance.

It was still early, but word was already spreading about

the grandeur of the new hotel. Hagen had hoped the place might begin to turn a profit within a year or so.

But once he put his new plan in place, there was no reason why he could not pay off his bank loan by the end of the month.

He was glad to see Rube Miller cut his way through the crowd to where Hagen stood.

"Evening, Mr. Hagen." The man's breath always smelled from the tobacco he often chewed. "What can I do for you?"

"You ever work a big board, Rube?"

"A big board?" the pit boss repeated. "You mean the kind they have at racetracks?"

"The same principle, but different in this case. I'm envisioning something closer to a bare knuckles match, but much bigger. Grander, in keeping with our hotel's theme."

Rube gave it a moment of consideration. "I know how they work and I'm sure I can figure it out if you wanted. What do you have in mind?"

"We're about to find out." Hagen pulled over an empty chair from one of the poker tables. "Help me get everyone's attention."

Hagen climbed atop the chair as Rube began to bellow, "Ladies and gentlemen. May I have your attention, please."

In addition to being a skilled gambler, Miller also had an ability to project his voice like an opera singer Hagen had once heard back in New York. "Mr. Adam Hagen, owner and proprietor of The Laramie Grand Hotel, would like to make an important announcement."

Hagen kept his balance on the chair as the entire gaming floor gradually grew still. Dealers held on to dice and cards. The man at the roulette wheel took the marble ball from play. Even the cattlemen standing back at the bar turned from their drinks to hear what their host had to say.

Hagen had always loved to be the center of attention. "I'm afraid I don't have the same booming voice as Mr. Miller here, but I hope you'll all be able to hear me because I think you'll like what I have to say. I've just received word from a trusted source that a dangerous villain is in our midst."

Many of his customers began to whisper to each other. Some of the cattlemen called for the man to be strung up, even though they had no idea who or where he was. That was good. *Hook them with fear, then offer them relief.*

Hagen held up his hands to quiet them. "You're in no immediate danger, I assure you. But I thought you might like to know that none other than the outlaw Ben Washington has been spotted in a nearby township not an hour's ride from here."

Mention of Ben Washington's name had the desired effect. Women clutched their pearls and gamblers took renewed stock of the chips they still had in front of them.

Hagen was glad to have their interest but had to be careful not to let them get too far ahead of themselves. "I know Ben Washington is no stranger to any of you here. He has spent the past five years riding roughshod over not only this territory, but practically every settlement from here to California. There isn't a stage he won't rob, a train he won't take by force, or a lawman he won't hesitate to gun down should he dare to stand in his way." Hagen held up a solitary finger. "Until now."

More murmurs began as Hagen continued to speak. "I think Mr. Washington has made sport of us for too long, and I say it's high time that someone make sport of him. That is why I have directed Mr. Rube Miller here to begin taking wagers on this infernal scoundrel's capture. The pot will be at least one-thousand dollars to whomever bets correctly on whether or not our own brave Sheriff Buck Trammel will successfully bring Ben Washington back to Laramie. Mr. Miller will also be taking side bets on whether or not Sheriff Trammel brings him back alive or dead."

Hagen saw Rube begin to give orders to his assistant, Oren, as a cheer went up throughout the gaming hall at the prospect of betting for or against the outlaw Ben Washington.

Hagen waved for his customers to become quiet. Many of the gamblers told their neighbors to be quiet as they were eager to hear the next part of the stakes.

"I'll begin the pot at a thousand dollars, but it can go much higher than that depending on how many bets we receive. And since it's no secret that Sheriff Trammel is a personal friend of mine, I'm sure you'll understand that we will not be accepting any bets involving his possible demise. We will begin taking wagers within the hour. Mr. Miller will make another announcement at that time. But be sure to make your wagers quickly, as I'm expecting to hear word of Washington's capture or escape before midnight." He bowed slightly at the waist. "Thank you and good luck."

Hagen jumped down from his chair as men holding cash and poker chips began to rush toward him and Miller. He pulled Rube close and spoke directly in his ear over the growing shouts of eager bettors.

"Discourage them from betting against Trammel at first. That'll only make them eager to drive up the odds. Take the bet after a while but be quiet about it."

Hagen pushed past the growing mob as some of the

men he employed to keep the drunks in line waded into the crowd that threatened to overwhelm Rube.

Hagen laughed to himself as he made it to the relative peace of the hotel lobby. He decided he would take a late dinner up in his room. Making money always managed to give him quite an appetite.

CHAPTER 4

Trammel was glad to find the streets of Laramie were as quiet as he had left them as he led Washington and Blake back into town. Every window in The Laramie Grand Hotel across the thoroughfare from City Hall still burned bright, but no one seemed to be out of order.

The only people he saw on the boardwalks were couples out for an easy stroll around town after a late dinner. Deputy Bush waved to the sheriff and the men with him as he went about on his nightly patrol.

Trammel rounded the corner of City Hall and found Hawkeye smoking a cigarette in front of the large iron gates that had just been installed there. The old gates had been destroyed during the jail break a few months before. The new doors were sturdier and much easier to open and close.

Hawkeye tossed away his smoke when he saw the sheriff and the two men approaching. "Mercy," Hawkeye said as he came to take hold of Washington's horse. "You really got him."

"Looks that way," Trammel said as he and Blake climbed down from their mounts.

Hawkeye looked at the prisoner draped over the saddle. "He dead?"

"He only wishes he was." Trammel took a set of keys from his saddlebag and began to open the heavy lock on the gate. "Help Blake get him into a cell, then have Doc Carson take a look at him if he's still around. If he's not, he can tend to him when he comes back for his midnight rounds."

Blake undid the rope binding Washington's hands and feet beneath the barrel of the horse and let the outlaw spill out of the saddle onto his head. Washington yelped as Blake and Hawkeye pulled him to his feet.

"No call to be gentle with this one," Blake told Hawkeye. "He won't break."

Hawkeye helped the outlaw get up, but Trammel could see something was on his mind. The boy had never been able to hide his feelings when something was bothering him. It was one of the many reasons why he trusted him. "What's the matter? Something happen while we were gone?"

Hawkeye shied away like the kid he was. "Nothing bad. Well, nothing *too* bad, I guess. Might not even be bad at all, come to think of it. Guess that'll have to depend on how you take it. Can I tell you after I help Blake?"

Trammel unlocked the gates and pushed them open. Unlike the old gates, they swung easily and silently on their hinges. "Be quick about it. And come straight back here. I'll be getting the horses settled."

Blake and Hawkeye brought Washington to the side door of the jail while Trammel led the three horses toward the livery in the yard. Old Bob, the black man who tended to the horses, came out of his room to meet him. Trammel still winced when he saw the eyepatch he had sported since the riot. He had lost an eye in the melee for simply being in the wrong place at the wrong time.

"Evening, Bob," Trammel greeted him. "Hope we didn't wake you. We got back from Woodbine quicker than I expected."

Bob gladly took the reins of the three horses from the sheriff. "Was that Ben Washington I saw them bringing into the jail just now?"

"It was, but I'd appreciate it if you didn't tell anyone. I don't want people knowing he's here until we've got him settled."

"I don't have to tell anyone because everyone already knows," Bob said as he led the horses to their stalls. "You're the talk of the town again, Sheriff. And this time, it's in a good way."

Trammel's broad shoulders sagged as he looked to the sky. Now he knew what Hawkeye had been afraid to say. "Hagen got Hawkeye to tell him I was after Washington, didn't he?"

"Don't know where Mr. Hagen heard it, but he heard it sure enough," Bob answered from inside the livery. "Made himself quite a killing, too, though not in his usual manner, I'm glad to say."

Trammel heard the side door of the jail creak closed and saw Hawkeye standing beside it, toeing the ground with his boot. He did not look up when Trammel walked over to him.

"Guess Old Bob already told you how stupid I am."

Trammel was not angry with Hawkeye but wanted to teach him a lesson. "How did Hagen get it out of you?"

"After you left, I went over to the hotel to tell him to make sure he didn't let his cattleman friends get out of hand. He wondered why you weren't telling him yourself and, before I knew it, I was telling him about how you'd gone after Washington. He was worried about you, boss. He would've helped you if you needed it, just like he always has."

"After helping himself first," Trammel reminded him. "What happened after you told him?"

"He promised me he wouldn't tell anyone about it, but word must've gotten out because next thing I know, it's all over town that they're taking bets about whether or not you'd bring Washington back. They even took side bets on if he'd be dead or alive." Hawkeye scratched his chin. "I would've stopped them if I thought it was against the law, but none of the others thought it was. Pretty soon, there was a line all the way out into the street of folks looking to make a wager. Me and Charlie Root and Jimmy Brillheart minded the line, but everyone behaved themselves. That's why I said nothing bad happened." His face grew red with embarrassment. "Besides me letting my big mouth get away from me, that is."

Trammel could see Hawkeye was already punishing himself and did not want to add to it. "How'd the betting go? For or against me?"

Hawkeye shrugged. "Three-to-one against from what I heard, though don't hold me to it because I don't know for sure."

Trammel was glad to have disappointed the good people of Laramie yet again. "I'm more concerned about what you learned from all of this."

"To not be so free with my words."

"To anyone," Trammel said. "There were a lot of men in my office who heard about Washington, so word about what I was doing was bound to get out eventually. You know how they like to talk. But you've got to watch what you say to your friends just as much as you have to watch what you say to strangers. The less you say in this line of work, the better. For you and the men who are counting on you. Understand?"

Hawkeye nodded. "I do now."

"Good. You can think that over while you help Bob muck out the stalls for the next week."

He did not expect an argument from Hawkeye and did not get one. "Yes, sir. I deserve it."

Now that it was settled, Trammel was eager to let it pass. "You and Blake get Washington in a cell?"

"Yes, sir. We even hung up some blankets on the bars to keep the others from looking at him. Blake kept Washington's hands bound behind his back until you told us otherwise. He even put a gag in his mouth, saying he'd done the same to that poor rancher back in Woodbine."

Trammel imagined he would've done the same thing had he been in Blake's shoes. "Go back inside and see if Blake needs you to do anything. I'm headed over to the station to send a wire to the marshal's office in Cheyenne about Washington. I suspect they'll want to send a deputy to come for him as soon as they're able. From what Peyton said, it's liable to be a week or so before someone gets here. If you're done with your punishment by then, I'll take you with us. Show you around Cheyenne a bit. I've never been there myself, but I hear it's a nice town."

The prospect of a trip, even with a known outlaw in tow, was enough to brighten the young man's spirits. "I'll do a week's worth of mucking in a day if it means I can come with you."

Trammel told him to get one door of the iron gate while he got the other. "And no more smoking. It'll stop your growth. Folks are liable to think poorly of this town if they see a midget running around with a deputy's star."

* * *

After sending off his wire, Trammel decided to stop by The Laramie Grand to pay Adam Hagen a visit. He had not set foot inside the place since construction had stopped, and found it was as gaudy as he had expected it to be.

The man behind the front desk stood straighter as he watched Trammel approach. Mr. Lee was chubby and cheerful, a welcoming face to greet weary travelers after a long journey by horse, stagecoach, or train. He always put considerable effort into trying to look at the scar that ran down the side of Trammel's face.

"Good evening, Sheriff. What can I do for you?"

"Tell me which one is Hagen's room."

The clerk ran a finger under his collar. "Mr. Hagen didn't tell me he was expecting any guests this evening. If you give me a moment, I'll have someone run up and—"

"That wasn't a question. Tell me what room he's in."

"Suite two-oh-two. At the top of the stairs, then—"

Trammel was already on his way. "Thanks. I'll find it."

He took the stairs two at a time, found the suite at the top of the stairs and did not bother knocking before going inside.

He found Adam Hagen pointing a Colt at him from behind several piles of small slips of paper on his desk.

Hagen lowered the pistol and tossed it on his desk in disgust. "It's only you. Just my luck."

Trammel noticed Hagen was paler than usual and his eyes looked odd. "What happened to you? I thought you'd be celebrating your big bet."

"I *was* celebrating." He gestured toward a bottle of champagne before lowering his head into his hands. "Now I've got a screaming headache, and I think I might be sick. The champagne must be off. I'm already hungover and it's barely nine o'clock yet. I was hoping you might be an assassin or at least a robber who could put me out of my misery."

Trammel had no sympathy for him. "You got Hawkeye to tell you I'd gone after Ben Washington, then opened betting on if he'd escape. You put the kid in a bad spot, Adam. He's over at the jail beating himself up over it right now."

"This ought to make him feel better." Hagen took a small money bag from his desk and tossed it to Trammel. "There's a hundred in gold pieces in there. His share of the take so far and it's still rolling in."

Trammel could tell by the weight of the bag that it probably held that much. Hagen never lied when it came to money. "It's not about the money. It's about the precedent you set tonight."

Hagen slowly lifted his head. "'Precedent,' he says. My, someone's been listening to the adults speak. If you keep going at this rate, you'll be reciting Shakespearean sonnets and the Gettysburg Address in the city square."

Trammel knew he might not have had the same level of education Hagen had received at West Point, but he never doubted his own intelligence in other matters. "I'll be reciting more at your trial if you pull something like that again. No more bets on how I do my job, Hagen. It might give people funny ideas about making sure the outcome goes in their favor."

Hagen rolled his neck, causing some of the cartilage and bones to pop. "Why don't you admit what this is really all about? You're up for election next month. You don't want your oldest friend making waves. You want to keep the boat nice and steady until you're officially in office."

Trammel had never cared much for politics. His time as the sheriff of Laramie had done nothing to change that. "I care more about someone betting big that Washington gets himself killed on his way to Cheyenne and tries to make their bet pay off. I don't want people betting on what happens outside your gambling dens. You make enough from your poker and table games all over town as it is."

Hagen placed his hands on his stomach and suppressed a belch. "There's another fancy word from you, Steve. 'Enough.' We've never agreed on the definition of that word, have we? In fact, it's always been at the root of any disagreement between us. You think such a concept exists. I don't. You think there's a certain amount of money I can make that will satisfy me. I only think I'll have enough when I'm dead. I'll keep on looking for more until they lower me into the ground and not a moment sooner."

Trammel had no interest in wasting any more time debating him. He knew Hagen would just keep throwing words at him like he always did, so he began to leave, but not before he issued a final warning. "No more bets about Washington or me or my men. Understand?"

"I'm afraid it's too late for that." Hagen raised his chin at him. "The last round of betting was such an overwhelming success that I had to start another book on Washington's overall fate. My patrons might've rioted otherwise, and I knew you wouldn't have wanted that."

Trammel stopped before he reached the door. "What did you do?"

"Those who feared they might lose money on Washington's capture were eager to make some of it back," Hagen explained. "They demanded to bet to see if you would bring Washington safely to trial in Cheyenne. His gang is still out there somewhere, you know. It's a fact some of my customers found intriguing. They even insisted on placing side bets on the exact date when he would hang. At this rate, I'm going to run out of space in my safe pretty soon. I might even have to buy a couple of barrels to move the money over to the bank."

Trammel knew some men would bet on anything, but this was too much. "You're not serious."

"For all my many faults, you know I never joke about money," Hagen reminded him. "If it's any consolation, your success in bringing Washington in alive has put the odds overwhelmingly in your favor. They're betting heavily that you'll get him to Cheyenne alive. You should take heart in their confidence. It shows you have a good chance of winning your election next month."

Trammel felt his anger begin to grow. "You took their money. You can give it back."

"Quite to the contrary." Hagen picked up his pistol from the desk and slid it back into its holster on his hip. "They'd be quite cross with me if I did. I've even sent a wire to several newspapers that I'm taking out an advertisement in their next editions. By this time next week, I expect bets from all over the country to come pouring in. I've certainly sweetened the pot some. A cash prize of ten thousand dollars."

Hagen laughed. "I wish you could see the look of indignation on your face right now. Don't be so glum, Steve. Washington and his kind have benefited from inflicting misery on others for years. Why shouldn't the rest of us have a chance to earn a profit at his expense for once? Since you claim to love justice so much, I'd have thought you above all people would've enjoyed the irony of the situation."

Trammel and Hagen had found themselves on the opposite sides of a problem many times since their first meeting in Wichita years before, but this was the first time when Trammel found himself truly angry at his friend. "If any trouble comes of this, if one of my men so much as sprains an ankle because of what you've done, I'll make sure you pay in more than gold."

"And if the money keeps rolling in like it has been, I'll be able to afford it. Now, if you're done threatening me, I have work to do." Hagen took a pile of slips and began to sift through them. "Give my love to Emily. You should bring her to dinner here sometime. The food's really quite good."

Trammel did not bother to close the door behind him when he left.

CHAPTER 5

The next morning, George Mahaffey knew there were only three reasons why Ben Washington always left him in charge of the Washington Gang in his absence.

The first was that, at almost forty, he was the next-oldest member of the group.

The second was that he and Ben had formed what had later become the Washington Gang back when they were rustling cattle in Kansas after Lee's surrender.

The third reason, one that came in handy from time to time, was that he was the only one beside Ben Washington himself who could read.

He regretted that skill now as he read the unwelcome news in the morning paper behind Johnson's Livery in a town outside Cheyenne.

"Well?" Dib Bishop, the youngest outlaw, prodded as Mahaffey read and reread the article. "Aren't you going to tell us what it says?"

The news was so bad that Mahaffey decided to break it to them in pieces so they would fully understand it. "Looks like Ben's gone and finally gotten himself caught, boys. Says here that it happened outside of Laramie a couple of days ago."

"Laramie?" Coleman asked. Mahaffey knew Coleman tended to be the most cautious of the bunch. "What would the boss be doing way over there? I thought he was supposed to come meet us here tomorrow so we could all ride down to Colorado together."

Mahaffey knew the reason and cursed himself for not thinking of it earlier. He might have been able to stop Washington if he had. "His family used to own land there. Remember when we were holed up in Bauersville a few weeks back? Ben ran into an old friend of his from when he was a kid. Him and the fella got to talking about the old days and about this new family that was now living in his family's old house. He said the bank sold it to them cheap. Cheaper than what Ben's family owed on the place."

Mahaffey lowered the paper and fought the urge to throw it into the small cook fire they had built for their coffee. "Guess it set to gnawing at him worse than I realized, and he got it in his head that he ought to do something about it."

Mahaffey pushed his hat farther back on his head. It was all so clear to him now that it was too late to be of much use. "I knew he was acting peculiar since that conversation, but I didn't think he'd do something this reckless. If I had, I might've been able to find a way to stop him."

Tim had been riding with Washington and Mahaffey since their early days. "You couldn't have stopped Ben even if you'd known what he was up to. He's never been one to let himself get talked out of an idea, bad or otherwise. Does that paper say how it happened? Who got him?"

That was the part Mahaffey was struggling with the most. The part that made Ben's predicament even worse. "It says the local constable rode into Laramie and brought Sheriff Trammel back with him. He's the one who took

Ben in, boys. Buck Trammel's got Ben locked in a cell in City Hall as we speak."

Mahaffey saw the gloom that descended on the rest of the gang. He knew their first thoughts upon hearing Ben had gotten caught was to find a way to get him out of prison.

But knowing Buck Trammel was the one who had him gave them justifiable pause.

"Trammel." Dietrich poked the small cook fire with a long stick. "Of all the lawmen in the territory it could've been, why'd it have to be him?"

"Bad luck," Mahaffey supposed. "Springing a man of Ben's notoriety was never going to be easy but going against the likes of Trammel only makes it that much harder."

Hank Classet, usually the quietest in the group, surprised Mahaffey by speaking up. "It's still one man against the ten of us, George. We all know Trammel's a tough customer, sure, but the numbers are still in our favor."

Besides Dib Bishop, Johnny Coombs was the second youngest member of the gang, and he said, "Numbers ain't the whole of it, Hank. It's not just Trammel we'd be going up against, but his deputies, too. They're all good men and they ain't afraid to fight. I saw them in action when I passed through Laramie about a year ago. And that was before Trammel was sheriff, but the same deputies are still there. They won't just roll over, not even for us."

Marcum had been a sharpshooter during the War Between the States and viewed the world from behind the gunsights of the Sharps rifle he carried. "Coombs is right for once. That jail's not exactly a canvas tent in the middle of nowhere. It's got thick walls and plenty of guards to mind the place. They fixed it up some after that jailbreak they had a few months back."

"I heard about that," Coombs said. "And I heard they got all the escapees back in their cells before noon, except for Lucien Clay, that is. Wasn't just the deputies' doing, either. The whole town helped to round them up. They'll fight, too, which doesn't help our chances of busting Ben out of there."

Marcum said, "No one's talking about leaving him there except you, Coombs."

Mahaffey felt the sour mood that had begun to settle over his men and did not like it. They were talking like they were already beaten before they had even tried to get Ben Washington free. "Let's quit worrying about what Trammel can do and start thinking about what we're going to do. We can't just let Ben rot in a cell, and we can't let them bring him to trial. He's as good as dead if we do. Folks have been looking to hang him for years."

"George is right," Barrett said. He was the rock of the gang. He did not excel at one thing but was reasonably good at everything. "The boss has always been good to us, boys. He never led us into a score we couldn't take and always made sure we had money in our pockets, even if there wasn't enough for him to take his rightful share. We can't give up on him now, no matter how tough Buck Trammel is supposed to be."

Dib Bishop's youthful temper flared. "To hear you tell it, I might think you're calling us cowards, Barrett. No one's talking about leaving Ben in a lurch. It's just that Trammel ain't the kind of man you go up against lightly."

"Dib's right." Roy Earnshaw had always served as the peacemaker of the group. When everyone else lost their heads, Earnshaw could be counted upon to keep his. "Every man who's ever gone against Trammel has either gotten lead or dead for his trouble. I heard they sent a whole army of Pinkertons after him a while back and he walked out without nary a scratch."

"Pinkerton men are from Chicago." Marcum leaned forward and placed the back of his hand against the coffee pot above the fire. It was not warm yet. "We'll give Trammel more trouble than a bunch of city boys could. Besides, a reputation doesn't make a man bulletproof."

"I didn't say it did," Earnshaw said. "Just said we have to be cautious about taking him on is all." He looked at Mahaffey. "What else did it say in that paper, George? I can tell there's something else gnawing at you."

Mahaffey knew he had never been good at hiding his troubles. It was why he had never been one to try his hand at playing cards.

He opened the paper and showed them an advertisement that filled an entire page. "Adam Hagen's taking bets on Ben's outcome. Says here he's accepting wagers by wire on when Ben will get convicted and when he'll hang." He handed the paper to Coleman in disgust, though he knew the man could not read. "It turns my stomach just to think about it."

Another uneasy quiet settled over the men as Coleman looked at the advertisement. "There ought to be a law against such a thing. Why, it ain't hardly decent!"

"That's rich coming from the likes of us." Tim got up and walked away from the men by the fire. "We've held up stagecoaches and pay wagons and trains between here and the Mississippi for years. Can hardly blame folks for wanting to make some sport of Ben's misfortune for a change."

The men began to grumble, but Roy Earnshaw waved them to be quiet. "None of this changes the fact that Ben's stuck in a cell and we've got to figure out a way of getting him out of there." He asked Mahaffey, "Did that article say anything about what they plan on doing with Ben next?"

Mahaffey took off his hat and ran his hands through his thinning hair. He hated being the one who had to do all the thinking, but fate had not given him much of a choice. He knew there had to be an answer somewhere in this mess, but for the moment, it eluded him.

"The paper said Trammel wired the marshal's office in Cheyenne. They're supposed to send someone to pick up Ben and bring him back to the capital for trial."

Yet, as he spoke, Mahaffey felt a cold stone of reality land in the middle of his stomach. He could feel the ripple of an idea reach the corners of his insides, but it disappeared before he could see it clearly.

He was still trying to understand it when Dietrich said, "Lefty Rollins used to be quite a marshal in his day. He's an old man now. He was all set to retire until Rob Moran got himself killed in Laramie. Rollins won't have the stomach to set out for a man like Ben on his own. He'll send one of his deputies for him instead. And I heard he's spread mighty thin at the moment. Trammel will probably ride back with whoever Rollins sends to make sure Ben gets to Cheyenne safely, but that'll take a week or more at least."

Marcum shrugged. "Don't see how it matters. It'll still only be two men against all of us. We've beaten worse odds, boys."

Mahaffey wished they would all keep their mouths shut long enough to let him think. He could sense the answer was close. Since talking it out had helped give him clarity earlier, he decided to give it another try.

"Earnshaw said something just now that stuck with me. How every man who's ever gone up against Trammel has gotten himself killed."

Dib Bishop said, "So? We already know that."

Coleman snapped at him. "Shut your mouth, you young pup. Let the man talk."

In the darkness of his mind, Mahaffey grabbed blindly for the idea and finally got hold of it. He wrestled it to the ground and saw it for what it truly was.

A possible answer to their problem.

"What if we figured out a way of going up against Trammel without having to face him?" The more he spoke, the more his idea began to make sense to him. "What if we could make Trammel not only come to us but bring Ben with him when he did?"

Tim stopped pacing. "I'd say that's a mighty tall order, George. Even for us."

"Yes, it is," Mahaffey decided. "But it's an order even taller than Buck Trammel himself."

Mahaffey took the pot of coffee from the fire and poured himself a cup. It might not be ready yet, but neither was his idea. *Yes,* he decided. *It just might be crazy enough to work.*

"Gather round, boys. I think I might have a way of saving Ben's hide and our own while we're at it."

CHAPTER 6

Leo Brandt cinched his saddle beneath the barrel of his horse while U.S. Marshal John "Lefty" Rollins, continued to talk at him.

"I'm sorry to have to do this to you, Leo, seeing as how you've just gotten back, but this isn't an ideal position I'm in. I know you just joined up with us a year ago, but I've got no one else who I can send to go fetch Ben Washington."

Brandt imagined he had heard the story at least ten times since he had brought his prisoner back from Rawlings the previous night. "Don't give it another thought, boss." Calling the older man by his nickname "Lefty" had never felt right to him. "I don't mind. I wouldn't have taken this job in the first place if I didn't like traveling so much."

The elderly marshal continued to speak as if he had not heard Brandt at all. "I wasn't planning on having my men spread all over the territory like this. You know I'd go with you if I thought I could, but my rheumatism has been hurting me something awful lately."

Brandt tightened the straps of the scabbard holding his Winchester. "Wouldn't be right to leave the town without a marshal anyway. You need to stay here and keep an eye on things. I'll be back with Washington before you know it."

Rollins continued to fret. "If it were any other prisoner, I'd just as soon as have you wait until Bell got back with the prison wagon. But he won't be back for another two weeks, and I don't like the idea of leaving a man like Ben Washington in Laramie for that long. Folks might think I need Buck Trammel to do my job for me."

Brandt tugged on the scabbard and found it was good and tight. "Justice delayed is justice denied."

Rollins said, "You be careful while you're down there in Laramie, Leo. It's a mighty dangerous place. It looks peaceable enough, but don't let all them pretty buildings and fancy people fool you. It's a bucket of blood. Rob Moran got himself shot by just standing on the street in broad daylight. I'd be on my porch in my rocking chair enjoying my pipe right now if he hadn't gone and gotten himself killed. And there's that prison break they had a while back."

Brandt might have been reasonably new to the territory, but he had heard all the stories about Laramie.

"It's a town where a man can find himself in a whole mess of trouble in the blink of an eye," Rollins went on. "You be sure to mind yourself while you're there."

Brandt appreciated the older man's concern. He intended on getting to town as soon as he could so he might have a chance to enjoy some of the good times he had heard could be had there. Visiting the new Laramie Grand, and its famous gambling floor, was top on his list.

But there was no reason to trouble Rollins with such ideas. It would only make him worry more than he already was. "I promise I'll be careful."

Another thought came to Rollins. "And don't let Buck

Trammel try to push you around, either. He's a good man.
A tough man, too, but he's a bully and headstrong. You're
the one toting the federal star, not him. Ben Washington is
your prisoner, not Trammel's. He does what you say, not
the other way around."

Brandt had never had the pleasure of meeting the infamous Buck Trammel before but certainly knew him by
reputation. In the year he had spent patrolling the western
part of the Wyoming Territory for Rollins, he had heard a
great deal about Trammel's exploits.

About how he was as quick with his fists as he was with
the Peacemaker he kept tucked in a shoulder rig under his
left arm. About how he was a man without fear and often
threw in with the likes of the infamous gambler Adam
Hagen to get the job done. Brandt was looking forward
to meeting both of them, particularly Hagen, when he
stopped by The Laramie Grand.

Realizing Rollins was far too consumed with worry to
remember that they had already discussed this, he decided
to humor the old marshal as he checked the bedroll at the
edge of his saddle.

"Trammel's sure to want to help guard Washington
when I bring him back here. Think I should let him do
that?"

"Can't see why not," Rollins said. "He's handy in a
fight, even if he usually happens to start them. He's always
there when it finishes, so feel free to bring him along." He
held up a crooked finger in warning. "But only if you want
to. You might make quicker time if it's just you and Washington alone. And be mindful of the Washington Gang.
They're still out there somewhere. I've heard tell they're
already down in Colorado, but there's no way of knowing
that for sure. You keep an eye out for anything out of the
ordinary both to and from Laramie."

"I won't forget." Brandt could not resist the urge to tease him a little. "I'll be sure to eat all my vegetables, wash behind my ears, and say my prayers before I turn in each evening, too."

"Don't be so glib about this," Rollins scolded him. "Sending you to fetch Washington is just about the most dangerous assignment I've ever had to give a man, and I've been doing this for almost thirty years now. Ben Washington is more than a handful on his own and with that gang of his on the prowl, it's even worse than that."

"I know, boss. I'll take every precaution."

With his tack secured, Brandt gave his gear a good look before he led his horse out from the livery and climbed into the saddle. It was a good, crisp spring day without a cloud or concern in the sky. "I plan on making it to Laramie well before dark." He recited his orders from Rollins before the marshal could repeat them. "I'll be sure to send you a wire as soon as I'm there. I'll send you another right before Trammel and I hit the trail with Washington, so you'll know when to expect us."

Rollins sagged a little. "Sounds like you have all the answers."

Brandt grinned. "Only because you already gave them to me." He offered his right hand down to him. "Thanks for the concern, boss. I promise I won't let you down."

Rollins eagerly shook his deputy's hand. "Be sure to mind yourself out there, Leo. I know you will."

Brandt touched the brim of his hat and brought his horse out onto the thoroughfare to begin his journey toward Laramie.

Brandt had been surprised by his mount's pace. He had not ridden the bay gelding at a gallop, but the animal had natural speed to him. He had not shown any signs of slowing down until they were two hours out of the capital. When he spotted a small stream up ahead, he decided this was as good a place as any for them to have a quick rest.

He found a clear spot among the lush overgrowth that lined both sides of the stream and climbed down. He stripped his saddle and tack from the gelding's back and set it down beneath a tree. The sun was high in the cloudless sky and not particularly strong, but years as a lawman had taught Leo Brandt that he should never pass up an idyllic spot to take a rest. A man could never be certain when he might have such a chance again on the trail.

While his horse drank eagerly from the creek, Brandt took his tobacco and paper from his saddlebag and began to build himself a smoke. When he was done, he took a match from his pocket, thumbed it alive, and lit his cigarette. He flicked the dead match into the stream and drew the smoke in deep as he took in his surroundings.

He had spent the past year or so running down dangerous men all over the territory for Lefty Rollins but had yet to grow tired of the majestic beauty that was Wyoming. Having lived most of his life in west Texas, Brandt had grown accustomed to the parched, arid landscape. The desert had a stark, wonderful quality all its own, even in wintertime.

But as he found himself rapidly approaching thirty, he started to believe the constant sun had begun to bake any hint of ambition or life from his soul. He knew there was more to life than just punching cattle and herding mustangs among the sage and sand of El Paso.

He had heard a great deal about the wilderness that was Wyoming, which was why he had decided it would be the ideal place for a new beginning. He had left Texas with little more than the clothes on his back, a bit of money he had saved, and a dot on a map. Cheyenne was where he would begin life anew.

Brandt had arrived in Cheyenne with the hope of taking the measure of the place before deciding where he would make his start. He quickly found himself volunteering as part of a posse the town marshal was pulling together to run down a man who had been too rough on one of the many sporting ladies in the capital.

After helping the posse catch the man, the town marshal hired Brandt on as a deputy and, before long, U.S. Marshal Lefty Rollins asked him to become one of his federals.

Brandt had never thought of becoming a lawman before, but quickly realized that it was not much different from corralling livestock. Herding men and animals both took a certain measure of vigilance and care. He had to be mindful to not let either slip away or let a predator get too close. He had to be ready to act quickly whenever the herd was threatened.

Now he was out here alone, enjoying a cigarette by a lazy creek, on his way to bringing in one of the most wanted men in the territory to trial. Life was certainly a trail that had plenty of odd twists and bends to it.

Brandt had not realized he had become lost in his own thoughts until the cigarette began to singe his fingers. He tossed it into the creek as he laughed at his own forgetfulness. He was becoming as scatterbrained as old Lefty back in Cheyenne and had wasted good tobacco in the process. He was not bothered by it. He was sure there were plenty of tobacco shops in Laramie who would be glad for his business.

As he went to pick up his tobacco and paper, he caught the glint of something in the thick overgrowth on the other side of the creek.

He forgot about his tobacco and made a move for his

rifle instead just as a line of men on horseback broke through the bushes and into the water. His own horse bolted at the approach of the strangers.

From behind him, Brandt heard a man call out, "Easy there, deputy. No one means you any harm."

Brandt looked around to see two men riding toward him as the others from the creek quickly closed in on him. Everyone was holding a pistol or a rifle except him.

The man on his side of the creek said, "Step away from your gear before someone gets themselves hurt."

Brandt backed away from his rifle but kept his right hand by the pistol on his hip. "That goes for you boys, too. I'm Deputy U.S. Marshal Leo Brandt out of Cheyenne. Who might you be?"

"I'm George Mahaffey," said the man out front. "And we already know who you are. Old Lefty fretted all over town last night about sending you out alone to any man willing to listen. Lucky for us, one of my boys heard him."

"Mahaffey?" Brandt repeated as the snout of one of the horses bumped into him. "You're one of Ben Washington's men."

"We all are," Mahaffey told him, "which is all the more reason why you'd be smart to dump your pistol on the ground. We came to talk, not to fight. If we hadn't, you'd already be long dead."

But Brandt knew he would be at the mercy of the outlaws if he did that. "My gun's staying right where it is and so are you until I get some answers. What are you boys doing here?"

He felt two lassos drop over him before he had a chance to pull his gun. The first one tightened around his feet while the other closed in around his shoulders, pinning his arms to his sides. He was pulled down on the ground as one of the men took his pistol from him and made quick work of binding his hands behind him with another rope.

"Glad we got that straightened out." Mahaffey spoke to the man beside him. "Coleman, ride out and fetch this boy's horse for him before it gets too far. We don't want the deputy having to walk the whole way, now do we? After all, he's our guest."

The outlaw dug his heels into his horse's sides as he went off in pursuit of Brandt's frightened gelding.

Mahaffey crossed his hands over his saddle horn as the man who had tied Brandt helped the deputy marshal get to his feet. "You sure picked a nice spot for a rest, deputy. Sorry we had to ride up and spoil it for you, but duty calls and all that."

"Duty?" Brandt tried to wriggle his hands free, but the knot only tightened. "Murder is more like it."

"Only if you push it in that direction," Mahaffey said. "We'll keep your hands tied behind you for now, but if you behave yourself, I'll see to it that we move them in front of you. If you give us any sass or try to get away, you'll get the back of my hand. Second time, we'll make you walk behind your horse until you're exhausted. We won't have time to stop, so we'll have to drag you. Ever see a man dragged through the dirt, deputy? After a mile or so, it ain't a pretty sight."

Brandt looked at each of the men surrounding him. They were all bearded and all had the same dead eyes as their leader. They had all taken lives before and did not look like they would hesitate to do it again. "Seeing a man hang isn't a pretty sight either, Mahaffey. You'd best turn me loose now before this gets out of hand."

Mahaffey laughed along with the others. "From where I'm sitting, deputy, everything's already in hand. My hand."

Coleman returned trailing Brandt's horse by his reins. "He didn't get too far, George."

"Get the saddle on him." Then Mahaffey spoke to the man holding Brandt's arm. "You ought to acquaint yourself with Mr. Dietrich there. Try to be nice to him. He's going to be keeping an eye on you while the rest of us go about our business. He'll be the one who decides on how you're treated during your stay with us."

Dietrich pulled Brandt toward the horse as Coleman placed the saddle on the horse. Both men helped him climb up into the saddle and set his feet in the stirrups. Brandt might have tried to ride away, but Dietrich kept tight hold of the reins as he got back on his own horse.

Mahaffey said, "You mind what I told you about what'll happen to you if you cause any trouble. I'd like to trade you healthy, but if you happen to be missing a few teeth more or less, it won't drive down the bargaining price any."

Now Brandt understood what this was all about. "You plan on using me to get Ben Washington free, don't you? I wouldn't count on getting much for me. Marshal Rollins won't agree to deal for me or anyone else you might grab. He'll sooner keep Washington in Laramie before that happens. He can always try him from there. Hang him, too. And when I don't send him a wire that I've reached Laramie safely, he'll ride out with a posse bigger than you boys have ever seen."

"You ain't that lucky," Mahaffey grinned. "Lefty Rollins is a man ten years past his prime and the town marshal in Cheyenne has no stomach for this kind of fight. Trammel might, but I'm counting on that." He pointed a gloved finger at him. "This is the last time I indulge that mouth of yours, Deputy. Any more sharp words out of you and you'll get the back of my hand for your trouble."

Mahaffey moved his horse past Brandt and spoke to two riders near the creek. "Dib, you're the youngest and the friendliest among us, so I've decided you'll be the one to deliver our message to Trammel."

Brandt put the young man at barely sixteen if he was even that old. He watched his smug expression fade to one of concern. "What do you want me to say? Trammel's just as likely to shoot me on sight than listen to me."

"Take one of your shirts from your saddle bag and put it on a stick," Mahaffey told him. "You'll ride into town under a flag of truce. Nobody'll be anxious to shoot a man who's only come to talk. His deputies might try to stop you, but tell them I sent you. Tell them you're there to speak to Trammel and only Trammel, not one of his men. I don't want this message getting watered down in the retelling. When you see the sheriff, tell him we've got Deputy U.S. Marshal Leo Brandt, but we're willing to trade. Tell him we'll return Brandt in exchange for Ben Washington. Listen to what he says and ride back here to tell me. That's all you have to do."

"That's all?" Dib said. "What if he doesn't let me go after I tell him all that?"

Brandt watched Mahaffey look at the man next to Dib. "He'll let you go because I'm sending Marcum here with you to watch over you. At a distance, of course. Make sure you hold up from going into town until after it's dark. That'll make Trammel less anxious to ride out looking to see if Marcum's really there. Tell Trammel that if Marcum doesn't see you riding out of town at first light that he'll start taking shots at people from the outskirts of town. That ought to make him think twice about holding on to you."

Brandt watched the man called Marcum smile. "That's the style, George. That's just what Ben would do."

"You do what I told you," Mahaffey told the two men, "and come right back. Don't let them talk you into agreeing to anything else." He drove his finger into Dib's chest. "You deliver the message to Trammel and get his answer." He poked Marcum in the chest. "And you make sure he gets out alive and bring him back without being followed. That clear?"

Both men said they understood before Mahaffey said to Dib, "You'd better get moving and don't forget to wait until after dark. Marcum and I have some things to discuss."

Brandt watched Dib ride his horse through the creek and set it to a gallop once he reached the other side.

Brandt saw Mahaffey waited until he had gotten well out of earshot before saying, "You remember that box canyon we've holed up in before? About an hour's ride from here?"

Marcum's grin grew wider. "I'm the one who found it, remember?"

"Then you should have no trouble finding it again. Make sure you bring Dib there once Trammel lets him go. I didn't want him knowing where we'll be in case Trammel tried to beat it out of him." Mahaffey took hold of the outlaw's arm. "Don't let anyone take you, Marcum. Ride off and leave Dib if you have to. We'll need you for whatever comes next."

"Save your worries for that squirt you're sending to Trammel," Marcum said. "He's the one who needs it. How many do you want me to pick off if Trammel doesn't let Dib go?"

The casual way he asked the question turned Brandt's stomach.

"Take down two of them to make your point, then wait as long as you can before coming to the canyon. Make sure no one follows you when you do. Trammel's a crafty one and I don't want us getting ourselves trapped with only one way in or out. Now, get."

The outlaw rode across the creek as Mahaffey returned to Brandt's side. "You hear all that, Deputy? Guess we're not as hopeless as you thought."

Brandt refused to allow his rising panic to take hold of him. "It doesn't matter what any of us think now, Mahaffey. Only what Trammel thinks."

Mahaffey rode out to the front of the group as the rest of the men followed him. "You'd better hope the sheriff thinks the right way. You'll pay if he doesn't."

Dietrich pulled Brandt's horse behind his own.

CHAPTER 7

Buck Trammel had not been aware he had been pushing the food around his plate until Emily said something about it.

"What's wrong, Steve? Do you really hate my cooking that much?"

Trammel set his fork aside. "No, honey. The food's fine. It's me who's wrong. Guess I've got a lot on my mind is all."

Dr. Emily Downs Trammel looked at her husband's plate. "The way you've been digging through those potatoes, you'd think you were digging a grave."

Trammel smiled. "I wish I was, depending on who it was for. Maybe I could bury my worries once and for all?"

"You? Not worry? I know better than to hope for the impossible."

Trammel knew she had a point. "Guess I always find something to pick over, don't I? If it's not one thing it's the other."

Emily lowered her fork to her plate. "I thought you'd be able to take life a bit easier when you became sheriff of Laramie. I was hoping having all those deputies around to help you would let you enjoy life a bit more. But it's been one thing after another ever since the day they swore you in. First, Rob gets killed, then that business with Lucien Clay. Then the jailbreak. You were better for a while until Ben Washington rode into our lives."

She patted her mouth with her napkin and placed it on the table beside her plate. "I'm beginning to think you enjoy being distracted from me."

The thought of Emily taking second place to anyone or anything had never entered his mind. But he supposed life's choices were never as stark as that. It was not like a court of law where both sides of a case were heard before a jury rendered a decision and a judge issued a sentence.

Life, particularly a married life, was about the small choices he made each day to allow his worries to build up between them.

Trammel reached across the table and gently took her hand in his. "I was doing a good job of leaving my work at the jail for a while, wasn't I?"

"For a while," Emily allowed. "But when Ben Washington showed up, you went right back to the way you were before. And if it wasn't Washington, it would be Adam Hagen. You always wondered what he was up to and if his new hotel would ruin the town. It always seems to be something else." She looked down into her lap. "Something other than me."

Trammel tried to put her mind at ease. "You knew who I was when we got married. You knew my job was important to me. Just like being a doctor is important to you."

"But there's a difference between the law and medicine, Steve. I can diagnose a patient and treat what ails them. Sometimes they get better. Sometimes they die. That's part of life. But there never seems to be an end to your troubles. There's always someone who needs to be locked up or chased down or shot up. It doesn't always have to be you who does it, but it always somehow turns out that way."

Trammel could practically feel her sadness and hated being the cause of it. He never could stand to see her this glum on his account. "After I got rid of Lucien, I let the others do more. I even let Blake handle more so I could be home for dinner most nights."

"I wouldn't call racing through your meal so you can rush back to City Hall to check the night watch 'being home.' You barely say a word to me. It feels like it's just another chore on your list of things to do each day."

Trammel caressed her hand. "Nothing about you is ever a chore. Seeing you is the only bright part of my day."

She slid her hand from his and folded it on her lap. "It sure doesn't feel like that. I used to be able to tell myself otherwise, that I was just being silly, but it's not so simple anymore. It's all just so different now."

Trammel's heart sank as he watched a single tear run down her cheek and drop into her lap. Emily had always been a woman of strong emotions, but she rarely cried. He hated himself for being the cause of it and wanted to do something about it.

"I got a wire from Lefty Rollins this morning. He's sending a deputy to come pick up Ben Washington. After I help him get Washington back to Cheyenne for trial, I'll come back. We can go on that vacation you've been talking about. We'll go to St. Louis to see that doctor you mentioned. The one who might be able to do something about this scar on my face."

He hoped that might be enough to bring her around, but she only continued to look down at her lap. "You don't care about your scar, and you don't even want to go to St. Louis. This isn't about going on a vacation, Steve. This is about you and me and our life together. I never used to mind sharing you with the worst people in the territory, but it's different now. You'll always find a reason to put yourself in harm's way, and I'm always going to be the one who has to just accept it. It's not fair. Not anymore."

Emily may not have moved since they had begun to talk, but he could feel her slipping away from him. He got up from his chair and took a knee beside her. He could not remember a time when she seemed so sad. "If it was any other prisoner, I'd let Blake and some of the others take him to Cheyenne for me, but this is Ben Washington. He's got a gang of men who'll stop at nothing to get him free of this if they can and I can't let that happen."

Another tear dropped into Emily's hands. "And after it's Washington, it'll be someone else. Your election is in a month, and you haven't even asked a single person to vote for you."

"You know I've never been much of a back-slapper." He thumbed the scar on his face. "And looking like this, I'd probably scare more babies than I could kiss."

She stifled a sob as she looked away from him. He was beginning to grow concerned when he heard a loud knock at the door.

"Sheriff?" It was Blake. "I hate to bother you during supper, but it's real important."

Trammel scowled at the door. He did not dare think about leaving Emily in such a state. "Not now. I'll be over at the jail later. You can tell me then."

But Blake persisted. "I wish I could, boss, but this can't keep. It won't wait that long."

He tried to comfort his wife, but she pulled away from him as she got up from the table. "Just go, Steve. You'll just be too worried about what Blake needs to listen to anything I say anyway."

Trammel remained on his knee as she picked up their plates and took them into the kitchen. He wanted to tell her she was wrong. He wanted to tell her that she was all he cared about. That the town could wait.

But they both knew that was not true, and he had never lied to her before.

He got to his feet and opened the door to find Blake standing on his porch. "This had better be good."

"Sorry for disturbing you like this," Blake said, "but we've got real trouble. You got another telegram from Marshal Rollins in Cheyenne. He's asking if Deputy Brandt got to town. He's worried about him and seems to have good reason."

Trammel could not believe Blake had seen fit to interrupt him for something so trivial. "How should I know where he is? He probably got drunk somewhere and is sleeping it off."

"I thought that, too, until a young fella rode into town just now. Said he's here under a flag of truce. Got a shirt on a stick and everything."

Trammel wondered if Blake was drunk. He was not making sense. "A what?"

"A flag of truce he calls it," Blake said. "And that ain't the half of it. He says he's been sent by the Washington Gang with orders to only speak to you. I've got a couple of our boys watching him while I came to get you."

Trammel was beginning to understand why Blake had seen fit to interrupt his supper. "It's got to have something to do with Brandt being missing, doesn't it?"

"I can't say that for certain," Blake admitted, "but figured it was important enough to trouble you because of it. I would've left you in peace if I thought otherwise."

"And you were right to do it." Trammel took his hat from the peg by the door, his shoulder rig from the newel post at the stairs, and pulled the door shut behind him. "Sorry about being angry. Emily and I had an argument."

"Think nothing of it. Makes me glad I'm a bachelor."

Trammel shrugged into his shoulder holster as he joined Blake in walking along the thoroughfare. When they rounded the corner, he could see a good-sized crowd had already begun to gather in front of City Hall.

"You ever seen this idiot with the flag before?" Trammel asked his deputy as he shifted his Peacemaker under his left arm. "What does he look like?"

"Young," Blake said as he struggled to keep pace with the much taller sheriff. "Younger than Hawkeye, would be my guess. Looks like you could keep him in a bath for a week and the grime would still stay on him. I can't say for certain if he's one of Washington's men or not, but he seems to be telling the truth."

Trammel did not like to see so many citizens gathering around the young man with a message. Even the hint of the Washington Gang being anywhere near Laramie could be enough to start a panic. And with Hagen entertaining his cattleman's association over at The Laramie Grand, he knew things could get out of hand in a hurry.

"Let's go see what this youngster has to say for himself."

Trammel knifed his way through the growing crowd, knocking civilians aside without stopping to apologize.

He found a scrawny, flea-bitten young man talking to one of the civilians. He held a stick with a gray shirt affixed to it as if it were Old Glory itself.

The boy stopped talking to the townsman when he saw Trammel charging his way. "My name is Dib Bishop, Sheriff Trammel, and I've come to—"

Trammel batted away the stick and snatched Bishop by the back of the neck. He half-shoved, half-carried the boy up the stairs to City Hall as Blake and the deputies kept the crowd back.

Dib tried to get free but could not break Trammel's grip. "You've got no call to treat me like this, Sheriff. I come with a message under a flag of truce from the Washington Gang."

"I heard you the first time." Trammel called for Blake, and the deputy ran up the stairs to join them. When Blake reached the top, the sheriff shoved Bishop at him. "Lock this kid in shackles and take him up to my office. Keep him there until I come to get him."

Blake took hold of the boy as Trammel took the stairs down to the jail. "Where are you going?"

Trammel motioned for the guard to open the door to the cells. "To get some answers before I get lies from that pup."

Dr. Carson came out of his office when he heard the prisoners begin to raise a holler. It was already an hour past mealtime, so there was no call for any excitement.

It was only when he saw Sheriff Trammel heading his way that he understood the cause of the uproar.

"Evening, Sheriff," Carson said as he joined Trammel in the aisle between the cells. "We weren't expecting you to stop by this evening. What's the occasion?"

"Answers," Trammel said as he walked past him without stopping. An iron ring of keys jangled at his side. "Follow me."

Carson had seen that dark look on Trammel's face many times before and was familiar with the violence that often followed it. "Who are you planning to question? And will I need my medical bag?"

"A burlap sack will be more useful if he lies to me."

Carson was not surprised when Trammel stopped outside Ben Washington's cell. Blankets were still in place to prevent the other inmates from seeing the famous outlaw inside. The men cheered and banged the bars of their cells as Trammel searched for the right key on the ring.

He turned to them and shouted, "The next man who makes a sound will answer to me."

Carson knew most of the inmates had lived through the jailbreak. They knew Trammel's temper was a force to be as much feared as respected. The men gradually calmed down as Trammel found the right key.

The sheriff opened the lock and threw open the door. Carson kept the door from banging shut again as Trammel tore the blanket down and fell on Ben Washington.

Carson watched as Trammel snatched the prisoner by the collar and pinned him to the cot. Washington's legs flailed wildly as he tried in vain to pry the larger man's hands from his throat.

"The name Dib Bishop mean anything to you, Washington?"

Trammel let up just enough pressure on Washington's throat to allow him to respond. "I don't have to tell you anything."

Carson closed his eyes. That was the worst possible answer Washington could give.

He heard the man choke as Trammel tightened his grip. "Say that again and I'll hurt you. Does Dib Bishop ride with your bunch?"

Washington coughed as Trammel relaxed his grip. "What if he does? What's it to you?"

"Means nothing to me, but someone sent that idiot here

with a message for me. Who's in charge of your gang when you're not around?"

Carson watched Washington flash a prideful grin. "That'd be George Mahaffey. And he wouldn't have shown his hand like that unless he wanted you to see it. You're in trouble, Trammel. Worse trouble than you know."

Trammel kept his weight off Washington's windpipe. "He rode in alone and without supplies, so the rest are bound to be close. Where could they be?"

"Can't say for certain," Washington said. "How about you and I ride out together. See if we can't find them?"

Trammel threw his forearm across Washington's neck and put his considerable weight behind it. "You don't have to tell me anything, and I don't have to keep seeing you're fed. Tell me where they're hiding out or you'll spend the rest of your time here hog-tied and gagged."

He let up enough to allow Washington to say, "They could be anywhere! I know a hundred places within half a day's ride of here and there's probably a hundred more I don't know about. If I give you the wrong one, you'll think I'm lying and beat me. If I tell you something too soon, you'll think I'm lying and beat me anyway. I'm in for a thumping anyway, so I might as well keep my mouth shut and take it."

Trammel released him and stood over him. "How many men ride with you besides Mahaffey?"

Washington rose onto his elbows. "Fifty. Maybe a hundred. Maybe only one. You won't believe what I tell you, so don't expect me to tell you the truth."

Washington flinched when Trammel slapped his hand against the wall just above his head. "The deputy marshal they sent to bring you to Cheyenne is missing, Washington, and I think your boys grabbed him. You'd better hope he's still alive because if he's not, I'm going to make sure you pay for it."

Washington's grin turned into a defiant sneer. "How? They can only hang me once."

Carson did not expect Trammel to leave it at that but was glad when the sheriff walked out of the cell. He pushed past the doctor and said, "Lock him in and stay close, doc. I might need you sooner than Washington would like."

Carson stepped outside, quietly closed the cell door and locked it.

Washington laughed out at the doctor from the cot. "Where are you going, doc? Ain't you gonna give me something to soothe my throat? A little whiskey, maybe?"

Carson might have taken pity on the outlaw had he been someone else. But Ben Washington was far beyond any emotion the doctor might be able to spare for him. "Your throat will be fine. Wouldn't hurt for you to pray a little, though."

"No thanks. I'd prefer the whiskey."

"I'm sure you would." Carson removed the key from the lock. "But if Trammel sees fit to come back down here, only God will be able to save you then, not me."

"He can't do that." Washington laughed. "That would be against the law."

Carson heard the guard close the iron door that led up to City Hall. "Against the law, maybe, but not Trammel's law."

CHAPTER 8

Deputy Blake ignored Dib Bishop's babbling while he waited for Sheriff Trammel to return to his office.

"He can't do this to me," Bishop kept repeating. "I rode in here under a flag of truce."

"Quiet," Blake told him. "Save it for when the sheriff gets up here."

Blake did not know when Trammel would get there and that was what troubled him. He often did not understand what the sheriff did or why these days. It was not so much that Blake thought he should be included in his decisions, but it would help if he could follow his reasoning.

He remembered how he and Trammel had gotten off to a rocky start when Rob Moran had picked Buck Trammel to replace him as sheriff of Laramie County. Blake had worked with Moran for more than five years. He knew the county better than anyone and the people in it. He had never thought the job was his for the taking but thought he had earned consideration for the office. The other deputies had thought so, too. But Rob Moran had made up his mind and any lingering resentment Blake had about the decision was cast aside the moment Moran had been shot dead on the front steps of City Hall.

Trammel had been a difficult man to like at first. He did not have a welcoming nature, but Blake and the others had grown to respect him. It was difficult not to have regard for a man willing to put his life at risk for others.

Over time, Blake had grown to feel a certain loyalty for him. When the town elders turned against Trammel for pursuing Lucien Clay after the jailbreak instead of staying in Laramie to restore order, Blake had spoken up for Trammel. He and the other deputies had even gone as far as threatening to quit if they fired Trammel.

But Trammel had not been making sense lately, and Blake was beginning to wonder why. Ben Washington was one of the most wanted men in the territory, and Blake could have ridden out and taken him in alone. A man trapped with a family in a cabin was not difficult to bring down.

But Trammel had not only insisted on going with Blake, but he had also decided to leave young Hawkeye in charge while they were gone. The other deputies had resented the decision, and Blake could not blame them.

Had Trammel been another man, he might have thought it had something to do with the upcoming election for sheriff. But Trammel had never been much of a politician, which Blake saw as a problem. For all of his strength and bravery, it took more than guns and fists to keep a town in line. A place had law and order because the people respected the law and remained orderly. They only did that if they respected the men who had the power to enforce the law.

More than a few people in town had told Blake that they no longer thought Trammel was the right man for the job. They wanted someone they understood and who understood them. The sheriff's closeness with Adam

Hagen was an ongoing concern, though the town elders knew men like Hagen were a necessary evil.

Blake hoped this business with Washington and his gang was cleared up soon. He would hate to see Trammel lose his job because he was too busy doing it.

Blake heard Trammel's heavy footfalls on the stairs. He could tell by the pattern that the sheriff was coming with a full head of steam. Whatever he had gotten Ben Washington to tell him was not good news.

Trammel did not stop when he pushed open his office door and headed straight for Dib Bishop's chair.

The young man raised his shackled wrists as if they might be enough to keep Trammel away. "I came here under a flag of truce to deliver a message from the Washington Gang."

"Your flag doesn't mean anything." Trammel leaned on the arms of Bishop's chair, causing the boy to cringe away from him. "We're not soldiers, and this isn't war. George Mahaffey sent you, didn't he?"

Bishop remained coiled against the back of his chair. "How'd you know that?"

"You'd be surprised by what I know," Trammel told him. "Your leader is real chatty. Tell me what you came here to say and if you lie, I'm going to be angry."

Trammel pushed back a bit to give the kid some room. "George wants you to know that he has Deputy Brandt. He grabbed him on the road between here and Cheyenne, but I can't tell you where he's holding him because I don't know. He wants to trade Brandt for Ben. If you let Ben go, he'll let the deputy go."

"And if I don't?"

Bishop swallowed. "He didn't tell me that much. He

just wants you to give me your answer. By tomorrow morning. He wants me to ride back at first light."

Trammel closed in again. "Return where?"

"A creek about an hour from here," Bishop told him. "But he won't be keeping Brandt there for long. They rode off after he sent me here, and they're long gone by now. You can beat me all night and I won't tell you where because I don't know, and that's the truth."

Trammel looked over at Blake. "Any idea where this creek might be?"

Blake wished he did. "Could be anywhere, boss, but I think he's telling the truth."

Trammel returned his attention to Bishop. "What makes you think you're riding out of here in the morning? Since Mahaffey likes taking captives, maybe I'll take one of my own."

"He already thought of that." Bishop chanced a look at him. "That's why he sent Marcum to watch over my back trail. He figured you'd understand what that meant."

Trammel looked back at Blake again. "That name mean anything to you?"

Blake was beginning to admire how Mahaffey thought. "Marcum's a sharpshooter said to ride with Washington. He's supposed to be pretty good, and I've never heard anyone say anything to the contrary."

Bishop added, "He's supposed to start shooting people from the edge of town if you don't turn me loose in the morning. Alone. He said you might not be afraid to die, but you won't want anyone else getting themselves shot on account of your stubbornness. If I don't ride out of here all by my lonesome, Marcum is gonna start dropping folks and you won't be able to stop him before he does."

Blake thought the sheriff might hit him but was glad

when Trammel pushed himself off the chair and backed away from the boy.

"Mahaffey told you to say all that, did he?"

Dib Bishop sat upright in his chair again. His confidence had returned. "He not only said it, but he also meant it. I'd sure hate to be in your shoes, Sheriff."

"You'll be hating the ones you're in soon enough." Trammel came over to Blake. "What do you make of him?"

Blake was glad to tell him. "I think this little rat is telling the truth as he knows it. Marcum's a known killer and won't mind shooting a few civilians if he has to. As for whether or not I think Mahaffey will let Brandt go if you give him Washington, that's not for me to say."

"No. That decision is all up to me." He looked down at Bishop. "I'm not so sure he's really with Washington's bunch. You've seen how close I've gotten to Ben the past couple of days. I can't see his men trusting a flea-bitten mutt like this with a job this big."

Dib Bishop almost came out of his chair. "I'm man enough to ride with Ben and hold my own, too. He'd never say otherwise."

Trammel ignored him. "I bet this little trail rat doesn't even know how many men ride with Washington."

Bishop jutted his chin up at the sheriff. "Ten men and each one of them alone is tough enough to put your big carcass in the ground."

Trammel smiled. "Thanks. Ben wouldn't tell me how many were out there with you, but you just did."

Bishop leapt from his chair, but Blake cut him off and grabbed him. "Where do you want me to keep him, boss?"

"Don't put him downstairs," Trammel said. "He'll just yelp all night for Washington. You'd better talk to Old Bob and stick him in one of the stalls. Make sure you pair him up with a horse that doesn't like noise. That ought to keep him quiet enough until I figure out what to do with him."

Bishop tried to break free from Blake, but the deputy easily pulled him from the office as Bishop yelled to Trammel, "You do that, Sheriff. You think long and hard about what you're gonna do next because a lot of lives depend on it. Yours least of all."

Trammel shut the office door in his face as Blake dragged him toward the stairs.

Once the door was closed, Bishop began to move under his own power. "I don't know what all the fuss is about him. He ain't much.".

"Sure he is, kid." Blake led him down the stairs. "I hope you don't find out he's everything they say he is and more."

CHAPTER 9

Adam Hagen had lived through sieges before, but never one like this. Instead of firing bullets or arrows, frantic gamblers waved betting slips and money at him. They may not have been singing death songs or cutting loose with rebel yells but shouting the bets they wanted to place was almost as rattling.

Hagen was glad that his guards were there to keep his customers from storming the small platform they had hastily built at the side of the casino floor. He had been caught up in the commotion while walking through the lobby and did not know what had caused this sudden rush in betting.

"Has another war broken out?" Hagen asked Rube over the shouts of the gambling hall.

"It's the Washington Gang, boss. They've grabbed Leo Brandt on the trail."

Hagen considered himself an informed man, but he had no idea who Miller was talking about. "Who the devil is Leo Brandt?"

Miller leaned closer and spoke louder. "A deputy U.S. Marshal out of Cheyenne. Lefty Rollins sent him here to pick up Washington and bring him back for trial. We just heard that Ben's men sent a messenger to talk to Trammel. They want to trade Washington for Brandt. They said they'll kill the deputy if Trammel doesn't make the trade." He pointed down at the throng of men clamoring for their attention. "They must've heard about it and want to bet accordingly."

Hagen was thrilled they wanted to give him their money but knew how quickly excitement could devolve into anger. A bump perceived as a shove could start a brawl. One misunderstanding would return The Laramie Grand back to its former name. The Tinder Box. The only thing worse than the destruction would be the knowledge that Buck Trammel had been right to warn against accepting wagers on the Washington matter.

Amid the growing chaos, Hagen spotted Wayne Carter standing just beside the platform. He had not seen the man since the gathering in his suite the night before. He appeared to be as unaffected by the pushing and shoving as a man standing beneath an awning in a rainstorm.

Hagen noted Carter was not as well-dressed as the other cattlemen. He sported a brown derby and coat to match. He had his thumbs tucked in his gun belt and Hagen spotted a pistol on his right hip, though he did not appear to be eager to use it.

Hagen held up his hands and shouted for his customers to be quiet. When they refused to cooperate, he drew his pistol from his hip and aimed it at the ceiling. He had no intention of shooting, of course. The plaster work had cost him a small fortune, but the sight of the gun had the desired quieting effect on the crowd.

"Gentlemen," Hagen shouted, "I need you all to remain calm for a moment. I understand there has been a development in the Washington matter that might affect the odds. As I've only just learned of this, I must ask you to be patient with us while we find out exactly what has happened. I ask you to give us two hours to investigate so we can offer revised, correct odds for all concerned. The Laramie Grand has a reputation for offering the best and fairest odds in the territory. I assure you that Mr. Miller and his men will be glad to take your bets as soon as we know more. Until then, the gaming tables will remain open and there's still plenty of whiskey to help you pass the time. In fact, the next drink is on the house."

The prospect of free liquor was enough to cause even the most ardent gambler among them to rush across the gaming floor to the bar.

Everyone except for Wayne Carter, who remained behind.

Hagen pulled Miller closer to him. "You hold the fort while I go talk to Trammel. He'll know what's happened. I'll be back with news as soon as I can."

Rube Miller looked relieved. "Sounds good to me. I thought they were going to stampede us there for a moment."

Hagen had another concern beside a horde of rowdy gamblers. "Did you hear back from New Orleans about the Carter boys yet."

"Nope. I sent the wire, but no answer. I've been too busy with all these Washington bets to send another wire. But I've had some of our boys watching him and his brothers. They said at least one of them has been around the floor all day and night, but no one's seen them so much as take a drink or place a bet or even talk to any of Janine's girls. They just watch. I think you're right about them, boss. I don't like the attention they're paying to how we do things."

Hagen patted his arm before he stepped down from the platform. He found Wayne Carter waiting for him with a broad smile beneath his drooping moustache. "That was a fine bit of speech-making on your part, Mr. Hagen. I didn't think you'd be able to turn them so quick. I'd have lost good money betting exactly on the opposite result."

"I wish you had," Hagen said. "It would've been the first bet either you or your brothers would have placed since you arrived here days ago."

Carter grinned. "I thought you had someone keeping an eye on us."

"I make it my business to know everything that goes on in all of my places. You and your brothers seem to prefer to keep your own company. Kind of undermines your purpose for coming to a cattleman's convention, doesn't it?"

"That would depend on my purpose for being here," Carter said. "My true purpose. And I think you've figured out by now that me and my brothers aren't really ranchers."

Hagen was glad Carter was finally being honest about it. "Consider me intrigued, but I'm afraid your reasons will have to remain a mystery to me for a bit longer. I'm running late for an appointment. I'm sure we can find time to talk later."

Hagen moved away and Carter followed. "I know you're quite a busy man, but I think you'll find my reasons for being here are important. Would you mind if I walk with you?"

"By all means, but I'll have to insist that you tell me your real name if you do. This Carter business was never too convincing."

"Fair enough. My real name is Jean LeBlanc, but I always go by Wayne."

The name Wayne Carter had meant nothing to Hagen, but LeBlanc was quite a different story. He remembered the brothers had started off as pool hall toughs who quickly graduated to working as hired guns for some of the more undesirable gambling dens in New Orleans. "You boys were just beginning to make a name for yourselves when my time in New Orleans came to an unfortunate end. Your reputation precedes you, sir. My compliments."

"As has yours, Mr. Hagen," LeBlanc said. "My brothers and I weren't surprised to see you'd built yourself quite a business here in Laramie. We figured it was finally time for us to pay you a visit and introduce ourselves to you properly."

"I never turn down an opportunity to make a new friend or two." Hagen waved to one of his blackjack dealers as they walked by. "But we both know you're not here to sample my whiskey or try your luck at my tables. Why are you really here?"

LeBlanc smiled. "The oldest reason there is."

Hagen smiled, too. "Sorry to disappoint you, Wayne, but you're hardly my type."

"The second oldest reason, then. Money. Lots of it. You have it. My brothers and I can help you make more of it. Much more."

Hagen had figured as much. "What can you offer me that I don't already have? Muscle? I've got plenty of men on my payroll who can manage that side of the business. Bouncers? There's no shortage of ruffians in Laramie. I suppose I could always use a few more dealers for my tables if you're interested."

"We kind of had our heart set on something better."

"Didn't we all?" Hagen sighed. "I was going to be a captain of industry."

"And look at you now," LeBlanc said. "Everyone has a run of bad luck now and then. Some runs longer than others. Some have it sooner rather than later."

Hagen had been wondering when the conversation

would take a nasty turn. "Let me guess. You and your brothers can assure me that my good fortune will continue in exchange for a cut of the house take. Nothing too greedy at first. Perhaps five percent or so split between the five of you with the promise of increasing it to ten percent within the first year."

"I was thinking of something closer to twenty percent to start," LeBlanc said. "Me and my brothers are worth it. You can ask Big Littlejohn down in New Orleans if you don't believe me. He'll be more than happy to vouch for what my brothers and I can do for a place."

"Littlejohn?" Hagen laughed. "Is that old pimp still toddling around? I heard he was dead years ago."

LeBlanc did not laugh. "He's more than a pimp these days. He's got most of New Orleans in his pocket. Me and my brothers helped put it there for him."

"I didn't know he was that enterprising." Hagen led him past another blackjack table as customers groaned when the dealer flipped his card, revealing he had a perfect twenty-one. "Whatever he's got going on down there is nothing like I have up here."

"I know," LeBlanc said. "My brothers have spent the past few days watching all of your places, Mr. Hagen, and you're lucky we came along when we did. We've noticed many cracks we can help you fill."

"Is that so?" Hagen asked as they headed toward the lobby. "Give me an example."

"I could give you several, but let's talk about the way you move your money around this place. You have men dressed as waiters collect it on a tray and move it into the side door back there where you count it. A blind man could see it. That's not exactly what I'd call subtle, and it wouldn't take much for someone to force their way into the back room."

Hagen had decided to collect the money that way by design. "I prefer style over subtlety in a gambling den. The clerks dress the same as the waiters in my dining room to create a certain look. In New Orleans, I believe they called it 'ambiance.'"

"They still do," LeBlanc said. "I call it careless. The door to the counting room isn't even guarded. With all the money pouring in from these Ben Washington bets you're taking, I'm surprised someone hasn't tried to rip you off by now."

"Feel free to test your theory any time you wish," Hagen said. "But I can assure you that if you do, you won't like what you find waiting for you on the other side of that door."

Hagen was glad his mockery had taken some of the shine from LeBlanc's brass.

LeBlanc said, "Seeing as how much work you put into this place, it would be a shame if someone came along and tried to steal from you. It wouldn't look good, what with all these rich cattlemen running around. Something like a robbery would flat out ruin all their fun, not to mention the damage it would do to your reputation. And just when you're starting to make something of yourself again, too. I bet people have already begun to forget about that business with your father. Not everyone believed his death was old age. Your family turning on you started some nasty rumors that you might've helped the old fella die. Rumors like that have a way of catching on, especially if you don't have someone like me to keep them from sparking."

Hagen resented this Royal Street thug daring to remind

him of what people had said about him. Of what many still said.

LeBlanc had just crossed a line he did not know was there. He was no longer an amusement, but a threat. "Temper, Mr. LeBlanc. No need to get testy when you were doing so well at making your point."

"My point speaks for itself," LeBlanc said. "You already control all the best places in town, and I hear you've got Sheriff Trammel eating out of the palm of your hand. You could have the whole territory in your hip pocket if you play it right. You're a smart man, but you're only one man. My brothers and I could help you double what you're already making. By this time next year, we could have you stretch all the way down to Denver. Why turn down a chance to help you get back some of what your family took from you."

Hagen led him into the lobby. "It'll take much more than thuggery to make that happen."

"But without thuggery, you don't have a prayer. You'd be surprised at how useful the LeBlanc brothers can be to a man like you."

Hagen walked to the front desk. "Not to mention how vengeful they can be if scorned, I'm sure." He turned his back to LeBlanc as he summoned over Mr. Lee, the head clerk and asked to see the guest register.

LeBlanc kept his distance, looking over the lobby. "I thought you had to go see the sheriff?"

"I do, but this won't take long," Hagen said as he turned his back to LeBlanc as he casually slid the bone-handle knife from its sheath beneath his brocade vest. "As you've already learned for yourself, I like to keep a close eye on things."

Hagen spoke to Mr. Lee as he looked over the ledger

with his left hand and slipped the blade under his right sleeve. "Looks like we've got another full house tonight."

"It'll be like that for the next month, Mr. Hagen," the head clerk said proudly. "Word about the Grand's prominence has spread through the territory like wildfire."

His blade now ready for use, Hagen turned the ledger back toward Mr. Lee. "My compliments to you and your clerks. Keep up the good work."

Hagen led LeBlanc out the front door and onto the boardwalk. The street was relatively quiet, almost abandoned. "I take it you've been too busy looking for ways to rob me blind to have had the opportunity to meet Sheriff Trammel."

LeBlanc stayed a few steps behind him. "I like to stay away from the law when I can."

"As do I," Hagen said. "Neither Trammel nor I would be caught dead being seen talking to each other in public, which is why we usually meet in the livery behind the hotel." Hagen beckoned LeBlanc to follow him into the alley. "I think now would be a good time for me to introduce you to him, seeing as how we'll all be working closely together."

LeBlanc hesitated as Hagen stepped into the dark alley beside the hotel. "You really think I'm dumb enough to walk in there with you?"

Hagen doubled back to him as he waved off the idea. "Look at you being as skittish as a foal. Don't sell yourself short, Wayne."

He plunged the knife into LeBlanc's side as he grabbed the man's gun, pulled it from his holster and tossed it behind him into the alley. "I know you're much dumber than that. Any man with a lick of sense in him would be smart enough not to ever threaten me."

He took LeBlanc by the shirt and pulled him with him into the darkness before pushing him against the wall of the hotel. "Make a sound and I promise I'll make this far more painful than it has to be."

"You're out of your mind!" LeBlanc struggled to grab the knife handle, but Hagen used it to keep him pinned in place.

"And you're out of your depth," Hagen whispered. "A man in my line of work comes to expect the occasional shakedown now and then. It comes with the territory. But I resent a cut-rate operator like you coming into my town to lean on me for a piece of my action. And that bit about threatening me in my own joint? That's just downright insulting. You've hurt my feelings, LeBlanc. Now I'm going to hurt you."

LeBlanc tried to swing at Hagen, but the gambler dodged the blow and plunged the knife deeper in the man's side. Hagen put his free hand over LeBlanc's mouth as the wounded man said, "You won't get away with this. You're a dead man, Hagen. My brothers won't just let this go. They'll bring down everything you love in this world."

Hagen pushed LeBlanc even flatter against the wall. "So many have said, yet here I am. I wouldn't put much faith in your kin. Once word gets out about what happened to you, they'll make themselves scarce. They and everyone like them will learn that The Laramie Grand is no easy target and Adam Hagen is nobody's pigeon."

Hagen grabbed LeBlanc by the collar and used the knife to steer him deeper into the dark recesses of the alley. "Don't be so glum about this. You walked into my place as just another grifter looking for a piece of the pie. By this time tomorrow, you'll be a legend. An example of what will happen to any tinhorn and crook with similar dreams of swiping an easy buck at my expense."

"My brothers," LeBlanc said as he stumbled backward. "They'll . . . they'll avenge me."

Hagen pushed him toward the back where the cooks dumped their refuse. It seemed like a fitting final resting place for the career of a man such as LeBlanc to end. "From garbage you came. To garbage you shall return."

CHAPTER 10

"I don't like this, George," Tim said to Mahaffey. "I don't like anything about it one bit.

George Mahaffey took a sip of coffee as he watched the flames of the cook fire dance. Normally, there was nothing he enjoyed better than sitting beside a good fire at the end of a long day. He liked to use the quiet time to set his troubles aside while he lost himself in the flames. Ben Washington liked the men of his gang to rest when they could manage it so they would be fresh for whatever awaited them in the day ahead. Mahaffey thought Ben did his best thinking while the rest of the gang slept.

But Ben Washington was in jail, so the burden of leadership fell to Mahaffey. The enjoyment of a quiet cup of coffee would have to wait. "What don't you like, Tim?"

"Him." The outlaw pointed at Deputy Brandt, who was sitting on the ground at the edge of the fire. "I don't like the idea of leaving him with his hands tied in front of him like that. Might give him ideas about running off in the middle of the night."

Mahaffey had thought that might be the case. Tim had always been a worrier. "His legs are bound, and he's got almost ten men sleeping around him. There's only one way into this canyon and one way out. He won't be going anywhere. Not with you standing watch up on those rocks like you're supposed to be doing now."

"I'm watching, all right. I just don't like what I see." Tim kept looking over at the defenseless lawman on the ground. "He came with us a bit too easy for my tastes. And the way he just sits there watching everyone in camp is downright unsettling if you ask me."

"But no one asked you, did they?" Mahaffey said. "What do you expect him to do? Play the fiddle and dance? Sing songs? His hands and feet are tied, and they're going to stay that way until Dib and Johnny get back here with Trammel's answer tomorrow. You've got more to worry about from a coyote sneaking up on us than you do from him. Now get to standing watch before I lose my patience."

"I'm going," Tim said as he got to his feet and picked up his rifle. "But if that fella does anything stupid, I'll put a bullet in his belly for his trouble."

Mahaffey allowed him to have the last word as he watched Tim walk up the incline among the rocks to begin his watch.

Brandt cleared his throat. "I guess your friend doesn't like me much."

Mahaffey swirled his cup to soak up the coffee grinds in the bottom. "He doesn't have to like you. He just has to keep on doing what he's told. And so do you. The less we hear from you, the better. Keep quiet and get some sleep if you know what's good for you."

Brandt held out his bound hands toward the warmth of the fire. "Doesn't make it easy on you, though. Being in charge of all these men like this. I can tell you don't care for it much."

Mahaffey did not know he was that easy to read. "I don't

care much for any of this business. And right now, all I care about is getting Ben back here where he belongs."

"Seeing as how my life depends on it," Brandt said, "that's all I care about, too. Say, I heard you boys got your start rustling cattle in Nebraska. I put in a fair amount of time in the saddle myself. Down in El Paso before I came up here. You boys ever get that far south in your travels?"

Mahaffey knew what Brandt was trying to do. He wanted to keep the conversation going in the hope that they might form a kind of friendship. He was banking on sentiment being enough to make Mahaffey or some of the others hesitate if it came time to kill him.

"You can save your breath, lawman." Mahaffey sipped his coffee. "Chatting me up won't do you a lick of good. Tomorrow is going to be here soon enough and what's going to happen will happen. You'll either go on living or you'll be dead. All the words you throw at me now isn't going to change that one tiny bit."

"I didn't expect they would." Brandt kept his hands near the fire. "Just trying to pass the time is all."

Mahaffey drained the rest of his coffee. "You don't think we'll actually go ahead with it, do you? Kill you, I mean."

Brandt grew quiet as he thought it over. "I'd like to think you wouldn't like to do it. But as for whether or not you would, I can't tell yet. I don't know you well enough, except by reputation."

"Well maybe I can give you something to chew over while you try to sleep." Mahaffey reached for the coffee pot and poured himself another cup. "You're nothing to me and you're nothing to the men scattered around you, either. You're not a friend or a deputy or somebody's son, or husband, or brother. You're no different than a chip on a poker table, and I'll cash you in if it'll help get Ben out of this fix he's found himself in. Whether it means us handing you over to Trammel or putting one right between the eyes, it's all the same to us."

"At least I know where I stand." Brandt rubbed his bound hands as best he could. "You ever come up against the likes of Sheriff Trammel before?"

Mahaffey had not pegged Brandt to be such a talker. "No, but I know the kind of man he is. We've faced down plenty of men like him and we're all still here to tell the tale. We'll be here long after tomorrow, too."

"I guess," Brandt allowed, "but it was different then, wasn't it. You had Ben to see you through all those other times."

Mahaffey glared at him from across the fire. The deputy had finally found a way to get inside his mind and plant a seed of doubt.

Brandt kept talking. "You know he'll never trade me for Washington. He'd sooner hang your friend in his cell in Laramie than turn him over. I don't mean anything to Trammel. He's never met me and probably hasn't even heard of me before tonight. He'll say I knew the risks when I let Lefty Rollins pin a deputy's star on my shirt."

"And he'd be right." Mahaffey's joints popped as he got a leg under himself and stood. The chilly night air had settled into his bones, causing them to ache. "But, for your sake, let's hope you're wrong about Trammel. You seem like a decent enough kid. I'd hate to have to kill you on account of another man's stubbornness. But I will if he makes me." He looked out at the men bedded down on the ground around them. "And so will any of them."

Mahaffey took his coffee with him as he went to where he had placed his saddle and blanket just beyond the reach of the fire light. He did not expect Trammel to come looking for them in the dark, but it paid to be careful.

The outlaw gave Brandt a final word of caution before he turned in for the night. "And don't get any ideas about running off. There's not a sound sleeper in the bunch. If they hear so much as a snake slithering in the dark, they're liable to come up firing. And don't forget about what Tim said about putting a bullet in your belly. See to it that you don't give him the chance."

Leo Brandt smiled. "And here I was thinking you didn't care about what happened to me."

Mahaffey set his cup on the ground as he unrolled his blanket. "I'll care until Dib and Johnny get back. After that, we'll see."

Buck Trammel may have been looking out the window of his office but did not see much of anything beyond his own reflection. Not the lights of The Laramie Grand across the thoroughfare. Not even the night that had settled over Laramie. He was too lost in his thoughts as he turned Leo Brandt's deputy star on his desk like he turned over the problem in his mind. He had found it while searching Bishop's saddlebags after questioning him.

He had an impossible choice to make. Ben Washington for Leo Brandt. The most wanted man in the territory in exchange for a deputy with barely a year's worth of experience. A man he did not know. A good man for a bad one.

It was not much of a choice at all, which was what troubled Trammel most. A man's life hung in the balance, but it was not as simple as that. If he let Washington go, every outlaw's brother and friend would grab any lawman they could and make the same demand.

Buck Trammel could not live with that outcome. But he did not know if he could live with an innocent man's blood on his hands.

Come first light, he would have to give Dib Bishop an answer before he let him ride out of town. If he held Bishop in a cell, that sharpshooter Marcum may very well start shooting innocent people on the street. He could order people to remain indoors, but that would make his deputies a target. He could not even order his men to follow Bishop out of town, for he was sure Marcum would put a bullet in any man who tried to follow him and Bishop back to wherever Mahaffey was holding Leo Brandt.

And there was yet another problem to consider. Once word spread that the dreaded Washington Gang was somewhere near Laramie, panic would spread through town. No matter how Trammel flipped the coin, death won.

He was pulled from the depths of his thoughts when Adam Hagen entered his office, waving a white handkerchief.

"I come to parlay under a flag of truce." Hagen grinned. "I understand that's the fashionable way to approach you now."

Trammel was in no mood for Hagen's nonsense. "Go away, Adam. I'm busy."

"You're not, but you soon will be." Hagen pocketed his handkerchief as he leaned against Trammel's desk. "I came to tell you that word has already gotten out that Washington's men are close. The streets are quiet now, but the good people of Laramie will have themselves worked into quite a frenzy about it by morning. You'd best get your brooding in now while you can."

Trammel gripped Brandt's badge tighter. "I'm not brooding. I'm thinking."

"Of course," Hagen deferred. "I heard about Mahaffey's demands. I didn't know if there was much to the rumors, but I can see now that there is."

Now, Trammel knew why Hagen had paid him a visit. "Guess you're here to get a better fix on the odds."

"That's certainly part of it," Hagen admitted. "Mostly I'm here out of concern for you. You're in quite a bad way, Buck. I don't envy your position."

Trammel tossed the deputy's star on his desk and ran his hands over his face. "If I don't let Washington go, they'll kill Brandt. If I don't let their idiot messenger go, Marcum will start shooting people on the street until I do. If I keep Washington here, I might have a town full of scared citizens begging me to get rid of him. I can't move him to Cheyenne and the town might lynch him if I keep him downstairs. Seems like whatever I decide, someone dies."

Hagen picked up Brandt's badge and began to examine it. "I suppose that's one way of looking at it."

Trammel looked up from his hands. "What's that supposed to mean?"

Hagen palmed the badge as he walked over to the window. "It means that the answer has been staring you right in the face this entire time and you don't even know it."

Trammel's chair creaked as he leaned forward. "What answer?"

"You're looking at this situation like a lawman, Buck." He tapped the window with Brandt's star. "If you look at it like a gambler, the answer is pretty obvious."

Trammel knew how Hagen liked to twist words. "How obvious?"

"To borrow a tried-and-true poker term," Hagen said,

"this Mahaffey character is bluffing. Even worse, he's bluffing blind, and you seem content to let him get away with it."

Trammel's hopes of an obvious solution faded. "I'm in no mood for another gambling lesson right now."

"Then think of it as a lesson in strategy instead," Hagen explained. "Mahaffey has been running the table on you so far. First, he sends a boy to tell you he wants Washington in exchange for Brandt. You're supposed to give him your answer or he'll kill Brandt, right? If you don't let his messenger go in the morning, he's got a man out there who'll shoot people until you release him. Let's assume all of that is true." Hagen threw open his hands. "The solution is clear. You call Mahaffey's bluff. You call it by not giving him an answer at all."

Trammel's first instinct was to tell Hagen he was wasting his time. That he was out of his mind.

But was he?

The gambler smiled. "Did the imbecile with the flag tell you what would happen if you just sent him on his way at first light?"

Trammel thought over their earlier conversation. "No. He just said they'd kill Brandt if I didn't agree to let Washington go."

"There's the answer. Mahaffey's bluffing. You call his bluff by simply staying silent. He won't be expecting that. Bishop and Marcum certainly won't be expecting it and they won't know how to react. Rather than risking Mahaffey's anger, they'll do nothing."

Trammel got up from his chair and walked away from Hagen. He'd had just about enough of his nonsense. "This isn't a courtroom, Adam. Mahaffey won't buy that he lost just because he didn't use the right words."

"You mean semantics," Hagen said. "And you're right. It won't buy us anything except something that's invaluable to you right now. Time. And time may lead to an opportunity."

Trammel's head was beginning to ache. "How?"

Hagen said, "You turn Bishop loose in the morning just like they want. Let him and Marcum ride off back to wherever they're keeping Brandt to deliver your answer, or at least your lack of one. I'll hang back at a good distance and track them after they've left. I'll find out where they are, ride back here and, together, we get some men and rescue Brandt. Or at least try."

Trammel knew there had to be more to it than that. It could not be that simple. "Why shouldn't all of us ride out after them?"

"It won't work. They'd spot a group of riders from miles away. They'll be looking for you, not me. And, if you might forgive me for bragging a little, we both know I'm a much better tracker than you."

Trammel had seen Hagen in action. He knew what the man could do on horseback and knew better than to question his abilities. But placing Brandt's life in the hands of a gambler, even if it was Hagen, was risky. "I'll send Blake with you."

Hagen shook his head. "You'll need him here with you to keep order in town. I almost had a riot on my hands over at my place when they wanted to place bets on the new developments. How do you think the average civilian will feel once they realize there's a gang of infamous murderous thugs within a day's ride of here? The people will be expecting you to assure them all is well in hand. You'll want to be the one who gives them that assurance, especially with your election coming up next month."

Trammel pounded his desk in frustration. "Hang my election. There's a man's life at stake!"

"You're right and it's not just Brandt's life we're talking about," Hagen said. "During Clay's jail break, you saw how quickly this town can tear itself apart. What happens if they think handing over Washington is the only way to save their own skin? What happens if they decide to take matters into their own hands and rush the jail? Blake is a fine deputy, but he's not you. You've faced down an angry mob before and you're the only one who can do it now."

Hagen placed Brandt's deputy badge on Trammel's desk. "I'm not making you any promises, Steve. Maybe I'm wrong and Marcum will start shooting anyway. Maybe Mahaffey will kill Brandt in a fit of rage. But handing Washington over isn't the answer, so in a mess of truly rotten choices, I think you'll find my idea is the best one for now."

Trammel hated the idea of relying on another man to do his job for him, even if that man was Adam Hagen. But if there was a better way, he could not see it.

"You really think you can track them and stay out of sight?"

"I grew up here," Hagen reminded him. "I probably know the land better than they do. They'll never know I was even there until all of us ride in guns blazing."

"And you'll come right back when you find out where they're hiding Brandt. You won't try to rescue him on your own."

"I'm the gambler here," Hagen said. "I hear Washington rides with as many as ten men. I won't go up against odds like that."

Trammel saw that he had no choice but to trust him. "Can you be ready to ride before first light?"

"With bells on." Hagen saw his joke had fallen flat and added. "Not actual bells, I promise."

"Make sure that's the last of the funny business, Adam. No flair, none of your usual Hagen flourishes. Go out, find them, and come straight back here."

"I'll be sure to fly as straight as an arrow on the wind." Hagen touched the brim of his hat and began to leave when he paused at the door. "By the way, you might want to send one of your deputies around to the alley behind my place. Seems someone got themselves knifed tonight." He shrugged. "It happens sometimes. See you in the morning."

Trammel knew there had to be more to the story but doubted Hagen would tell him.

"Blake!" the sheriff called out for his deputy. "Get in here. I've got something that needs tending to."

CHAPTER 11

The sun had not yet risen when Trammel followed Blake and Hawkeye as they led Dib Bishop out of the stall. There, Old Bob stood waiting with Bishop's horse, the animal saddled and ready to go.

"That's far enough," Trammel told his deputies. "Let him go."

Blake and Hawkeye released Bishop with a shove in the general direction of his horse.

Despite having spent the previous evening locked in a stall, the younger man had plenty of spite left in him. "I sure hope you've got something good to tell me, Sheriff. I think your friend Brandt could use some good news right now. I doubt he slept much last night."

Trammel pointed at the horse. "Get up there and ride on before I change my mind."

Bishop pulled himself up into the saddle and took the reins from Ben before the liveryman went to open the courtyard gate. "When do you want to make the exchange for Washington and Brandt?"

Trammel knew he was taking a risk as he said, "Tell Mahaffey I don't have an answer for him. I haven't made up my mind yet, but I'll let him know when I do."

Bishop turned his horse to face him. "What do you mean you don't have an answer? That's as good as telling him no. George ain't gonna like that, and Brandt will like it even less."

"George should've thought about that before he sent you here to make a spectacle of yourself. You called a lot of attention to yourself by riding in here with your shirt on a stick. The whole town's scared that the Washington Gang is close by, so I'm going to be busy keeping them from panicking for the next day or so. I'm not asking him to like it. I'm just telling you how it is. If he kills Brandt on account of that, it's no fault of mine. Now, get going and be sure you take Marcum with you when you do. Move!"

Bishop and his horse flinched before both turned and rode out of the courtyard at a brisk pace.

The three lawmen watched the young outlaw head east as Old Bob went to close the gate behind him.

"Want me to follow him?" Hawkeye asked.

"I'll go," Blake said. "I can track him at a further distance than you."

Trammel headed off an argument about each man's tracking ability before it started. "I've already got someone doing that. I need both of you here with me in town. Folks will be waking up soon and are bound to be fretful about the Washington Gang being so close."

Blake looked like he wanted to say something, but quickly changed his mind. "I got a lot of questions about that while I was tending to that fella who got himself stabbed behind The Laramie Grand last night. I'd say folks were more concerned than worried about it."

Trammel knew a night full of nightmares about the gang would change that. "They'll get themselves worked up into a lather when they gossip about it over their morning coffee. They're apt to start looking for a way to make the Washington Gang leave them alone. We have to stay close to keep Washington from being lynched."

Blake shook his head. "It's a funny thing having to protect an outlaw from the people he's fed on for years."

"He's in our custody," Trammel said, "so it's up to us to make sure he lives long enough to go to trial."

"Where he'll hang anyway," Hawkeye said.

Trammel hoped that would be the case. "If there's any justice."

He beckoned his deputies to follow him through the open gate and into the throughfare, where he pointed at the four streets that led to City Hall.

"Blake, I want you, Hawkeye, and one of the others to go to every business in town. Round up every empty wagon you can find and put one at the mouth of each of these streets."

Blake joined Trammel in looking over the area. "You want us to set up a cattle chute. A choke point that makes it tougher for people to stay in a herd."

"If that's what they call it out here." Trammel was glad Blake understood his plan. "We used something like it for marches back in New York and Chicago. A barrier makes folks think twice about bunching up in one place. Every second counts when a mob starts to gather. I've seen them take on a life of their own. The sooner we can break it up, the less likely trouble will start."

"You sure you want to go to all that trouble, boss?" Hawkeye asked. "The street looks peaceful enough for now."

But Trammel could sense trouble brewing somewhere out among the slumbering town. The scar on his face ached the way it always did whenever snow or rain was in the air. "I'd rather have them and not need them than need them and not have them. Don't force any of the shops to give you their wagons, though. That'll only make folks think we're expecting trouble. After you get the wagons in place, I want you to spread our men around the area in front of City Hall. But don't let them form a straight line. That'll only give people ideas. I want them seen and ready to move in if they have to. I'll let you know what to do next if it comes to that."

"You will?" Blake looked up at him. "I figured you'd want to be out tracking Bishop and Marcum back to wherever they're holding Brandt."

"I go where I'm needed," Trammel told him. "And I'm needed right here. There'll be plenty of time to worry about Brandt once we have things buttoned up here."

Trammel never liked to talk too much about something. The more he gave air to an idea, the more likely it was to fail. "The town's starting to wake up. You two had better get busy with those wagons."

As Blake and Hawkeye went off to carry out their orders, Trammel saw Mayor Walt Holm walking toward him from across the thoroughfare. Trammel had always found him to be an entirely unremarkable man in every way except for the depth of his corruption.

The two men had managed to keep clear of each other since Clay's jailbreak a few months before. Not even the capture of the most wanted man in the territory had been enough to bring Holm out of his law office. The mayor's friendship with Clay and the role he was rumored to have played in his escape had almost cost him his position, but memories were short in Laramie. It appeared he would run unopposed in next month's election.

"Sheriff," Holm called out to him. "I want a word with you."

Trammel had threatened to take the corrupt politician's reputation away from him but had been unable to do so.

Even Hagen had fallen short on his threats to ruin him. Holm would remain mayor simply because no one else seemed to want the position.

"Nice for you to show up for a change," Trammel told him. "Whatever you've got to say, make it quick. I've got a lot to do today."

"That's why I'm here," Holm said. "I've already spoken to several people in town in the past few hours. They're all concerned about this Washington Gang business. Is it true that they sent a messenger and that they're holding one of Rollins's men captive?"

"It's true as far as I know," Trammel told him. "Don't worry. I'm handling it."

"How? I've got the right to know. I'm still the mayor of Laramie."

Trammel had worked with quite a few politicians in his day, but Holm had a lack of decency that would have made a Manhattan ward boss blush. "You think I'm dumb enough to tell you anything? After everything you've done?"

The mayor held up his hands. "I'm here to help, not argue with you, Trammel. We might not like each other, but the people are worried and they're asking me what will happen next. Are you actually considering handing over Ben Washington to his gang?"

"The short answer is no, and if you try to get me to think otherwise, I'll kick you from one end of this street to the other."

Again, Holm offered no resistance. "You know what should be done far better than I could ever hope to, sheriff. But the people I've spoken with may not agree with your decision. They think it's better to make the trade, save the deputy, and get these outlaws as far away from Laramie as possible. They're afraid the gang might ride into town and try to release him if you don't. Scars are still fresh from . . . the Clay incident."

Trammel put a finer point on it. "You mean from the jailbreak you helped Clay pull off."

"Judge me if you want," the mayor said. "I suppose that's your right. But I pray you never find yourself in a similar position against such a man. One where you're faced with nothing but unpleasant choices no matter which way you turn."

Trammel saw no point in arguing with Holm, especially since he might prove useful in calming the town. "How worked up would you say the people are? Enough to cause trouble?"

"They're scared, which makes them unpredictable," Holm admitted. "A few boisterous rabble-rousers in the group could push them even further toward desperation. Tell me what I can do, and I'll do it."

Trammel was in no position to be proud. He would need all the help he could get, even from Holm. "You want to help? Show your face around town. The dining halls and cafes. Even the saloons. Tell people there's nothing to worry about. Tell them to be vigilant about spotting strangers they see, but that they shouldn't panic. Tell them this will all blow over in a couple of days. Tell them they have my word and if they have any worries, they should come see me in my office."

"Is that true?" Holm asked. "About this blowing over in a couple of days?"

Trammel did not know, but there was no use in admitting that to Holm. "It'll be over, one way or the other."

"Sounds like I have a job to do." Holm touched the brim of his hat and moved away. "I'll do my best."

Trammel could not resist getting in one last jab at Holm. "Just pretend you've got a big payoff waiting for you at the end of this. That usually does the trick where you're concerned."

Holm stopped walking for a moment before continuing on his way.

Trammel had hoped he might have goaded Holm into doing something stupid and was almost sorry he had failed.

From the window of their room at The Bradley Hotel, Burt LeBlanc stepped away from the window overlooking the thoroughfare. "Trammel's up to something, boys. He's got his men running all over town and, from what I just saw, I think he just got into an argument with the mayor."

"They're probably out looking for us." Jim LeBlanc took another swig of whiskey from the bottle. He was the second eldest among the brothers, but rarely acted like it. "We shouldn't have run when you told us to, Burt. We should've made Wayne take one of us with him when he braced Hagen like he did. He might still be alive if we'd insisted."

Burt might have been the middle child of the LeBlanc brothers, but sometimes he felt like the oldest. "I didn't make us do anything, remember? We were just doing what Wayne told us to do. He wanted us out of there before he leaned on Hagen in case things got rough. Looks like he was right. He usually was."

"I still can't believe he's dead," Rick LeBlanc said from his chair against the wall. "The notion that he got himself killed by a two-bit card sharp burns me something awful. He wasn't killed by some drunk. Hagen's the only one who could've gotten over on Wayne like that. He never let anyone get that close to him. And what was he supposed to be doing back there in the first place unless he was tricked into going there. The whole thing stinks, and it's turning my stomach."

Burt was struggling with the loss as much as his brothers but dared not show it. The time for mourning would come one day. Now was the time to figure out what their next move would be. "Quit that kind of talk. It won't do us any good now. We've got to think, not waste time being angry."

Don LeBlanc pounded the uneven table he sat at. "I warned Wayne that Hagen was no pushover and now we're all paying the price for it. I told him he shouldn't face him alone, but he always knew better than the rest of us. It was his stubbornness that was his ending and it'll be ours, too, if we don't get out of here right now."

Burt heard his brother Virgil gag into a chamber pot on the other side of the dingy room. He was the youngest of the brothers and had always looked up to Wayne as something of a hero. It was Virgil who had insisted on going to look for Wayne despite their orders to remain in the hotel across the street. He was the only one of the brothers who had risked being seen when his body had been found behind The Laramie Grand.

"I wish I never saw him like that," Virgil moaned. "Thrown away like he was nothing. All of them times he saved us. All of them fellas he killed, and he winds up dead in a godforsaken dump like Laramie."

Burt wished for a lot of things, too. He wished they had remained in New Orleans. They had a good thing going with Big Littlejohn. In a few years, they might have been able to carve out a piece of the city for themselves. Maybe push Littlejohn out altogether.

But Wayne had been growing restless for a while. He had always wanted something the LeBlanc brothers could finally call their own and had begun to fear they would never have it by working for someone else.

His plan to try to fool Hagen by posing as a bunch of cattlemen had never made much sense to Burt, but he had gone along with it because Wayne had been sure his plan would work. He had thought it would be the perfect way for them to blend in while they looked over Hagen's gambling hall for a way they could either work for Hagen or rip the place off.

Now they were on the run and their brother was dead. Everything they owned in the world except for their guns and ammunition was still up in their room at The Laramie Grand. Wayne had told them to leave it all behind out of fear that the sight of luggage would have tipped off Hagen that something was about to happen. They had managed to sneak down the back stairs without much notice. He was sure Hagen's men had already cleared out the room by now.

Burt was glad he had thought to grab his bag of safe-cracking tools and the dynamite when they fled, not that any of it would do much good now. Looking out the window would be the closest any LeBlanc brother ever got to The Laramie Grand.

Jim LeBlanc set his bottle on the uneven table beside the bed. "Wayne always had his reasons for doing whatever he did, boys. He wanted us to have something of our own. It was a decent plan. Admirable, even."

"Until it wasn't," Donald added. "Now he's dead and we're stuck. Whatever scheme he was cooking up died with him."

"That's no way to talk." Rick got up from the table and began pacing the room. He was the second oldest and, next to Wayne, had been the thinker in the family. "Wayne might be gone, but we're still alive. He wouldn't have

wanted us to just up and quit like this. To sit in this dump
and feel sorry for ourselves. We're still LeBlanc men and
LeBlanc men always get what we go after." He looked
across the room at Burt. "He talked to you the most out of
all of us. He was thinking about hitting Hagen's safe,
wasn't he?"

"That was part of it," Burt admitted. "But after we had
a chance to look it over, he knew getting it open was going
to be a lot harder than he thought. You should've seen that
thing. This was no stagecoach strong box, boys. The door
is bigger than me. Wider, too. It's as solid as some bank
vaults I've seen, and I've seen plenty of those. That's why
Wayne decided to try to get us steady jobs in Hagen's
places. Get us a piece of the action." He sagged against
the wall. "I wouldn't count on cracking the safe. I don't
think I could do it even if I had the chance."

Rick stopped pacing. "You don't *think* you can do it, or
you *know* you can't do it? There's a difference. An important one at that."

Burt hesitated. "Any safe can be opened eventually,
but it takes time to do it right. To do it quiet. It doesn't
matter anyway because, after what happened to Wayne,
none of us will be able to get within ten yards of that hotel
again. Hagen's probably given them orders to shoot us
dead on sight."

"Don't be so sure." Rick grew quiet the way he always
did when he thought he was on to something. "They don't
know we're LeBlanc boys. The only two of us who were
ever seen together at any time were Wayne and you, remember? We were careful about that. As far as his guards
know, we're just guests in the hotel. I never saw them
watch us go into our rooms. Did any of you?"

He looked at each of his brothers in turn, and all of
them agreed they had not. Burt had kept an eye out

whenever he came out of or entered the room. He had not seen anyone, either.

Rick said, "I think it's high time we quit worrying about what Hagen *might* do and for us to decide what we're going to do to avenge our dead brother."

Rick pointed at Burt. "I'm asking you if you could get that safe open if you had enough time." He gestured at the bag full of sawdust and dynamite. "Could you cut one of them sticks open and burn your way through it?"

Burt knew it was not as simple as that. "Dynamite will work on just about anything, but not this. That thing's got a lock the likes of which I've never seen before. Hagen said it's even got some kind of clock in it that only allows it to be open at certain times. I've never worked on something that fancy. Sure, I could use the dynamite, but I'd have to use so much that it would wreck half the hotel and still might not put a dent in the thing."

Rick began to grow frustrated and started to pace. "Now that Wayne is gone, you're the only one of us who knows how to open a safe. If you can't blow it up, how much time would you need with the lock? An hour? A day?"

Burt had always left such details to Wayne to figure out but tried to put a time on it for Rick's sake. "A couple of hours at least, but there's still that timing part to worry about. I don't even know what one of those looks like."

"Forget about that," Rick said. "Sounds like you're going to need at least a few hours to get it open. It'll be up to the rest of us to make sure you get it."

From beside the washbasin, Virgil wiped his mouth with the back of his hand. "We don't have to waste time on that, Rick. If you want to get back at Hagen, let's do it quick. We can hit the counting room, grab as much as we can, and get out of there."

Rick turned on his younger brother. "Why don't you

stick your head back in that bowl where it belongs? That's a great idea. Why should we steal thousands when we could get hundreds? We'll be risking our necks no matter what we go after. I'd rather get shot with a whole turkey under my arm, not just a bony wing."

From his spot on the bed, Jim said, "Rick's got a point. We've been taking scraps from folks our whole lives. Hagen has probably pulled in more money in the last day from those Washington Gang bets he's taking than he was expecting to make in a year. I'd hate to leave that much money on the table, especially considering what it's already cost us. Wayne's life was worth more to me than a few hundred dollars."

Burt wished he could have felt as confident in the idea of a big payday as the rest of his brothers. But they had not seen the safe. He had. He knew what they were up against, and he did not think he could get it open without Wayne.

But Rick seemed to be doing all of the thinking for the family. He asked Burt, "Did Hagen tell you what times the safe could be opened?"

"Yeah," Burt said. "Right after he told me the combination. Hagen's not that stupid, Rick."

"I'm just thinking out loud is all." Rick ran his finger across his chin as he continued to think it over. "I wonder when Hagen set that safe to open. It could be for a few hours at night or first thing in the morning."

He snapped his fingers at his brother Don. "Wayne had you watching the street in front of the hotel most of the time. Did you ever see anyone leave and head for the bank and come back again?"

Don said, "That fat clerk at the front desk left every morning at ten o'clock on the nose. He never made much of a show of what he was doing, but he always looked a lot heavier going than he did when he came back. It looked to me like he stashed the money under his coat. Always had a man walking behind him when he did it, too, and always took a different way there. But each time I followed him, he always went to the back door of the bank where someone was waiting to let him in."

"There's the answer," Virgil said. "At ten o'clock this morning, we knock the clerk over the head, take the money off him, and run."

Rick held up his hand to silence him. "Don't think so much, Virg. You're not good at it." He slowly lowered his hand. "But Hagen's a thinker, isn't he? Smart, too. Maybe smart enough to make us think he's smarter than he really is." He said to Burt, "You said he had that safe behind his desk. Big as life for all the world to see."

"He sure was mighty proud of it," Burt remembered. "He wouldn't stop talking about it the whole time we were in his suite. It was almost as if he was daring someone to crack it."

"Talked a lot for something so important to him, didn't he? Like maybe he said too much."

Before Burt could ask him what he meant, Rick took his coat from the back of his chair. "I've had enough of all this talk. Feels like I'm just going around chasing my tail in circles. I'm going to get a look at that hotel for myself."

Burt felt a spark of panic rise up in him. "You can't do that! They'll be looking for us in there, especially now that Wayne's dead."

"Hogwash," Rick said as he got into his coat. "We didn't check in together and no one saw us together at one time. I'd bet they don't know who I am. I'm willing to bet my life on it. And, depending on what I find over there, I'll be willing to bet your lives, too. We owe it to Wayne to try."

Rick took the bottle from the night table next to Jim. "I want you boys dressed and ready to get moving at a moment's notice. Burt, get your stuff ready, including the dynamite. Stay by that window until I get back. We might not have a moment to lose when I do, and we may have to move quick. That means you, too, Virg. You can get sick all you want after we're done."

The remaining brothers looked at Burt after Rick left the room.

Jim said, "He always was tough to stop once he got a full head of steam going."

Don said, "He's right about us never being seen together, though. Maybe they really don't know who we are. That would sure change things in our favor, wouldn't it, Burt?"

But Burt did not think so. "Nothing's going to change how thick that safe is. Nothing's going to make it easier to open, no matter how much Rick thinks different."

Virgil bent over the basin again. "I think I'm going to be sick."

Burt might have joined him if he thought it might have done him any good.

CHAPTER 12

Adam Hagen remained crouched behind a headstone in the graveyard as he watched Dib Bishop ride past him. He was not hiding as much as he was trying to prevent the young man from seeing his face. He did not want to risk trouble later in case they happened to meet. Anonymity could have its uses in the right situation.

Hagen waited for the boy to ride up the hill at the end of the road out of Laramie. He got to his horse beside the chapel and rode in the opposite direction. He was sure that the sharpshooter Marcum was on the lookout for anyone who might be following Bishop. He would grow suspicious if no one in town was moving, so Hagen planned to make a long circle out of town before riding back to pick up Bishop's trail. It beat sitting in a graveyard waiting for the long minutes to slowly tick away.

Hagen rode along the thoroughfare and grew troubled by the clusters of citizens he saw along the way. Laramie had always been a busy place in the morning with shop-keepers and tradesmen eager to get a head start on the new day. All but a few shops remained closed as people huddled together, undoubtedly discussing the prospect of the Washington Gang being so close to their fair town. He hoped Trammel followed his advice and remained in Laramie. The people would need his steady hand—not to mention his reputation for violence—to keep order among a frightened populace.

He rode out of town for a mile before he made a sweeping arc back toward where he had last seen Bishop. He kept an eye on the overgrowth for any sign of Marcum and his long gun. He was glad there was no sign of the sharpshooter anywhere.

He slowed his horse to a lope as he found Bishop's tracks and began to follow them. He allowed his mount to move at its own pace in case the outlaws looked back to see if anyone had dared to follow them. Time was not on his side, much less on Deputy Brandt's side, but rushing could get both of them killed.

He continued to follow Bishop's tracks until his horse's shoeprints mingled with those of a second rider. Hagen read the ground and determined the two outlaws had continued on into the flatlands outside of Laramie before breaking north.

Hagen grinned. *These boys are careful.*

He had not been in this part of the territory in years but began to call some familiar landmarks to mind. There was a lazy creek up ahead, followed by any number of places where Mahaffey and his men might be holding Brandt prisoner. Deep pine woods. A box canyon. A few caves closer in the direction of Cheyenne, too.

Hagen reined his horse to a stop when he saw the tracks disappear in the dirt. He climbed down from his horse to study the ground closely. He looked around him and saw a lopsided bush off the side of the trail and went to examine it. He saw the place where a knife had cut away a branch. The wood was still light and tender. He ran his finger over the spot. It was fresh.

"Someone's trying to cover their tracks by trailing a bush behind them," Hagen said to himself. He doubted a man like Trammel would have seen it, but Hagen had. *Smart, but not smart enough. Not even close.*

Hagen got back in the saddle and continued to ride toward where he remembered the creek to have been. He found it about half a mile ahead and decided it would be best if he walked his horse across it. Splashing through it would make noise, which would only give him away if Bishop and Marcum happened to be close.

Hagen ducked when he heard the unmistakable sound of a Sharps rifle boom across the land. He pulled his Winchester from the scabbard on his saddle and brought the horse off the trail to a cluster of bushes lining the water's edge.

He watched the terrain as he wrapped the reins around a branch in the hope he might see where the shot had come from.

A second shot filled the air and he saw a puff of gun smoke climb into the air about a hundred yards to his left on the far side of the creek. That, he knew, must be Marcum.

But what was he shooting at?

Hagen kept his head down as he peered out in the general direction of where Marcum had been aiming. He saw a riderless horse slowing in the distance about two hundred yards farther away.

"You get him?" Hagen heard a young voice say. He took that to be Bishop.

"I got him the first time." Hagen thought that must be Marcum. "The second time was just to make sure he's dead. I needed the practice."

"Good," Bishop cheered. "Was it Trammel? I'd sure like to see that big jackass dead."

"That fella's too old to have been Trammel," Marcum said. "Too small. He came from the direction of Cheyenne. Trammel couldn't have ridden around us that fast."

Hagen crouched lower behind the bushes as the two men stood. Dib Bishop was about half a foot shorter than Marcum and had a much lighter complexion. The sharpshooter had a thick black beard and wore a permanent squint beneath a faded slouch hat.

Hagen gripped his Winchester tightly as he fought the urge to shoot both men. He could easily hit them from this distance, but he had not come to kill. He had only come to follow.

"I don't know who that fella was," Marcum said, "but he won't be bothering us anymore. We'd best be moving on."

Bishop was not quick to follow. "You sure we shouldn't go over and make sure he's dead?"

"I told you he was, didn't I?" Marcum sounded annoyed. "Besides, George is gonna want to hear that bad news you've got for him right quick, and I don't aim to be the one who makes him sore about us being late."

Hagen remained low as he watched the two outlaws get back on the horses they had hidden among the overgrowth and ride away at a good gallop. He remained there, concerned about the fate of whomever Marcum had shot, until the sound of their hooves died away. He chanced a quick look over the bushes before standing up to his full height. Bishop and Marcum were long gone.

Hagen untethered his horse from the branch and led it across the creek as slowly and as quietly as he could manage.

He stopped by a tree on the far side and, after he was sure the outlaws were out of sight, climbed atop his horse and rode toward the riderless horse in the distance.

He could see the animal was limping as it favored his right foreleg. Hagen knew it was the kind of injury that was a death sentence for a horse. He only hoped the rider fared better.

Hagen saw the rider thirty yards away on the ground amid the tall grass of the hillside. He was clutching at the left side of his stomach as blood had already begun to spread on his shirt.

Marcum's description of his target had been right. For although he had not seen Lefty Rollins in more than a decade, he imagined the old lawman must be pushing seventy by now.

Hagen pulled his horse to a stop and dropped to the ground. He pulled some bandages he kept in his saddle-bag and rushed to tend to the wounded marshal.

The older man's eyes grew wide with recognition when he got a good look at his rescuer.

"Adam Hagen!" Rollins spat. "I should've known you'd be wrapped up in this somehow. Where's Deputy Brandt?"

Hagen took a knee beside Rollins and tried to pry his hands away from the wound. "Nice to see you, too, Lefty. Sorry it has to be under such circumstances."

He struggled to get the marshal to allow him to look at his wound. "I suppose I have you to thank for this hole in me. You always were a lousy shot. Always used to close your eyes when it came time to pull the trigger."

"I was eight years old." Hagen tore away the soaked part of the shirt. He saw that Marcum's fifty-caliber bullet had taken a decent chunk out of Rollins's side. "And it wasn't me who shot you. I would've had the decency to finish you off quicker than this. Quit struggling and let me tend to you."

Rollins relented and allowed Hagen to examine the wound. "Where's Brandt?"

"I don't know, but the man who shot you does. I was following them from Laramie when you got in the way. Don't you think you're a bit too old to be playing hero?"

"Looks like I'm still young enough to stop a bullet." Rollins stifled a yell as Hagen patted away the blood. "And who are you to question me playing a hero? You never used to stick your neck out for anyone, which was a source of endless disappointment to your dear pa. Don't tell me you've gone and found Jesus or the like."

"You'll be shaking hands with him soon unless you shut up and let me try to save your life."

Hagen knew most people found Rollins to be a folksy, easy-going sort. Unfortunately, Hagen had never seen that side of him. Rollins had always shared King Charles Hagen's poor opinion of his adopted son.

Hagen told him to hold the bandage in place while he went back to his horse, retrieved his canteen and a flask of whiskey. He returned and poured the water over the wound to clear the blood so he could get a better look at it. "Looks like you're human after all. I always figured you to be full of nothing but tobacco juice and sawdust."

Rollins barely managed to bite off a scream as the water hit his wound.

Hagen took little pleasure in his discomfort. "Steel yourself old man, because this next part's going to hurt me a lot more than it hurts you. Go ahead and scream your head off if you want. No one's around to hear you."

Hagen poured liquor on the wound and, this time, Rollins bellowed from the pain.

Hagen began to wind the bandage around the marshal's waist as tightly as he could. "I don't know what you're yelping about. That's good scotch. Had it brought all the way from Scotland, too. I hate the idea of wasting it on an old coot like you."

When he recovered, Rollins said through clenched teeth, "How bad is it?"

"Bad, but not as bad as it ought to be." Hagen glanced back at Rollins's wounded horse. "I think your saddle horn might've deflected the bullet a bit. Your horse doesn't look too good, though."

Rollins cursed. "The first shot hit the ground, but I think he caught a piece of it in the leg. I was climbing down when the second shot knocked me flat."

"Good thing you're so spry or he might've put that shot through your head. That was Marcum shooting at you."

"I figured as much," Rollins seethed. "Lousy Washington Gang. I never should've let Brandt ride out here alone. Did you see where they rode to?"

"I saw it," Hagen said as he began to tie the bandage, "and I plan on following them, too. That means I'm going to have to leave you here while I do it. When I find out where they're holding Brandt, I'll ride back to Laramie to get Trammel and the others to save Brandt. I'll try to bring a doctor back with us to tend to you."

"You won't be doing anything of the kind."

Normally, Hagen enjoyed his reputation as a renegade, but neither Brandt nor Rollins had time for such nonsense. "Don't believe everything you've heard about me. I'm not nearly the monster I'm supposed to be."

"I didn't mean that." Rollins pressed the barrel of his pistol against Hagen's left ribs. "I mean you ain't leaving me here. You're going to find Brandt and you're taking me with you."

Hagen had always admired Rollins's legendary grit, but

this was taking pride too far. He balled his right hand into a fist and held it in front of the marshal's face.

"You've got a hole in your side about the size of this. If you stand up, you'll die, much less try to ride a horse. I don't have time to coddle you, and Brandt doesn't have that kind of time, either. If you really want to save him, you'll stay here like I told you."

"I didn't ride all this way to die in the grass. One of my men is being held out there somewhere and I aim to get him." Rollins thumbed back the hammer on his pistol. "If you won't take me, then I reckon I'll just have to shoot you and take your horse, seeing as how mine is lame."

Hagen could tell Rollins was serious. "I told you I'm just going to find out where they are and ride back to Laramie."

"And I'll stay behind and keep an eye on them until you get back." Rollins swallowed hard. "If I die, I'll die doing my duty, not out here in the wilderness like some deer."

Hagen wondered if men lost their common sense when they pinned a star on their shirt. "Have it your way, but when you pass out, I won't be stopping to put a blanket under your head."

Rollins slowly lowered the hammer of his pistol. "No need to stop on my account. Just give me a hand up so I can tend to my horse properly. He's a good animal and doesn't deserve to suffer."

Hagen got up and offered his hand to help Rollins up. He thought the old marshal would pass out from the effort. He was surprised when the man pulled himself up, and even more surprised when he kept his footing.

Rollins kept his left arm against his side, holding the bandage in place, as he staggered over to his horse. He bit through the pain as he tried to stand upright.

The horse, its right foreleg curled above the ground,

lowered his head and looked away as if it knew what was about to happen.

Rollins aimed his pistol at the wounded animal. "They always know when it's their time, don't they?"

"The smart ones do." Hagen tried to wipe the blood and dirt from his own hands. "There's something to be said about knowing when you're beaten."

"Yeah." Rollins took careful aim at the horse, then pulled the trigger. "Guess it's a good thing I'm stupid."

CHAPTER 13

Trammel remained inside the front door of City Hall while he and Mayor Holm watched a sparse crowd of citizens begin to gather down in the thoroughfare.

Blake and Hawkeye had managed to move only three wagons to block the main artery of the town, but they were doing what Trammel had intended. In order to reach City Hall, people would have to snake around to the side streets and come out on one of the other avenues. The added effort had made most people think better of it.

Trammel knew it was far from a military fortification, but it helped keep the casual observer and rabble-rouser at bay. If trouble started, no one would be able to later claim that they had found themselves in front of City Hall by accident.

Trammel did not bother to look at the mayor as he said, "Looks like you didn't do much to calm their concerns, Walt."

"I did more than you know," Holm said. "That crowd would be twice what it is if it weren't for me. What you see down there right now are just the curious. The idle agitators who always come around whenever there's a whiff of trouble in the air. You won't find any organized resistance, though. No banners and no scores of men taking to the streets. It was your influence we have to thank for that. Most folks said they felt better knowing you were around."

Trammel had always been suspicious of compliments, especially from politicians. "Don't see as how I had anything to do with it. I haven't left this building all morning."

"You didn't have to," Holm told him. "Almost every large group in town is willing to give you the benefit of the doubt that you can keep them safe from Washington's men. You're the message. I was just the messenger."

Trammel had never liked Walt Holm, but there was no denying he had a knack for knowing how to handle people. "Just when I start to think you're useless, you manage to do something that proves me wrong."

Holm bowed slightly at the waist. "I'll take that as a compliment. Remember, even a broken clock is right twice a day."

"That depends on which one of us is the broken clock."

Holm nodded out at the thoroughfare. "Neither of us can afford to be broken in the face of that. If you need me, I'll be upstairs in my office."

Trammel waited for Holm to leave before he said to Blake, "Looks like we've got a few stragglers starting to bunch up in the middle down there. Have the men move in to send them on their way. I don't want to encourage anyone to do the same."

Blake went out to the top step of City Hall and signaled the deputies he had positioned throughout the street to move in. The citizens in the thoroughfare held their ground for a moment, arguing with Trammel's men before ultimately deciding their grievance was not worth spending the rest of the day in a cell.

As Blake went down to talk to the deputies, Hawkeye joined Trammel in the doorway and watched the street. "I know it might just be my imagination, but I can feel things beginning to turn against us."

"It's not your imagination," Trammel said. "That's your experience talking. There are more of them than there were an hour ago. They'll come and go like that all day, stop for a bit until we run them off. Any real trouble won't come until after dark. People tend to act up after dark when it's harder to see their faces. We can keep the crowd under control as long as we don't let them knot up and get brave. Let's just hope Adam comes back with some good news about Brandt soon."

Hawkeye said, "I've already got our horses picked out down in the livery. I even got a fresh one for Mr. Hagen. I figure his will just about be played out when he gets here."

"You're not going anywhere," Trammel said. "I need you here with Blake to keep an eye on the town. The danger won't stop just because Adam finds the Washington Gang. Folks here will still be afraid, and I want them to see we're still here to protect them."

When Hawkeye looked down at his boots, Trammel knew the kid had something on his mind. He did not have to wait long to hear it

"People don't care about me, boss. It's you they're afraid of. And if something were to happen to you while you were saving that deputy, it'd take a hundred deputies to restore order. I don't like being disagreeable, but I think you ought to let me go instead of you."

Trammel was convinced there must be something new in the town's water that caused those closest to him to start questioning his decisions. First Emily, then Hagen, and now Hawkeye.

He tried to choose his next words carefully for he did not want an argument. "There may be trouble here. There's definitely going to be trouble when we free Brandt. I know you can fight, but it's not your fight. It's mine."

"Your fight's here in town with the people who pay you, boss. Freeing a federal deputy who got himself caught doesn't count near as much as Laramie does. People in town will want you here, and they won't like you leaving them when they need you most."

Trammel could feel his patience begin to slip away from him. "You've been talking to Emily, haven't you?"

"No, but I'm not surprised if she said the same thing," Hawkeye admitted. "I've worked really hard to keep you alive over the years. Bled some over it, too. I'd hate to see all of that effort go to waste. I'd hate to see you lose your election next month because you were doing what's right instead of your duty."

Trammel had not expected such deep thinking from his young deputy. He had certainly changed from the shy boy he had first met on the streets of Blackstone into a man with ideas of his own. Trammel wanted to think he'd had something to do with Hawkeye's growth, even now when it was inconvenient.

"Saving Brandt and ending the Washington Gang is right and my duty. Making tough choices is part of the job. If I lose my job because people think I picked wrong, then maybe I deserve to lose that damned election."

"Brandt knew the risks when he rode down here to bring Ben Washington back to Cheyenne," Hawkeye said. "The people have a right to be scared about his gang looking to come free him, just like they have a right to expect you to stay here to protect him. Send me and some of the others with Mr. Hagen, boss. You know it's the right thing to do."

Trammel felt the scar that ran down the length of his nose begin to ache like it always did whenever he faced a tough decision. It ached more these days than usual.

He stepped outside and began to walk down the steps. "We'll figure out what to do when Hagen gets back. For now, we'd better get down there and show our faces. I'd like to head off trouble before it starts for once."

Rick LeBlanc felt a surge of excitement as he threaded his way through the crowd toward The Laramie Grand. He did not see people in the street as a problem, but rather a possible benefit for the plan that was quickly growing in his mind.

He remembered that he had resented Wayne for having chosen Burt to join him at the fancy parties with the fine liquor while he and the other brothers had been relegated to observing Hagen's operation. But, as usual, Wayne had been right.

Rick had thought hitting the counting room would have been the best and easiest play for the brothers to make, but now he knew the safe in Hagen's suite was the true prize. He was confident Burt would find a way to open it if he had enough time to do it. It was up to Rick and his brothers to give him that time. The only question was how.

He knew part of the answer might lie among all the people who had gathered in the street. Rick heard them murmuring about the threat of the Washington Gang. Some said the gang had been seen on the outskirts of town and might ride in at any moment to free their leader. Rick took heart in the nervous looks of the deputies who kept a wary eye on the nervous citizens. It would only take a small spark to set the town ablaze in panic. He hoped it would not come to that. Not for Laramie's sake, but for the sake of his scheme. Stealing money was only good if he lived long enough to spend it.

Rick may not have joined Wayne and Burt for the party in Hagen's suite, but he had spent some time looking at the lock on Hagen's door. Hagen had taken precautions. He remembered it as being different from the others in the hotel. It was a sturdy metal number, and the door was thick. It would not pop open with a quick pick or a hard shoulder against it.

That meant he would have to find someone to open it for him. He doubted Hagen would oblige but knew someone who might.

Rick made his way up the front steps of the hotel, where men he recognized as Hagen men now stood guard. He had counted ten armed gunmen when he had been watching the hotel and there were eight of them on the steps. That left only two inside. That was good.

He went to the front desk and was glad the fat clerk did not appear to recognize him. He had always been lucky when it came to blending in. "I was wondering if Mr. Hagen might be around?"

The clerk did not look up from the mail he was sorting. "I'm sorry, sir, but Mr. Hagen isn't here at the moment. Is there something I can help you with?"

Not for what Rick LeBlanc had in mind. "Thanks. I'll check back later. No message."

Rick moved through the lobby and into the gaming floor. It was a more subdued setting than he had seen in previous days. Most of the poker tables were empty and only one roulette wheel had any business. The blackjack tables were empty, and one of the dealers looked asleep on his feet. That would not have happened had Hagen been wise enough to hire the LeBlanc boys to run things for him.

He spotted only a few men standing at the bar in conversation. They were cattlemen, undoubtedly talking about the current trouble facing the town.

Rick's confidence in his budding idea grew with each step as he headed toward the side where Rube Miller stood on a platform in front of a chalkboard that listed the latest odds on the Washington affair. Like the clerk at the front desk, he was busy sorting through telegrams, probably from out-of-town bettors looking to get a piece of the Washington action. He was too consumed with his accounting to notice LeBlanc's quick approach.

And there was not an armed thug anywhere in sight.

Miller did not see Rick until he was already on the platform and on his side of the table.

"I'm sorry, sir, but customers aren't allowed back here. Kindly step around to the other side if you wish to place a wager and I'll be happy to help you."

"Don't worry about that. I've already placed my bet."

Rick knelt as if to tie his shoe and removed a stiletto from his boot. He already had the blade against Miller's considerable belly before the pit boss realized what was happening. "I've placed it all on me."

Miller did not react. He kept his hands still as he looked down at the telegrams. "If this is a robbery, you've made a terrible mistake. I don't have any money here as you can see."

"I didn't come here for money," LeBlanc said. "I'm here for you. And as long as you stay nice and quiet and do exactly what I tell you to do, I won't gut you the way your boss gutted my brother last night."

"LeBlanc." Miller whispered the name as if it were a curse. "Which one are you?"

"The one who's going to kill you if you don't do exactly what I tell you. And don't think any of your tough guys will be able to save you. They're all out front watching the street. That means it's just you and me."

"There's one in the back," Miller said. "You won't get away with this. Walk away now before you get yourself killed."

"We're not going in the back," Rick told him. "We're going upstairs where we can chat in private." He pushed the side of the blade harder against Miller's gut. "Get up and walk to the back stairs. The same ones I've seen the maids use. And don't try anything stupid along the way. I know how this place works almost as well as you do."

"Just take it easy," Miller said as LeBlanc kept the knife against his kidney. "You'll get no trouble from me. There's no reason why anyone has to be hurt."

"I'll remember you said that. Now, move."

The two men walked to the back of the gaming floor and up the back staircase. None of the customers or the bartenders paid them any mind and Miller did nothing to attract their attention.

When it was just the two of them on the stairs, Rick said, "When we get to Hagen's suite, you're going to open the door and step inside."

"I can't do that," Miller told him. "I don't have the key. Only Mr. Hagen has that, and he's not here."

"Nice try. You're his pit boss and you manage the money. I know you have a key, and I know you can open that safe so you can keep the loot inside. You open it for him, and now you're going to open it for me."

When they reached the second landing, Rick shifted the blade so the point was pressed against the side of Miller's stomach. He made the man stop before he took a quick look up and down the hallway. Since no one was there, he pushed Miller in the direction of Hagen's suite.

"Get your key out and open that door. And don't get any ideas about causing trouble once we're inside. I can kill you just as easily in there as I can out here."

Miller silently took out his set of keys and began to fumble them loudly.

Rick pressed the blade hard against Miller's shirt. "Quit making noise and get it open."

Miller found the right key and, as soon as he opened the door, Rick shoved him hard inside and quickly heeled the door closed behind him. He delivered a swift kick to Miller's ribs, causing him to roll over on his side as Rick took a slow look around the suite.

The room was as plush and ornate as many houses of ill repute he had seen back home in New Orleans. The safe was exactly where he had expected to find it. Right behind Hagen's equally gaudy desk.

He dragged Miller to his feet and pushed him toward the safe. "You're almost done. Now all you have to do is open the safe and you can spend the rest of the day relaxing tied up on the floor over there."

Miller was still panting from the blow to his side. "I already told you I can't do that. I don't have the combination. Mr. Hagen is the only one who has that. And it's a timed lock besides. I couldn't open it until five o'clock tonight even if I had the combination, which I don't. He told your brothers the same thing a few nights ago."

"I've never heard of a timed lock on a safe this size, even if it's a custom-built job." Rick kept hold of him and brought the knife to Miller's left cheek. "Stop lying to me and get to work, because if you can't open the safe, you're not useful to me. And I don't like keeping people around who aren't useful."

Rick watched how Miller's hand shook as he began to work the dial. He turned it around three times, grabbed the handle, and tried to pull it down.

It did not budge.

"See?" Miller said. "I told you no one can open it until tonight."

Rick cut loose with a stream of curses before he slammed Miller's head against the safe door. As Miller dropped to his knees, Rick delivered a swift kick to his temple. Miller's body sagged, and he was out cold.

He dragged Miller out from behind the desk, grabbed one of the thick cords that kept the drapes tied back and used them to bind the unconscious man's hands and feet. He used Miller's necktie to gag him while he thought about his next move.

At least he was now in Hagen's suite. This battle was not over yet.

Rick tried the handle of the safe and found that it still would not move. Burt and Wayne had been the safe experts of the family, but he had been with them on several jobs back home. He ran his hands along the door, looking for a gap he could use to pry it open, but it was pointless. Burt had been right. It would take a fair amount of time to open it without the combination. There had to be a way.

Rick went to the window and saw that it had a commanding view of the heart of Laramie. Not only City Hall and the deputies breaking up the crowd down on the street, but of The Bradley Hotel, too. He could see the room where his brothers were staying. He saw Burt was keeping watch at the window, just as Rick had told him to.

Rick squinted up at the sun shining down into the room and had a flash of an idea.

He ran into Hagen's bedroom, looking for anything that might catch the sunlight. He found a small hand mirror on a table next to the wash basin. Hagen's vanity just might serve as his undoing after all.

He grabbed the hand mirror and went back out to the front room. He opened the window to the street and stepped aside to catch the sunlight to avoid anyone seeing him from below. He moved the mirror back and forth in the direction of Burt's window. After flashing him several times, Rick waved across to him.

Fortunately, Burt had seen him and quickly opened his window, too.

Rick emphatically waved his arm, hoping his brother understood that he wanted them to join him. When Burt stepped back inside, Virgil replaced him at the window. Rick hoped the boy would not get sick while looking outside. He would only draw unwanted attention by spoiling someone's hat and coat below.

He watched Burt walk across the street alone, keeping an eye on Hagen's window as he moved past the townspeople milling around him. Rick gestured for him to go to the side alley and Burt acknowledged him with a tip of his hat.

Rick ran back into Hagen's bedroom and opened the window, overlooking the alley where Burt was waiting. Fearing that Hagen's men might hear them in the counting room directly below him, Rick kept it brief.

"Bring our guns here. Your tools and the other stuff, too. I'll lower something you can put them in, and I'll pull them up through the window. Come one at a time from the back stairs. Don't draw attention."

Burt frustrated him by asking, "Why can't we just bring them up there ourselves?"

Rick could not explain to him that four men walking through the lobby armed with rifles and pistols would not be the best of ideas.

"Just do as I told you and be quick about it. Time's wasting."

He kept the window open as he looked around the bedroom for something he could use to bring the weapons and tools up to the suite. He was close to getting the payday he and his family had been looking for. He only wished Wayne had lived to see it.

CHAPTER 14

Mahaffey kicked dirt in the air as he walked away from Bishop and Marcum. He had not been counting on such an answer from Trammel.

"You're sure he didn't tell you anything else?" he asked Bishop. "You didn't hear him say something that might help us, even while you were locked up."

"He had me locked in a horse stall the whole night, boss. There wasn't much of anything to see or hear besides the grunts and groans of that deaf old mare he stuck me with. Then, this morning, he turned me loose like I'd just stopped by for a friendly visit. All Trammel said was that he was thinking about your offer. He didn't tell me how he was gonna tell you when he made up his mind even though I asked him."

Mahaffey knew he only had himself to blame. He should have risked going himself instead of sending a boy to do a man's job. He should have forced him to make the trade by being ready to attack Laramie, even though he did not think he had enough men to do it. Trammel would not have known he was bluffing, and the gang's reputation for ruthlessness might have made him believe it.

He was beginning to think he should have waited to try

to grab Ben when they brought him back to Cheyenne for his trial, but they would have been expecting that. No matter what he decided, he seemed to just be moving in a great big circle with nothing to show for it except a federal deputy no one seemed to care much about saving.

From his spot on the ground, Leo Brandt said, "Sorry about the bad news, boys. Guess I'm not worth as much as you'd hoped."

Mahaffey kicked dirt in the prisoner's face. "You'd do well to keep your mouth shut."

Roy Earnshaw was the only member of the gang to step forward and pull Mahaffey aside. "How do you want us to handle this, George? We can't let Brandt go and we can't stay here."

Mahaffey did not need to add another problem to his list. "Why not? We've got plenty of supplies, it's close to Laramie, and this canyon's easy to defend. I don't aim to give up a good hideout just to look for another."

But Earnshaw persisted. "We need to go because it stands to reason that someone might've followed Dib and Johnny here."

Marcum took offense to that. "No one followed us here, Earnshaw. We only saw one fella dogging us from the direction of Cheyenne, not Laramie. I put him down as sure as you're standing there."

Earnshaw turned to face him. "And what about after you killed him? I'll bet you two were hellbent for leather to get here as soon as the shots died away. Were you as careful about watching your back trail after the creek or do you just think you were?"

Mahaffey read the answer in their expressions. Earnshaw was right. They had not been careful.

Earnshaw continued. "Even if no one was following

you before then, someone could track you here now. It's only smart to play it safe by moving the whole outfit to a new spot. That pine forest is closest. We could set up there in an hour or two while we think this through. There's good cover in there, George, and we won't be boxed-in like we are here."

Mahaffey's head began to spin from all the options. How did Ben keep track of so much at once? "Everyone just quit talking while I think this over. Everyone talking at once is worse than a bunch of hens in a barnyard."

He silently counted the number of men looking at him and did not like what he saw. "Who's keeping watch up in the rocks?"

Jim Barrett slowly raised his hand. "I guess I should be, but I came in with Dib and Marcum when they showed up. I wanted to hear what they had to say for myself."

Mahaffey charged at him. "I don't care about what you hear, you idiot. I only care about what you see. Get up on those rocks where you belong. Now!"

Barrett muttered apologies as he began to leave, but Marcum stopped him. "I'll go up for you, Jim. You stay here." He glanced at Earnshaw. "The air down here is getting too thick for my taste."

As Marcum began to make his way up the hillside, Barrett and the rest of the Washington men looked to Mahaffey for answers he did not have. He had not thought this far ahead. He would have gladly traded places with Ben Washington right about then.

The last person in the canyon Mahaffey wanted to hear from was Leo Brandt. Which, given how poorly the day had started, was the only man willing to speak up. "I might have a way to get us all out of this."

Earnshaw brought the butt of his rifle down hard across

Brandt's jaw. "I thought he told you to keep your mouth shut."

Mahaffey pushed his friend aside. "Let him talk, Roy. Everyone else around here has something to say. I've got a messenger without a message, a sharpshooter who doesn't think he can be tracked, a lookout man who likes to listen instead of keeping an eye out, and my oldest friend who thinks we ought to run. Brandt might as well join in the fun. He's the only one who hasn't disappointed me yet, so give him a chance."

Brandt worked a tooth loose and spat it out away from Mahaffey. "I was just going to say that you've got another option."

"Let me guess," Mahaffey mocked. "You think I ought to send my boys out to gather hawk wings and tie them together so we can all just fly out of here."

"Actually, I was thinking of something more practical than that," Brandt said. "Something that'll save you a lot of trouble and just might buy all of you some time."

Mahaffey folded his arms across his chest. "Well? I'm listening."

Brandt shut his eyes and winced as he said, "Don't hit me, but you ought to think about letting me go."

Earnshaw brought up his rifle butt to strike him again, but Mahaffey stopped him before he could. "I told you to let him talk."

Brandt did. "Trammel can't know about that fella you shot yet, so I'm the only reason why Trammel would bother coming after you. If you keep me, you've got to keep an eye on me. You know Trammel's only stalling for time, and Earnshaw is right. There's a good chance someone from Laramie can track Bishop and Marcum here even if they were careful. If you hold on to me, you'll have to worry about me slowing you down or trying to escape."

Mahaffey knew there was another way. "We could just shoot you now and leave you here."

"You surely could," Brandt admitted, "but what would that get you? If you cut me loose now, I can ride on to Laramie or go back to Cheyenne, whatever you think's best. It'll be enough to make Trammel stay in town while you figure out what to do next."

"Let you go just like that," Earnshaw repeated. "I suppose you'll be expecting us to give you your guns back, too, if you promise you won't shoot at us after. What kind of fools do you take us for?"

"You can give me my horse and guns on account that they belong to me," Brandt said, "but you can keep all my bullets. Once I'm gone, you boys can ride off wherever you like. I won't know where you're going, so you don't have to worry about me leading them to you."

Coleman stepped forward. "That's the dumbest thing I ever heard. You'd tell Trammel about us. Tell him our names and what we look like."

Brandt said, "Trammel and every lawman for a thousand miles already know who you are, Coleman. They've got your names and descriptions, too. I've seen the wanted flyers on you in the marshal's office ever since I came to Cheyenne. The town marshal's office, too. I can't tell them anything they don't already know and have known for a long time."

Earnshaw pulled his rifle away from Mahaffey's grip. "Let me shut him up, George. He's just trying to save his own skin."

"You're damned right I am," Brandt admitted. "But saving my skin doesn't cost you anything. And unless your friend on lookout duty sends up a holler that a posse is coming, it sounds like I'm more trouble to you than I'm worth. Let me go and move off and it'll buy you much more time with Trammel. You know I'm right."

Hank Classet said, "You expect us to just give up on saving Ben just like that?"

"Of course not," Brandt said. "No one expects you to. But Trammel won't be expecting to see me ride into town alone, either. I've never met the man, and I'm not promising I can stall him. You wouldn't believe me if I said I could. But when he didn't give you an answer, he did something you weren't counting on. If you do the same, it'll throw him off and put the weight back where it belongs. On Ben Washington."

Earnshaw raised his rifle again and Brandt covered his head. "He's already locked up! How much worse could it get for him?"

This time, Mahaffey did not need to stop Earnshaw from striking him. The outlaw slowly lowered the rifle on his own.

For the first time that morning, Mahaffey thought he finally had something close to a solution to at least one of his problems. He walked away from the others and around behind Brandt. He felt the eyes of his fellow outlaws follow him as he moved and found himself speaking without thinking.

"I've never been the brains of this outfit, boys. I never said I was. Ben always did the thinking for all of us. You know as much about this mess as I do, and you're all risking as much as I am by being here. So, I put it to you. Who among you thinks we should hold on to Brandt or let him go?"

Ben Washington had never once asked the men for their opinion, and they all looked equally puzzled by the prospect of offering it now.

Tim spoke first. "We all figure you're the one in charge, George. We'll abide by whatever you decide."

Mahaffey shook his head. "No. Not this time. This is too important. Each man has an equal say. Don't be shy. Tell me what you think."

He saw the men continued to struggle with what they should do, so he decided to make it easy on them.

"Every man who thinks we ought to let Brandt go, raise your hand."

Five of the men slowly did.

"Every man who thinks we should keep him, raise your hand."

Earnshaw was the only one who did. The others just looked at the ground.

Mahaffey looked down at Brandt, who had not shown any reaction to the news. "Looks like today is your lucky day, Deputy."

Brandt kept his hands and head low. Mahaffey saw he understood that the men may have voted, but his fate was still in Mahaffey's hands. He did not want to risk any sign of emotion that might risk his freedom. *Smart man.*

Mahaffey told Earnshaw to follow him. "Let's go over there and talk about how we ought to do this."

They had only managed to take a few steps when a single shot echoed through the box canyon.

Hagen figured Lefty Rollins had refused to pass out from the hole in his side purely out of spite. The old man had been hanging on to him without so much as a grunt as they had followed Bishop and Marcum's trail to a box canyon he decided was almost exactly halfway between Cheyenne and Laramie.

"I thought this is where we'd find them," Rollins said

weakly. "It's just far away enough from anything to serve their purposes."

"You're alive." Hagen brought his horse to a stop and looked back at the marshal. Rollins's face was pale, and his mouth hung open. He looked like he might pass out at any moment. "You've been quiet for so long that I thought you might've gone and died on me."

"Not yet, but I'll be needing some help in getting down from this horse."

Hagen was off the saddle first and saw Rollins had already bled through the bandages around his middle, but not as much as he had expected.

He took the marshal's arm and watched him bite off the pain as he half slid, half fell off the back of the horse. Rollins did not fight him as he brought him over to the shade of a tree just off the trail. It was not a warm day, but the wounded man was sweating profusely as his body worked hard to replace all of the blood he had lost.

Hagen knew Rollins still had his pride despite his sorry condition. "I'll need you to mind the horse and keep a look out for anyone trying to sneak around me. I'm going to take a look over that ridge to see if Brandt and the others are down there."

He thought Rollins had heard him but could not be sure. He tied his horse around another tree a good distance from the marshal and crept toward the canyon wall. He had taken his field glasses from his saddlebag but left his rifle behind. He did not want to risk the temptation of using it against Mahaffey and his men. Trammel had made Hagen promise not to do anything foolish. To observe, not act. And since ten-to-one were lousy odds, especially with a captive's life in the balance, he had decided to heed the sheriff's advice for once.

Hagen peered over the side of the canyon and saw

several men clustered below. He focused his binoculars and counted ten men in total. And although he had never seen the deputy before, it was easy to see which one was Brandt. He was the only one on the ground. His hands and feet bound.

A man he took to be Mahaffey loomed over his prisoner as he faced the other men of the Washington Gang. He was too far away to hear what they were saying, but they appeared to be taking some kind of vote. Some raised their hands. Some did not. He searched the faces in the group to see if Bishop and Marcum were among them.

He found Bishop lingering at the back of the outlaws. The rest of his comrades had dark, thick beards but none of them wore a slouched hat like the one he had seen Marcum wearing when he had shot Rollins. *Where was he?*

Marcum was glad he had been smart enough to leave the canyon when he did. Earnshaw had always been a loudmouth. He liked to hear himself talk, especially when Ben or George was around to hear him. He had never known him to not have an opinion on any subject at hand, be it where to hit a stagecoach line or which breed of cattle was best or how a man should clean his guns.

And he had been all too glad to point out that he and Bishop had forgotten to cover their trail in their haste to get back to the hideout after shooting that old codger by the creek.

During his time with the Army of Virginia, Marcum had learned that predictability was the surest way to get a man killed. So, when he reached the path that led directly to the top of the canyon where Mahaffey had ordered other men to stand watch, he decided to move off to the left. He walked slowly through the vegetation that grew wild there, looking for anyone or anything that was out of place.

He had stopped when he saw bushes near the trail rustle and heard what sounded like the snort of a horse. Earnshaw had been right. Someone had tracked him back to the canyon.

Marcum crept forward through the overgrowth, careful not to snap any twigs or branches as he headed toward the road. He thought there was only one mount out there, but he needed to be sure.

Marcum paused to listen and, when he was reasonably certain there was only one horse out there, moved out into the open. His long Sharps was at the ready. It was only good for one shot, but the way he could shoot and at that distance, once would prove to be more than enough. He would easily go to the six-gun on his belt if he had to.

He moved away from the bushes, preferring to stay on the quiet packed dirt of the trail as he worked his way back toward the lip of the canyon.

He saw a stranger observing Mahaffey and the others on his belly. He was still looking through a pair of binoculars and had not heard Marcum approach. And, at this range, he would not hear anything ever again.

He was bringing his rifle to his shoulder when he heard a sound off to his right. His mind told him a branch had snapped, but his instinct told him it was a far more familiar sound.

He looked left and found the old man he had left on the hillside aiming a pistol at him from beneath a tree.

Marcum dropped his rifle as he tried to dive away, but the old man squeezed the trigger before the Sharps hit the ground. Marcum felt a searing pain in his jaw for only an instant.

And then he felt nothing at all.

* * *

When he heard the shot from behind him, Hagen dropped his field glasses over the wall as he drew his pistol while rolling on his back.

He saw Marcum fall to the dirt. And given the condition of his head, there was no question that the sharpshooter was already dead.

Hagen scrambled to his feet and ran back to check on Rollins. He found the old marshal with his smoking pistol across his stomach, panting from the effort of having just killed a man.

"You hit?" Hagen asked as he rushed to check on him.

"Don't bother about me," Rollins shouted. "I'm dead anyway. Get on that horse and ride. They'll be on you in a minute. I'll keep them off you as best I can. Just go! Tell Trammel where they are and get Brandt out alive."

Though Hagen had never liked Rollins, he hated the idea of leaving him for the Washington gang to find. But he could not get him on the horse and get away before Mahaffey and the others got him. The marshal would have to take his chances with the outlaws.

Hagen pulled the reins free from the branch, jumped in the saddle and heeled his horse into a gallop. He rode as fast and as low as he could manage and did not dare look back.

Chapter 15

"They're building up to something," Deputy Blake told Trammel as they stood at the base of the stairs up to City Hall. "They've been quiet for a while, but they're too quiet now."

Trammel had been watching the scene unfold and, as usual, Blake was right. Men had stopped trying to form in front of City Hall and instead had begun to congregate on one of the side streets beside The Laramie Grand. The hotel's thugs had worked with Trammel's deputies to keep people away from the entrance, but their interest stopped at the property line.

He had seen men passing among the crowd from one side of the street to the other. No one had started shouting and no one appeared armed, but Trammel knew the crowd was large enough to easily overwhelm his deputies if he allowed their numbers to grow unchecked. He had to do something or at least try.

He told Blake, "I'm going over to talk to them. Have the men ready to move back here to the hall if things take a turn. Move them back into the jail and do your best to keep anyone from getting into the courtyard. Let them tear the offices upstairs to pieces if they want, but don't let them grab Washington. No matter what happens."

Blake said, "No matter what?"

Trammel had chosen his words carefully. "I'd rather have to explain a bullet in his head to a judge than see him swing from a tree. Or, even worse, traded for Brandt."

"I'll do my best."

"I don't want your best," Trammel said over his shoulder as he began to walk. "I just want you to do it."

Trammel took his time as he walked alone toward the crowd. He wanted them to see him. To know he was coming their way.

He saw Hawkeye standing at the edge of the side street. He had been helping the other deputies keep people penned in.

"What do you want me to do, boss?" he asked Trammel.

The sheriff walked past him. "Whatever Blake tells you to do. Keep your eyes on him and don't worry about me. I'll be fine."

The men out at the front of the group stepped back as Trammel drew nearer. Someone had placed several small crates in the street to form a crooked platform, probably for one of the more vocal among them to give some kind of speech.

Trammel made a show of easily stomping them into splinters before walking over the broken wood. At more than six-and-a-half-feet tall, he did not need any help to be seen or heard.

People began shouting questions at him before he had a chance to speak.

"Is it true, Sheriff? Is Washington's gang ready to ride in here and attack us?"

"Are you gonna give them Washington, Sheriff? Are you gonna save the town?"

"Give 'em what they want, Trammel!" another shouted. "We've had enough bloodshed in Laramie! Turn him loose!"

Trammel waited until the last question died away before he decided it was time to address them. "I know you've been talking about this all day, so now it's time you hear the truth from me. Ben Washington's gang has taken a deputy U.S. Marshal hostage. They wanted to trade him for Washington. They didn't threaten the town, and I won't let them threaten it. I let the man they'd sent go at first light this morning with the understanding he wouldn't be followed. They threatened to kill the deputy if we did. We think they're somewhere between here and Cheyenne, but I don't know that for certain. But what I do know is that none of them is anywhere near Laramie. No one's looking to kill you. No one's going to burn the town. They're not waiting outside to ride into us, either. They didn't even threaten to do that. Anyone who tells you anything different is either lying to you or just plain wrong. The town isn't in any more danger than it was last week or yesterday. You people pay me to keep you safe and that's exactly what I'm going to keep on doing. You've got my word on that."

A man from the middle of the men in front shouted back, "Those are mighty big words, Sheriff, but what if those Washington boys have other ideas in mind?"

Trammel did not often like to use his size to his advantage, but at times like this, it came in handy. He slowly stepped toward the man, and those around him were eager to back away.

Trammel had seen this man several times in town since becoming sheriff. He was a freight driver who did not even live in Laramie. He was short and lean and about half of Trammel's size.

The sheriff looked down at him as he spoke loud enough for everyone else to hear him. "If the Washington Gang is dumb enough to try to take him, I'll just have to stop them."

The freighter did his best to hold his ground. "What if they just ride over you?"

"You ever see anyone ride over me yet?"

The freighter kept looking up at him. "There's a first time for everything."

"Not that. And not today." He looked out over the crowd as he said, "You've got nothing to worry about, so you'd all best go on home. Keep your doors locked if it makes you feel any better. If you see any strangers lurking around, come get me or one of my men if you can and we'll look into it. That's it. Off the street. Everyone."

He remained among them until those around him began to move away. Those behind them followed suit and so did the rest at the back until almost everyone had left, even the loudmouthed freight driver. He kept standing where he was in case anyone had any other questions, but if they did, they took them with them.

And when he was certain that the threat had passed, he began to walk back to City Hall as calmly as he had left it. He saw Hagen's gunmen still standing watch in front of The Laramie Grand. "That goes for you boys, too. Back inside where you belong. I'll tell you if I need you."

Blake joined him in the center of the street. "That went better than I'd thought it would."

Trammel knew he might have thrown water on the fire, but it would only take one spark to set it off again. "Keep an eye out."

Blake fell in beside him. "At least you didn't have to kill anyone this time."

"The day's not over yet."

* * *

Rick LeBlanc turned from the window, ready to fire, when he heard the suite door burst open. He lowered his pistol when he saw it was only Virgil and Don returning to the room.

"Shut that door," he ordered his brothers. "I told you idiots to knock first before busting in here. I almost shot you dead."

Neither of the two LeBlanc brothers took notice of Rick's annoyance.

Don said, "You were right about all of our stuff being gone from our room."

"Even our clothes," Virgil added.

Rick did not see that as a good enough excuse for them to have rushed back into the suite without knocking. "With what's liable to be in that safe Burt is working on, you boys can buy all the clothes you'll ever need."

"The clothes ain't the concern," Don said. "All of our bags are gone. The same bags we were gonna use to haul all this money out of here."

Baggage was the least of Rick's worries at the moment, but he looked down at Rube Miller, whom he had kept bound and gagged on the floor. "You got any idea where our stuff is?"

Miller shook his head, but Rick was not sure he believed him. It was not important, anyway. "We won't have anything to haul unless Burt gets that safe open. That means you two nitwits had better keep quiet. Get in the bedroom and help Jim with what he's doing. And try not to make too much noise. Keep the door closed. Burt here is trying to concentrate."

When the brothers did as he had told them, Rick resisted

the urge to question Burt on his progress with getting the safe open. He was glad his brother had remembered to bring his bag of tools and dynamite with him when Wayne had ordered them to flee The Laramie Grand the day before.

Rick looked out the window and down at the crowd in the street. No one was shouting yet, but they were getting louder. He had never been one to pray, but he hoped any trouble on the street happened when he and his brothers were ready to leave with the money.

Getting the firearms up to the suite had gone better than Rick had expected. Burt had brought a rope up to him while the others had wrapped their rifles in a blanket down in the alley. He had pulled them through the window while they slipped inside from the back stairs.

The safe was another story. Rick watched Burt use an old doctor's stethoscope to listen to the tumblers as he worked the dial to find the right combination of numbers. It required patience and silence, both of which had been in short supply in Hagen's suite for the past several minutes. The noise from the growing crowd outside was not helping matters.

Burt ripped the stethoscope from his ears in disgust. "It just doesn't make any sense. I can hear the dial turning but it's not catching anything."

Rick had feared that might be the case. "Maybe it's that timer you said Hagen has on it."

Burt stood up and arched his back. He pointed down at Miller. "Take that gag out of his mouth. I want to ask him something."

Rick obliged but placed the barrel of his pistol against Miller's head. "You shout, I shoot."

Burt asked Miller, "What time is this thing set to open?"

"This evening," Miller whispered.

Rick pushed the barrel harder against Miller's head. "My brother asked you what time. Tell him."

"Six o'clock," Miller blurted out. "Just like I told you before."

Rick cursed and pulled the gag back into Miller's mouth. "He's lying. He told me five o'clock when he let us in here. He won't tell us anything useful."

But Burt did not look as discouraged as his brother. "How'd you get in here? The door didn't look busted to me."

Rick said, "Miller used his key. Why?"

Burt knelt beside Miller and began to search the bound man's pockets. He found the keys in his coat and began to examine them.

Rick had not paid any attention to them at first, but now he saw a key that looked different from the others on the ring. It was thicker than the rest and had ridges. And where the others had an "E" shape at the end of it, this one was in the shape of an "H."

Burt examined it closely. "What does this one open?"

Rick undid the gag enough for Miller to say, "I don't know. It was on the ring when Mr. Hagen gave it to me when he hired me on. I've never used it before."

Burt turned back to the safe and Rick replaced Miller's gag. Rick could tell his brother was on to something as he tapped the odd key against his palm.

"He's lying," Burt said. "And I'll bet I know why."

Rick looked on as his brother attacked the safe with a renewed vigor. He ran his hands over the top of the bookcase that had been built around the safe. Then he checked the sides before he felt under the lip of the lowest shelf.

He stopped and his eyes brightened. "There's a lock down here. I knew there had to be something."

Rick watched Burt place his head flat on the floor and look beneath the shelf. "There it is." He slid the strange key into the lock and, with some effort, managed to turn it. They both heard something metallic slide somewhere deep inside the safe.

Rick looked down at Miller, who had turned his face away.

Burt got up and worked the dial. This time even Rick could hear the tumbler tick.

Rick could hardly keep from cheering. "You did it, little brother!"

"I did something." Burt quickly put the stethoscope back in his ears. "Still don't have it open yet."

Rick let him work as he turned his attention back to the street in time to see Buck Trammel talking to the crowd. He hoped this might be when the trouble started, but his hopes faded when the group began to break up and drift away. So much for leaving in the middle of a riot. The brothers had managed to get into The Laramie Grand easily. Getting out would prove much harder without a distraction from outside.

Harder, Rick knew, but far from impossible.

He watched Trammel stop to speak to the gunmen from the hotel before he and one of his deputies walked back across the thoroughfare toward City Hall. He had heard Trammel was a big man, but he looked even larger when he stood next to someone. He would do his best to keep his brothers as far away from him as possible whenever they made their escape. He allowed himself to begin thinking about how they could get away without being noticed.

"Got it!" Burt exclaimed.

Rick forgot about the world outside as he watched his brother grab the safe door's handle and pull it down.

He stepped away from the window as Burt pulled the iron door open.

Behind it was another door with three more combination locks, just like the one on the front.

Rick looked down at Miller, who did his best to try to duck his head against his body as if he expected to be struck again.

Burt placed his hands on his hips as he examined the newest obstacles in his path. "Looks like I've still got some work to do. But don't worry. I'll get it."

Rick poked Miller's sore ribs with the tip of his shoe. "You'd better hope he does, because it'll go bad for you if he doesn't."

CHAPTER 16

Mahaffey held on to Brandt's arm as they looked down at the dead old man beneath the tree. "You know him?"

Brandt dropped to his knees beside the corpse. "That's Marshal Rollins."

"Your boss," Tim said.

"My friend," Brandt answered. "I guess this is Marcum's doing."

Dib Bishop began to say something, but Mahaffey waved him to be quiet. The young man was not always careful with his words, and Brandt was taking the loss of Rollins hard. He did not want to risk the deputy doing something stupid, like going for the boy. His hands might still be tied in front of him, but he could do some damage if he had a mind to try.

Mahaffey said, "Marcum shot this man when he and Bishop were coming here. Marcum thought he'd killed him then, but it looks like he was wrong. And judging by the size of that hole in Marcum's face, I'd say old Rollins here made him pay for his mistake."

"He was a fighter." Brandt rested his hands on Rollins's chest. Dib had already taken the marshal's gun when he and Hank Classet had ridden up to take a look around after they had heard the shot. "A stubborn, brave old man."

Mahaffey had never shed a tear for a dead lawman, but he felt a twinge of sympathy for Brandt. Mahaffey did not have much experience with loss. He had seen plenty of men die. He had killed a fair number of them. But he had never lost a relative or anyone he considered a friend. He had seen how death affected other men and imagined it must be a pain that was different from anything he had ever experienced. It was why he rarely allowed himself to grow attached to anyone.

Barrett said, "We lost a man, too, boss. Marcum was a top hand."

The other voiced their agreement.

Mahaffey said, "This ain't a contest. There's plenty of bad feeling to go around for everyone. Marcum should've made sure this old codger was dead, but he didn't. Let that be a lesson to the rest of us. Pay your respects to him if you want but be quick about it. We've got to get out of here."

He told Brandt, "I can let you have a few moments with him to say your goodbyes but that's all. There's bound to be more men coming this way, and we have to move on. That also means we won't have time to bury him or Marcum, either."

"I said everything I had to say to him when he was alive." Brandt stood up without any help. "He won't be able to hear it now." He lowered his head. "Guess this means you won't be letting me go."

"Not yet," Mahaffey admitted. "Maybe later when we get clear of here, but we'll be taking you with us for now."

He took Brandt by the arm and handed him over to Tim. "Don't be harder on him than you have to. You boys head for the pines. Me and Earnshaw need to talk some things over."

Some of the men grumbled a complaint, but Mahaffey spoke over them. "I know Brandt heard us planning to go there, but we're going anyway. I didn't say we're staying there. We'll ride through and head somewhere else. We'll be harder to track in the pines. You boys had your chance at voting earlier and only a few of you had the good sense to do it. Go on like I told you. We'll be along in a bit."

Tim got Brandt on his horse, and the men rode on with their prisoner in the middle of the group.

Roy Earnshaw held his rifle loosely at his side as he used his thumb to push his hat farther back on his head. "How'd you know I wanted to talk to you?"

"Figured you would," Mahaffey said. "It's kind of hard to ride with a man all these years without getting to know him a little." He nodded down at the corpse. "Besides, I know you understand what happened here."

"The others know it, too. They just didn't say anything."

Mahaffey knew what had been left unsaid. "There's no sign of his horse and there's no way he could've walked all the way here from the creek with that hole Marcum put in him."

Earnshaw pointed at the ground. "And there's fresh tracks heading back in the direction of the creek. Given the spacing of them, I'd say whoever it was tore out of here at a good clip after Marcum was hit."

"I saw that, too." Mahaffey took the canteen from his saddle, rinsed out his mouth, and spat it down at Marcum's body. His and Dib's mistake could cost the whole gang dearly. "That means Rollins must've had someone bring him here. You were right about Dib and Johnny being sloppy about their tracks. And whoever got away knows how many we are, and they'll come ready when they do. Buck Trammel will be riding right out front."

Earnshaw said, "There's plenty of places between here and Laramie we could ambush a posse, George. We could double back and hit them at the creek."

Mahaffey knew he had never been much of a planner, but he had made a decision at the beginning of all this, and he was going to stick to it. "We aimed to stay away from Trammel if we could, and that's just what we're gonna keep doing. And we're holding on to Brandt. Trammel will be coming for blood once he finds out Rollins is dead. Cutting him loose won't delay him now."

"You're not forgetting about Ben are you, George? We're only in this mess because of him. We can't free him if we keep running away every time something goes wrong."

Mahaffey scratched at his chin. No, he had not forgotten about Ben. He had not been able to think about anything else since he had learned of his capture. He hated feeling like this. Scared and tense all the time. No matter which way he moved, he felt stuck.

But something Earnshaw had said earlier struck a chord in him. "Who's the fastest rider we've got?"

Earnshaw gave it some thought. "Dib, probably, but he'll be too rattled by the loss of Marcum to be much good. He's liable to try to find a way to make up for him leaving a trail and getting Marcum killed. Why? What do you have in mind?"

"Set Dib aside. Who's next fastest?"

"Coombs," Earnshaw said. "Why?"

"I don't know yet." Mahaffey gathered up his reigns as he began to get on his horse. "But I'll let you know when it comes to me."

* * *

It was already well past noon when Trammel heard Hawkeye call up to him from the bottom of the staircase in City Hall. "Better come quick, Sheriff. Mr. Hagen is back."

Trammel rushed down the stairs and reached the courtyard just as Hagen was climbing down from his horse. The animal was slick with sweat and breathing heavy.

"Did you find them?" Trammel asked Hagen as Old Bob led the weary animal away.

"I found more than I bargained for." Hagen accepted a canteen from Hawkeye and drank deeply. He wiped his mouth with the back of his hand. "Lefty Rollins is dead."

Of all the names he had expected Hagen to say, he had not been counting on that one. "Lefty? He's supposed to be in Cheyenne. How'd he die?"

"He got worried about Brandt and set out to find him on his own," Hagen told him. "Marcum and Bishop spotted him while I was tracking them, and Marcum took a chunk out of his side with that cannon he carries around with him. His horse was hit, so we had to ride double while we tracked them to a box canyon west of the creek. We ran into some trouble from Marcum, who I guess Mahaffey sent to be their lookout. He came across Rollins, and the old man killed him. I figure he saved my life."

"But you said Rollins is dead," Hawkeye said.

"He was still alive when I hightailed it out of there, but that hole in his side was bigger than my fist. I hate to say it, but I imagine he's bound to be long dead by now."

Trammel did not like to hear that a good man like Rollins had met such an end, but he was more concerned about the gang and the deputy they were holding captive. "Did you have time to see if Brandt was still alive."

"He is." Hagen took another drink from the canteen.

"Or at least he was when I took off. I got a good look at the whole gang down in the canyon. There's ten of them, not counting Marcum, of course. They had Brandt's arms and legs tied, but he was breathing. I don't know if that's changed since I left."

Hawkeye spoke as Hagen drank. "I'll get a fresh horse for Mr. Hagen, then we can ride out after them, boss."

Trammel grabbed the boy's arm before he got too carried away. "Get inside and tell Blake and the others what happened. Stay in there and send Blake down here. I want to talk to him."

But Hawkeye was slow to move. "I know where that canyon is, boss. It's only about an hour's ride from here if we take this shortcut I know. We could have them in hand by suppertime."

Trammel glared down at him. "I've got enough on my mind without any sass from you. I gave you an order, Deputy. Do as I tell you."

Hawkeye ducked his head and ran back to the side door of the jail.

Hagen grinned after him. "Why, Buck, I do believe that boy's beginning to stand up to you."

"And at the worst time, too." He'd worry about Hawkeye's independent streak later. "How many men do you think we'll need to hit that canyon."

"None because they won't be there," Hagen said. "They would've heard the shot and are bound to have come looking to see what happened. They didn't come after me, so I figure they've already grabbed Brandt and moved on."

Trammel imagined they had. "Where do you think they'd go?"

"No shortage of places to hide in that part of the territory, and I'll bet Mahaffey knows them all like the back of his hand."

Knowing how cunning Mahaffey could be did not make Trammel's situation any easier. He decided to ask the same question differently. "Fine. Where would you go if you were them?"

"There's a pine forest that's closest to the canyon. They could head in there, slow walk their horses along the roots. It's pretty dark in there, and we'd have a tough time picking up their track. There are plenty of places where they could hit us from the trees, too. You could have fifty men spread out in that forest and not see them until you were right on top of them."

Trammel remembered how tough it had been to follow Lucien Clay through a forest. He was not anxious to face the likes of the Washington Gang on similar ground.

Hagen continued. "If it were me, I'd do something no one was expecting. Mahaffey knows we'll be coming after him, so I'd lie in wait somewhere between here and that canyon. Maybe at the same creek where Marcum shot Rollins. There's good cover there and some water to cross. And given how I've heard they fight, they would cut us down to size before we got near them, then make a run for it. Might even get away."

Trammel rarely believed much of what Hagen said, but he knew how to read the land better than anyone the sheriff had ever met. "How many men would we need to do the job?"

"Thirty good men, not just the eager and the brave. And even if we had them, which we don't, I still wouldn't give much for our chances."

Trammel saw Blake walk through the open courtyard gate. "Hawkeye told me what happened. Said you wanted to see me. What do you want to do?"

That was the problem. Trammel did not know what to

do. If he took every deputy he had and a few volunteers, they might have a chance.

But that would mean leaving Laramie without any law just when he had managed to quiet the town. He could not rely on Old Bob and the prison guards to keep Washington safe from a mob of angry citizens, and he could not trust Mayor Holm to keep the town calm without Trammel's men around to back him up.

Whatever element of surprise Trammel might have once had was now gone. Mahaffey thinking Trammel might go after him was much different from knowing he was coming. They might just kill Brandt anyway if it looked like they would lose.

No matter how many ways he looked at the problem, he was left with only rotten choices. There was only one thing he could do.

"No one's doing nothing. We're all going to stay right here in town. And so is Washington."

Hagen toasted him with his canteen. "Good thinking, Buck. I wasn't expecting you to say that."

Blake's eyes narrowed. "You mean you're just going to let a band of murderers go free? They killed a federal marshal and they're holding one of his deputies captive. We can't let that stand, boss, and you've got no right to ask us to."

"I know what they've done, Blake. I know what they're expecting us to do, too, which is why we're not going to do it. They know the land better than us, and they can fight better than we can. I'm not going to throw away good lives after bad only to leave the town wide open while we do it. Chasing Mahaffey's bunch won't get us anywhere. If they want a fight, we can best fight them here."

Blake did not seem to understand him. "You've never gone up against a bunch like these before. They could kill

Brandt or worse. They could start sending him back to us in pieces. What do you think the town will do then?"

Trammel could not control what Mahaffey did. He could only control what happened in Laramie. And that was exactly what he was doing. "I'm going over to the telegraph office to wire Washington about Rollins. I'm going to ask them if there's a judge nearby who can hold a trial. We're going to have Ben Washington tried right here in Laramie where we can keep an eye on him."

Trammel walked away as Blake asked, "We can hide here if you want, but where does that leave Brandt?"

"Exactly where he's been since yesterday," Trammel answered. "He's a sworn officer of the law. He knew the risks when he pinned that star on his shirt, same as Rollins knew them."

"Brandt's one of us." Blake's voice grew narrow and sharp. "If you're too scared to get him, the least you can do is let some of us go instead."

Trammel stopped walking.

Hagen slowly lowered his canteen. "You'd better make yourself scarce while you still can, Blake. It looks like you just went a step too far."

But Blake remained where he was. "If Trammel doesn't have the stomach to go against the likes of Mahaffey, he won't do anything to me."

Trammel turned around and Hagen moved between them. "Steady now, Steve. His blood is up and so is yours. Now is not the time for this. Go send your wire and cool down."

But Trammel knew he would not cool down. He could hear his own blood roar in his veins. The muscles in his clenched jaw popped and he felt his hands ball into fists. He lost sight of everything around him. The courtyard. The stables and horses behind Blake. Even Hagen was just a blur. He locked eyes with Sherwood Blake, and he saw how the deputy's face twitched as he tried to remain brave in the face of the avalanche of violence that was about to overwhelm him.

Hagen chanced another step forward. "You can't hurt him. Blake's a good man and you're going to need him."

"No, I won't. I only want men with me who have some sense in their heads." He pointed at the deputy. "Take off that star and drop it on the ground before I rip it off you. You don't work for me anymore."

Blake unpinned the star and dropped it. "I was going to quit anyway. And so will the others. We've had a bellyful of you and your harebrained ideas, and we're not going to take it anymore. When I leave, they'll leave with me. Every last one of them."

"You can leave, but the gun's city property. It stays here."

Blake's hand moved toward the belt. "How about you come over here and get it?"

Hagen drew his pistol before Blake's hand reached halfway to the buckle. He aimed at the center of the deputy's forehead. "Careful, Blake. I'm fond of you, and I'd hate to have to kill you, but I will. Don't do anything stupid."

Blake sneered at them as he began to unbuckle his belt. "That's the way it's always been, hasn't it? The lawman and the gunman. The sheriff and the gambler. The two of you sticking up for each other no matter what." He let the belt drop to the ground and held his hands out from his sides. "You're going to regret this, Trammel. I'm gonna see to it that you do."

"See to it from another town," Trammel said. "If you're still here in an hour, I'll kill you where I find you. Get out of here while you still can."

Blake took his time walking around Hagen and Trammel before passing through the courtyard gate for the last time.

Hagen holstered his pistol. "Send your telegram and go see Emily for a bit. You'll feel different when you've had a chance to calm down."

Trammel blinked away the anger that had almost consumed him. "I don't have time to feel different. I feel fine."

And as Hagen watched his friend leave, he found himself almost believing him.

CHAPTER 17

Adam Hagen had never been the type who paid aging much attention. He was still a relatively young man and imagined time would eventually catch up to him when it was good and ready.

But as he walked back to his hotel, he began to feel every step of the many hard miles he had ridden in his quest to get back to Laramie as soon as possible. His legs ached, and his shoulders were sore. A slight twinge at the small of his back told him he was in for quite a bit of pain for the next few days. He could not allow that to stop him, for although Ben Washington would remain in a cell, there was much preparation to do for the inevitable fight that was to come.

He knew that once word about what had happened with the Washington Gang began to spread, bettors at The Laramie Grand would be eager to place bets on the new outcome. He might even have to hire on more men to keep order on the gaming floor.

Other troubles were bound to pop up. He imagined the town would once again grow restless when they learned of the death of Marshal Lefty Rollins and that Deputy Brandt remained a captive. Fear would come to a boil when they heard the Washington Gang was on the move somewhere close by. Hagen doubted Mahaffey and his bunch would come anywhere near Laramie. They were used to fighting in the open, not on the narrow streets of a town.

But Hagen also knew that people were bound to think differently about it. Civilians were not prone to allowing something as trifling as common sense to interfere with a good panic. The next few days would be challenging indeed.

Which was all the more reason why Hagen was eager to go up to his suite, pull off his boots, and take a long nap. Rube Miller could go on running things until he had the chance to regain his strength and warm his belly with some of that good scotch. Perhaps toast the memory of Lefty Rollins while he did it.

Hagen spotted two of his guards sitting on the wide front porch of the hotel. Each man held his rifle low against his side. Both men were on the tall side, lean and good with a gun. They had long faces and dark moustaches, just like all the gunmen who worked for him.

One was named Fuller and the other was called Knothe. He did not know which one was which and chose not to embarrass himself by guessing.

"Afternoon, Mr. Hagen," they greeted in unison.

"Keep a sharp eye out, boys. There's bound to be some excitement soon. Where's Mr. Miller?"

"Haven't seen him," one of them said. "We've been minding the front. Got another two at the back. The front desk might know where he is."

Hagen passed between them and went to the front desk. Mr. Lee's fleshy face brightened into a smile. "Welcome back, Mr. Hagen. It's certainly been quite a busy day so far."

"You don't know the half of it. Where's Mr. Miller?"

"I haven't seen him in quite some time." He looked

back at the large, ornate brass clock that sat atop the mail slots for the guest rooms. "In fact, I haven't seen him in more than an hour. I'm sure he's inside manning the chalk boards for the Washington matter. He was doing quite a brisk business earlier this morning, last I checked."

Hagen was too tired to traipse through the gaming floor, offer fake smiles to the customers who wanted to speak to him, and glad-hand the high rollers. And since he was the boss, he had the benefit of options.

"Send someone to find him and have him come up to my suite as soon as possible. I want to get some sleep, so tell him to be quick about it."

He began to walk up the stairs and found himself grateful he had taken the suite at the top of the first landing as his own. He remembered how Rube Miller had seen it as an odd choice at first, given how close it was to the center of the hotel. Virtually every guest would pass by his doors on their way up to their rooms at all hours of the day and night, which made it the least private suite in the hotel.

But Hagen had not wanted privacy. He had wanted to be at the very heart of the operation. He learned much from the casual conversations and the mumblings of the drunks who passed by his door. He could gauge how well the place was doing without having to solely rely on others to feed him what they wanted to tell him.

Hagen took his key from his pocket and began to open the door to his suite.

He caught a rush of movement inside. The safe door was open.

Reflex made Hagen reach for the gun on his hip as he dropped to a crouch. Sight of a man with a Winchester made him dive to the side just as a bullet struck the half-opened door, shutting it instantly.

Two more bullets pierced the wall and hit the carpet as

Hagen, Colt in hand, dashed for cover behind the stairs. The two guards from the front rushed up from the lobby, their rifles at their shoulders.

"Stay back," Hagen told them. "Someone just took a shot at me."

"From where?" one of the gunmen asked.

"My suite." The words did not sound real to him as the weight of the situation finally settled on him. "Good God. I think I'm being robbed!"

Hagen removed his hat and chanced a quick look over the top stair. The door to his suite was closed, but not all the way.

From inside the suite, a man called out, "That you out there, Hagen?"

"It's me. You're a lousy shot, whoever you are. You didn't come close to hitting me."

"Play it smart and I won't have to hit you at all. Or your friend, neither. Mr. Miller's in here keeping us company."

Of course, Miller would be in there. They must have grabbed him down on the gaming floor. They had made him use his key to open the door without drawing much attention. They would have had to destroy the door to open it otherwise.

"Is he alive?" Hagen shouted back.

"He is for now but doing poorly. I don't think he can take another beating."

One of his guards rose to the next stair below him. "That door's still open, Mr. Hagen. Me and Knothe can bust in there and end this before they get dug in."

Hagen pushed him down. "They're already dug in and have been for quite some time. They've got my safe open and have taken cover behind it. We'll be cut to pieces if we try to rush them now." He told Knothe, "Get the rest of the boys together in the lobby, then come back here. I need to find out more about this character."

As Knothe went on his way, the man inside the suite called out, "You still out there, Hagen?"

"As long as you're in there, I'm not going anywhere," Hagen said. "Let me guess. You must be one of the LeBlanc brothers."

"You're a pretty smart man for a drunk," the man laughed.

Hagen almost wished he were drunk now. "Which one are you? I imagine Burt's probably the one who got my safe open, isn't he?"

"The name's Rick," the man yelled back, "and we're all in here as one big happy family. This old safe of yours wasn't nearly as tough as you made it out to be. All that fancy talk about timers and such almost had my brother cowed, but not me."

Hagen regretted not using the timer, but it was always such a chore to have to wait for the right time to put his money in his own safe. But now was not the time for regret. He was playing a high-stakes game of poker with an angry brother bent on greed and revenge.

He decided to follow some of his own advice to Trammel. He would play the man and not the cards in front of him. "Sounds like you had this pretty well thought out, Rick. Wayne told me you were the brains of the outfit. Almost as sharp as him. You're fashionable, too. Taking hostages seems to be all the rage in Wyoming these days. First the Washington Gang takes Brandt, now you boys grab Miller. Guess you never thought you'd be called fashionable, did you?"

"And we're going to be a lot more fashionable once we leave here with all your money. How much do you have in there? We're down to the last lock so we'll find out soon enough. Telling me now would save us a lot of time counting it later."

"A hundred thousand," Hagen lied. "Not that you'll live long enough to spend it. But I'm not a man who likes to hold a grudge, so I'll make a deal with you. Climb out the window, leave Miller where he is, and I promise I won't come looking for you. We'll call it even for what happened with your brother." He decided to add something to the pot for the sake of the other LeBlanc brothers who might be listening. "Do it now and I'll have a thousand dollars put into the saddlebags of your horses. That ought to help you overcome your grief."

Rick cut loose with a sharp laugh. "We're greedy, not grieving, Hagen. What kind of fools do you take us for? We're not dumb enough to take five of something when we could have a hundred of everything. So, unless you want your friend Miller here to start serenading you with his screams, here's what you're gonna do for us. You're going to send one of your boys to get our horses and tack out of the livery of this fancy hotel of yours. You're gonna have them brought to the alley, even Wayne's. You're gonna put a ladder up to the window so we can climb down—with not just your money, but with your friend Miller. When we get clear and we're sure you don't have anyone following us, we'll let him go and we'll be on our way."

Hagen suppressed a yawn. He really could have used that nap. "You're banking on Miller meaning something to me. Making him open my suite to you has decreased his worth considerably. What if I don't care about what happens to him?"

"You care," Rick said. "If you didn't, you would've had your men rush us by now." He whispered to someone, and the suite door was pushed shut. The lock thrown.

"The time for that is over," Rick went on. "Give us

what we want, and we all walk away from this clean. You can always make more money."

Hagen had tried to flatter him. Now it was time to frighten him. "When you boys were down in New Orleans, did you ever come to hear about me?"

"We did," Rick shouted back, "but we were just starting to make a name for ourselves back then. If we'd known you were such an easy mark, we would've taken a run at you earlier than now."

Hagen wished they had. They would have been long dead. "Then I'm sure you know I've never allowed anyone to steal from me and live. You boys won't be any different. I'll have your horses brought to the alley just like you want. If you leave now, I'll let you live. If not, you'll meet a worse fate than Wayne did. He died terribly, but I'm sure you've already heard that."

Rick laughed again. "We know how to take care of ourselves. But you'd best get those horses ready anyway. Mr. Miller will thank you for it."

Hagen winced as he heard a thud followed by a scream he assumed belonged to Rube Miller.

Hagen moved down to a lower step as Fuller kept watching the door. "What do you make of it, Mr. Hagen?"

Hagen ran his fingers over his scalp. "I think I killed the wrong LeBlanc."

Trammel balled up the telegram the clerk handed to him as he stormed out of the telegraph office. He had read some dumb ideas from back east, but this was one for the ages.

"Steve," he heard Emily say as she came to him. "One of my patients told me Adam is back. Is it true? Lefty Rollins is dead?"

Seeing her again reminded him of how he had left their

last conversation at the dinner table. How unpleasant it had been. He never liked quarrelling with her, especially now with everything going so wrong all at once.

He led her off the boardwalk and away from any citizens who might overhear them. "Not so loud. I'm trying to keep the lid on this place. And yes, it's true. Lefty got killed by one of Washington's bunch. The man who shot him is dead, too, according to Adam."

"That poor old man," Emily said. "I hope he didn't suffer."

"He died as well as he could've wanted," Trammel said. "He died doing his job. His duty."

Emily frowned as she looked at the balled-up telegram in his hand. "Is that more bad news?"

Trammel knew she did not like him to share his troubles with her, but since she had asked, he had to tell her. "I sent a message to Washington, D.C., to tell them Lefty was dead and to send a judge here to Laramie so we could have the trial here."

Her eyes brightened. "That was a good idea. What did they say?"

"That Judge Delker is already in Cheyenne and that's where he's going to stay. They're afraid it's too dangerous for him to come here, so we're going to have to bring Ben Washington to Cheyenne after all. Gang or no gang."

Emily had the same reaction as Trammel had upon reading the news. "But why can't you keep him here until they send more deputy marshals to pick him up and bring him back? Ben Washington is their responsibility, not yours."

Trammel knew the next part would be the hardest for her. "I told them that, but the nearest deputy is a three-day ride from here. Instead of changing their mind, they decided to make Washington my responsibility. They've made me Acting U.S. Marshal for the territory."

Emily brought her hand up to her mouth. "Oh, Steve." He could not tell whether she was happy or saddened by the news.

He handed the telegram to her. "It's actually Temporary Acting U.S. Marshal. It'll stay that way until the deputies get back to Cheyenne since I'm the closest lawman to the capital. They'll figure out who'll get it later after the trial, but for now, I'm the one."

He could remember a time when he would have been honored by the assignment. But after all that happened in the past day, it felt like a cruel joke. "I'm a sheriff without deputies and a marshal without deputies. It's just me and Hawkeye, I guess."

She took his hand in her own. "What do you mean? What happened?"

"I got into a fight with Blake. He wanted to ride out after the Washington Gang after we found out they'd killed Rollins. I knew they'd be expecting that, so I decided to keep everyone here. I thought the folks back in Washington would've agreed to have the trial here, but that's not the case."

She smiled up at him. "You mean you did your best to stay here instead."

Trammel smiled back. "Guess your words made more of a dent in that hard head of mine than you thought. Charging out after them just didn't make any sense. Blake called me a coward and I fired him because of it."

Emily's smile faded. "But you didn't hit him, did you?"

"Adam stopped it from going that far," Trammel admitted, "but Blake's popular with the men. When he leaves, they'll go with him. It'll just be me and Hawkeye left to mind the town. I turned them back once, but it won't be so easy the second time around."

She held his hand tightly. "You know, I didn't get a chance to say everything I wanted to say when we fought over dinner."

Trammel was eager to move past that. "I was wrong. I could see you were upset, but I wasn't thinking."

"I wasn't upset," she told him. "It's just like I told you about everything being different now. I was going to say that you and I have always been able to live through the dangers of your job. But things are different now because it's not just about you and me anymore."

Trammel knew that much was certain. "You're right. Laramie's a whole lot bigger than Blackstone."

She stepped forward and pressed his hand against her stomach. "And it's about to get a little bigger still."

Trammel did not understand. She was far from heavy and had always ate little until the last couple of weeks.

And then the realization of what she had meant overwhelmed him and he dropped to a knee. Her stomach was a bit rounder than normal. "You mean it? But I didn't think you could."

"So did I." She beamed. "But it looks like I was wrong. Some doctor I turned out to be."

Any thoughts of Ben Washington and his gang and Judge Delker and Sherwood Blake left him. All that mattered was Emily and the tiny life he now knew was growing within her.

He stood up again and gathered her close to him. He did not care about protecting Laramie or Cheyenne or anyone else except her and the baby. Their baby. "This changes everything. It'll all be different from now on."

He could hear Emily quietly weep against his shirt. "After our last fight, I didn't know if you'd be happy."

Trammel had not known what true happiness had felt like before meeting Emily. But what he felt in that moment was something so much beyond happiness that he could not describe it. It was as though a piece of him he had not known was missing had fallen into place.

"I'll get this mess with Washington figured out, and I'll hire on new men. Good men. Maybe one who can take my place before the baby comes."

Emily eased away enough to look up at him. "Laramie already has a good man, Steve. It has you and it doesn't know how lucky it is to have you. I want you to keep your mind on your work just like you've always done. You've got a lot to live for, Sheriff Trammel."

He took her up in his arms again. "I already did even before you told me."

He shut his eyes as he heard someone running toward him along the boardwalk. He had heard that gait before.

"Sorry, boss," Hawkeye said. "I hate to bother you, but there's trouble over at The Laramie Grand."

Trammel lifted his head from Emily's. "Can't Hagen's men take care of it?"

"It's not that simple," Hawkeye persisted. "Someone's broken into his room. They're stealing his money and are holding Rube Miller captive."

Trammel did not want to let Emily go. He did not want to let this moment escape him. He wanted to feel like this forever and let the world go on tearing itself apart.

But Emily gently pulled away from him. "Go, Steve. You have a job to do, and I still have a room full of patients to tend to. I'll see you when it's over."

Trammel kissed both her hands before he joined Hawkeye on the boardwalk and began to head to The Laramie Grand. He was still dizzy from Emily's news but tried to focus on the problem at hand. "You see any sign of Blake around?"

"Saw him and the others heading over to the livery when I came looking for you," Hawkeye told him. "I called out to them, but I don't think they heard me. I figured getting you was more important."

"You did right," Trammel said. "How many were with him?"

"All of them," Hawkeye said. "Johnny Welch, Charlie Root, Brillheart, and Bush, too. It's not like them to just ignore me like that. I wonder what I did to make them so angry."

Trammel figured Hawkeye had not yet heard about his fight with Blake in the courtyard. Blake had made good on his promise to leave and pull the rest of his friends with them. That would leave Trammel and Hawkeye alone to protect the town with growing dangers everywhere he turned.

He did not have time to explain it all to Hawkeye but knew the boy could be relied upon to deliver whatever message Trammel gave him. And he could only think of one gesture that might be strong enough to keep Blake and the others from leaving town.

He unpinned the sheriff's star from his shirt and handed it to Hawkeye. "I want you to run over to the livery and give this to Blake. Tell him he can keep it if he stays."

Hawkeye held the star as if Trammel had just handed him an anvil. "But this is your star, boss."

"Just give it to him. And have him and the others get their rifles and meet us at the hotel. Tell them to be quick about it. We've got a night's work ahead of us."

CHAPTER 18

Mahaffey kept Brandt by his side as the outlaws walked their horses through the gnarled, raised roots that ran along the ground of the pine forest.

Brandt said, "Guess I ought to thank you for cutting my hands free, but I'm too low for gratitude at the moment."

"Can't say as I blame you," Mahaffey said. "Seems like you and Rollins were close."

"Not close, but I respected him, and I'd like to think he respected me, too."

Mahaffey understood the sentiment. He imagined that just about summed up how he felt about Bob Washington. "If it's any comfort, we always did our best to stay out of his way. That man hauled in a lot of good friends of ours. Came close to roping us a time or two." That last part was a lie, but he thought it might make Brandt feel better.

"Lefty would've given you all a tough go of it if he'd been healthy back at that canyon," Brandt said. "He wasn't one to let a little thing like being outnumbered stop him. It's just a shame he died the way he did."

Mahaffey might not be mourning the loss of Marcum, but he would not apologize for his actions, either. He had shot Rollins in order to protect the group. "I only wish he'd been finished off clean. It would've saved the old boy a lot of needless suffering. You, too, considering how we were just about to let you go." He was curious about something. "Would you have really gone back to Laramie or Cheyenne like you'd promised?"

"I might not have if you let me leave with some bullets," Brandt admitted, "but without them, I wouldn't have stood a chance against you boys. I'd have no choice but to head straight for civilization."

Mahaffey certainly could not expect Brandt to forget about all that had happened since the gang had grabbed him on the road to Laramie. But a lot had happened since then. Two good men were dead with the promise of more before this was over. And his bid to free Ben Washington was as far from a certainty now as it had been at the beginning.

"I guess you blame me for Rollins getting killed."

"I should," Brandt admitted, "but you didn't pull the trigger. Marcum did and now he's dead because Rollins killed him. I'd say that just about makes them even. You had a hand in it, but you're not entirely to blame."

Mahaffey appreciated the deputy's honesty. "Nothing's going to change if I keep you here, is it? You don't think Trammel will bend."

"Men like you and Trammel don't bend," Brandt said. "They don't run, and they don't give up. They fight their way out of trouble because that's the only way they know how to win. There's no middle ground to be had here, George. The situation just doesn't allow for it. You want Ben free. Trammel won't give you that and you can't accept anything less. I'm just caught in the middle of it. As for which one of you will win, I have no idea."

Mahaffey knew Brandt was right. Trammel had proven to be craftier than he had expected. Nothing would change unless one side did something drastic to change things. He needed to plan his gang's next move carefully and saw only one way that might buy them the time they needed.

He asked Brandt, "If I let you go when we get clear of these pines, do I have your word you'll head straight back to Cheyenne? That you won't try to track us and that you'll wire Trammel that you're safe?"

Brandt thought for a while before he answered. "You going to give me my guns without my bullets?"

Unlike his current standoff with Trammel, there was middle ground here. "Yeah. Guns, no bullets."

"Then I promise I'll do that. But if we cross paths again on account of this Washington business, I won't let up on you or your men. I won't expect you to let up on me, either. Any accounts between us will be even."

Mahaffey imagined neither man could expect anything more from the other than that.

The two navigated the rest of the way through the forest in silence until they reached the top of the hill, where Mahaffey raised his hand and drew the band of outlaws to a stop.

"This is where we let Brandt go, boys." He checked the position of the sun through the tall pines and pointed due north. "You keep riding in that straight line, and you ought to hit Cheyenne in an hour or two." He held out his hand to Brandt. "I lived up to my end of the bargain. I'm counting on you to do the same. Hope there's no hard feelings."

Brandt regarded Mahaffey's hand as the outlaws looked on, before shaking it. "No soft feelings, either."

Mahaffey grinned. "I wouldn't expect there to be." He told Earnshaw, "Take his bullets and give him back his guns. Check his saddlebags again to make sure there's nothing in them he can use against us. I know you already checked but do it again."

Earnshaw took Brandt's Colt from his belt, pocketed the bullets, then levered the rounds from his Winchester until it was empty before handing both guns to the deputy.

Mahaffey said, "I'll expect you to keep both of these holstered until you reach Cheyenne. I'll have to shoot you if I see different."

Brandt put the empty pistol on his hip and the empty rifle in the scabbard on his saddle. "I gave you my word, didn't I?"

"And I've just given you mine."

Earnshaw shook hands with Brandt. "Sorry about hitting you earlier. See you in Hell, Deputy Brandt."

"You can save me a seat." Brandt touched the brim of his hat to the others. "I wish I could say it was a pleasure, but we'd all know I was lying. Let's just say I'm grateful you treated me decent enough, considering the circumstances."

Coleman said, "Thanks for not making us kill you. Next time we see you will be different."

"That goes for all of us." Brandt climbed into the saddle and rode out of the pines and in the same direction Mahaffey had pointed out to him.

Earnshaw stood next to Mahaffey as they watched the deputy ride into the clearing. "You sure letting him go like that was a good idea, George?"

"What harm could it do now?" Mahaffey said. "Trammel won't be expecting that, which is good for us. Gives us time to figure out how we're going to get Ben out."

Hank Classet said, "They only had our descriptions before, but Brandt knows our faces. We might've been able to blend in when they put Ben on trial, but not with Brandt around. He'll pick us out for sure."

But Mahaffey had already considered that. "Then I guess we'd better stay out of Cheyenne, hadn't we?"

Coombs stepped forward. "I sure hope that doesn't mean you're thinking of letting Ben swing."

"Just the opposite," Mahaffey told him. "We're doing what we probably should've done from the beginning. We're going to Laramie, boys. We're going to see just how sturdy that jail is for ourselves."

He spoke over the approving cheer that went through the men. "But we're going to be smart about it. We're not just riding into them. We're going to need a plan. One that works. Dib, I want you to lead us back the way we came. I want to be there by nightfall so we can take a look around the place."

Dib led the others back through the pines as Earnshaw asked Mahaffey, "What are you up to, George?"

"Can't say that I know," Mahaffey told him. "But I hope to figure it out before we get there."

Trammel pushed past the guards at the entrance of The Laramie Grand. "Where's Hagen?"

"Just up those stairs," one of the riflemen said. "He's up there right now in front of his suite."

Trammel entered the lobby and saw two more guards keeping curious bettors inside the gaming floor.

Had he not known about the robbery, Trammel might have thought Hagen and his guard, Fuller, had decided to lounge on the main staircase.

"Ah, you're here," Hagen greeted Trammel when he saw him. "Now we can start the party."

Trammel was not in a joking mood. "Hawkeye told me what happened but didn't have many details."

While Fuller kept an eye on the suite, Hagen said, "It appears that the remaining LeBlanc brothers are in the process of ripping me off as we speak."

Trammel had no idea who they were. He had never heard that name before. "Sounds French. They friends of yours from New Orleans?"

"In a sense, but not directly. It was their brother who got himself knifed to death out back last night. They seem to be blaming me for his death. He was probably killed while trying to figure out how he and his family could rob me blind. I was going to send flowers, but that's entirely out of the question now."

Trammel could never understand how Hagen could be so casual about money. He asked Fuller, "How many are in there?"

"Five brothers and a hostage," Fuller said. "They've got Rube Miller. One of them is getting the safe open and another has a rifle. He's fairly good with it, too. He knew enough to take a shot at the boss at the door and through the wall. There are three others in there with him. They're probably armed, too, but I don't know that for sure."

That was not good enough for Trammel. "What are they doing in there? Sitting around and smoking cigars while they watch their brother work on the safe?"

"Probably drinking my good scotch while they're at it." Hagen sighed. "I heard banging a little while ago. They must've taken to hacking the safe. They're wasting their time."

"Just sitting here letting them work is a waste of time, too," Trammel said. "You put anyone on the buildings across the street to see what's happening inside?"

Fuller said, "We've had our hands full keeping the crowd back here. They're all trying to lay bets on what happens next, but with Mr. Miller inside, there's only one other man who can run the book. We almost had a riot on our hands before my men got here. Even worse than yesterday."

Trammel thought it was just as well that Hagen's men

had stayed out of the way. It gave his men more room to maneuver. "I've got some deputies coming. We'll handle it from here."

Hagen seemed amused. "And just how do you plan on handling this? Charging in there with guns blazing? They're not going anywhere, and they'd need a case of dynamite to put a dent in that safe. There's also Rube's life to consider. They'll get tired before long and make a mistake. That's when we'll pounce."

It was not often that Trammel found himself with an advantage over Hagen, but this was one of those rare instances. "You might know what you're talking about when we're outdoors, but I've handled plenty of problems like this. I guess you don't want to let them leave with the money."

Hagen frowned. "Comedy isn't your strong suit, Buck. What did you have in mind?"

Trammel would wait to tell him specifics when the time came. "Sounds like they're dug in there pretty deep. Getting them out could be messy."

Hagen shrugged. "Whatever it takes within reason. But I've grown rather fond of Rube. I'd like him to come though this unharmed if possible."

"That'll be up to LeBlanc."

From inside the suite, a man shouted, "I can hear you talking out there. Who's that new voice belong to?"

"Which one is he?" Trammel asked Hagen.

"Rick LeBlanc," Fuller said.

Hagen added, "The aggrieved brother of the recently departed Wayne. He appears to be the brains of the operation."

Trammel yelled back. "This is Sheriff Trammel of Laramie. You'll be dealing with me from here on in."

"Sheriff Trammel." Rick laughed. "Hagen's lackey. I

was wondering when you'd show up. I saw you scare off those people on the street earlier. Me and my brothers won't be that easy to scatter. We'll give you all you can handle and plenty more."

Trammel ignored the insult. "Come out with your hands up and empty, LeBlanc. No one has to die here tonight."

A sharp scream from inside the suite cut through the three men crouched on the stairs.

Rick called back, "Old Rube here doesn't seem to think much about that idea. He's in a lot of pain, Sheriff. I don't think he can take much more of this. I think he needs a doctor. I hear your woman's a doctor, Trammel. How about you send that pretty lady in here to keep us company."

Trammel rose up as he drew his Peacemaker from under his left arm and fired six shots at the lock. The bullets splintered the wood and caused the door to swing a few inches inward.

Trammel opened the cylinder, dumped out the spent bullets into his hand and began feeding fresh ones from the loops on his belt. "That's the last warning you're going to get, LeBlanc. And this is your last chance to end this peacefully. I can't guarantee your safety if this goes on any longer."

"And I can't guarantee yours," Rick yelled. "Shooting a door is different than pulling that with me. The door won't shoot back, and I've got a nice big safe here to give me all the cover I need."

Hagen pulled Trammel down to the cover of the stairs. "He's not lying, Buck. That safe door is thick enough to stop a cannon ball. I ought to know. I designed it myself."

But Trammel had no intention of going anywhere near the safe.

"Boss," Hawkeye called out to him from the lobby below. "I got the others, just like you wanted."

Trammel finished filling the cylinder and flicked it shut before tucking it away. "You two stay here. I'm going to see about ending this right now."

CHAPTER 19

Trammel followed Hawkeye out onto the porch where Blake and the other deputies who had left with him stood waiting. Their pistols were on their hips and their rifles in their hands.

An hour ago, he might have resented them for taking Blake's side in this. But although he had come to think of them as his men, they never were. They had always followed Blake, and that would never change.

Each of them was wearing their stars except for Blake, who was holding the sheriff's star Hawkeye had given him.

"Hawkeye said you sent this for me," Blake said. "What's the matter, Trammel? Too proud to ask me to come back yourself?"

"Didn't have time," Trammel said. "I still don't. We've got five men up in Hagen's suite right now. They're trying to rob his safe, and they're holding Rube Miller hostage. They're threatening to kill him if we don't let them ride off with him and the money. I figured you boys might want to do something about that." ·

Blake held up the sheriff's star. "That still doesn't explain this."

"I'm sure Hawkeye already told you," Trammel said.

"That's yours free and clear as soon as this Washington mess is cleared up. You've wanted it long enough and now it's yours. I hope you're happy."

Blake looked back inside the hotel. "Does what's going on in there have anything to do with Washington?"

"No. It's a problem between Hagen and a bunch of guests at his hotel. The LeBlanc brothers. I don't know the details, and I don't care. All I know is that we can't let them walk out of here with Miller or the money. Seeing as how all of you still have some back pay coming, I thought you'd want the chance to earn it."

"We don't run from fights, unlike some people around here." Blake handed the star back to Trammel. "We can talk about that later. What are we going to do about the mess up there?"

Trammel beckoned the others to follow him to the corner of the porch, where he pointed out the fine goods shop across from the hotel. "I want you boys to work your way up onto the roof over there. Be careful because one of them is probably watching the windows. I want you to get ready to move, but I don't want you to go until Hawkeye gives you the signal. When he does, bust out and start shooting into Hagen's suite. You know which one it is?"

"I do," Deputy Brillheart said. "Second floor. The one with the balcony overlooking the thoroughfare. I watched them when they brought the safe up there. They had to use a winch to lift it up there in pieces."

Trammel had only been in the suite once but knew Brillheart was right about the location. "His bedroom faces the alley. I'll bet some of the brothers are bound to be in there. And if they're not, they'll come running once one of you starts shooting through the windows. You all know what Rube Miller looks like, don't you?"

All the deputies said they did.

"He's not part of this, so try not to hit him. When Hawkeye gives the signal, start shooting. Me and Hagen will go in through the door and take on the two at the safe and anyone else who comes running out. We do this right, and it'll be over before you have to reload. Any questions?"

Blake said, "Hagen know we'll be shooting up his room? He just spent a lot of money finishing it. He won't like us ruining all those fancy furnishings he has."

"He'll like losing his money a lot less." Trammel added, "And recent problems between you and me aside, I'd appreciate it if you boys didn't shoot me or Hagen while you're at it."

The deputies laughed, even Blake.

Blake told the others, "There's no way we can see Hawkeye from the roof, so we'll set up a system. Jim, I want you to stand in the doorway of the shop and wait for Hawkeye's signal. Welch, you give it to Root who'll give it to me on the landing. When I open up, I want Root and Welch to run up the stairs and get ready to fire while I reload. Clear them out of the bedroom, but don't fire into the office." He looked up at Trammel. "That way, there'll be no danger to you or anyone else who comes through the door. You'll be nice and safe."

Trammel swallowed the anger that rose in his gullet. "You and I are going to have a nice, long talk when this is over."

Blake walked around him and off the porch. "I'll be looking forward to it."

While the rest of the deputies dashed across the alley to the fine goods store, Hawkeye followed Trammel back into the hotel where Hagen's guard, Fuller, was waiting. "What are you and your men going to do, Sheriff?"

"Hawkeye is going to stay down here and tell me when Blake and the others are in position on the roof of the store across the alley," Trammel said. "When they are, I'll have Hawkeye signal them to start shooting into Hagen's bedroom. That'll distract the LeBlanc boys long enough for us to hit the door and surprise them as well as we can expect, given that they know we'll be coming."

Hawkeye remained in the lobby as Fuller and Trammel walked up the stairs. There was no sign of Hagen anywhere.

"Where's your boss?" Trammel asked Fuller.

"He got restless and went to listen at the door. I think they must've moved a chair to keep it closed."

Trammel knew a chair would make it more difficult to get inside, but far from impossible. "I'll need you on the stairs to give Hawkeye the signal to the others to start shooting. Think you can do that for me?"

Fuller stopped halfway up the stairs. "I'll be ready."

Trammel continued up to the second floor where Hagen was listening at the door to his suite.

Hagen was smiling as he whispered, "I've heard them talking. They're having trouble opening the third lock because they opened them out of order. I've been hearing more banging in the last few minutes, so I think they're getting desperate."

Trammel was more concerned about the door to the suite than the door to Hagen's safe. "What do you think they used to block this thing?"

"A chair. It's too heavy for them to have tilted it under the knob, so it'll slide out of the way. When are we going in?"

"Right now."

Trammel saw Fuller waving at him from the stairs and knew Blake must be in position on the roof. The sheriff drew his Peacemaker and gave a curt nod to Fuller, who, in turn, did the same to Hawkeye down in the lobby.

In his mind's eye, he saw Hawkeye run out to the street,

give the signal to his deputies who relayed it from one to the other until Blake burst onto the roof. He had envisioned it perfectly as the sound of gunfire shattering window glass began right on time.

Trammel and Hagen had been in such situations so many times before that each knew what the other would do without having to discuss it first.

The big sheriff hit the door, knocking it and the chair blocking it aside while Hagen drew his pistol and rushed in behind him.

Trammel braced for the sound of gunfire to greet them as they rushed into the room, but all he heard was Blake's shots from across the street.

When he looked into the suite, Trammel saw why LeBlanc had not opened fire.

There was nothing to shoot at. The safe door behind Hagen's desk hung open and abandoned. There was no sign of Rube Miller and the door to Hagen's bedroom had been closed.

"They must be in there," Trammel told him.

Hagen ran to open one of the windows facing the alley, waved his hat to get Blake's attention to stop firing. He called out to the deputy on the roof. "Can you see into the bedroom?"

Trammel kept an eye on the bedroom door as Hagen returned from the window. "He can't see inside. They must have closed the curtains." He went to the safe. "They weren't able to get it open. That's a relief." He sniffed the air. "They enjoyed my cigars, though."

But Trammel would not be relieved until he knew what was going on inside the bedroom. "The LeBlancs didn't fire back."

Hagen closed the safe door and joined Trammel. "Maybe Blake hit them all."

"Each shot a kill shot? Firing blind? He's not that lucky. This isn't right."

Before Hagen could stop him, Trammel walked down the short hallways and tried the knob. It turned. It was unlocked.

Hagen readied his pistol and motioned for Trammel to push in the door and fall flat to give him a clear shot into the bedroom.

Trammel pushed in the door and hit the floor. He swept the room with his Peacemaker as Hagen stepped around him.

The floor inside the bedroom was littered with mattress stuffing, shattered glass from the window and plaster dust.

Trammel saw a crowbar beside a gaping hole in the lower half of the wall beside Hagen's bed. The LeBlanc boys had busted through the wall and had already escaped into the room next door.

Hagen leapt over the sheriff as he got to his feet. "That's where all that noise was coming from. They were making an escape!"

As Trammel stopped in the hallway, Fuller was already running behind Hagen down the hall. The door to the room next to Hagen's suite was open. They must have snuck out as soon as Blake had started shooting.

Trammel caught Hawkeye when his deputy was half-way up the stairs. "The LeBlancs are getting away. Get the others to spread out on the outside of town. Stop anyone riding out. Stop everyone you don't recognize. They've probably split up."

Trammel ran down the hall and rounded the corner as gunshots erupted from somewhere behind the hotel. He rumbled down the back staircase and was swarmed by a rush of maids, cooks, and waiters running toward him. He dodged them as he moved toward the open back door beside the kitchen.

A bullet struck the doorframe, and Trammel dodged back inside. He chanced a quick look outside and saw Hagen crouched against the side of the building. Fuller was laid out flat on his back on the ground. A neat hole through the center of his forehead.

Trammel holstered his pistol as he ran to pick up the dead man's rifle and joined Hagen at the corner of the building.

"They were waiting for us when we got outside, then scattered like chickens," Hagen reported. "Rick is bringing up the rear with Rube Miller. They just ran down the back alley beyond that fence over there. I think they're trying to get to their horses in the livery."

"I've got Blake and his men trying to block off the town." Trammel checked the rifle and saw it was still loaded. "Follow me."

Trammel rounded the corner and was heading for the fence when a man came out from behind one of the stores on the thoroughfare and fired at him. The sheriff dropped to a knee and shot the man high in the chest before he could dive for cover. The wounded man cried out as he fell. His rifle clattered onto the street.

The LeBlanc man shouted as he clutched his chest, "They got me boys. They're coming for you now, Rick!"

Trammel levered in a fresh round as he moved to the sparse cover offered by a low wooden fence. He was about to look around it and up the alley when a bullet crashed through the wood just above his head, filling the air with wooden splinters.

Hagen dashed out from behind the hotel and snapped off two shots as he reached the back of the building on the far side of the alley.

To Trammel, Hagen yelled, "You hurt?"

Trammel wiped at his eyes with his sleeve. His vision was watery, but at least the sleeve was not bloody. "I'm fine."

He heard the sound of boots scraping along the dirt before another shot rang out from the alley. This time Hagen had been the target.

Hagen took a quick look around the corner of the building before moving into the alley. Trammel followed.

He saw Rick LeBlanc had his arm around Rube Miller's neck as he dragged his captive backward toward the hotel livery. He was holding a rifle in his right hand and had it aimed in Hagen and Trammel's direction.

"Get going, boys," he yelled back to his brothers. "I'll hold them off."

"We're not going without you," one of them called back.

"Don't worry about me," Rick said. "I told you what to do, now do it."

Three horses broke out from the livery. A rifle shot from above rang out as the first rider pitched forward and dropped from the saddle while the two remaining LeBlanc men sped away.

Trammel knew that must have been Blake firing from the rooftop of the store next to the hotel.

Hagen kept his pistol aimed at Rick as he continued to slowly approach him. "Looks like you're running out of brothers, LeBlanc. I wonder which one that was. The one Trammel shot was just a boy."

"You'll pay for that," Rick said as he dragged Miller backward with him. "You'll all pay for what you've done here today."

Trammel had the Winchester at his shoulder, trying to get a clear shot at LeBlanc. But this was not his rifle, and he was not sure how accurate it was. He was still too far away to try a shot with his Peacemaker, so he could only join Hagen in continuing to crowd LeBlanc and his captive.

Hagen kept advancing. "Sneaking out of my room the way you did was awfully smart, Rick. I don't know how you did it without making much noise, but I'm impressed."

"My brothers and I have gotten out of tighter squeezes than this." Rick squeezed Miller's neck tighter, causing the pit boss to yelp. The right side of his face was swollen and already beginning to bruise from the earlier beatings he had suffered. "If you care about your friend here, you two will back up and let me ride out of here or I'll quit being gentle with him."

Hagen laughed. "I don't know how you expect to get him up on a horse, much less yourself, before one of us cuts you down. You haven't thought this through, have you?"

"I don't think your man lying dead back behind the hotel would agree with you." He slowly swept the rifle back and forth between Hagen and Trammel as he moved. "I could end either one of you right now if I wanted, but I don't have to. I've already won."

Trammel wished he would stay still for just a second, but LeBlanc kept moving. "You can only hit one of us before the other drops you. You squeeze that trigger and you'll be dead right after."

"You'd be right." Rick pulled Miller closer as he kept their heads next to each other. "But I won't have to shoot anyone. I've done my damage."

Trammel saw Rick's eyes flicker to somewhere above and behind them. Back to the hotel. He was too smart to fall for that old trick. "Quit playing games, LeBlanc. You've got nowhere to go."

LeBlanc grinned. "No, but Hagen's money does. Guess your ears were still ringing from all that shooting back there that you didn't hear the fuse we lit. We would've liked to bring some of that dynamite with us, but we were in a hurry and traveling light."

Hagen's step faltered, but Trammel kept moving.

The gambler looked back at his hotel. "You're lying. No fuse is that long. It would've gone up by now."

"Not if I used one of those fancy cigars and a box of matches to make it burn slower under that nice desk of yours. I'd say it ought to be just about ready to go at any moment. Since I couldn't get your money, I decided to take something else from you in exchange for Wayne. Your hotel."

Rick LeBlanc pushed Miller at Trammel, blocking his shot as a loud explosion split the air behind them just before a wall of heat knocked them flat on the ground. Trammel fell on top of Miller as wood and plaster and glass rained down on the alley, pelting his back with debris.

Smoke billowed over them, filling Trammel's lungs and stinging his eyes. He began to choke as he rolled off Miller and tried to sit up, remembering that LeBlanc was still close by.

He peered through the smoke and found Hagen sitting against the wall, looking back at his hotel. The left side of The Laramie Grand had been engulfed in thick smoke highlighted from angry orange flames below it. Large chunks of broken wooden beams thrown into the sky by the explosion had just begun to land on the buildings around it.

Trammel shook Hagen by the shoulders. "Are you hurt?"

But the gambler could not take his eyes from the sight of his ruined hotel. It was not until Trammel heard the sound of screaming horses that he looked toward the hotel livery. A large piece of flaming debris had crashed through the roof and a fire was beginning to burn.

Trammel gagged on the thickening smoke as he struggled to his feet and stumbled to the livery. He found the stable hand crushed beneath a fallen beam as the hay around him began to burn.

Trammel began to pull open each of the stall doors as the terrified horses bolted, fleeing the growing flames above them. The smoke grew thicker still as he watched the last of the animals run free into the growing chaos of the street. Bells of the fire brigade rang out as men and women rushed to the scene.

Trammel's stomach lurched as he moved back into the alley. He knew he had to get Miller and Hagen out of there before they were smothered to death by the thickening smoke.

He kept his arm over his nose and mouth as he felt his way along the wall back toward them. The smoke cleared in time for him to see Hagen push Miller away from him as he brought his pistol under his chin.

Trammel smacked the Colt from the gambler's hand and fired a straight left hand into Hagen's jaw, knocking him out. He grabbed Hagen by the back of the shirt as he helped Miller get to his feet. Miller tried to help as Trammel lifted Hagen over his shoulder and carried him out to the cleaner air of the thoroughfare. His knees buckled from the effort just as he reached the boardwalk.

Citizens clamored around to take Hagen from him and ease Trammel to the ground. Some tended to Miller before he, too, collapsed.

Trammel knew he did not have time for this. The Laramie Grand was on fire. He had to know what had happened to Blake, Hawkeye, and the others. He had a town to take care of. There would be hurt who needed rescuing and dead to be seen to. Someone had to restore order to the madness.

But despite all the people trying to keep him still, Trammel willed himself to stand anyway as a bout of deep coughing knocked him flat again. He managed to whisper two words before the world slipped away from him. "Emily. Baby."

CHAPTER 20

Deputy Leo Brandt did not go back to Cheyenne as he had promised. With Rollins dead, he knew there was nothing left for him there.

He had ridden in that direction until he was sure he was out of sight of Mahaffey and the others, then took the long way back to Laramie.

Despite how weary he and his horse might be, Brandt had refused to stop to rest at the same creek where he had been captured. He forced himself to continue on to the place where Ben Washington was being held. Laramie.

He ignored his own growing hunger and kept riding until he got close to town.

At first, he found the scent of burning wood he had caught on the wind to be comforting. He imagined a homesteader somewhere nearby must be preparing a fire for their supper. But the smell only grew thicker the closer he got to Laramie. It soon became a thick, acrid stench that stung his nostrils.

It was only when he rode atop a rise on the outskirts of town that he finally saw the thick smoke billowing high into the afternoon sky. This was no humble cook fire. He smelled death in the air.

Brandt forced the horse to move faster than it wanted as he urged it on toward town. He wondered how Mahaffey and his men could have caused so much destruction so quickly. He had heard Laramie's City Hall was a great stone building. It would not burn like this. He quickly realized that was impossible, even for them.

Brandt began to hear shouts and urgent voices coming from the town as he got closer. And as he reached that first street, he finally understood what had happened.

Townspeople with clothes blackened by smoke and soot were everywhere. They cast uneasy glances up at the stranger on horseback as he rode by. The sights and sounds caused his horse to fight the bit and he was afraid it might panic and throw him. He climbed down and led it the rest of the way.

He found himself on what looked to be the main thoroughfare of the town and while he had never been on a battlefield, he imagined one must look similar to what he saw now.

The street was littered with debris of every description. Charred wood and glass were everywhere as ash continued to fall on everything like filthy snow. Everywhere he looked was either gray or black and it was difficult for him to tell the people from their surroundings.

At the center of it all was the remnants of a once great building that looked as though it had recently been a hotel. It had been reduced to a hulking, smoldering ruin. It reminded him of a deck of playing cards that had been toppled over by a careless child. The left side of it had been obliterated. The floors above it had crashed down upon the rest, leaving charred broken rafters to jut out from the smoke like fingers curled in agony.

The entire front of the building beside it had been

crushed, leaving only the rear part of it intact. It looked like a dollhouse he had once seen in a store window in Cheyenne. Blackened floorboards and beams protruded out from it like matchsticks.

A steady stream of smoke continued to rise from the charred right side of the hotel. Torn drapery fluttered out from broken windows like a forgotten nightmare. He doubted an inch of the place had escaped the flames.

Brandt peered through the smoke that now stung his eyes and saw two men carrying someone out through a gaping hole where large windows may have once been. He was too far away to see if it was a man or a woman. He did not know whether the person was living or dead and was not sure it mattered.

Men and women tended to the coughing injured wherever they could. Blackened sheets covered lumps in the street he assumed were people who had died in the fire. He forced himself to stop counting when he reached twenty. There were clearly many more.

Leo Brandt had never been one for prayer, but he found himself praying for these people now.

He had not known anyone was standing behind him until he had been pushed. He turned to see a woman, her hair undone and her skin and clothes dark from smoke, chastising him.

"Don't just stand there and gawk. Pitch in. There's plenty of folks who need helpin'!"

She moved off among the ruin of her town, leaving him to look over the street around him. And everywhere he looked were broken people and destruction.

He spotted a stone building on the other side of the thoroughfare and the brass plaque that read "City Hall." He pulled his horse in that direction, careful to stay as close to the boardwalk as he could. The debris was not nearly as dense there.

He found a man sitting alone on the stone steps. The left side of his face was heavily bandaged, and the top of his scalp was singed. He did not blame the man for taking long pulls on the bottle of whiskey he drank from now. He imagined the pain must be excruciating.

Brandt tried to think of something meaningful to say to this man, but words no longer had much meaning for him. He simply asked, "What happened here?"

The man took another long drink of whiskey. "Explosion. About five sticks of dynamite near as I can figure. Could be more, but it was enough to do all that." He looked at him with his good eye. "What's it to you?"

"I'm Leo Brandt. Deputy U.S. Marshal."

"Brandt." The man said it as though the name had some meaning to him. "The prodigal deputy. I'm a deputy, too, or at least I used to be. I don't know anymore. Name's Blake."

Brandt could not bear to look at the street anymore. "Some of Washington's men grabbed me on my way here. I—"

Blake waved him quiet. "I know all about it. You ought to see the sheriff if he's still alive. He was last time I saw him." He gestured across toward the hotel. "You'll find him over there pulling people out of the hotel. I was helping him a little while ago until he ordered me away. Not many left to save anymore. He's still at it, though."

Brandt looked across at the building. That must be The Laramie Grand he had heard so much about. "How will I find him?"

"Just look for the biggest man in the bunch. He's real hard to miss, even now. You can leave your horse here if you want. I'll keep an eye on him, which ought to be easy since I've only got one left."

Brandt felt foolish standing there unscathed with his horse, so he led the animal to the side and wrapped the rein around its leg before he went to find Trammel.

He spotted the sheriff as he stepped out through a shattered window. His face and clothes were smeared black, and it was difficult to tell where his skin ended and his clothes began.

He was carrying the lifeless body of a woman who appeared to be wearing the apron of a maid. Brandt noticed one of her shoes was missing.

He watched Trammel hand her over to two men waiting outside the hotel with a canvas stretcher. He saw a line of stretcher bearers trudging back to the hotel. All of their stretchers were empty.

Brandt cleared his throat as he said, "Sheriff Trammel?"

The large man stopped before heading back inside the wreckage. "Who's asking?"

"Leo Brandt."

Trammel slowly turned as if awakened from a deep sleep. "I told these boys to get a wagon to help carry these people out of here, but they won't listen to me. Guess they prefer to do it themselves. Seems like a wasted effort to me. The dead don't mind. They don't mind anything. They're lucky."

Brandt watched the men carry the woman away. "I'm sorry about what happened here, Sheriff. I just got to town."

Trammel kept looking at the woman being carried off. "I found her curled up in a ball in the back stairwell. I wonder if she knew what had happened or if she didn't have a chance. She had a bag of sheets in a bag next to her.

She was just doing her job one minute and was dead the next. No reason for it, really."

Brandt began to step up onto the porch. "I be glad to help some if you want."

Trammel raised his hand to stop him. "No call for that. You said your name is Brandt? I thought you were with Washington's men. What are you doing here?"

"They let me go as soon as we cleared the pine forest. Lefty Rollins is dead."

"I know." Trammel leaned against the side of the ruined building. He looked like he might fall asleep standing up. "That all happened this morning, didn't it? It's still today. Funny how long a day can get. How so much can happen in only a few hours."

Brandt did not know the sheriff except by reputation, but it was clear he was not in his right mind. He could hardly think less of him for that. "You look like you've been at this awhile, sheriff. How about you let me take you back to your office? You look like you could use the rest."

Trammel looked back into the ruined hotel. Brandt could see the remnants of what appeared to be a front desk and ruined carpet beneath a collapsed ceiling. He could not think anyone could have survived that, but people had lived through worse.

Trammel scratched at a scar that ran down the length of his face. Brandt did not think it was a fresh wound. "I'd better get you over to Doc Carson. Let him have a look at you. You look well enough, but your brains might be scrambled some. Mahaffey's men are a tough bunch."

Brandt doubted anyone had ever felt sorry for Sheriff Buck Trammel before, but he found himself feeling so now. "I don't know where I could find him, but I'd appreciate it if you could bring me to him."

He let Trammel lead the way as he stepped over the debris and began walking back toward City Hall. He wanted to keep the man talking in the hopes it might clear his mind a little. "Do you know how it happened? Your deputy told me it was dynamite."

Trammel stopped walking. "Which deputy told you that?"

"He said his name was Blake." Brandt pointed at the man still sitting on the stairs. "I saw him when I first got to town just now."

Trammel looked across at the stairs where Blake was still sitting. "Some thieves were trying to break into Hagen's safe. They couldn't get it open, so they lit a bunch of dynamite they'd brought with them. They figured they'd get away before it blew. Some of them did, I think." He pointed at the crushed building next to the hotel. "Blake was up there on the roof when it happened. Got burned pretty bad. The rest were already down on the street when it happened. They got cut up some, but at least they're alive. They're around here somewhere." He brought his hands to his mouth as he called out, "Hawkeye! Where are you?"

Brandt urged him to keep walking toward City Hall. He had to get him off the street. Had to get him care. "He's probably up in your office with the others. They're bound to be waiting for you there."

Trammel resumed walking. "At least I got the horses out of the livery before it went up. Couldn't save the stable hand, though. He was already dead when I got there. I hope he died as quickly as the maid. Doesn't seem right a man should lose his life just because he was tending to horses. Doing a job shouldn't cost a man his life." He looked in Brandt's direction but did not seem to see him.

"You ever hear horses scream? It's not a pretty sound. It'll stay with me for a while. I'm glad I was able to save them."

Brandt looked up when he heard a woman call out Trammel's name and saw her running toward them from beside City Hall. Her clothes were not as blackened as the other people's he had seen in town, but her apron was bloody.

"Steve," the woman said as she put her arm around him. "You said you were going straight up to your office. I was just going to check on you. Where have you been?"

"There's still work to be done, Emily. People who need to be taken out of the hotel."

"You've already done enough for now. Leave that work to the others." She looked around Trammel at Brandt. "Who are you?"

"Deputy Leo Brandt, ma'am."

"And I'm the sheriff's wife. Help me get him inside. He was behind the hotel when it went up and hasn't been right since. I guess none of us have."

Brandt did not crowd Trammel but stayed close to him as they walked up the stairs of City Hall. Brandt glanced back at Deputy Blake, whose head was down as he clung to his bottle of whiskey.

Brandt joined the Trammels as they went up to his office, where Emily sat him down on the couch. "Just lie down and close your eyes for a moment. I'll go get you some water. Please don't leave this time. Do it for me?"

She forced the issue by lifting Trammel's legs onto the couch. She ushered Brandt outside. The sheriff's eyes closed, and he was asleep before she gently closed the office door behind her.

Once in the hallway, she brought a trembling hand to her mouth. "He's not well."

Brandt tried his best to comfort her. "He seems all right. Just a bit confused is all."

Emily choked back tears. "He's got a concussion, but he won't stay still. I had him down in the courtyard with me tending to the wounded, but he keeps thinking there are people who need saving in the hotel. He forgets everyone's been pulled out of there already. And we've got so many hurt that I can't keep an eye on him. Will you do it for me? Will you make sure he rests. I'd be forever grateful."

"I'll come right back here after I get him that water you promised him." He let her lead as he walked down the stairs with her, unsure of where they were going. "Are there many people injured?"

"The worst hurt are gone now." She leaned on the railing as she took the steps slowly. "Heaven forgive me for saying it, but they're better off for it. By some miracle, all of the deputies made it out alive. Poor Blake lost an eye and suffered some terrible burns, but he'll live. The wounded are scattered all over town. There wasn't a single place where we could keep them all. Hawkeye and the others are trying to get a number on the hurt and dead. We're treating more than thirty people here and some of them won't live to see morning. Thank God for Doc Carson. He was a doctor in the war. I've never seen this much carnage in all my life."

Brandt wished he could have said something that might make her feel better, but words failed him. "If I can help in any way, other than just looking after the sheriff, I'm here, ma'am."

"You'll be sorry you made that offer, deputy. My husband told me about what happened to Marshal Rollins. You have my condolences. I understand he was a good man."

Brandt appreciated the sentiment. "Looks like we've all lost a lot of good people today."

She led him back outside and down the stairs. Deputy Blake was nowhere in sight, but an empty bottle of whiskey was on the step where he had been sitting.

Emily asked, "Is that your horse down there?"

"It is. He's had a long journey."

"Bring him with you around back to the courtyard. There's a stable back there where the deputies keep their mounts. Old Bob will take good care of him."

She waited while Brandt unwrapped the rein from the foreleg and led it around the corner to the courtyard gates.

The sights he had just seen on the streets of Laramie had not prepared him for what he found there. The moans of pain and misery reached him first. The stench was close behind it. He saw wounded men and women of all description on cots that had been hastily set up in crooked lines. Doctors and volunteers tended to people suffering from scorched skin and blisters from the intense heat of the explosion.

Emily broke away to stop a man from falling out of his cot. He was about to lean on a right arm that was no longer there. Unnatural sags beneath the blankets of other patients betrayed missing arms and legs. The few who were conscious coughed constantly, which only aggravated the pain in their bandaged heads or hands.

Besides the doctors and nurses looking after the injured, Brandt saw only one man who seemed relatively unharmed. He was not on a cot but sitting against the courtyard wall. He was a fair-haired man with sharp features and blue eyes that stared off at nothing. The right side of his jaw looked swollen and bruised. His clothes looked like they had been expensive once, but they were ruined now.

Brandt stopped in front of him and asked, "You need anything, mister?"

The man on the ground did not look at him. Only at the pistol on his hip. "I'd be grateful if you let me borrow your gun. I've got some unfinished business to tend to."

Emily pushed past Brandt and said to the man, "That's enough of that nonsense, Adam. If Doc Carson hears you talking like that, he'll lock you in a cell for your own good."

"I might wind up there anyway after today." There was no tone to his voice. "I probably deserve it."

"No, you don't." Emily bent at the knees and peered at him. "None of this is your fault, Adam. The only man responsible for this is the man who set off all that dynamite. We've got enough maimed folks around here without you adding yourself to the toll. People who need rest and care." She took him by the arm and tried to pull him up. "What you need is a purpose and that's just what I'm going to give you. Help Deputy Brandt here get his horse taken care of and bring some water up to Steve. He's in his office right now and would like to see you. It'd do you both some good."

Hagen slowly stood on his own without any help from Emily. "Your name's Brandt?"

Emily moved away and the deputy forced a grin for Hagen's benefit. "Didn't know I was so popular."

"I was the one who found Rollins and brought him to the box canyon. I saw you down there with Bishop and the others. How'd you escape?"

"I didn't," Brandt admitted. "They let me go after they walked their horses through the pine forest. They made me promise to head straight back to Cheyenne, but I didn't think any promise made to an outlaw was worth keeping."

"Yes." Hagen began to drift again. "I suppose you're right. Rollins is dead, isn't he?"

"Found him where I imagine you left him. Right beneath a tree. His Colt was still in his hand when we got there."

"He died well." Hagen looked around at the injured people on the cots all around them. "Not everyone was as lucky today."

Emily interrupted them by handing Hagen a small bucket of water. "Make yourself useful and bring that up to Steve. He might be sleeping when you get there, but he'll be glad to see you when he wakes up." She took the reins from Brandt. "Go with him, Deputy. Make sure he doesn't do anything foolish. He's not himself, either."

Brandt assured him he would as she led his horse back to the stables. He tried to take the bucket from Hagen, but the man walked away.

He was not thinking when he asked, "Were you in the hotel when it happened?"

"I was outside with Trammel when it blew up. I just opened the place about a month ago. It's a shame, really. All because a man wanted to pay me back for killing his no-good brother. Because he couldn't get into the safe in my room."

Hagen gave a sharp laugh, but there was no humor in it. "All this death and horror and the safe made it through without a scratch. I saw it from the street, you know. The damned thing crashed right down through the floor and landed without so much as a dent. I should've built the whole place out of iron instead of plaster and wood. Next time I will. If there is a next time. Are you sure you won't let me borrow your gun? It's really for the best if you would."

Hagen had said it so blandly that Brandt was not sure he had heard him correctly. "Wouldn't do you much good if I did." He slowly slid the pistol from its holster and opened the cylinder. "Mahaffey didn't let me ride off with any bullets."

Hagen stumbled, but Brandt helped steady him. "Just my luck."

Neither man saw the lone rider passing the courtyard entrance before he dug his heels into his horse and sped away.

CHAPTER 21

In the clearing where they had set up camp just outside of Laramie, George Mahaffey asked Tim to repeat what he had just told them. He had sent him to scout out the town when they saw the plume of smoke rising at a distance. His report was too important to leave unexplained.

"A fire? You're sure?"

"No doubt about it," Tim confirmed as he poured himself some coffee from the small cook fire. "The whole side of one of the buildings in the center of town looked like a cannonball tore right through them. There were pieces of it scattered all over the street. The whole front of a smaller building beside it looked like it had been cut clean off of it, too. I saw the dead on the street beneath sheets and blankets."

Earnshaw asked, "How many did you see?"

"I counted thirty," Tim said, "but they were still bringing bodies out of the building and carrying them away on stretchers. There were too many wounded to count, but there sure was a lot of them. Women, too. Folks were tending to a bunch on cots in this courtyard they've got next to City Hall. They were all hurt really bad. And the smell was something awful." He cleared out his nostrils into the fire.

"I never want to smell anything that bad again. I ain't seen anything like it since the war. Not even when we derailed that train a few years back."

Earnshaw asked Tim, "Was the jail damaged, too?" He looked to Dib Bishop. "It's in the basement of that City Hall they've got, isn't it? That's where they're holding Ben."

"That's where it is," Dib Bishop confirmed. "And if that courtyard is packed as tight as Tim says it is, that means a lot of people got hurt."

Tim continued with his story. "After I looked the town over, I got a couple of old timers to tell me what had happened. They said The Laramie Grand had been blown to bits, but they didn't know why or who did it. They heard there were over a hundred dead and so many injured that they had to bring them to a whole bunch of different places all over town. No one place was big enough to take care of them all under one roof."

Mahaffey and the gang were no strangers to the awesome power of dynamite. They had seen the damage a single stick could do in a mine, to railroad tracks, and to a strongbox. It would've taken more than one stick to cause the kind of destruction Tim had just described.

The criminal in Mahaffey was curious about why anyone would bring dynamite to a hotel, but not enough to blind him to the opportunity this disaster had presented. If anything, Laramie's newfound hardship had changed his thinking about how they could free Ben Washington.

The town had taken a serious beating and the best way to win any fight was to kick a man when he was down. Notions of fair play and decency did not apply to outlaws. His odds of freeing Ben Washington had just improved dramatically.

"These old timers you spoke to tell you anything about

what happened to Trammel?" Mahaffey asked. "He still alive?"

Tim said, "They'd heard he'd gotten hurt in the blast, but they saw him walking around since. One of his deputies lost an eye and a couple were burned, but they're all alive." The outlaw hesitated for a moment before adding, "I saw something else while I rode by City Hall. Something you won't like. Leo Brandt was in the courtyard helping some wounded fella."

Hank Classet looked up from the fire. "You're sure it was Brandt?"

"I'm just as sure it was him as I am that he didn't see me. I didn't tell the old timers who I was, either. No one knows we're out here, boss."

Dietrich spat into the dirt. "The rotten weasel. I knew we should've shot him and left him back in the pines."

Mahaffey was not disappointed in his former captive. He had not expected the deputy to keep his word about going back to Cheyenne. "Brandt being in Laramie doesn't change what we came here to do, boys. We aimed to get Ben out of there, and that's exactly what we're going to do."

Earnshaw frowned. "Riding into town was a bad idea before and it hasn't gotten any better, George. The town's still standing, and I don't care how many wounded there are, we're still outnumbered by plenty. That fire or whatever it was hasn't changed that."

Mahaffey was starting to wonder if his old friend had finally lost his killer instinct. He could remember a time when Ben had to practically throw a rope around Earnshaw to keep him from doing something dangerous. Maybe the years had started to catch up to Earnshaw. He was glad they had not caught up to him yet. For his own sake as well as Ben's.

"You don't see it, do you, Earnshaw? This isn't a tragedy. It's a blessing."

Earnshaw's eyes narrowed. "Blessing? How do you figure? They've got wounded in the courtyard right next to the jail. We'll never be able to bust in there now."

Mahaffey was almost embarrassed for his old friend. He was sorry that he had to explain it to him. "That town is flat on the ground right now. All the fight has just been pounded right out of them. Trammel and his deputies are hurt, so now's the time to make our move before they can catch their breath. We're going to hit City Hall and get Ben out of there, boys. And we're going to do it this very night. The odds have never been more in our favor."

He enjoyed watching the expressions on the faces of the men slowly change from doubt to confidence. They were beginning to come around to his way of thinking.

Everyone, that is, except Earnshaw. He gripped his rifle tightly and dropped to a crouch as he whispered, "You hear that? Someone's out there."

Mahaffey and the others drew their pistols and turned to the same direction Earnshaw was facing.

A man's voice called out from the darkness, "Hello in the camp. There's three of us coming in. We're armed and we're keeping our hands where you can see them."

Every member of the Washington Gang raised their guns and aimed in the direction of the voice.

Mahaffey answered, "Make sure you come in real slow, mister. If you know what's good for you."

He watched as three horses stepped into the clearing. The lead rider had his hands up, as did the two men behind him. None of them were wearing badges and did not look like deputies.

"That's far enough," Mahaffey told him when they were ten yards away. "What are you doing here?"

"Name's Rick LeBlanc," the lead rider said. "We saw your man riding through town just now, and we took the liberty of following him back here. There weren't too many men on horseback down there today, so we got curious. Seeing as how we're kind of on the run ourselves, we mean you no harm. We've already caused our share of trouble for one day."

Earnshaw kept his rifle aimed up at Rick. "How do you figure?"

"Your friend there has just been telling you all about our handiwork down in Laramie. That burned out building? Those wounded? All our doing." He gestured to the rider behind him. "It was my brother's dynamite that caused it."

"That so?" Mahaffey knew it was easy for a man to take credit for another's bad deeds, especially when there was no one around to call him a liar. "Why'd you blow up the hotel?"

"Because we couldn't get into Hagen's safe," Rick told him. "And because Hagen killed our brother, Wayne, last night. We didn't set off to burn the place down, but it seemed like a good idea when the safe wouldn't open."

Mahaffey told the men to lower their guns while Earnshaw kept his rifle trained on Rick. "Sounds awfully severe to kill all those people over one lousy brother."

"A man will get all sorts of crazy notions in his head when his brother gets killed. Like you boys looking to spring Ben Washington from jail and he's not even your kin. Besides, I wouldn't expect the Washington Gang to shed any tears over a few dead civilians. I heard you boys are supposed to be the bitter end."

Earnshaw adjusted his rifle. "I reckon we're bitter enough to take care of the likes of you without breaking a sweat."

Rick kept his hands in the air. "We didn't come up here to fight, boys. We came here to see if you'd let us join up with you. Figured we could throw in with you."

Mahaffey gestured for Earnshaw to lower the Winchester. "We don't need you and we don't want you."

"Sounds to us like you do," Rick said. "We heard you boys talking while we were sizing you up back there in the bushes. You're looking to bust your friend out of jail now that you think Trammel and his men are hurting." He slowly shook his head. "It won't be as easy as you think."

Mahaffey admired the stranger's gall, even if he did not like it. "No one said it was going to be easy."

"But the way you're thinking will only get you and all your men killed," Rick said. "Mind if I lower my hands while I tell you why?"

Mahaffey saw his men may have lowered their guns, but they still held them at their sides. "Go ahead, but talk fast. We're anxious to get started, so if we have to kill you, we'd just as soon do it now."

Rick and his brothers lowered their hands. "No need for anyone to die. Not me or any of your men. From what I overheard just now, you're thinking about riding into that courtyard, taking the wounded as hostages, and forcing them to let Ben go. Did I get that much right?"

Mahaffey did not appreciate being that easy to figure out. He had not gotten around to telling his men what he had been thinking. "It's the general idea."

"A bad one because it won't work," Rick explained. "Trammel might be hurt, but he's not dead. You can't get at him by taking captives. Believe me, I tried that. I had the pit boss of The Laramie Grand bound and gagged in Hagen's suite while my brother Burt here was trying to get that safe open. I threatened to kill him if Trammel tried coming after us. I even set to beating on Miller enough to make him cry out just to prove I was serious. You know what Trammel did? Had his men start shooting at us while he and Hagen busted through the door." Rick smiled in admiration. "He's one tough customer, that Trammel. Smarter than he looks."

Dib Bishop spoke up. "How'd you boys manage to get away before the whole place went up?"

"I always like to have a back way out whenever we pull a score, so I had my brother Jim here bust a hole in the bedroom wall so we could get out through the room next door. We were already out of there when Trammel's men started shooting. Took the pit boss with us when we left. Trammel and Hagen caught up to us in the alley and killed two of my brothers while we were trying to get away. Good thing I rigged a delayed fuse to burn the way I did, or else we might not be having this conversation with you fine gentlemen." Rick looked at Mahaffey. "And you wouldn't have this chance to free your friend. I could be forgiven for expecting a bit of gratitude right about now."

Mahaffey had taken just about as much sass as he could stand from the stranger. "You can expect a bullet in the belly unless you start making some sense really quick."

Rick leaned forward in the saddle. "How's this for sense? While you and your men have been moving Deputy Brandt all over the territory, my brothers and I have been watching how Laramie works. We've seen and heard how Trammel does things. Threatening a bunch of wounded civilians won't get you anywhere with the likes of him. He and his deputies would just fire down on you from City Hall and believe me when I tell you he won't miss. One of them shot my brother out of the saddle while he was getting away. You'll all be dead, and Ben Washington will still be behind bars. That seems like a waste from where I'm sitting."

Earnshaw looked as frustrated as Mahaffey felt. "So far, all you've done is tell us what we can't do. You haven't said what we should be doing. I'm starting to think you just like to hear yourself talk. You're wasting time we don't have."

Mahaffey saw the others begin to raise their guns, causing Rick to quickly say, "You can only beat Trammel's men if you spread them out all over town. You can't hit the courtyard and expect him to just roll over. The town was already on edge about you being around before the hotel blew up, so you have to use that to your advantage. Cause trouble in different parts of town at the same time. Make the deputies run from one place to the other and cut them down one by one."

"We're outgunned," Coombs told him.

"Which is why you hit and run and hit again." Rick spoke directly to Mahaffey. "You tried to draw Trammel out when you grabbed Brandt, but he didn't go for it. The people are tired, and his deputies are exhausted. They won't put up much of a fight, especially if you don't give them anything to shoot at. You can whittle the deputies down one at a time. You might even catch Trammel in a moment of weakness and end this quick. Getting whoever's left to let Ben go free will be much easier if there's not any law left to stop you. And if it all breaks your way, you'd not only have Ben but an entire town ripe for the taking."

Mahaffey moved between the men and the LeBlanc brothers. He was beginning to appreciate the way Rick thought. "You got any ideas on where we could hit them first?"

"It just so happens that I do." He tapped his temple. "It's right up here. And if you let me get down from this horse, I'll be happy to draw it in the dirt so you can see it, too."

Mahaffey beckoned him and his brothers to dismount. But as Rick went to take a stick from the fire, the outlaw grabbed his arm. "What are you doing this for, LeBlanc? We're going into Laramie to free a man, not rob a bank or a gambling hall. You came here to get steal money, not this.

Rick pulled his arm free. "I also came into town with five brothers. I'm leaving with only two. Buck Trammel and Adam Hagen owe me a debt no amount of money could repay now. I intend to collect tonight with or without your help."

LeBlanc squatted by the fire, took a stick, and began to draw a square representing the town in the dirt. "Gather around, boys, and let me show you how we're going to spring your friend free."

CHAPTER 22

Given Trammel's condition, the mayor had summoned Hagen and Brandt to Trammel's office to discuss the latest figures of dead and wounded.

Trammel remained on the couch as Hagen and Brandt sat in front of the desk while Mayor Holm began to read from a sheet of paper.

"The latest count provided by Doctor Emily Trammel stands at more than thirty people dead. Since we haven't been able to reach those closest to the blast, we should expect that number to only go higher in the days ahead. One-hundred-and-ten wounded with the vast majority of them suffering from severe burns and broken bones caused by fire and debris. Several people rescued from the hotel have since lost limbs."

Trammel said, "Including Deputy Sherwood Blake, who lost an eye."

Holm sighed as he removed the glasses from his nose and placed them on his desk. "An unmitigated disaster any way you look at it. And I thought Clay's jailbreak was the worst thing that could ever happen to this town. I suppose we should be grateful that there were no children injured in all of this. I don't think the town could recover if there had been."

Hagen sagged in his chair. "I take full responsibility for what happened. The dead and the dying are on my head."

Trammel was surprised by how quickly Holm shut down that kind of talk. "This is no time for misguided chivalry, Adam. You won't win any points with anyone here by falling on your sword. It wasn't your dynamite, and it wasn't your fault."

"It wouldn't have happened if I'd been in the hotel where I belong instead of out looking for Brandt." He glanced over at the deputy. "No offense."

"None taken," Brandt said.

Mayor Holm said, "You might have a point if you had been out gallivanting somewhere, but Trammel tells me you were tracking the Washington Gang in the hopes of freeing Deputy Brandt here."

"And I'm grateful to you," Brandt said. "I truly am."

Holm continued. "My strong dislike for both you and Trammel aside, no one can blame either of you for this. How's your head, Sheriff? I understand you weren't quite yourself earlier."

"I'm fine as far as it goes. So are my men. Even Blake insisted on going out on patrol tonight with the others. I'm proud of them."

"As you should be," Holm confirmed. "It'll do the people good to see the law is still keeping an eye on the town despite all of this." He drummed his fingers on the arm of his chair. "However, there are some nasty rumors sprouting up that the Washington Gang may have had something to do with this. I've done my best to nip that kind of talk in the bud, but between us, there's no reason to suspect them of being part of it, is there?"

"None," Brandt said. "They only let me go when we

were through the pines across the creek. I didn't get here until after it happened. There's no way they could've reached Laramie much before I did, not even with hard riding. Besides, they were aiming to stay away from town. I was with them for a long while. I didn't see any dynamite around and they never mentioned anything about the LeBlanc boys."

Trammel had already gotten the full story from Hagen earlier. "The LeBlanc boys out of New Orleans did this. They came to town as part of Adam's cattlemen's convention, even though they don't have any cattle. They spent the last few days looking the town over, hoping to get Adam to hire them on as part of his operation. When they saw how much money he was getting by taking bets on this Washington business, they got greedy and decided to go after the safe. Their older brother Wayne got himself killed behind the hotel last night. They blamed Hagen for doing it."

Holm cocked an eyebrow as he looked at Hagen. "Well? Did you kill him?"

Hagen looked away.

Trammel continued, "From what Rick LeBlanc said before he got away, when they couldn't open Hagen's safe, they lit all the dynamite they had to bring down the hotel. He said if they couldn't get Adam's money in one way, they'd cost him something in another."

Holm drummed his fingers on the arm of his chair again. "Any sign of this Rick LeBlanc or his remaining brothers anywhere in town?"

Trammel said, "I killed one of them in the alley and Blake shot another LeBlanc who was trying to escape from the livery. It looks like Rick and his two remaining brothers got away in the confusion after the explosion. I'd have my men look for them—"

"But they don't know what they look like," Hagen spat, "and neither do I. They were careful to never allow themselves to be seen together. I only know Wayne and his brother Burt and now Rick. Either of the other two brothers could walk in here right now and I wouldn't know them." He pounded his own leg in frustration. "I allowed myself to get rolled in my own place by a bunch of Cajun grifters."

Holm folded his hands on his desk. "I'm sure you'll exact a measure of revenge when the opportunity presents itself, Adam, but we have other concerns at present. That's the other reason why I wanted to meet with all of you tonight. Laramie was troubled when they thought the Washington men were going to ride into town and start shooting everyone. After they've had time to get over the initial shock of what's happened here today, some will be looking to blame someone for it. I don't think I have to tell any of you what a potent combination fear and anger can be. Add whiskey to the mix and it gets even worse. That is why we need to take some drastic but necessary steps to keep order at all costs."

Trammel could see where Holm was headed. "Don't do this, Walt. We're not up for it."

The mayor continued. "I'll be imposing a curfew starting tomorrow night. I want all saloons to close at seven o'clock. No one will be allowed on the streets after eight. LeBlanc and Washington thugs aren't the only criminals we have in Laramie, and I don't want anyone getting the idea they can take advantage of the situation."

Trammel said, "My men haven't had a chance to rest since this happened. Blake's hurt bad and the others have been helping out where they can all over town. They'll be pretty ragged by morning. You can order a curfew if it makes you feel any better, but enforcing it will be a tall order."

"Which is why I'll start asking for volunteers to help you out tomorrow. I'm sure there won't be any shortage of willing men looking to protect their homes and families for a short while. That should give your deputies some time to rest and tend to their injuries." He looked at Hagen. "Any objections to closing your saloons early?"

"Whatever you think is best. I don't have it in me to fight you."

Holm said to Brandt, "Deputy, I hope I can expect you to help out wherever we need you. Having a federal man in town could go far in allowing us to keep everyone calm."

"A federal man who got himself captured by the Washington Gang probably won't make people feel any safer, but I'll do whatever you and Sheriff Trammel want."

"Then it's settled." Holm stood to leave. "I'm sure you men have a long night ahead of you. I plan on making the rounds to see how the rest of the town is faring. I should be easy enough to find if you need me."

Trammel waited until Holm left before resuming his seat at his desk. He opened his top drawer, found Brandt's star, and handed it to him. "You ought to have this back. Dib Bishop had it on him when he came to deliver Mahaffey's demands about you." He had to remind himself that it had only been a day since Bishop had been in his office. It felt like a lifetime ago.

Brandt pinned the star on his shirt. "What do you want me to do now?"

"Wait until Hawkeye gets back," Trammel told him. "Have him take you around town. He'll show you the places you ought to keep your eye on. The streets are pretty straight in all directions, so you won't have to worry about getting lost. Do anything he asks of you."

A thought nagged at the back of Trammel's mind. "You have any idea where Mahaffey was taking his men?"

"No, but I wish I did. They told me to ride straight on for Cheyenne, but with Lefty gone, I figured it would be best if I came back here to help you with Washington. I'm kind of glad I did."

Trammel fought through the fog in his mind to remember the details of what Brandt had told him earlier. "They caught you at the creek, took you to a box canyon, then led you through the pines before letting you go."

"That's right," Brandt confirmed. "And those are the only hiding places they talked about around me. They said they had other spots, but they were careful not to tell me where they were. They're a sharp outfit, Sheriff. They don't make mistakes, and they're good at what they do."

Hagen said, "They didn't get to be the most wanted men in Wyoming for nothing. Think they might come back here? Maybe try to take advantage of the situation to free Ben?"

"I'd say anything's possible with Mahaffey," Brandt said. "That whole gang is dead set on finding a way to get Ben out of jail. I think Mahaffey was hoping to wait you out somewhere between here and Cheyenne and grab Ben while you moved him. He might have someone keeping an eye on the town for him. I wouldn't put it past him to cause some trouble here if he thinks it could help him free Washington."

Trammel knew whatever Mahaffey *might* do was not as important as what already needed to be done in Laramie. He hoped he and his men would be ready if the gang set their sights on the town.

But Trammel had a more pressing concern before him now. He told Brandt, "I'd be grateful if you went down to the courtyard and checked on Emily for me. I need to talk to Adam in private."

Brandt left without another word, leaving Trammel and Hagen alone.

He told the gambler, "You'd better hurry up about getting your mind right, Adam. I need you."

But Hagen kept staring at something before him that Trammel could not see. "I burned down my father's house to spite his memory and now someone has burned down my hotel to spite me. It's funny how life always seems to find a way to balance the books, isn't it? Sometimes in the cruelest of ways. Justice may be blind, but she's rarely kind."

During his time as a Pinkerton, Trammel had seen how a tragedy could compel a man into confessing his sins. He could not allow Hagen to slide down into that abyss. He would risk losing him forever, and he did not have the time to pull him up from it. "Stop beating yourself up about this. You still run most of the saloons in town. You aren't exactly penniless."

"I have money," Hagen admitted, "but little value. I borrowed every penny I could against everything I have. It'll take me years to pay off a building reduced to rubble, if ever. And that doesn't begin to cover what others have lost. Did you happen to see where the safe wound up?"

Trammel had not. He had been too busy removing the dead from the first floor of the hotel, and there had been much to do. "Can't say that I did. Didn't have the time."

"I did," Hagen said. "It crashed straight through the floor and is standing upright at this very moment. A bit charred, but not a dent on it. I can't understand why LeBlanc did that. He had us dead to rights in the alley. I didn't even know what he looked like until that moment. He could've gotten away and tried to finish me off another time. He could've shot me in the alley. All those people didn't have to pay for his hatred of me."

"Hate costs everyone something, Adam. Just like it cost you your family and your fortune. But you've got more than you think. You could've pulled up stakes and left Wyoming when your family turned on you. You didn't. You decided to stay here and rebuild your life once. You'll rebuild from this."

Hagen did not wipe away the tears that began to run down his face. "After all the men I've killed and for all the reasons why, you'd think the deaths of my employees wouldn't affect me this much, but they do. I can still see Mr. Lee's fat face whenever I close my eyes. He was always smiling. I can't believe he's dead."

"I've never seen you kill without a good reason," Trammel told him. "Not even when I didn't agree with it. You're not the reason why they're dead. Rick LeBlanc and his brothers did this and, together, we're going to make them pay. That much I can promise you."

Hagen smiled as the last tear dropped from his face. "I never took you for an optimist."

"And I never took you for a quitter. Besides, I've got plenty of reason to be an optimist despite everything that's happened." He figured Hagen could use a bit of good news. "Emily is going to have a baby."

Trammel watched Hagen's expression change from one of profound sadness to complete joy. "That explains the change in you. How long have you known?"

"She told me right before Hawkeye told me about what was happening at the hotel. She caught me as I was leaving the telegraph office. I'm glad she told me when she did. It carried me through a pretty dark day."

"As it should. What wonderful news. I shamelessly nominate myself as godfather, of course."

"I'm glad to hear you say that." Trammel opened his top drawer again, took Hagen's pistol and placed it on the desk. "It's yours if you promise not to do anything stupid with it."

Hagen picked up the gun and slid it in the holster on his hip. "That darkness has passed."

"Good. You'd better visit all your saloons and let them know about Holm's curfew tomorrow night. I'm going to check around town. See how they're faring."

The two men left Trammel's office together when they heard rifle fire and screams echo up to them from the street.

CHAPTER 23

As Trammel and Hagen ran down the steps of City Hall together, they heard people screaming and pointing in the directions from where they heard shots. They were pointing everywhere.

Trammel recognized one of the men as being a clerk from one of the general stores in town picking himself off the ground and asked him, "What happened?"

"One fella rode right through here from the east and another from the west. They were just shooting at folks and didn't seem to care who they hit. Then, another came up from the north and set to firing into the courtyard. They didn't stop, Sheriff. They just kept on going."

Hagen pushed Trammel toward the corner. "Go to the courtyard and check on Emily. I'll get some of my men to start looking for those riders."

The two men broke in opposite directions, with Hagen going left to one of his saloons and Trammel heading for Emily in the courtyard.

Trammel found Brandt at the open gate looking up the street. "A rider just poured six shots in here, Sheriff. I would've shot back, but my pistol's empty."

Trammel ran past him as he looked for Emily. "You'll

find a couple of boxes of bullets in my desk. Bring them both down here. Rifles, too."

Now in the courtyard, Trammel saw nurses tending to a doctor who had been wounded in the shoulder. Doc Carson was tending to an amputee on a cot who had been hit in the stomach. Emily was treating a nurse on the ground who had been shot in the back.

She saw her husband approaching. "Help me get her to the table, Steve. She's hurt bad."

As Trammel bent to lift her, he saw the bullet wound in her chest and the vacant look in the young woman's eyes. He picked her up anyway and carried her over to the operating table that had been set up near the stable. When he set her lifeless body down, Emily gasped when she finally saw she was dead.

"She's gone." Trammel gently took Emily's arm. "Are you hurt? Were you shot?"

She continued to look down at the nurse. "She barely left my side the entire day. She was standing next to me just now when the shooting started. I thought she just fell. I—"

Trammel knew she was slipping into shock as he quickly ran his hands over her body. He was glad his hand came away clean.

He took his wife by both shoulders and moved her away from the dead woman on the table. "She's gone but there are plenty of other people who need your help. Doc Carson's tending to a belly wound right over there. Go to him. Go now!"

He eased her in toward the doctor and she went without question.

Trammel picked up the nurse's body and carried her over to a rare spot of clear ground beside the wall. He was sure others would have better use for the operating table now that she was beyond care.

Old Bob brought out two saddled horses from the stables and led them over to Trammel. "I started getting them ready as soon as I heard them shots. Figured you and Brandt could use them."

Trammel climbed into the saddle and took the reins from him. "Don't saddle any more mounts. If any deputies come back, tell them I want them to stay here to guard City Hall. The Washingtons are trying to draw us out so they can take a run at freeing Ben. They can't let that happen. Close these gates behind me and don't open them up for anyone."

The black man said he understood, and Trammel rode past the wounded and out to the street, where Brandt was waiting for him with his rifle.

He handed the Winchester up to the sheriff. "Careful. It's loaded."

Trammel gave Brandt the reins of his horse. "Reload and mount up. Shoot at any man you see on a horse."

Old Bob shut and locked the large iron gate behind them as Brandt got onto his horse. "What'll you be doing?"

"Everything I can." Trammel dug his heels into the flanks of his mount and ran to the sound of gunfire echoing through the streets of Laramie.

The dam had finally broken. The town was under attack.

Adam Hagen was only half a block away from one of his smaller saloons, The Rosie O'Grady, when a rider rounded the corner and brought his horse to a sliding stop.

Hagen knew he had been seen.

Hagen drew and fired three times, striking the man in

the chest. The rider pulled his horse around and began to ride in the other direction as Hagen ran after him. His next shot went wide, but his next two hit the man in the back. He slumped forward in the saddle but kept riding.

Hagen jogged to the saloon and leapt over the men who had taken cover on the boardwalk. He saw his bartender crouched behind the bar with a coach gun in his hand. "What do you want me to do, Mr. Hagen?"

"The town's under attack by Washington's men." Hagen continued on to his office in the back. "Lock that door and shoot anyone who tries to come in here. I'll go out the back way."

The barman slid across the bar and locked the door. "How many of them are there?"

"I don't know, but there's at least one who won't be riding out again."

Hagen unlocked his office door and took down a Winchester from the rack above his desk. He did not have to check if it was loaded. He always kept all of his guns loaded. He took down a box of cartridges for his Colt, dumped out the spent bullets and began reloading the pistol. When finished, he took a handful of bullets and put them in his pocket. He was sure he would have use for them soon.

He holstered his Colt, picked up his rifle, and left the saloon by the back door. Gunshots followed by screams and breaking glass sounded from all over town.

Gunfire sounded nearby, and he knew someone must have cornered one of the gunmen on the street. He ran down the alley in that direction where he saw Hawkeye with Deputy Welch had taken cover behind the corner of one of the stores on the side street. Bullets peppered the brickwork only inches from them.

Hagen cut loose with a sharp whistle to get Hawkeye's attention.

The young deputy shouted over to him, "I shot the horse out from under one of them. He's dug in right over there."

A single shot struck the boardwalk in front of them, sending splinters of wood up into their faces. Both deputies cried out and fell back against the wall, rubbing at their eyes.

Hagen remained still as he watched and listened for what would happen next. He heard boots scrape on the dirt of the street as the marauder began to quickly close in on them.

Hagen took a quick look around the corner. He was hoping it was a LeBlanc brother, but when he saw the heavy beard, he knew it must be one of Mahaffey's men.

The gunman raised his rifle as he began to round the corner at a wide angle. "You tinhorns just killed a good horse."

Hagen stepped out, his Winchester at his shoulder and fired. The shot struck the Mahaffey man in the left shoulder, jerking him back as he fell to the ground.

Hagen fired twice as he rushed out to close the gap between him and the man he had just shot. Both of his shots missed, hitting the ground on either side of the gunman's head.

The gunman tried to raise his rifle as Hagen kicked it away from him, then pinned his arm to the street. His left arm was useless.

Hagen carefully aimed the Winchester down at his head. "Which one are you?"

"Coombs." The man did his best to look defiantly up at the rifle. "What does it matter?"

"It matters to me." Hagen levered in a fresh round to finish him off as a bullet struck him in the right hip.

The impact knocked Hagen backward and he let himself fall as more bullets filled the air around him.

Hagen held on to his rifle as rough hands grabbed his shoulder and pulled him back into the alley.

Deputy Welch moved past him and fired back at the men until his pistol emptied. More bullets chased him back to cover.

"That's Dib Bishop out there," Welch said as he emptied the gun and began to quickly reload it with bullets from his belt. "He's pulling the other one back to safety."

"Coombs is the name of the one I shot." Hagen thrust his Winchester at him. "Use this, but be careful. It bucks higher than I remembered."

Welch took Hagen's rifle as Hawkeye looked at Hagen's wound. "It looks like he got you in the middle, Mr. Hagen. I'll undo your belt so I can get a better look at it."

Hagen pushed his hand away. "Not unless you buy me dinner first. Don't worry about me."

Welch crept out into the street. "They're gone, but they couldn't have gotten far."

Hagen tried to sit up, but the pain was too great. "You two go after them. I'll be fine where I am. You can come back for me later."

Both deputies knew their duty and neither argued with him. They ran out into the night to run down the men who had dared to attack the town.

The irony of his predicament was not lost on Hagen. He had tried to take his own life twice that day, only to have one of Mahaffey's men try to do it for him.

Hagen did not consider such ideas now. He still had plenty of killing left to do.

* * *

Trammel caught a blur of movement in front of him as a rider sped from one side of the thoroughfare to the other. He ignored the plaintive cries for help from the citizens as he rode by them, urging more speed out of his horse as he took the corner in pursuit.

Trammel saw the rider running down the center of the street, shooting down at those who had been caught outside when the shooting started.

Trammel knew he could not hit much from the back of a speeding horse, so he pulled hard on the reins to bring his horse to a short stop as he took careful aim at the man terrorizing the civilians.

He raised his rifle and fired once, levering in a fresh round without waiting to see if he had hit his target. He fired again as another shot came from behind him. He turned in the saddle to see a second rider speeding toward him.

The rider he had been shooting at had turned and begun to charge back in his direction. They were trying to catch Trammel in a cross fire.

The sheriff snapped the reins and rode as low as a big man could while his confused horse gave him all the speed it had. The rider in front of him closed in fast, snapping off shots from his pistol at Trammel as he bounced in the saddle.

Trammel fired in the man's general direction, but the shot went wide and struck a porch post instead of the man racing toward him. As they met, Trammel leaned as far to the left as he dared and swung the rifle into the rider's chest as hard as he could manage.

The impact was hard enough to rip both of them from their saddles, sending them crashing to the street below. Trammel lost his grip on his rifle when he hit the ground.

The rider who had been chasing him from behind shot at Trammel as he ran by without stopping. The sheriff saw the man he had knocked from his horse lunge for his pistol. Trammel kicked it away just before the man swept his leg out from under him.

The man pulled a blade from his belt and tried to bring it down on Trammel's middle. The sheriff brought up his knees in time to knock the knife aside. He grabbed hold of the man's wrists and wrenched him hard to the left. The blade dropped as Trammel delivered a hard knee to the man's ribs.

His attacker rolled free as people broke from the cover they had taken and descended on the man, pummeling him as he tried to stand. He pushed his way through them and began to run away as they gave chase.

"Get out of the way!" Trammel bellowed as he drew his Peacemaker from beneath his left arm, but the people were too close to his target for him to get a clean shot, so Trammel had no choice but to run after them.

The gunman stopped short and easily knocked them aside as he launched himself into Trammel's middle. He rode the bigger man to the ground and made a play for his gun.

Trammel kept his right arm extended, far away from the man's reach as he tried to pry the gun from his fingers. He grabbed the man by the back of the neck as he rolled, pinning him to the ground as he pulled his gun hand free. He brought the butt of his pistol down hard on the side of the man's head, rendering him unconscious.

The townspeople who had been knocked aside quickly gathered around Trammel as he pulled the man's arms behind him. "Someone give me something to tie him up with and get him back to the jail."

A man took off his belt and handed it down to the

sheriff. "Use this. I don't think anyone'll notice if my drawers fall down in all this excitement."

Trammel quickly wrapped the belt tightly around the prisoner's wrists and helped the citizens get him to his feet. "Make sure you don't kill him. I want him alive."

He did not like the idea of allowing townspeople to take control of a prisoner, but when he heard more gunshots come from deeper in the town, he knew he still had a lot of work to do.

He picked up his rifle and jogged to his horse who had stopped about halfway down the street. He practically leapt into the saddle and sped off to rejoin the fray.

CHAPTER 24

As he struggled to keep his eyes focused in the dark, Deputy Sherwood Blake wished he had not drunk as much as he had. The pain in his scalp and face had begun to return as the excitement caused the numbing effects of the whiskey to quickly recede.

He had been drinking in The Corner Saloon—which was not actually on the corner of a street—when the shooting had started. Bullets had shattered the saloon's front window as the men who had been so curious about his injuries only a moment before began to drop to the floor. Blake had fallen with them, half from instinct and half from the liquor.

He had heard a rider race past the saloon as he continued shooting down at people on the street. Blake did not pause to check on his fellow patrons as he crawled over them and began to make his way outside. He had just reached the boardwalk when another rider opened fire, causing him to dive back into the saloon. The door had saved at least two rounds from hitting him, possibly more.

Blake tried to shake his head clear now as he moved forward, but it only made the pain from his burns grow worse. Shots and shouts from other parts of town reached him as he slid along the wall of the saloon in slow pursuit of the gunmen. He saw citizens tending to each other as he tried to make sense of what was happening all around him. Someone had decided to lay siege to the town, and, through his haze of pain and drink, Blake knew it had to be the Washington Gang. He had counted only three LeBlanc boys escape from the livery behind The Laramie Grand and doubted they had enough men to conduct such an attack on their own. The Washington men had probably been drawn by the smoke and destruction they had seen from the outskirts of town. They had decided to make the most of a dire situation.

His Colt in hand, Blake checked an alley as he stepped from one boardwalk to another. He passed a woman using a kerchief to try to stop the bleeding from a bullet hole in another woman's shoulder. A man in the middle of the street cried out as he cradled his leg. A young boy on the opposite side of the street wept as he pushed against another fallen man to get up.

Blake heard a commotion of gunfire at the next corner and began to run in that direction, but dizziness overcame him. The street tilted violently beneath him, and Blake tilted with it, landing flat on his side before he slid off the boardwalk.

A man on horseback must have heard him hit the ground, for he brought his horse around and rode back to him. His pistol was aimed down at Blake, but he did not fire.

To Blake, it felt like man and horse had been standing over him for hours before he finally said, "I recognize you. You're one of Trammel's deputies, ain't you? Where's your star?"

Blake wanted to raise his pistol, but the man and dark sky above him kept twitching in and out of focus. He thought he might get sick, so he closed his eyes. "What's it to you?"

"Nothing, I guess," the man said. "And don't worry. I ain't gonna kill you."

The boy up the street who had been willing his father to stand continued to wail for help. A single shot from the rider looming over Blake quieted the street.

"I ain't gonna kill you because I need you alive," the rider said. "I need you to tell Trammel that this is only the beginning. Me and my men are going to keep on hitting this place day and night until you give over Ben Washington. You'll never know how I'll hit or when and you won't have a moment's rest until Ben goes free. Tell him to put Ben on a horse and let him ride off. Tell him that's the only way all of this will end. Think you can remember all that? I hope you can. You smell like a whiskey barrel."

With his eyes still closed, Blake raised his pistol toward the sound of the rider's voice. "Here's something to remember me by."

Blake heard horse and rider bolt off before he could manage to squeeze the trigger. He fired anyway. He was sure his bullet sailed harmlessly into the sky, but it felt good to do something to set the outlaw on edge.

"You've got fight in you," the man yelled back as he rode away. "I'll make sure I save you for last."

Blake lowered his pistol and tried to roll himself upright. He did not know where Trammel was but began to stagger toward the sound of distant gunfire. He was sure the sheriff could not be far.

Mahaffey rode to the end of the street and was glad to see all of his men had gathered where they had been told to gather. They were relatively unharmed, though Coombs was holding onto his shoulder. A quick count showed him two were missing. "Where's Hank? Where's Jim LeBlanc?"

Earnshaw said, "I saw Hank tangling with the sheriff a few streets back. You told us not to double back for anyone, so I didn't. He's either dead or captured."

Rick LeBlanc brought his horse around. "I saw my brother riding straight out of town. He looked like he was hurt bad. We've got to find him and get him back to camp before they catch up to us."

A bullet creased the air between them, and LeBlanc heeled his horse into a gallop. Mahaffey hung back to see where the shot had come from while the rest of his men followed LeBlanc.

Mahaffey saw the dark outline of a large man on a sorrel charging his way. He knew that had to be Trammel.

Another slender figure was riding up the street right behind him and, despite the darkness and the distance, Mahaffey recognized him as Leo Brandt.

Mahaffey steadied his mount as he took careful aim with his pistol at the charging Trammel and fired into the center of the sheriff's bulk. He paused just long enough to see the animal pitch forward, throwing Trammel over its head as rider and horse crashed to the ground.

Mahaffey snapped the reins and spurred the horse after the others, wondering if Brandt would be foolish enough to continue to give chase. He rounded the corner on the road at the edge of town and kept going through the overgrowth alongside the dirt path that wound back to where his men had set up camp. He paused behind a large rock on the side of the path and holstered his pistol as he drew his Winchester from the saddle scabbard.

He heard a horse galloping toward him and took aim in the darkness. When the sound grew closer, Mahaffey cut loose with three shots before racing off to catch up to the others. He glanced behind him as he fled, unsure if he had struck Brandt. All he knew was that the deputy was no longer after him. He had made his point.

After a mile or so, when it was clear no one was chasing them, Mahaffey saw his men had stopped in a clearing where Earnshaw had taken hold of a riderless horse.

When he stopped beside them, he saw Jim LeBlanc's body on the ground. The horse had belonged to him in life.

Rick LeBlanc looked down at his brother while Burt LeBlanc wiped at his eyes with his sleeve.

"He was trying to get to our camp," Rick said through gritted teeth. "That's the third brother I've lost to this town. I'll make them pay for this. I'll make them pay dearly. All of them."

Mahaffey kept looking around to see if anyone was coming after them. They were still too close to town for his tastes. "We'll be paying dearly ourselves unless we keep moving. Let's get going, boys. There's no point in making this easy for them."

The men rode out, including both remaining LeBlanc brothers. Mahaffey caught up to Rick LeBlanc as they rode away from his brother. "I'm sorry about what happened to Joe. I didn't know him well, but he seemed like a fine man."

"His name was Jim, and he wasn't a fine man at all. He was a lousy drunk and a schemer, but he was still my brother. But Burt and I would be dead right now if he hadn't thought to break through the wall of Hagen's room."

Mahaffey knew they had more pressing concerns than one man's grief. "We'll have to camp somewhere else tonight. We can't risk having anyone track us there come the morning."

Rick's tone was cold as he said, "Some outlaw you

turned out to be. I was thinking we should wait a couple of hours and hit them again around midnight. Make them pay for what they did to Jim."

Mahaffey resisted the urge to knock the man out of his saddle. "This isn't a game, LeBlanc, and this isn't about revenge. These horses need rest and so do my men. We need to count up our ammunition and see how much we've got before we plan on another go-round. I told one of Trammel's deputies that we're going to keep doing this until they release Ben. We've got to give some time for that message to spread so they see there's only one way out of this for them. We need to let fear take root before we strike again."

LeBlanc continued to ride through the darkness. "You're the one who said we should kick them while they're down and they're down right now, Mahaffey."

"We did that," Mahaffey said. "But my men and I have done this kind of thing before. It cost us two good men and a lot of bullets. We have to take that into account before we can even think of hitting them again. An empty gun's not much good to anyone. You'd do well to remember that."

Mahaffey could practically feel LeBlanc sneer at him in the darkness. "I'm not some kid who needs teaching, Mahaffey. Me and my brothers have done this kind of thing long before we ever heard of you."

"Smacking around pimps and drunks in New Orleans is different than raiding a town," Mahaffey told him. "Fear takes time. And there's also our supplies to consider. I figure they'll last us one more day at most. We'll need to find a way to stock up soon if this goes on for much longer."

"I'm sure you've got plenty of ideas on how to get more," LeBlanc said. "We can hunt for our food if we have to."

"We can," Mahaffey allowed, "but unless you're handy with a bow and arrow, hunting takes bullets. Every shot we use is one less we'll have against the town."

"Then we'll just have to get more, won't we?"

Mahaffey had an idea of how they could get more but kept it to himself. He decided the less LeBlanc knew about what he thought the better for all concerned.

CHAPTER 25

"I've been seeing entirely too much of you lately, Hagen," Doc Carson said as he finished stitching up the wound in the gambler's hip. "You're lucky that bullet passed straight through you without hitting a bowel or your bladder. The bullet struck your hip bone and kept on going. I expect you'll have a limp for a month or so, but you'll probably live. Can't do anything about the scar, though. Good thing you're not a vain man."

Hagen did not mind the doctor's teasing. He did not even mind being shot. The laudanum Doc Carson had given him had taken effect. "It'll be just another scar to add to my collection. The ladies will be impressed."

Doc Carson glanced at him over the top of his spectacles. "The kind of ladies you attract are only interested in the amount of money in your pocket, not the scars on your body."

Hagen grinned through the discomfort as Carson continued stitching him shut. "You sound jealous, Doc. You ought to come around one of my places sometime. I'll be sure to find you a suitable companion. A lady who has some patience for a man of your advanced years."

"No thanks." Carson snipped the last stitch. "I've already

got enough ailments without having one of your soiled doves adding to the list."

Hagen saw Trammel rap on the open door of the prison doctor's office. Blake was right behind him.

"How's the patient?" the sheriff asked. "I heard him talking just now, so his mouth must still work."

Doc Carson placed the scissors in a bucket of solution while he washed his hands in another bucket. "He'll be fine. There's always the risk of infection, of course, but Hagen here usually has enough alcohol in his system to kill almost anything." The doctor looked past Trammel at Deputy Blake. "How are you faring, Sherwood? I can see you're in an awful lot of pain. You should've taken my advice and rested."

Blake pawed at the bandages on his face. "Been medicating myself since I left, doc. Guess that's part of the problem."

"I know. I can smell you from here." Carson finished washing and began to dry his hands, before he took a small bottle from the cabinet above the wash basin. He handed it to Blake. "Take that when you sober up some, but be careful. It's laudanum. It'll dull the pain but if you take it in your state, you might fall asleep and not wake up again. Sleep's the best medicine you can have right now, Deputy. Your body will heal itself in time if you allow it." He looked away before adding, "I'm sorry I couldn't do more to save your eye."

"No reason for you to be sorry, Doc. I know you did the best you could."

Hagen saw the doctor did not appear to take much comfort in that.

As Carson began to leave, he told Trammel, "Don't let him take that stuff until he sobers up. If you need me, I'll be out in the courtyard tending to several new patients who need my attention."

Trammel gently pulled Blake into the office with him and set him on a chair as Hagen clasped his hands behind his head. He had once made a small fortune peddling laudanum to his customers up in Blackstone but had never sampled the stuff personally. He had always thought there was something unseemly about becoming addicted to his own product.

"We're a great pair, you and me," Hagen said to Blake. "With your missing eye and my limp, we could make a fairly decent pirate. What do you say you and I head down to New Orleans, get ourselves a frigate, and become the terrors of the high seas?"

Trammel crossed his arms. "How much of that stuff did Doc Carson give you?"

"Enough to melt all my troubles away."

Trammel grunted. "Too bad the doc doesn't have enough to give a dose to everyone in town. It might help folks feel better about the state of things."

Hagen felt foolish for feeling so good while he was surrounded by such misery. He forced himself to remember all that had happened and why he had to be stitched up. "It was Washington's men who hit us, Buck. I shot a man I think was one of the LeBlanc boys, but he got away despite my best efforts. I shot another man named Coombs, but Dib Bishop managed to save his life by putting a hole in me."

"Hawkeye told me all about it," Trammel said. "I managed to grab another one on the street. He goes by the name of Hank Classet. And Blake here had his own run-in with Mahaffey."

"And lived to tell the tale, I see," Hagen observed. "It's not like Mahaffey to leave a loose end dangling like that."

Blake lowered his bandaged head into his hands. "He only let me live because he wanted me to deliver a message to Buck." He looked up at Trammel for approval to continue speaking, and the sheriff gave it to him. "He said he and his gang will keep hitting us like this until we let Washington go. He said more people will die until we do."

Hagen felt the reality of the situation begin to crowd out whatever relief the opium had bestowed upon him. "We put a dent in them. I killed one and wounded another. How bad did they hit us?"

"At least twelve wounded," Trammel told him, "but I imagine the number will go higher. One man was shot dead right in front of his boy. I thought there'd be more. Bush and Brillheart got nicked, but they're still able to fight. Mahaffey knew exactly when to hit us and how."

Hagen knew that was the case. "Sounds like he's far craftier than we gave him credit for."

Trammel nodded. "One would start shooting up a street before a second rider followed behind a few seconds later to hit people as they came out from cover. I found Mahaffey and the others at the edge of town and tried to go after them when one of them shot out the horse from under me. At least I think it was Mahaffey, but they've all got those beards, so it's tough to know which one is which. Brandt went after them while I was down, but almost rode into a wall of lead. It's a miracle that he's alive."

Hagen was glad to hear it. "And Hawkeye?"

"He's doing what he can while I'm in here with you, but as you'd expect, the mood in town has taken a dark turn."

"With the promise of it growing still darker," Hagen said. "This wasn't blind luck on Mahaffey's part. I've seen this kind of run-and-gun strategy when I was down in New Orleans. The LeBlanc boys have joined up with Washington's bunch. That only compounds our already long list of concerns."

Hagen watched Trammel struggling with his thoughts and decided to make it easier on him. "You take a run at questioning the man you captured yet? He ought to be able to tell you where Mahaffey and the men are camped."

"It wouldn't do any good," Trammel said. "I can't trust what he tells me, and I don't have enough men to check it for myself. I need every man I've got to stay here and keep an eye out for trouble both inside and outside of town. This raid is exactly what folks feared might happen and I wouldn't be surprised if someone starts acting up because of it."

Blake sat up as straight as he could manage given his condition. "Me and the boys can handle anything those outlaws throw at us. The LeBlanc boys won't make a difference. They won't catch us flat the next time they ride into us."

Trammel looked away. "You're half-blind with pain and on your way to suffering from an epic hangover come morning. Bush and Brillheart are wounded, and none of you have gotten any sleep since this whole mess started. Go out and tell them I've ordered them to get some rest here at City Hall. You can set up some cots in the courtroom if necessary. Make sure you get some rest for yourself, too. Tell the men I'll wake them if I need them."

Blake winced as he got to his feet and left Doc Carson's office without another word.

Hagen waited until he had left before saying, "I've seen men laid up for weeks in better condition than him. It's a wonder he's still standing."

"He can get better after this is over. If he lives that long."

Hagen heard a troubling tone in his friend's voice. "I hope you're not actually thinking about giving in to Mahaffey's demands. You're not thinking of letting Washington go, are you?"

"Of course not," Trammel said, "but I don't know how much more this town can take. The mayor got them to trust me to keep them safe. They won't trust me after this, and I can't blame them. Mahaffey said he'll hit us again and I believe him. There's no reason for him not to, and there's not much I can do to stop him."

"You can try to track him come morning," Hagen offered. "With me laid up and Blake in no condition, Hawkeye could track them."

"I can't let him risk it," Trammel said. "If they grabbed him, they'd use him against me. All I can do is react to whatever Mahaffey does next and it's impossible to win that way. One more attack, and the people will revolt against the closest target. Me."

It was at times like these that Hagen regretted that he had never been able to get Trammel to think like a gambler. He saw the world in black and white. Something was either lawful or illegal to him. A man was either a criminal to be charged or a civilian in need of his protection. There was only right and wrong and no room for any consideration to the contrary. Such a philosophy limited the way he viewed a problem.

"You can't beat men like Mahaffey by throwing something in their way, Buck," Hagen said. "They're used to hitting whatever's in front of them until it breaks or buckles. They're good at it, too. And when you find yourself up against a man like that, you have to just let it happen. But you've got more of an edge than you think."

"Yeah," Trammel said. "The only edge I see is the one right against my throat."

"The same one you've had all this time. The same one you had when Dib Bishop gave you Mahaffey's demands. You're still holding the same cards you had then. You still have something they want. You have Ben Washington. And the only way you might be able to stop them is if you make them risk what they want most."

Hagen watched a new idea dawn on Trammel's face. Many discounted his intelligence due to his toughness and size, but Hagen had seen how quickly the big man could catch on to a notion once it was presented to him properly. Just as Hagen had presented it to him now.

"You mean I should use Washington as a shield, don't you."

"In a way. And if you'll pull up a chair, I'll tell you how I would pull it off if I were in your boots."

Trammel picked up the chair and placed it beside the examination table. "Oh, you're already in this right along with me, Adam. The whole town is."

"All the more reason why you should sit down and listen, for none of us have a moment to lose."

George Mahaffey could tell by the way Earnshaw was frowning that his inventory of their situation was dire. He beckoned Mahaffey to follow him away from the small cook fire they had built.

Earnshaw kept his voice low as he said, "Each man's got about twenty bullets between them, more or less. That includes bullets for their rifles and their pistols."

Mahaffey could not believe the number was that low. "What about what was in the dead LeBlanc man's saddle-bags? Jim or Joe or whatever his name was."

"I already factored that in."

Mahaffey cursed quietly to himself.

Earnshaw continued. "The good news is that we can make the food last three more days if we have to and we've got plenty of water to go around."

Mahaffey looked around for answers in the darkness. "Things are worse than I thought."

"I figure we've got enough bullets to last us maybe one more run at the town, but that's pushing it. They'll be expecting us next time, so it won't be as easy to get away as it was before."

"I wasn't planning on hitting them the same way again," Mahaffey told him. "I was thinking of setting up outside of town and taking random shots like I'd ordered Marcum to do. Keep them off balance that way. They won't know what to expect from us after that."

Earnshaw considered that tactic. "We might manage to get a few of them before they run for cover. Let's be generous and say each man gets one citizen apiece on his first shot, which they won't. That'll make our ammunition situation even worse. No matter how you look at it, we need more bullets, George. There's just no way around it."

Mahaffey may not have been as good a thinker as Ben Washington, but he was not an imbecile. "I know what the problem is, Roy. I just don't have an answer for it."

"There's only two answers to our troubles," Earnshaw explained. "The first is to ride over to Woodbine and get what we need from the general store there. It's small and there's no law to speak of that'll stand in our way, just an old constable."

Mahaffey knew the township where Ben had been captured might be relatively close, but a ride like that would tire their already worn-out horses. The fight was here in Laramie. He wanted to keep it here, which limited his options.

"It's close, but not as close as Laramie. We'll have to get food and bullets down there."

Earnshaw was quiet for a moment. "That would be easier, but it's risky. We'd have to be careful about who we picked to ride into Laramie. Dib's out because some folks are bound to have already gotten a good look at him when you sent him there with that message. The two LeBlanc brothers are out for the same reason. You can't go either, George. Trammel might've seen you at the edge of town last night."

Mahaffey knew it had been too dark for anyone to have gotten a good look at him, but there was no reason to take chances. "Do you think anyone saw you last night?"

Earnshaw shook his head. "I kept shooting and riding. I didn't stop long enough for anyone to get a good look at me. I'll be happy to go, but I'll need some money. All the general stores are bound to be swamped with people looking to buy bullets to defend themselves. They'll be on the lookout for thieves and looters."

Mahaffey dug into his pocket and handed Earnshaw a fistful of coins. "Slip into town tonight and see what you can take. Take Coombs with you. I know he's got a hole in his shoulder, but he's steady. Get as much ammunition as you can carry. Go to different stores if you have to. If you don't think you can break in somewhere without getting caught, buy them first thing in the morning and come right back. The food and other supplies we need can wait. The bullets can't."

Earnshaw pocketed the coins. "Burt's better with locks than Coombs. He'd be the better choice if you want me breaking in someplace."

"Someone might remember him. Coombs is good enough."

Mahaffey was glad Earnshaw was not in the mood

to debate. "I'll be back as soon as I can with whatever I can get."

Mahaffey grabbed him before he walked away. "Be careful, Roy. I can't spare another man. Not even you."

Earnshaw grinned. "I didn't know you cared."

Mahaffey stood by the edge of the fire as he watched Earnshaw and Coombs mount up and ride off toward Laramie. It would have been too dark and dangerous for some, but he knew Earnshaw could have made the trip blindfolded.

Dib Bishop helped himself to another cup of coffee as he asked Mahaffey, "Where they off to?"

"To save our hides, Dib. In a way."

CHAPTER 26

Hawkeye suppressed a yawn as he sat watch in front of Kilroy's General Store.

At first, he had questioned Trammel's idea of sending deputies to mind the stores all over town. He had thought it would be a better idea if all the deputies holed up in City Hall in case the Washington Gang made a run at the jail. Hawkeye certainly could have used the sleep.

But he had seen the wisdom in Trammel's decision as soon as he had seen the group in front of Kilroy's. About twenty of Laramie's citizens had already formed a line along the boardwalk, eager to be there as soon as the store opened in the morning.

Arn Tully, one of those at the front of the men waiting to buy supplies, asked Hawkeye, "Can't you have that hard-headed jackass Kilroy open his store for us? I don't enjoy the prospect of sleeping out here all night."

Hawkeye had already tried to discuss it with the stubborn Scotsman. "He won't budge, Arn. He's as stubborn as a mule on the subject. He said he needs his rest, and he'll open for business at eight in the morning. Not a minute sooner."

Tully grumbled as he pulled his horse blanket around

his shoulders, careful to keep it from touching the man beside him. "It just doesn't seem right for him to hold out on us like this. Can't you make him open up? We've all got the money to pay for what we need."

"That's the problem," said the man next to Tully. "He oughtn't to be allowed to charge us for bullets in the first place. How's a man expected to protect himself, what with the likes of the Washington Gang on the war path and all if he doesn't have bullets?"

"All the stores in town are closed," Hawkeye reminded them. "The owners came to an agreement. I'm not arguing with you, just telling you like it is. I don't like being out here more than you do."

He was glad the men decided to quit complaining and huddle beneath their blankets in a bit to get some sleep. It had been a long day for everyone in Laramie. The longest Hawkeye could remember.

Hawkeye had nodded off several times in the two hours he had been guarding the store, but constantly snapped awake. There was an uneasy mood on the streets of Laramie that evening. The stench of the fire from The Laramie Grand still hung in the air. The stretcher bearers had resumed their grisly work once the shooting had stopped and, every so often, another pair would lope by Kilroy's General Store as they carried the dead to the church graveyard at the end of the street.

Hawkeye could still hear the sound of little Tommy Holley's sobs as the men came to carry his father away. It was a small wonder that no one else had been killed during the robbery, but Ed Holley had been quite a loss. The carpenter had been popular. He always charged a fair price for quality work and, unlike many of his neighbors, had never been known to speak ill of anyone. The people had taken the loss of the good man poorly and Hawkeye imagined there would be some sort of public outcry for justice once the sun came up the next morning.

But for now, Hawkeye knew the people of Laramie passed an uneasy night among the charred ruins of a grand hotel. The added terror visited upon them by a band of ruthless outlaws would not help them sleep any better.

He felt himself begin to nod off once more when he heard a sound from somewhere deep inside the general store. He looked at the men on the boardwalk to see if any of them had heard it, too, but all of them were fast asleep beneath whatever blankets they had brought with them.

Hawkeye peered through the windows to see if Kilroy might have come down from his room in the loft to make a late-night inventory of his goods but saw no hint of a lamplight in the dark interior of the store.

But he did see a shadow pass by the back door. It was quickly followed by another.

Someone was trying to either break into Kilroy's or had already done it.

Rifle in hand, Hawkeye eased out of the chair and slowly crept off the boardwalk, careful to not wake any of the customers. He swiftly moved down the alley between the store and the rooming house beside it. Something scurried away from him in the alley as he moved, and a cat sprang forward to give chase.

Hawkeye paused when he reached the mouth of the alley and took a quick look around the backyard. He saw the back door of the general store open less than an inch. He knew Angus Kilroy always made sure all of his doors were locked before he turned in for the night. Whoever had broken in had been careful about it.

Hawkeye thought about going back to ask one of the men to run and get one of the deputies, but the robbers would likely be gone before any help arrived. He knew he was on his own.

He swept around the corner and used the barrel of his rifle to push the door wide open. He stood to the side of the doorframe as he called out, "I know you're in there. You'd best come out with your hands up or I'll shoot."

A shotgun blast obliterated a large chunk of the back door as Hawkeye ducked for cover. Another blast lit up the inside of the store, sending shot through the gaping doorway.

Hawkeye never liked to fire blind, but he had no choice. He stuck his rifle through the doorway and snapped off two quick rounds into the darkness.

Curses and shuffling feet on creaking floorboards followed and he knew the robbers were trying to escape through the front of the store.

As Hawkeye moved inside, Angus Kilroy was running down the stairs from his room as he bellowed, "Thieves! Looters! Stop them!"

The storeowner knocked Hawkeye aside without stopping as he leveled his own shotgun at the outlines of the fleeing men. "Stop right there or I'll—"

Hawkeye grabbed hold of the shopkeeper's robe as three bullets struck him in the chest. The door up at the front flew open as Kilroy tumbled backward and over the deputy.

Hawkeye did not stop to check the shopkeeper's condition as he got to his feet and ran through the length of the general store.

The men who had been sleeping outside were wide awake as Hawkeye saw the last of the robbers dart down the alley next to the store. The deputy skidded to a stop and ran back inside, hoping to catch them as they came out of the alley. He leapt over Kilroy and bolted outside.

Bullets bit into the wood and the mud around him, causing Hawkeye to drop flat on the ground. He looked up in time to see the men making a mad dash toward a pair of horses waiting for them behind the shops.

He sat up, brought his Winchester to his shoulder, and fired into the center of the shapes. He kept firing as the men scrambled onto their horses and rode out toward the thoroughfare.

Hawkeye got to his feet and began to chase after them. He ran through the far alley and out onto the street, where he saw the thieves moving away at a good gallop.

He levered in a fresh round and emptied his Winchester in their direction.

His rifle empty, he looked to see if one of them had dropped from the saddle, but both of them continued on until they cleared the town and disappeared into the night.

Sheriff Trammel called out to him as he ran toward him from City Hall. His rifle was at his side. "What happened?"

Hawkeye struggled to catch his breath. "Two fellas just broke into Kilroy's store. Came in the back, shot Kilroy, and took off. I could've sworn I hit them, but they kept on going. Want me to go after them?"

Trammel shook his head. "We've got bigger troubles. Come on."

He followed the sheriff as he ran through the alley and to the back of the general store. He only slowed when he reached the back door and stepped inside. Shards of glass crunched beneath his boots. Trammel found a lantern hanging beside the doorframe, thumbed a match alive and lit it.

Hawkeye watched as Trammel began to move through the store, the lamp offering the only light in the place. Its amber glow revealed Angus Kilroy slumped on the floor of his storeroom just as Hawkeye had left him. His eyes were vacant and the three holes in the center of his chest no longer bled.

The deputy felt his legs grow weak. He had been sent to protect the store and now the owner was dead.

Trammel swept the lamp to the shelves, revealing every box of bullets had been taken. A few loose cartridges littered the floor around Kilroy's corpse, but not many.

"There's no way those boys could've taken all of those bullets," Hawkeye said. "They didn't have the time."

Trammel moved into the main part of the store. He lifted the lamp to reveal a vacant spot behind the counter where Kilroy kept the bullets he sold. There was not a box in sight.

The sheriff set the lamp on the counter. "You see anyone loitering outside before they broke in?"

Hawkeye hated to say the words. "About twenty of them had lined up for the night. They wanted to be the first in line to buy ammunition when the store opened in the morning."

The young deputy knew what this meant. Yesterday, no one would've dreamed of taking something without paying for it. They would have rushed to tend to Kilroy instead of robbing him blind.

But a day was a long time in Wyoming. And that day had been the longest in recent memory.

Trammel scowled as he looked over the rest of the store. "Think you can remember any of them?"

"All of them. Arn Tulley and some of his friends."

Trammel placed his hands on his hips. "This is bad, Hawkeye. Real bad. It means the looting has already begun."

Hawkeye knew that now the cork of disorder had been

pulled, the town might very well drown in its own fear. "What do you want me to do, boss?"

"Get out there and bring back one of those stretchers. It won't do anyone any good seeing Kilroy like this. We'll worry about running down the looters later."

As Hawkeye began to leave, Trammel called out to him, "And don't go blaming yourself for this. Guilt won't do us any good now."

Hawkeye moved off into the night, unsure if he entirely believed that.

Unlike the other members of the Washington gang, Mahaffey had not tried to get any sleep. His mind was too busy puzzling over what might happen if Earnshaw and Coombs did not return with those bullets.

He and the others were dug in too deep now to just give up on freeing Ben Washington. The men would turn on him if he even suggested it. And after raising havoc in Laramie, running away would not do any of them much good. Buck Trammel would still hunt him to the ends of the earth to make them pay for what they had done to his town. He had bet his life on getting Ben Washington free. There was no way he could turn back now even if he wanted to.

Mahaffey threw his blanket aside when he heard riders approaching the camp. Some of the others woke, too. The sound of hammers being thumbed back sounded like crickets on a summer's evening.

He walked to the edge of the firelight as Earnshaw and Coombs rode in. Coombs's hat was gone, and his left shoulder was caked in blood.

Earnshaw was all smiles when he handed a bulging

blanket down to Mahaffey. "We got what we could, George. I think it'll be enough to see us through for a while."

The men broke from their bedding and began to eagerly look through the loot the others had brought.

Rick LeBlanc did not join them. He pointed at Coombs's wound and said, "Looks like you boys ran into some trouble."

"This one's barely a scratch," Coombs said as he climbed down from the saddle. He took Earnshaw's horse and walked them both over to where the other animals had been tied up. "A boy with a rifle got me this time. He got lucky is all."

Mahaffey was not as casual about it as Coombs. He had been shot twice that evening, which was quite a number, even for a Washington man. "What happened down there?"

Earnshaw knelt by the fire and poured himself a cup of coffee. "Coombs got the door open easy enough, but we didn't know they had a deputy posted out front guarding the place. I guess we must've been louder than we'd thought because he tried to stop us. The shop owner, too, but he's dead now. The deputy who chased us started shooting all over creation. That kid's got reflexes like a cat. I thought we had him dead for certain, but I don't think we hit him. He managed to wing Coombs while we were escaping, but like he said, it's just a scratch."

Mahaffey looked past him into the darkness. "Think anyone followed you here?"

"Not this time," Earnshaw assured him. "I made sure we were careful. That boy deputy we mentioned chased us on foot for a bit, but no one rode after us. They might try to track us in the morning, but I wouldn't count on it. They'll still be licking their wounds from that beating we gave them earlier."

Mahaffey wished he could be as confident as his friend.

He had seen many towns crumble under such pressures. But he had seen just as many come together and fight off whatever threatened them. Trammel would not have to lead a posse after them. Laramie just might have enough hotheads to give it a go on their own. It was tough to predict how a man might react when he feared for his life, so Mahaffey decided not to waste time worrying about it.

He caught the men beginning to divide the ammunition between them and shouted, "Anyone who took anything had better put it back. Let Earnshaw count it first. I want to know how much we've got. This isn't over until Ben is with us. I don't want to be caught short again. That means you boys'll have to be more careful with your shots next time."

The outlaws began to reluctantly place the boxes they had taken back on the blanket.

Earnshaw kept his voice low as he said to Mahaffey, "I thought we were going to sit up on the town and shoot at them from a distance in the morning."

"And I thought grabbing Brandt would've been enough to get Ben free," Mahaffey said. "Looks like we can't count much on reason when it comes to Laramie, so you'd best get busy counting cartridges."

Earnshaw finished his coffee before settling beside the blanket to take store of what they had stolen.

Mahaffey looked out in the direction of Laramie, though he knew he was too far away to see the town from where he was. He wondered what Buck Trammel was doing just then. Wondered how he was preparing the town for the coming day. Wondered if he was even considering letting Ben Washington go and if the town might force his hand to do so.

Trammel was boxed in and knew it. Outlaws on the outskirts and frightened townspeople at his door. Would his pride make him hold on to Ben despite what it might cost him? Would he continue to play it smart and hold on to Washington until the last man stood? How much was he willing to pay to keep Ben as his prisoner, considering he had already lost so much already?

Mahaffey did not know the answers but imagined he would find out come sunrise.

CHAPTER 27

As the sun began to rise over Laramie the next morning, Leo Brandt felt the pangs of panic surge through him. Not over what Mahaffey and his men might do next, but over what Buck Trammel had said he was about to do.

Trammel might have been half a foot taller and fifty pounds heavier, but Brandt blocked the sheriff's path to keep him from leaving his office.

The sheriff loomed over him. His lantern jaw was set on edge. "Get out of the way before you get hurt, Brandt."

But Brandt would not move. "I can't let you do this, Trammel. It's not legal and it's not right."

He was surprised to see Mayor Holm rise from his chair and stand beside Trammel. "Legal? We're well beyond the boundaries of the law right now, Deputy. This town's got a knife at its throat and the sheriff's proposition is the only hope we have. It's the one way I can see that has even the slightest chance of stopping another attack from Mahaffey and his men."

Brandt put all of his weight against the door. "But Washington isn't your prisoner. He's mine and I can't allow him to be treated like this. Keep a gun on him. Shoot him if they storm the jail, but what you're talking about doing is just plain wrong."

He watched Trammel ball his large hands into fists at his sides. "They've already hit us twice in one night. We've lost good men the people liked. I can't fight the town and Mahaffey at the same time. I don't have the men, and I don't have the inclination. If they want Washington free, that's what they'll get, but they'll get it my way. And it'll cost them everything if they try."

Brandt might not have known Trammel long, but he had heard plenty about him since he had arrived in Wyoming. He had seen enough since coming to Laramie to know this could not possibly be Trammel's idea. "This isn't your way, Buck. It's Hagen's way. You weren't talking like this until after Doc Carson patched him up. This is his revenge for losing his hotel, not yours."

"It's my plan," Trammel said, "and it's my town. Move."

But Brandt kept holding on to the doorknob. "What if something goes wrong? What if something happens and Washington winds up getting killed? You won't be responsible for that. I will."

Holm said, "I'm the mayor of Laramie, and I'll take full responsibility. You can tell anyone who asks that you never had a choice. I'll be happy to put that in writing if it'll make you feel any better. I'll even say that we forced you to do this. We can tell them anything you want when it's over, assuming any of us are alive afterwards. And our survival is far from a certainty, Deputy."

Brandt thought he could see the scar on Trammel's face grow redder as the sheriff struggled to continue to keep hold of his temper. "Mahaffey cleared out a lot of Kilroy's supply last night. He and his men can hunt for their food. They can stay out there for days, maybe even a week before we get any help, which we won't."

"You don't know that for certain," Brandt said. "You haven't even tried to send a wire since this started."

Holm walked away from them and went to the window. "You might as well tell him, Buck."

Trammel said, "I tried to send a wire after the fire, but the line's been cut since yesterday. The clerk at the telegraph office has just been going through the motions to keep folks from panicking. No one is coming to help us, Brandt, so we have to help ourselves. And that's exactly what I'm going to do."

The sheriff took a slow step forward and loomed over Brandt. "Are you going to move out of my way or am I going to have to move you?"

Brandt swallowed hard. He knew he did not stand much of a chance if Trammel laid into him, but he would give it whatever he had.

He lowered his hand to the pistol on his hip. "One more step and we'll both regret it."

From his spot at the window, Mayor Holm said, "No cause for that, gentlemen. Hawkeye and Blake have already gotten started."

Brandt slid out from between Trammel and the door and went to the window to look for himself.

In the hours before dawn, Trammel had ordered the thoroughfare to be turned into a veritable fortress. Wagons from every shop in town had been placed at the four intersections of each street leading to City Hall. Deputies with rifles manned each wagon. Brandt thought Trammel had been wise to order it done.

But what he saw happening down on the street was nothing short of barbaric.

A noose had been strung up from one of the charred beams that jutted out from the ruins of The Laramie Grand, forming a crude gallows. Smoke continued to rise from the charred wood as Blake and Hawkeye struggled to lead a bound Ben Washington to a horse that stood waiting beneath the noose. Someone had thought to place blinders on the mare.

He watched Adam Hagen rise from his chair beside the animal to applaud the approach of the imprisoned outlaw.

Brandt pounded the glass hard enough to crack it. "This is wrong."

"It might not be right," Holm said as he left the office. "But given our circumstances, I'm afraid it's necessary."

Brandt felt less than helpless as he watched Blake and Hawkeye force the noose around Washington's neck as Hagen began to raise it. The rope remained taut, forcing the outlaw to climb into the saddle before being strangled to death. Blake helped Hagen retie the rope against a crooked burnt beam.

Brandt did not have to turn around to know Trammel was right behind him. He could feel the heat of the sheriff's anger pass through him. "If that horse gets spooked, it'll run off and Washington's neck will snap."

"Hagen picked that horse personally from the bunch we have in our stables," Trammel said. "He won't let it get spooked. But if Mahaffey and his men try anything stupid, it'll cost their boss his life. If you've got a better idea about keeping them out of here, I'm happy to hear it."

But Brandt did not have a better idea, which was what bothered him most of all. "What are you going to do with Hank Classet? You remember him. The man you captured last night? Are you going to tie him to a stake and threaten to burn him alive unless Mahaffey and the others surrender?"

"I'm going to let him go," Trammel said. "Since Mahaffey likes messengers so much, I'm going to make Hank one of mine. I want him to tell Mahaffey what he's up against. It might buy us some time."

Brandt turned to face him. "And what happens then? He stays out there and we're trapped in here? How long do you expect to keep Washington out in the street like that? How long until you think they'll leave? You know they won't leave because it's too late for that. They held me captive for more than a day and not even I know what they'll do then."

Trammel kept looking down at the ugly scene on display in the thoroughfare. "It takes as long as it takes. But they'll know what coming in here again will cost them, which is all I want."

Brandt tried to step around Trammel to leave, but the sheriff blocked his way. "Let's get one thing straight, Deputy. Washington's not your responsibility anymore. He's mine."

He watched Trammel dig a piece of paper out of his pocket and handed it to him. "That's one of the last wires that came in to town before the wire was cut. I let the folks back in Washington know what happened to Rollins. They named me acting U.S. Marshal for the territory. I didn't mention it before because so much was happening at once. So, whatever happens to Ben Washington is my responsibility, not yours. I can live with it if his death saves a single life in this town."

Brandt read the telegram, but the words had no effect on him about what he thought of what was happening down on the street. He balled up the telegram and tossed it aside as he tried to leave again.

And once more, Trammel blocked his way. "You don't have to like what I'm doing here, but you *will* obey my orders. And if you ever threaten to go for your gun again, I'll see to it you regret it."

Brandt pushed past him. "That goes for both of us."

Trammel led Hank Classet from his cell by the back of the neck. Doc Carson opened the side door to the court-yard, where many cots were still occupied by the wounded from the previous day's fire and last night's shootings.

Classet raised his hands to his nose to cover the stench. "We had nothing to do with what happened to these people."

Trammel kept him moving. "You'd be dead if I thought otherwise. The LeBlanc boys rode with you last night, didn't they?"

"Maybe they did and maybe they didn't," Classet said. "That beating you threw me has made me forgetful."

Trammel clipped him on the back of the head. The sound caught Emily's attention while she tended to one of the wounded. The glare she shot him made him regret it.

He kept Classet moving. "I asked you a question. The LeBlancs are with you, aren't they?"

"Three of them, and that's all I'm gonna tell you," Classet admitted as Trammel pushed him out onto the thoroughfare.

The prisoner stopped cold when he saw Ben Wash-ington sitting atop a horse beside the ruined hotel. He squinted when he saw the noose around his leader's neck.

"Ben?" Classet called out to the prisoner. "What have they done to you?"

Trammel gripped Classet by the collar and forced him away from Emily's line of sight. "When Mahaffey finds you, and I'm sure he will, tell him what you saw here today. Tell him that horse Washington's on is jumpy, so if a dog so much as barks anywhere near it or a fly bites its tail, that old mare will bolt like a colt and your boss will be dead a second later. Tell Mahaffey he's lost. Tell him to ride off and never bother this town again. Tell him if he does that, I won't come looking for him, but if he doesn't, he'll be sorry."

Trammel shoved Classet out into the street. "Get walking."

Classet staggered but turned to raise his shackled hands. "Ain't you gonna take these off first?"

"Let Mahaffey take them off for you." Trammel placed a hand on the butt of the Peacemaker holstered under his left shoulder. "Keep going before I change my mind."

Classet lowered his hands as he took off at a run and shouted over to Washington, "Don't worry about nothing, Ben. George will find a way to get you out of this."

Trammel pointed at Hawkeye, who was standing watch beside Hagen and Ben Washington. "Make sure he doesn't get lost on his way out of town. Then come right back."

As he watched Hawkeye jog over to take Classet by the arm, Trammel wondered if he was doing the right thing by letting the outlaw go. He did not know if giving Mahaffey yet another gun to use against him was smart, but Trammel had to stop any more bloodshed in town. He did not think his men could take it and knew the citizens of Laramie certainly could not.

Using Washington as a shield was the only way he could see to save the town, not only from the gang but from itself.

Only time would tell if he had made the right decision. Until then, all he could do was wait until Mahaffey made his next move.

* * *

Mahaffey had not been angry since Washington's capture until that moment. But seeing his leader being treated so poorly galled him something awful.

"Hank wasn't exaggerating," he said as he lowered his field glasses and handed them over to Earnshaw. "They've got Ben hung up there like they were fixing to butcher a dead deer."

Earnshaw took the glasses and looked for himself. "That old mare looks about ready for the glue pot. Ben's as good as dead if a horsefly so much as bites that horse's hindquarters. That's just got to be for show. Not even Trammel would think of keeping him out there long."

Mahaffey saw it differently. "Don't be so sure. He's afraid we'll come riding back into town. Keeping him trussed up like that is a good way to make us think twice about it."

Earnshaw slid away from the rock and so did Mahaffey. "What are we going to do about it? The boys won't stand for this. It'll be hard for us to hold them down now."

"I'm not looking to hold them down." Mahaffey began to walk back to the others. "I'm looking to turn them loose, but my way."

He found the men standing by their horses, watching him return from looking over Laramie. Each of them had a grim look in his eye, especially Hank. The men had found a way to break the chain, but the manacles on his wrists remained.

Mahaffey leveled with them. "I'm not going to try to put a shine on it, boys. Ben's facing a dire situation. Trammel has moved wagons to block the streets to City Hall. That's where he's got Ben staked out on an old mare, with a noose around his neck. He's got deputies with rifles guarding each wagon. This won't be easy."

Dib Bishop spoke up. "You're sure it's a mare? A dappled gray one with a short mane?"

"That sounds like the one," Mahaffey said. "She a friend of yours?"

His attempt at dark humor was lost on the boy. "That sounds like the same one Trammel stuck me in the stall with. She's real jumpy, fellas. She kept me up half the night. We've got to get Ben away from her now."

"Gee, why didn't any of us think of that?" Rick LeBlanc said.

That was just the kind of talk Mahaffey wanted to avoid. "You and your brother have helped us enough, LeBlanc. Saving Ben is our business, not yours. No one will think poorly of you if you and Bart decide to ride on and leave this to us."

"His name is Burt," Rick said. "And as the old saying goes, *'À cœur vaillant rien d'impossible.'* " Rick quickly translated from French to English, "To a valiant heart, nothing is impossible."

"I'll take it that means you boys are in." He looked at the others. He did not have to give any caution to the men who had ridden with him for so long against so much danger over the years. "The rest of you already know what we're up against. Hank was right about Ben. If we go charging in there like we did last night, he's as good as dead. But we can't just let him stay like that, so here's what I think we ought to do. Trammel has those wagons blocking off all the streets leading to City Hall. But he's also got all of his deputies manning those wagons, so at least we know where they are. We're going to use that against him."

"How?" Tim asked.

"By sticking to the same plan we've had since the beginning, just making it smaller." Mahaffey asked Rick LeBlanc, "How about you draw the town again for us? It'll help the boys know what I'm saying if they can see what I'm talking about."

LeBlanc picked up a stick and redrew Laramie in the dirt just as he had done before the raid the previous night. He even added an "X" to show the exact location where City Hall stood.

Mahaffey took the stick from him and carved twelve lines around the perimeter of the town. "If that looks like a clock, that's because it is. There are twelve numbers around a clock and there are eleven of us. We're going to spread ourselves out around the twelve points surrounding town and take shots from enough of a distance so we can get away if they take a run at us. Aim at people, businesses, anything you think that might set folks running."

Dib Bishop looked down at the scratches in the dirt. "From how far away?"

"A hundred yards wherever we can. That'll put us well within the range of our Winchesters and give us enough time to ride off when Trammel's men come after us."

He traced the movement with his stick in a clockwise position. "Each man will stay on his horse so he can shoot, ride away, and move to the next spot to his left where he fires again. One shot per man from each location. Eleven rounds in all."

Coleman was not pleased by what he saw. "That's not much of a plan, George. Trammel and his deputies are bound to be on us after the second shot, maybe the third." He pointed at the positions closest to City Hall. "They'll go after anyone who's stuck down there as sure as anything."

Dietrich added, "And that's where they've got Ben.

Trammel told Hank that horse will bolt if we start shooting and Dib agrees with him."

But Mahaffey had already taken that into account. "Trammel's been awfully cautious this whole time. He didn't come after us when we grabbed Brandt and I figure he won't risk it now. Not at first. He'll keep his men close at City Hall behind all of those wagons he's set up. That'll make them sitting targets for us for at least two shots, maybe as many as three before the shots they hear from us elsewhere bring at least a few of them running. The time we spend riding off and changing positions will make them think the threat is over. When they come out again, either to run for City Hall or another kind of cover, we'll hit them again. Once we have them whittled down to size, that's when we go in to get Ben."

Hank Classet picked up another stick and stuck it in the ground in front of where City Hall was supposed to be. "It's Ben I'm still worried about. He's liable to be the first to die before any of Trammel's men."

Mahaffey used his boot to erase the seventh spot on the circle. "That's why I'll be right there the entire time. The spot closest to Ben."

Rick LeBlanc looked over Mahaffey's shoulder. "There's a warehouse right there with a loft that gives you a good view of the street. If Trammel doesn't put a man up there, it'll give you an advantage."

Mahaffey said, "Then that's where I'll be keeping an eye on things while you boys shoot, ride to the next spot, shoot, and keep moving. Since it's closest to Ben, I won't shoot unless I have to. Trammel will hear the shots from all over town. He'll be torn between saving his people or keeping an eye on Ben."

He tossed the stick in the fire as he stood up. "If Trammel didn't have those wagons blocking the streets, maybe

I'd think different. I don't know what he'll do or when he'll do it, so we're gonna have to be ready to change things up as we go along. And yeah, this might get Ben killed anyway, but he'd rather die because of us than by a judge. Any man think different?"

He looked at each of the men for an objection, but none offered one.

"That's good. Just make sure your rifles are loaded and your pistols are ready. I want us mounted and riding in a few minutes."

Mahaffey kicked dirt on the fire as the men went to their horses and Earnshaw remained behind. "Splitting us up all over town isn't a good idea, George. It makes us easier to be picked off that way."

"It's already settled, Roy. If you had a better idea, you should've spoke up."

"I didn't want to sound like I was arguing with you in front of the others. We can take them on if we charge straight at them. They're boxed in behind those wagons. We can use that against them like we did outside Dodge City."

Mahaffey shoved him to be quiet. "And that's exactly what I plan on doing here after we soften them up with a few volleys first. I want Trammel's deputies rattled before we hit them. Our boys will be less likely to lose heart that way when the real fight comes. I'm counting on you, Roy. Can I count on you?"

"You always have before. No reason to stop now."

Mahaffey checked the remnants of the fire and was glad he did not see any burning embers. "Then let's get these men in position. There's lots to do."

CHAPTER 28

After telling Mayor Holm the latest about Hank Classet's release, Trammel took his rifle with him as he walked down the steps of City Hall to check on Hagen and Washington out in the thoroughfare. It had been more than an hour since they had released Hank and he was sure Mahaffey was bound to give them his answer at any moment.

Trammel found Hagen was sitting on a chair with the mare's reins tied to the chair leg. "How's your limp?"

"Sitting helps." Hagen looked up from the book he had been reading. "I've been keeping my mind on other things by reading to my new friend Ben here. He keeps telling me all the ways he's going to make me pay for what we're doing to him, and I keep reading to him from this anatomy book I took from Doc Carson's office. He doesn't seem to have much interest in hearing the part about *rigor mortis* and the wonders of what happens to the human body after death. Did you know that it only takes three weeks for a corpse to decompose? Depending on the climate, of course. I would've thought it would take longer, though I must admit that I've never stayed around long enough to see the process for myself."

Ben Washington strained against the rope around his neck. "I shouldn't have to listen to this nonsense."

Hagen tapped the reins of the horse with his foot, causing the animal to take a step forward. "Now, now," Hagen cautioned. "There's no call for being rude."

Trammel placed his hand on the mare's muzzle and pushed it backward. "See any sign of Ben's friends out there?"

"Can't say that I have," Hagen told him. "But I'm sure they've seen their leader staked out like a fatted calf. I expect them to think a long while before they take another run at us."

"Just keep your eyes on the horizon instead of in that book. There's no telling what Mahaffey might do next."

Ben Washington looked down at them from the back of the wagon. "I'll tell you what they'll do. They'll take their time figuring a way of how they're gonna get me out of this mess. They'll set up one of my men to shoot out this rope and, when they do, I'll dig my heels into this mare and ride off. It'll knock this chattering idiot plumb out of his chair, but he won't mind none seeing as how he'll be dead a second later when the next bullet lays him out flat." He threw a wink at Trammel. "That's when the fun really begins."

Trammel said, "That sharpshooter you're counting on for all this fancy shooting wouldn't happen to be named Marcum, would it?"

Washington looked away from him. His face did not betray the slightest emotion.

Trammel continued, "Sorry we have to tell you like this, but we've been too busy around here to let you know the latest. Marcum is dead. Lefty Rollins killed him. There's only one way this ends and it's with you swinging at the end of a rope. If not today, then after a judge passes

sentence on you. I hope you got a good look at Hank
Classet before he left because he's the last of your old
gang you'll ever see alive."

Trammel let go of the horse and, as he walked away,
told Hagen, "You send word for me if you see any trouble
coming."

"I'll be sure to send up a shot." He grinned up at Washington. "That'll be fun."

Mahaffey had always had a knack for being able to
judge distances fairly well, which came in handy now.

He led the men to the various spots from where he
wanted them to begin shooting around town and told
them where to set up. And since Rick LeBlanc was the
most familiar with the layout of the town, he told the men
where to shoot from and what feature to look out for when
they rotated to their next spot on the circle.

Dib was at the ninth spot and Coleman was at the tenth.
Mahaffey put Tim at the eleventh spot and Burt LeBlanc
at the farthest from the action at twelfth. The younger man
seemed the least capable of his men, so he wanted him to
start somewhere slow.

Mahaffey placed Dietrich at one o'clock, Hank Classet
at the second; Barrett at the third with Coombs at the
fourth position.

By the time they had finished placing all of the men in
a rough circle around Laramie, only Mahaffey, Earnshaw,
and Rick LeBlanc were left.

Mahaffey had saved the most prized spot in the circle
for his trusted friend. The fifth spot on his imaginary
circle around town. "Earnshaw, this is where you'll start.
Ride a hundred yards in and you'll have a perfect view of

City Hall. When I give the signal, shoot from your horse, then ride to the back of the courtyard. You might not see much action there, but you'll get all you can handle by the time you reach me over at the seven spot. I expect the writing will be on the wall by then, so be ready to change as I need you."

Earnshaw took his rifle in hand and began to ride the hundred yards in that direction. "I'll be waiting for your signal to start shooting."

Mahaffey and Rick LeBlanc rode to LeBlanc's spot at the sixth position, which was directly behind City Hall.

LeBlanc said, "I hope you're not expecting me to waste good ammunition by shooting at a wall."

Mahaffey did not appreciate how lightly the Cajun was taking this. "I want you to shoot at anyone you see before you ride to me over on seven, LeBlanc. If you don't see anyone to shoot at, don't waste the bullet. Wait for my signal, then get moving. I'll be waiting for you over at seven."

"Where I won't be shooting either," LeBlanc said. "Because of Ben's safety."

"You'll shoot if I tell you to shoot and hold your fire if I tell you to hold it. I haven't had any trouble from you before and now's not the time to start."

"No trouble," LeBlanc said as he rode toward his position. "Just trying to get a clearer picture of what you want me to do."

Mahaffey eyed LeBlanc, watching him ride off until he stopped behind a water trough less than half a street away from the back of City Hall. Right where he was supposed to be. He only hoped the man followed orders.

Mahaffey brought his horse around and rode to the

seven spot on his circle. He knew the men would be eager to start and did not want to keep them waiting.

Rick LeBlanc was more eager to start than most. He waited until he had heard Mahaffey ride away before he decided to make a plan of his own devising. He rode farther along the street and saw two wagons had been placed at an angle like arrowheads at the end of the street leading to the courtyard that ran next to City Hall. Trammel had not placed a deputy here. He must have thought the giant gates of the courtyard would discourage anyone from striking from there.

His mistake would be LeBlanc's gain, just as Mahaffey's foolishness had presented him with an opportunity to win the day. Not for Ben Washington, but for the memory of the brothers he had lost in Laramie.

LeBlanc got down from the saddle, tied his horse to a fence post and approached the wagons at a crouch. It offered a clear shot of the thoroughfare, with the blackened ruin of The Laramie Grand looming straight ahead. He saw Ben Washington atop a gray mare. The noose around his neck was tied to a charred beam of the hotel.

He saw Adam Hagen sitting beside the horse reading a book. Even sitting down, the man had a swagger to him that set LeBlanc's teeth on edge.

He raised his rifle and judged the distance between himself and Hagen. He put it at about almost two hundred yards, maybe a bit less. He knew he was not good enough with a rifle to make the shot, but there were other, more inviting targets.

He spotted Trammel much closer as he approached a wagon guarded by a deputy with a heavy bandage over half his face. He put the distance to him at little more than a hundred yards. He could always get to Hagen later.

LeBlanc shifted his aim to Trammel and grew still. He wanted to wait until Trammel was clear before he opened fire. He did not want the big sheriff to be able to reach the safety of the wagons.

He knew the others were waiting for Mahaffey to give them a signal, but the first shot of a fight was often like the first shot while drinking at a saloon. No one remembered the first one once the fun got started.

Trammel found Blake standing on the flatbed of one of the wagons he had ordered to block the street. The man's bandages were filthy from the previous night, and he had not changed them yet.

"How are you feeling?" Trammel asked.

"Better than I have any right to be, considering. And before you ask me, I've been taking it easy on the laudanum. That stuff packs quite a punch."

Trammel leaned against the wagon and looked up the deserted street. "Town's quiet. It's usually starting to come alive this time of the morning."

"Kilroy's death last night has them worried," Blake said. "None of them want you mistaking them for looters. You'll see them making the odd run to the stores once they open up, but folks will be careful about being bunched together in one place after Washington's raid."

"Is that what they're calling it?"

"Some are. Might be a good idea for you to walk around the town a bit as soon as things start opening up. Show them you're here. Keep them from worrying too much." He nodded over at Washington. "How long you plan on keeping him out there?"

Trammel was getting tired of answering that question. "I don't know yet. Don't tell me you're worried about Washington's health."

"Not Washington's," Blake said. "It's that mare I'm worried about. It's not good for an animal that old to stand still for too long. It's hard on her joints. And all that smoke is bad for her lungs. If you don't change her out of there regularly, she's bound to get pneumonia. That's as good as a death sentence for an animal."

Trammel had not thought of that. He had never been much of a horseman, but Hagen was. He should have mentioned it. "I'll talk to Old Bob and have him bring out a fresh horse from the stables every so often."

The sheriff scratched at the scar on his face. The next topic would be tricky. "How are the rest of the men doing? After yesterday, I mean. Over what happened before the fire."

Blake looked like he was enjoying watching the sheriff struggle. "You mean when they left after you and me growled at each other like a couple of wolves over a carcass?"

"Yeah. That part."

"They know their duty as well as I do, Sheriff. I didn't ask any of them to come with me when Hawkeye found us at the livery. I didn't have to ask them to stay afterwards, either, and that was before Hawkeye gave me your star. But now's not the time to talk about all that." He pointed at the bandages wrapped around half of his head and face. "A lot has changed since then."

"And some things haven't. The job's still yours if you want it. The folks back in Washington want me to take Lefty Rollins' place for the time being."

Blake's remaining eye narrowed. "I'd be inclined to

congratulate you, but I know you didn't want to get the job. Not like that."

Trammel was glad some things could remain unsaid. "Just keep it to yourself for now. I haven't gotten around to telling too many people about it. Emily knows. So do Hagen and Brandt. Now, you know it, too."

"Kind of surprised you told me at all, seeing as how we almost killed each other yesterday."

Trammel grinned. "Like you just said, a lot's happened since then."

He saw Hawkeye beginning to wave to him from behind a wagon on the other side of the thoroughfare. "I'd better go see what he wants. Keep your eyes open and let me know if you spot any trouble brewing."

Trammel only got a few steps away from the wagon when a bullet struck the ground at his feet.

The sheriff dove under Blake's wagon as another bullet struck just above him. He used his elbows to crawl beneath the axel through to the other side, where Blake helped him get to his feet.

"Looks like the Washington Gang is ready for another go," the deputy said. "Those shots came from the far end of the street by the courtyard."

Trammel feared for his wife, who was still in the court-yard tending to the sick and wounded from the previous day's fire. But she had a thick gate to protect her. He had to think of his men first.

He looked around to see if his deputies had moved behind the wagons for cover and was glad to see that each of them had. Hagen was squatting among the wreckage of his hotel beside Washington and the horse.

The sound of more rifle shots and screams began to reach him from other parts of town. Trammel may not have had the benefits of Hagen's West Point training, but even he knew what they were facing.

"Looks like they've got us surrounded." The flaw in his strategy was clear to him now. "And I've got us all bunched up here like ducks on a pond."

Blake took a quick glance over the top of the wagon. "They can't all have Sharps rifles, so they're already inside the town. What do you want me to do, boss?"

Trammel could only think of one thing that might give them a chance. "Have everyone get into the wagons. It'll give Mahaffey's men fewer targets to hit."

Blake opened the flatbed. "Where will you be?"

Trammel moved out toward the unguarded wagons near the courtyard. "Improving our chances."

CHAPTER 29

Mahaffey had not gotten into position yet when the men started firing. Someone had gotten nervous and opened up too early. He had wanted to get an idea of where Trammel's men in the street were so he could direct their fire as they rotated around the town. Everything had begun to fall apart before he was even in place.

And given the direction from where the first shot had come, he knew who was to blame. Rick LeBlanc. He knew he should have run off the hothead and his brothers when they first showed up in his camp. He would rather take the town with several good men instead of one he could not fully trust.

But it was too late for that now. If his plan was doomed to fail, all he could do was help it along.

He looked out at the thoroughfare and saw Ben was still atop the horse with the noose around his neck. Mahaffey slid his rifle from the scabbard on the saddle and took aim. A man was crouching among the ruins of the hotel. Only the top of his hat was visible.

He looked at the other wagons blocking the streets and saw all the other deputies had moved into the wagons for cover. *Smart.*

Mahaffey got off his horse and ran a few steps closer before dropping to a knee. A deputy had taken cover behind a wagon between Mahaffey's position and Washington. Mahaffey knew he would betray his position after he fired, so he took careful aim. His shot would bring the attention of every deputy, which meant Mahaffey would have to act fast.

As a second round of rifle shots rang out from other parts of town, Mahaffey fired at the deputy in the back of the closest wagon. The deputy fell back as Mahaffey levered in a second shot and hit him again, this time in the chest. The wounded deputy cried out as his comrades began shooting in Mahaffey's direction.

Mahaffey moved toward the cover of a nearby water trough as bullets rained down on the place where he had been kneeling only a moment before.

Water jumped as the shots from the deputies peppered the wooden trough. He knew he had been right not to lead a charge against them. These men could shoot.

He dropped to his stomach and crawled between the trough and the boardwalk as the sound of the shots faded.

He saw a young deputy running toward the wagon Mahaffey had just fired upon.

Mahaffey aimed quickly and fired, striking the young man in the right shoulder. The impact of the bullet was not enough to stop him from leaping into the back of the wagon to check on his friend.

More bullets struck the trough and the building behind him. Mahaffey ducked for cover again and looked through the windows. It was the warehouse LeBlanc had mentioned back in camp. He saw crates and boxes stacked inside.

When the shooting from the thoroughfare stopped once more, Mahaffey got up and bolted to the side of the building, looking for a way inside. He got around back, hoping to see Earnshaw or Blake riding toward him, but no one came. He found a back door was locked, put his shoulder into it, and popped it open. He found a ladder leading up to a loft to his right and began to quickly climb it as another round of rifle shot rang out through town. At least some of his men had followed his orders. He imagined they would begin to bunch up at LeBlanc's six o'clock position and would be drawn into whatever fighting was bound to be happening there.

He reached the loft and found a gaping frame that faced the thoroughfare. It was a perfect vantage point from where he could rain shots down onto the deputies. Their wagons would soon serve as their coffins.

From his spot in the wagon next to Blake, Leo Brandt saw Trammel run down the street as the gunman beside the courtyard took another shot at him.

Brandt caught a glimpse of the clean-shaven man and, since he did not recognize him as one of Mahaffey's men, knew he must be one of the LeBlanc brothers.

From one wagon over, Blake returned fire at LeBlanc, who easily ducked back behind the cover of the wagon. Brandt watched a rider about a hundred yards in the distance draw rein to a halt behind LeBlanc and recognized him as Earnshaw.

Brandt's face still ached from the blow from the outlaw's rifle butt the day before.

"We've got another one coming in!" Brandt called out to Blake.

Blake responded by shooting at the rider, causing him to drop awkwardly from his horse. And judging by the way he moved, it was clear Blake's shot had missed its mark.

Leo looked for LeBlanc, but there was no sign of him.

Was he still behind the wagons or had he seen Trammel trying to move around him?

Brandt took a shot at the last place he had seen LeBlanc and watched the ground for any movement. A flinch. Dirt kicked up from shuffling feet beneath the wagon.

He saw nothing besides splinters of wood flying up into the air.

LeBlanc must have moved behind the building, which meant Trammel was about to run into two guns instead of one. Brandt knew he could not let that happen.

Brandt leapt out of the wagon as a bullet slammed into it from the street in front of him. He dropped to a knee and saw a rider at the far end of the street moving to the right.

Brandt rushed his shot, trying to hit his target before the rider got away. He heard the horse scream and knew his bullet must have hit the animal instead of the human.

"Get back in the wagon!" Blake shouted at him. "That's an order."

But Brandt knew Trammel was still in trouble and continued to run toward the building at the corner. He crouched to peer under the wagons to see if LeBlanc or Earnshaw was there. He saw the long shadow of a man from behind the trough before it began to move. That would be Earnshaw.

Brandt dropped to his belly and brought his rifle up to his shoulder. More rifle fire sounded from all over town once more as Earnshaw moved out from behind the trough and ran toward the wagons blocking the street.

He heard Blake shooting at him, but Earnshaw kept on.

Brandt held his fire until Earnshaw stopped behind the wagon and peered over the top of it. Brandt's first shot struck him in the left shin, knocking his left leg out from under him. Earnshaw hit the ground, clutching his shattered leg.

The outlaw looked out from under the wagon and locked eyes with Brandt just before the deputy marshal's next shot was the last thing Earnshaw saw in this world.

Trammel was already in the alley when he saw the rider slow to a stop and drop from his horse. From where he was, the sheriff had no way of knowing if Blake had brought him down or if he had managed to reach safety. He did not know if Rick LeBlanc and the new man had opened fire on his men. He only knew they were still out there, and the lives of his deputies were at risk. Emily was behind the thick iron gates of the courtyard, so he knew she was relatively safe.

Trammel paused at the mouth of the alley to hear what was happening outside. Two shots close by, then the sound of boots running away on the packed dirt.

Trammel raised his rifle to his shoulder as he came out of the alley. He saw LeBlanc leaping over a dead man on the ground behind the wagons. One of his men fired as the fleeing gunman reached the safety of the stone wall of the City Hall courtyard.

LeBlanc was out of range for his deputies, but Trammel knew he still had a shot at him. His aim was spoiled when a bullet struck the building behind his head.

Trammel hit the ground in time to see one of Mahaffey's bearded riders racing toward him along the path a hundred yards away.

Before Trammel could take aim, another shot hit the dirt an inch from his head, throwing dirt into his eyes. Trammel fired blind as he began to scramble backward toward the safety of the alley.

He desperately wiped his eyes as he heard two sets of hooves pounding away from him. By the time his vision cleared enough for him to see, he found Brandt crouched beside one of the wagons blocking the street.

"You hit?" Brandt called out to him.

"Not yet. You?"

"Not yet. Mahaffey's got them moving around us in a circle like clockwork. If we wait for them here, we should be able to pick them off one by one as they come by."

Trammel doubted the outlaws would make it that easy for his men. "They'll catch on if they haven't already." He looked down at the dead man beside the wagon. "You recognize this one?"

"That's Earnshaw, Mahaffey's right hand. I took care of him. Coombs and the guy you chased off rode out around to the right before I could stop them. I think they're headed for that warehouse at the end of the street."

Trammel looked over the top of the wagon and saw his men scrambling on the far side of the thoroughfare near the ruined hotel.

Hagen was still crouched by Ben Washington's horse as the gambler yelled out to the deputies, "He's in the loft! Get under the wagons!"

Trammel did not understand why Hagen was yelling until he saw a rifle blast from the hayloft of the warehouse. One of Mahaffey's men must've gotten up there for a better angle to shoot down into the wagons. *But why hadn't Washington's horse run away yet?*

Trammel called out to Blake. "I need you over here to help Brandt cover this side. Shoot any man you see riding this way."

Blake dropped over the side of the wagon and ran to Trammel at a crouch. "One of them worked his way up into that loft over at the warehouse. We're gonna have a hell of a time getting him out of there."

Trammel ignored him as he looked over the scene. His

men were trapped beneath their wagons. They could not return fire if the Washington gang decided to close up on the town. The warehouse was at an angle that provided whoever was up there with a sweeping view of the thoroughfare. Unless his deputies remained flush against the wagons, they risked being picked off by whoever was up in the loft.

And with Coombs and LeBlanc riding in that direction, whoever was up there was about to get two more guns to help him butcher his deputies.

All of Trammel's deputies were on one side of the street. Trammel was the only one who had any hope of getting close enough to the warehouse without being seen.

He stayed flat against the wall as he began to move along the long shadow cast by the courtyard wall. He had to reach that warehouse quickly before more of his men got hurt.

The fire in Hawkeye's shoulder burned bright as he kept himself as flat as he could against the back wall of the wagon. The dead eyes of Deputy James Brillheart lingering on him did little to ease his nerves.

He was the only man in the thoroughfare with a clean shot straight up at the hayloft, but he could not raise his rifle or even his pistol. His right arm was dead against his side. Each time he chanced a look at Mr. Hagen crouched beside Washington's horse, he gestured for him to stay low.

He did not think he had been spotted by the man in the loft until the gunman said, "I guess this brat I've got pinned down here means something to you, doesn't he? He yours?"

"He's on my payroll just like all the others," Hagen

shouted back. "Which one of Ben's mutts are you? You wouldn't happen to be Mahaffey, would you?"

From his seat atop the horse, Ben Washington said, "Don't tell him anything, boys. Just get me out of here."

Hawkeye listened as Hagen continued to goad Mahaffey. "Here I am, taking bets on how tough the Washington Gang is supposed to be and you haven't hit anything you've shot at yet."

"Ask the dead fella in the wagon how good I shoot," the man in the loft yelled back. "I hope you're patient, because from what I see, you'll have a long wait for an answer."

Hawkeye saw Deputy Bush pop out from behind his wagon and fire a few shots up at the hayloft before moving back behind the wagon.

His effort was greeted by a laugh from the shooter. "Looks like these boys didn't listen to you about staying under those wagons. Won't matter. I'll plug them all anyway. That is, unless you're ready to turn Ben loose. Then we can all go about our business like none of this ever happened."

Hawkeye watched Hagen pat the neck of Washington's horse. "He's not going anywhere except at the end of this rope. And the longer this goes, the more inclined I am to smack this horse on the rump and send her back to the stables."

Hawkeye heard something else while Hagen and Mahaffey were barking at each other. Two horses had been riding hard somewhere behind him but stopped behind the warehouse. And since all of his fellow deputies were accounted for, Hawkeye knew they had to be Mahaffey's men.

He heard the men call to Mahaffey as they went inside the warehouse. "Don't shoot, George. It's Coombs and LeBlanc. Where do you want us?"

Hawkeye sagged against the wall. They were up against George Mahaffey himself.

"One of you watch the back while the other moves to the front door," Mahaffey yelled down to them. "They're working up to something, so be ready."

With Mahaffey distracted, Hawkeye knew this was his best chance to move. He grabbed his pistol in his left hand and used all of his remaining strength to fight through the pain as he lunged forward. He dove over Brillheart's corpse and spilled out of the back of the wagon. A bullet ricocheted somewhere above him as Hawkeye crawled beneath it. It was not the best position for him, but at least now he could see what was happening and could call out to the others what he saw.

He heard the front door of the warehouse bang open and could just make out the shape of a rifle barrel to the side of it.

"Morning, Hagen!" the gunman yelled. "I told you I'd be back."

"So, you did," Hagen answered. "Looks like you're still hiding behind something instead of having the sand to face me head on, Rick. Yesterday, you hid behind Rube in the alley. Today, you're cowering behind a door. How about you come out and settle this between us?"

"I'll be glad to oblige right after you let Washington go. We won't want that horse to get spooked in the cross fire, would we?"

"I'd be more worried about your nerves than about this horse if I were you, LeBlanc. This won't end well for you and your friends."

Hawkeye could not lie there, this close to their enemies, and continue to do nothing. His right arm might not be useful, but his left felt fine. He had good cover and could get off at least a couple of shots from here that might end this standoff.

He flopped over onto his stomach and raised his pistol to the left of the front door where he knew LeBlanc was standing. He fired three shots through the wall, which were quickly answered by several more that punched through the wooden slats of the flatbed above him.

The air filled with gunfire as Hagen and the deputies began to pepper the warehouse with a withering volley of bullets.

When the shots from above stopped, Hawkeye pushed himself out from under the back of the wagon. He kept his head low as he dashed to the next wagon behind him while Deputy Bush finished firing up at the hayloft. He grabbed Hawkeye and eased him down beneath the open tailgate.

Bush ducked as he began to reload his Winchester. "How bad are you hit?"

Other than knowing his right arm was useless, Hawkeye had not bothered taking his own condition into account. "Brillheart's dead."

"I figured. That shoulder of yours looks pretty bad."

Hawkeye left his pistol on the ground and felt at his wound with his left hand. "Doesn't seem to be much blood, but it hurts something awful. I can't move it, either."

"Think you're well enough to make it around to the other side on your own? Doc Carson and Doc Emily are still in the courtyard with the wounded. They'll see to you if you can get there. I'll give you all the cover I can from here."

Hawkeye grabbed Bush's arm before he could raise his rifle. "Don't waste the bullets until you have something to shoot at. They're not shooting back at us, are they?"

"No, they're not," Bush replied. "I wonder why. Think we got them just now?"

Both deputies got their answer when they heard the familiar sound of horses riding away.

Bush called out to the others, "They're running out the back. I'm going after them."

The deputy rose to give chase as Hagen called out, "Stay where you are, Bush. They want us to go after them. I need you covering our flank."

Bush reluctantly moved back behind the wagon. "Hawkeye's hit. He needs help."

Hagen said, "Can he walk?"

Bush helped ease Hawkeye up on his feet. "Barely."

"You'd best have Doc Carson look at that wound. Get going while it's quiet."

Hawkeye began to break for the courtyard when he saw Trammel running toward him. Trammel met him halfway and helped him the rest of the way.

The sheriff checked both sides of Hawkeye's shirt. "Looks like the bullet passed through you."

"Feels like it did, but I can't move my arm." For the first time since the shooting had started, he felt panic begin to creep into his belly. "I'm scared, boss."

"It'll take more than a little scratch like that to take you out of this fight. Keep moving. The two of us are mighty inviting targets out here."

Trammel led Hawkeye around the corner, past the wagons where Blake and Brandt were keeping an eye on the side street.

"That's the spirit, Hawkeye." Blake encouraged him. "You did fine back there."

Hawkeye did not share his friend's enthusiasm. "Brillheart's dead. The fella in the hayloft got him."

"I know," Trammel said. "And there was nothing you could do about that. Did I hear you right about them riding away from the warehouse just now?"

"They rode out the same way they came in." Hawkeye winced from the pain in his arm. "They didn't come our way, so I think they worked their way back behind City Hall. Bush wanted to chase after them on foot, but Mr. Hagen said no."

"I said no," Trammel told him as they rounded the corner. "I told him as much when he looked at me before he told you."

Trammel stopped when they reached the courtyard gate and pounded on the iron door. "This is Trammel. Open up. Hawkeye's been hit and needs attention."

The lock slid open and Old Bob stepped aside to let them in.

"Take good care of him, Bob," Trammel told the guard. "His right shoulder's pretty bad."

Emily rushed to Hawkeye's side. Her eyes were wide and full of worry. "We've been hearing the shots all morning. Is anyone else hurt out there?"

"Brillheart's dead," Hawkeye said. "I couldn't save him."

"This is no time for that type of talk," Emily told him. "Let's get you patched up."

And as Old Bob led Hawkeye to an empty cot among the other wounded still in the courtyard, Hawkeye saw Emily mouth the words "I love you" to Trammel.

Hawkeye did not see if the sheriff had replied in kind. Buck Trammel was not known to be a sentimental man.

CHAPTER 30

Mahaffey slowed his horse when he realized none of the deputies had ridden after them. LeBlanc and Coombs slowed as well.

"That was a close one, boss," Coombs said as he rode alongside him. "I didn't think they'd open up on us like that."

"They were giving cover to that boy who dove out of the wagon." But Mahaffey was puzzled by something else. Something that should have happened but had not.

He said to Coombs, "You were the last one in there when they started shooting. Did you see if Ben was still on the horse?"

"You mean before I had to crawl out of there on my belly?" Coombs asked. "Yeah, I saw him. He was still sitting on it last I saw."

That bothered Mahaffey. "They told Hank that the horse would bolt at the first shot, but it didn't. It just stood there the whole time."

Coombs said, "I saw its reins wrapped around a chair. Maybe it's a tame animal. It looked kind of old to me."

"That chair wouldn't have been enough to stop her from bolting, and I never saw a horse that didn't buck a little at the sound of gunfire. Even at the end of the war, they never got used to it."

LeBlanc said, "There could be a hundred reasons why the horse didn't move, and I don't care about a single one of them. I've still got a brother out there and you've got the rest of your gang to worry about. Start thinking about what you're going to do about them."

But Mahaffey had already begun to think about that when he was still up in the hayloft. He asked LeBlanc, "How was the six o'clock spot when you left it?"

"Earnshaw's dead," LeBlanc said. "Coombs came riding by when I was pinned down by the courtyard and got me out. I spotted two deputies there when I was at the front door of that warehouse."

News of Earnshaw's death hit Mahaffey hard, but there would be plenty of time to mourn his loss later. He still had the rest of his men—and Ben Washington—to save.

"Coombs, I'll need you to keep those two deputies pinned down while LeBlanc and I make a break for it. When you're done, join us at the edge of town. I'll gather the others and we'll find a place to hit them."

"That's crazy talk, Mahaffey," LeBlanc said. "Every one of those streets is a straight line. They'll shoot us like fish in a barrel if we go at them that way."

"I didn't say we were mounting a charge," Mahaffey snapped back. "I've lost all the men I plan on losing today. We'll come at them smart. Follow me."

Coombs raced ahead of them as Mahaffey loosened up on his reins. He said to LeBlanc, "I hope you can ride as good as you argue because you're going to need it."

LeBlanc dug his heels into his mount, racing off at a gallop as Mahaffey followed.

Coombs began shooting somewhere off to their left as both riders raced by, low across their saddles.

Mahaffey looked behind him as they rode clear and saw Coombs coming on quick. Two bullets in him and he was still riding strong.

But Mahaffey saw his luck run out when Coombs jerked upright, followed by two rifle blasts from behind the wagons. He continued on that way for a few more yards until he sagged and dropped to the ground.

Mahaffey turned his attention to the road ahead. Barrett and the others were still alive in front of him. And they still had a job to do.

"Looks like I just bagged my first one of the day," Blake said as he checked the body in the middle of the road. "You recognize this one?"

Brandt did. "His name is Coombs. Or at least it was."

He watched Blake go to the dead man's horse and began going through his saddlebags. "What are you doing?"

"He uses a Winchester '73 same as me." Blake dug out a box of bullets and tossed them over to Brandt, who caught them. "One for you and one for me. No reason to let good bullets go to waste. We'd best get back to our wagons."

"Trammel wants us to guard the road."

"Trammel didn't see those boys run by here just now," Blake said as he walked past him. "Those boys are probably stopping anyone else from coming this way. That means they'll be hitting us from one of the side streets next, and I aim to be ready when they do. Make sure your rifle's loaded, Leo. I'd wager you're gonna have more action than you can stand in a minute."

Brandt looked back toward the courtyard in time to see Trammel heading their way, shouting, "Reload and get ready, boys. They'll be coming at us head on. I want all of you on this side of your wagons. Be ready to move where you're needed."

"Told you," Blake said to Brandt as the federal deputy jogged over to join him. "Where do you think they'll hit us, Sheriff?"

"Wish I knew, but I doubt they'll keep us waiting. There are two fewer of them than when they started. Let's tilt the odds more in our favor."

Brandt checked the street his wagons blocked and saw it was deserted, so he caught up with Trammel. "What about the prisoner? Are you still going to leave Washington out here like bait? It didn't stop them from attacking us."

Trammel ignored Brandt as he continued to walk in a straight line toward Hagen, who was busy reloading his pistols.

"I'm glad something's finally happening around here," Hagen said. "I was beginning to get bored."

The sheriff pointed at Washington's horse. "Why is he still alive? I thought you said that horse would jump at the slightest sound."

Hagen slid his pistol back in the holster on his hip, moved within an inch of the horse's ear and screamed, "Run!"

The horse continued to nose at the dirt of the thoroughfare. It did not move a muscle.

"This poor old girl is as deaf as a post," Hagen said. "You didn't really think I'd want Washington dead by accident, did you? I knew you couldn't live with yourself if he hung." He tapped the mare's blinders. "That's why I put these on her. She'll move if I tell her to, don't worry. I'll be happy to kill Washington right now if you want. You can blame it all on me. Most people do."

Brandt saw his chance to stop an accident before it

happened. He said to Trammel, "We could explain a broken neck to a judge a lot better than a bullet hole, Sheriff. And since having Washington out here hasn't stopped an attack, I think it's best if we stick him back in his cell."

Trammel said, "Still worried about getting in trouble, aren't you, Brandt? Even after all this."

"Just trying to avoid us both facing a murder charge, because if he's killed when Mahaffey comes for him, that's exactly what we'll both be looking at. Maybe every man out here."

Brandt was glad when Hagen said, "Leo's got a point. Mahaffey called our bluff. Maybe it's time to take our chips off the table while we still can."

Trammel cursed as he went over and cut the rope of the outlaw's noose. Washington gasped and sagged in the saddle as he was finally able to draw a deep, fresh breath into his lungs.

Trammel handed the mare's reins to Brandt. "Take him back to the courtyard. Old Bob is guarding the door. Have him stick Washington back to his cell and keep him there."

Brandt was relieved as he took the horse's reins and led her along the thoroughfare. "I'm glad you finally listened to reason, Sheriff."

"He's a prisoner, not a pet, Deputy. Treat him accordingly. Then get to your post. Mahaffey will be back on us any minute."

When they were a good distance away from Trammel and Hagen, Washington said, "I owe you for this, Brandt. I can owe you a lot more if you just let me go."

"Save your breath, Washington. You don't have many left."

"The same could've been said about you when my men grabbed you. Mahaffey let you go, didn't he? He could've put a bullet in your brain, and no one would've known, but he didn't. I know I would've killed you if I'd been him. How does it feel owing an outlaw your life?"

"A lot better than sitting in the cell next to you if I let you go."

"Well, since gratitude doesn't work," Washington continued, "how about survival? Trammel's men aren't up to this fight, and you know it. You've seen Mahaffey and my boys. You know what they can do. Why, they'll ride right over Trammel and his deputies like they aren't even there once they set their minds to doing it. Let me go and maybe I'll even let you ride with me. You wouldn't just be saving your own life, but Trammel's and his deputies' lives, as well."

"And Hagen's," Brandt reminded him as they rounded the corner to the courtyard. "Don't forget him."

Washington laughed. "I've got something saved up special for that sick lunatic. Give me one good reason why you should stick with Trammel anyway. Let's say you live through this. He's your boss now, isn't he? Do you really want him telling you what to do for the next few years? Rollins is dead and you don't owe Trammel anything. At least you can make some real money if you're riding with me. It's not always like this. Me and the boys live pretty well, considering."

Brandt was glad to disappoint him. "What boys? Earnshaw is dead. Coombs and Marcum, too. Trammel's been up against worse than whoever Mahaffey's still got left."

"Like who?" Washington laughed again. "Pinkertons? An aging cripple like Lucien Clay was? Trammel's got one deputy dead, one out of the fight, and another with one eye missing. Two of mine could take down five of his on their best day and Trammel doesn't have that many. But I can make sure it doesn't come to that if you just let me go.

We'll all ride out of here and leave the territory forever if you do."

Brandt had reached the door of the courtyard and was about to knock but something made him stop. He did not dare admit why.

Washington seized on his hesitation. "Now you're thinking, Leo. I know Trammel's an easy man to admire. He's tough and honest and brave. But men like us have seen more than our share of this world. We know bravery and fairness don't count for much when compared to other men's lives. Guys like Trammel always find a way to make other men die for their mistakes. You don't have to end up like all the others. Sending me back to my cell is as good as signing a death warrant for your new friends. For yourself, too. You saw what happened to Rollins. There's no reason why you have to end up the same way. You think about that. Think about it long and hard before you bang on that door."

Brandt had only been in Laramie for a short while, but he had grown to care about Trammel and his men. About Hagen and Hawkeye and the other deputies, too. He had watched them overcome an explosion and fire and injury to put up a valiant fight to save their town. He had seen them risk everything to defend Laramie. The Washington Gang had already caused so much misery and destruction. Was the chance to put Ben Washington on trial really worth more suffering and death? Was justice really worth such a high price?

In his heart, Leo Brandt knew it was not. "I can't just let you go like that. Your hands are tied behind your back and your horse is practically lame. You heard Hagen say as much."

"I can ride this old girl with both hands and legs tied

behind my back. Tell them I dug my heels into the horse, made her buck, and knocked you down. There's no one around to call you a liar. I'll ride to my men, they'll cut me loose, and we'll be gone before you know it. I'm a man of my word, just like Mahaffey showed you he was a man of his. There's no shame in protecting friends, which is exactly what you'd be doing by letting me just ride on out of here."

Brandt flinched when the iron door swung open and Old Bob peered outside. "I thought I heard someone talking out here." He reached up to take Washington by the arm and pulled him down from the horse. "Don't you worry about this one, Mr. Brandt. I know just where he belongs. You can leave that old mare where she is. She won't go anywhere."

Washington smirked at Brandt as Old Bob led him through the open door. "Don't say you never had a chance, Leo. Whatever happens from here on in is on your head, not mine."

Brandt felt like a fool as Old Bob shut the iron door, leaving him alone holding on to the reins of a deaf old mare.

But he was not sure whether he felt foolish for letting Washington go back to his cell or for not allowing him to just ride away. Or if he had been a fool for even considering it at all.

He left the horse where it was and ran back to his wagon. Only time—and fate—would tell what kind of fool he really was.

Mahaffey and LeBlanc found Barrett first, then Dietrich and Burt LeBlanc as they were riding toward their next positions. They all rode together as they gathered Tim, Coleman, and finally, Dib Bishop. The outlaws and criminals formed a crooked arc around Mahaffey as he let them know the latest.

"Earnshaw and Coombs are dead," Mahaffey said. "Trammel has lost one deputy and another one's full of holes. They're all hiding behind some wagons at the far end of town in front of City Hall. They had Ben sitting on top of that horse with a noose around his neck when we left, but if that mare didn't move after all that shooting, I doubt she ever will. They must've plugged her ears with cotton or something. They know we'll be coming, so they've probably got him back in his cell for safe keeping. That makes it easier for what we've got to do next."

Barrett spoke first. "How do you want to handle it?"

"We've still got them outnumbered like we did before," Dib Bishop added.

"We do," Mahaffey said, "but we still can't just charge at them like we'd normally do. I was hoping we'd be able to draw them out by now, but so far, it looks like Trammel was the only one who came after us. They'll cut us down before we get close to them if we charge their positions. That means we've got to be smart about what we do next. We've got to make them think we're coming head on at them when we're not. It'll mean going on foot and collecting the horses later. It's risky, but I think we can pull it off."

LeBlanc pulled his horse away from the others. "All that's going to do is get your men killed, Mahaffey."

Mahaffey reached out to grab LeBlanc, but LeBlanc moved his horse out of reach as he said, "Your way will leave us afoot with half the town screaming for our heads.

What good is saving Ben if we can't escape afterwards. My way's simpler if you want to hear it."

Mahaffey went for the gun on his hip, but Bishop moved his horse next to him and grabbed his hand. "We've heard your side of things, George. Let LeBlanc talk. He's been right so far."

Each man grew still, even Rick LeBlanc. Mahaffey knew they had followed him until now, but with two of them dead, they would no longer follow him blindly. He had pushed their loyalty to the edge and now found himself somewhere beyond it.

He wrenched his hand free of Bishop's grip. "All right, LeBlanc. How about you tell us what you have in mind?"

Rick LeBlanc inched his horse closer to the others. "You boys don't know your local history, but I had a chance to hear all about it while I was watching this town for my brother Wayne. I heard how Lucien Clay got himself out of that jail by having a man climb over the courtyard wall, force his way in, and escape the same way. That's exactly what I want us to do right now."

Dietrich traded glances with his partners. "You aim for us to break into jail? We already thought of that. It can't be done."

"Normally not," LeBlanc agreed, "but that fire changed things. Trammel and his men are just waiting for us to come straight at them. I aim to let them go on waiting. And while they're watching the street, five of us ride our horses over to the wall and climb it while the rest of us stay with the horses and watch the street. Those big gates are meant to keep folks out, and I figure they're strong enough to do the same for Trammel. Four of us keep the wounded quiet while one of us gets the guards to open up the jail so we can get Ben and go."

"And what if they don't," Mahaffey said. "People don't always do what you expect them to do, even with a gun to their heads. What's to stop them from keeping that door shut and trapping you in the courtyard while Trammel and his men come to finish you off?"

"The guards will open when we threaten to start shooting the wounded," LeBlanc said. "If we do it right, we'll all get out of there with Ben before Trammel even knows what happened."

"And if he does?" Coleman asked. "We're trapped in there. You said as much yourself last night."

"Trapped, but with a courtyard full of hostages," LeBlanc said. "I like those odds. What about you?"

Mahaffey did not have to look at his men to know LeBlanc had already won them over. It was risky, but he had to admit it just might be crazy enough to work. He doubted Trammel would be expecting it.

And if they were destined to fail, Mahaffey had no choice but to help it fail as spectacularly as possible. "We can't go the normal way, so I'll lead us around the long way to the back. The deputies won't see us."

He shot a final glance at LeBlanc as he brought his horse around. "I sure hope you know what you're doing, Rick. Our lives depend on it."

"So does mine. And don't you forget that."

CHAPTER 31

Trammel found himself pacing back and forth between the wagons, willing both for the action to start and praying that it would not at the same time.

He paused next to Hagen, who now stood next to Deputy Charlie Root's wagon facing town.

"Where are they, Adam? Why aren't they coming?"

"Because that's exactly what they want us to ask," Hagen said. "It seems to me like they're waiting us out. I haven't heard a shot anywhere in town for the last several minutes. They're out there somewhere. Don't worry. They know we're down two men. Mahaffey's taking his time figuring out a way they can make one last run at us."

It was the quiet that bothered Trammel. He called out to Blake on his left. "You see anything on your side?"

"All quiet here," Blake answered. "Can't see so much as a mouse moving out there."

He shouted to Deputy Welch at the wagon on the opposite end by the warehouse. "See anything, Johnny?"

"Haven't seen or heard anything in a while here either."

Trammel knew Mahaffey would not just ride off and leave Washington behind. He still had more guns than Trammel, and Trammel still had Ben Washington. He had moved him back to the jail, of course, which he was sure Mahaffey must have seen by now.

The sheriff felt a coldness spread through the middle of his belly. Mahaffey had played it smart to this point. Why should he expect him to change tactics now?

Exactly.

Trammel tapped Hagen on the shoulder and silently motioned for the gambler to follow. Hagen did as Brandt left his wagon and began to approach them. "What's going on?"

Trammel pointed for the deputy to remain where he was. He did not want anyone else to think he was starting to imagine things in case he was wrong.

Hagen walked faster to keep up with Trammel's longer strides. "You think Mahaffey is about to make a play for the jail, don't you?"

The closer he got to the jail, the more he believed that could be the case. "He hasn't moved in a straight line since this whole thing started. I hope he's not as crafty as I think he is."

Trammel paused when they reached the corner of the courtyard by the wagons. He kept his rifle at his side as he looked around the courtyard wall.

He saw a bearded man lightly knocking on the iron door to the courtyard.

"It's Trammel," the man whispered. "Open up."

Trammel moved out from the corner as he heard the latch slide open while Trammel brought the Winchester to his shoulder. "Keep that door closed, Bob! It's not me."

Hagen was next to him, his pistol drawn.

The bearded man put his shoulder against the door as Trammel and Hagen fired at the same time. The man's weight fell against the door as Old Bob struggled to shut it once again.

Trammel rushed forward and slammed the butt of his

rifle into the back of the man's neck, knocking him down as the prison guard closed the door and threw the lock.

Trammel yelled through the door, "Don't open it again unless you're sure it's really me."

As Hagen moved along the side wall of the courtyard, Trammel snatched the pistol from the dying man's holster and tossed it aside. "Where are the rest of you?"

The man lifted his head for a moment, as though he was about to say something but thought better of it. He took whatever he knew with him as his eyes fluttered before his head sank to the ground.

Brandt rounded the corner, rifle in hand. "That's Mahaffey. You finally got him."

Trammel did not care who the dead man was. "Get back to the wagon," Trammel ordered him as he ran to join Hagen. "Keep an eye on the street."

But Brandt disobeyed, running past Trammel. Hagen tried to grab the deputy as he raced by, only to stop when he saw what was around the corner.

Brandt raised his rifle and managed to get off a single shot before he dove back behind the wall as several shots rang out.

"They're all there," Brandt shouted as he levered in a fresh round. "They're trying to climb over the wall!"

Hagen inched around the corner and began firing into the cluster of men and horses as Trammel dropped to a knee and joined in.

Trammel saw two men disappear over the top of the wall as the remaining men struggled to control their horses while they tried to return fire at the gambler and the sheriff. Of all the outlaws behind the courtyard, Trammel only recognized Dib Bishop and Hank Classet.

Trammel saw his bullet strike Classet in the chest,

causing him to rock back in the saddle as he brought his horse around to join the others already riding away.

Dib Bishop was still clinging to the top of the wall when two of Hagen's bullets found him. He lost his grip and landed hard on his back.

The rest of the outlaws rode away in a bunch, some twisting around to fire back at Trammel as they fled.

Brandt quickly began firing at the escaping men as screams began to rise up from the courtyard. The two men who had gotten over the top were in there.

Trammel's next shot slammed into the back of one of the outlaws, but the man remained upright as he rode away.

Hagen grabbed Trammel and pulled him back behind the wall. "Forget about them. They're already in the court-yard!"

Trammel had been too blinded by the fog of action to understand what had happened at first but remembered there were still scores of wounded from the fire in there.

Wounded who Doc Carson had been looking after. Doc Carson and Emily.

Trammel ran back to the courtyard door as Hagen began to reload his pistol while Brandt continued to fire after the escaping men.

Trammel began to shout for Old Bob while he pounded on the door. He only hoped that this time, the liveryman believed it was actually him.

Most days, Bob Irvington liked his job at the jail. The chores that some men found tedious were comforting to him. Each day was usually like every other. Routine was the norm. Wake the prisoners up. Feed them breakfast. Take them to the yard for an hour, then bring them back in. Mind them until supper and then wait until it was time to go to sleep. The pay was good and steady, and life had fallen into a predictable and easy rhythm. He even made a little extra money by looking after the horses of the deputies.

All of that had changed for a while after Lucien Clay's prison break, but the same old ways quickly returned once folks began to forget about it. Old Bob had been happy again until the day before when a quiet afternoon was rocked by a terrible explosion that tore through his part of town. The same courtyard where he had spent many a break chatting with the deputies about horses and life had become a hospital. He had not seen such pain and blood since his days as an orderly for the Union during the War Between the States.

But not even the sight of such misery had been too much for him to manage as the rhythm of tending to the injured had become just another part of his daily duties.

That was until the shooting had started outside that morning and Deputy Hawkeye had been brought in bleeding bad. Seeing Deputy Blake hurt after the explosion had bothered him, but Blake had always been a tough customer. If any of the men could take losing an eye in stride it was him.

The shooting outside had not even bothered him. He had lived through worse in the war.

But he had not been prepared for anyone to try to break into the prison again, so when he'd almost let one of them through the door, Old Bob was shaken by his own stupidity.

And when men started dropping over the side of the wall like spiders on a woodpile, he had been unsure of what to do. He was brought back to that bad night during the prison break when another man had dropped from the wall and cost Bob an eye.

Bob froze.

Edgar, a guard who had been working at the jail almost as long as Bob, had been the closest when that first man landed. A fair-haired outlaw had knocked him aside with his rifle before shooting him dead through the chest.

Bob had spent his life around killers and thought he knew the type, but this man's eyes were wide and wild. He had not only killed Edgar but had enjoyed doing it.

And when those same eyes set on Bob, the prison guard knew he was as good as dead. Screams rose from the wounded and Doc Emily as Bob began to reach for the rifle he had set aside to open the iron door to the courtyard.

Two bullets hit him in the chest, sending him flat against the iron gate.

Old Bob slowly slid to the ground, helpless as he watched another man come over the wall. He looked like the one who had killed Edgar but was darker and younger by a few years.

Bob's vision began to blur as he thought he felt a great pounding on the door he had sagged against.

"Bob, it's Trammel! Open the door. Open it now!"

Bob felt dizzy even though he knew he was flat on his backside. He saw the first gunman wildly look around the courtyard as Trammel continued to pound and call out above the screams, "Damn it, Bob! Open up!"

Bob's hearing grew thick as he heard one of the gunmen say to the other, "What'll we do now, Rick? They'll be in here any minute."

"Get over to that side door over there," Rick told him. "I'll hold off Trammel. I know just how to do it, too."

Despite his failing vision, Bob saw the one called Rick storm over to where Doc Emily and one of the nurses were trying to protect one of the wounded on a cot. He knocked the nurse aside before he grabbed hold of Doc Emily's arm and pulled her away from the cots.

Bob felt his strength begin to leave him as the pounding grew louder. He knew what he had to do but did not think he had the strength to do it.

He summoned all the will he had left and forced his arm up to the bolt and rocked toward his left to push it open.

He slumped to the side as Sheriff Trammel stepped over him and into the courtyard. His rifle led the way as Mr. Hagen came in right behind him, followed by Deputy Blake.

Bob was glad no one had wasted time tending to him, for the one called Rick had his arm around Doc Emily's throat.

The younger man by the door to the jail threw up his hands as he shouted, "Don't shoot! I surrender!"

Blake went over and pushed the man face first to the ground while the sheriff and Hagen kept their guns aimed at Rick. Bob knew this Rick might be crazy, but he had sand. He had seen men like him before. He would kill Doc Emily if he had to.

Bob heard the fear in Trammel's voice as the large man said, "Let her go, LeBlanc. You're a dead man if you don't."

Bob thought he heard LeBlanc give forth with a sound that was somewhere between a laugh and a growl. "Well, looks like I've finally grabbed on to someone who means something to you, Trammel."

Bob's stomach turned as he watched a look of recognition come over Rick. "Wait just a minute. She's in here tending to the sick. Your wife's a doctor, ain't she, Trammel? Don't tell me I went and grabbed your bride."

He grinned as he held her close. "I heard she was a beauty, but I didn't know she looked this good. Beautiful skin and a nice long neck on her." He pulled his arm tighter around her throat as he kept his pistol against her temple. "Would be a shame if you made me break it."

Bob watched a shudder go through the sheriff, just like it usually did when he was about to lose his temper. Like when he had almost killed Blake the day before.

"Let her go, or I swear to God, I'll kill you with my bare hands."

Thomas watched Mr. Hagen holster his pistol as he placed a hand on Trammel's rifle. "Steady now, Buck. No need for you to risk her life. You don't have to. I'm right here."

Bob saw Rick LeBlanc's eyes grew wider as he saw Hagen's gun on his hip. "You'd best listen to your gimpy friend here, Trammel. You wouldn't want your wife's death on your conscience. He's given up. So should you. Set that rifle down real nice and slow."

Hagen did not look at Trammel, only at LeBlanc. "This isn't a measure of surrender." Bob watched the gambler flex his right hand. He heard his fingers pop. "Think of it merely as a measure of timing."

Hagen's head bent forward just a bit. "Allow me to explain."

Bob blinked and missed seeing Hagen draw his pistol and fire, but he saw the red mist that shot out from the back of LeBlanc's head.

For a moment, Bob thought Mr. Hagen had missed LeBlanc entirely until he saw the man's grip on Doc Emily's neck weaken as he staggered back.

Bob saw Trammel burst forward and knock the pistol from LeBlanc's hand before the outlaw collapsed to the ground. He saw the sheriff take his wife in his arms before Mr. Hagen knelt, blocking his view. Hagen shouted to Blake, "Get Doc Carson out here. Bob needs help."

Bob hated that all of this had happened because he had been too slow. Too scared to move. "I did my best, Mr. Hagen. I tried, but I—"

Bob heard the side door of the jail open and saw Doc Carson running toward him as Mr. Hagen lifted him up in both hands. "You did just fine, Bob. Now shut up while the doc gets to working on you."

Old Bob could not remember the last time when he had been picked up like this. Not since he had been a baby, he supposed. It was the last thought he had before weariness carried him off into the darkness amid Doc Carson's shouting.

CHAPTER 32

Trammel did not think he could be happier than the moment Emily had told him he would be a father.

He was proven wrong when Blake told him that Old Bob had finally woken up.

Trammel rushed down the stairs from his office to find Emily sitting on the side of Bob's bed, with Blake, Hagen, and Brandt looking on.

He resisted the urge to shake the man's hand and settled for nudging his foot instead. "Welcome back. It's good to see you."

"Good to be seen," the guard rasped. He slowly looked at the faces who had gathered around him. "How long was I asleep?"

"More than a week," Emily said. "You had us worried for a while, but you're all better now."

Old Bob looked up at all of the faces smiling down at him. "You sure I'm still alive? You all look like you're at my funeral."

"Far from it," Hagen said. "A lot of good people would've been killed if you hadn't opened that door when you did."

Trammel placed a hand on Emily's shoulder. "We owe you, Bob. We owe you more than we could ever pay you."

"Did you get them?" Bob coughed from the effort of speaking. and Emily gave him a glass of water. "The men doing all that shooting, I mean. Did you get them all."

"We got enough of them," Trammel said. "Mahaffey and Rick LeBlanc. Dib Bishop, that scrawny kid who delivered the message, too. All dead. A few of the others besides."

"The rest all got away," Brandt said. "But they won't get far. We'll run them down eventually."

Trammel could see that Old Bob was more than just groggy. He was clearly not used to being the center of so much attention. "And Hawkeye?"

"He's fine," Emily said. "A little sore, but well. He's already up and about."

Bob tried to sit up, but the pain from the two wounds in his chest made him stop. "Edgar?"

They looked to Trammel to tell him. "He didn't make it. He was already gone by the time we got in there. But it was quick. He didn't feel any pain."

Bob accepted that as a lone tear ran down his cheek. "How long before I can get back to work, Sheriff? I know you'll be needing me."

"That'll be up to the sheriff to decide." Trammel placed a hand on Blake's shoulder. "Meet your new boss. Sherwood Blake, Sheriff of Laramie."

Trammel had never seen Blake smile before, but he was smiling now. Much of the hair from his scorched scalp had begun to return, though his skin still bore some damage from the fire. The black eyepatch he had chosen for his missing left eye suited him well.

"Take all the time you need," Blake told him. "Just concentrate on getting better. Your job will still be waiting for you whenever you're ready."

Old Bob looked confused. "If you're the sheriff, what's that make Sheriff Trammel?"

Trammel had not put on his star yet but decided Bob's progress was as good a time as any. He took it from his pocket and placed it in the guard's hand. "It's U.S. Marshal Trammel now. At least for the time being until they get someone else for the job. I'll be glad for the break. Emily and I are going to be busy up in Cheyenne after the baby comes."

Bob smiled as he blinked another tear away. "Life sure is funny like that, isn't it. Old friends leave us, and new ones come in every day."

Trammel gestured for everyone to leave. "We'd all better get moving to let this man get back to healing. You just keep working on getting better. Laramie needs you healthy, Bob. Don't let them down."

"Sounds like you're needed elsewhere," Old Bob answered. "The territory is lucky to have you."

Trammel wrapped his arm around Emily as the others filed out of his room. "We'll see about that."

TURN THE PAGE FOR AN EXCITING PREVIEW!

SLASH & PECOS ARE BACK!

**JOHNSTONE COUNTRY.
THE GOOD, THE BAD,
AND THE UTTERLY DEPRAVED**

**Slash and Pecos come face-to-face with the baddest
hombre they've ever known: a kill-crazy madman
who's paving the road to hell—with bloodlust.**

He blew into town like a tornado. A mysterious stranger
with money to burn, time to kill—and a sadistic streak as
wide as the Rio Grande. He says his name is Benson
and he's come to invest in the town's future. First, he
showers the banks and local businesses with cash. Then,
he hires a pair of drunks to fight and get arrested so he
can check out the local lawmen. After that, he warms up
to a lady of the evening—with deadly results.

That's just the beginning.

By the time Slash and Pecos return to town
after a quick-and-dirty cargo run, Benson has enlisted
half the outlaws in the territory for his own private army.
With the help of a corrupt colonel,
he's sent a veritable war wagon into the unprepared
town—wreaking havoc and slaughtering innocents,
with the brand of carnage one only sees on the battlefield. The local lawmen are quickly slaughtered. Even
the U.S. marshals are no match for the military precision
of Benson. With looters running amok and killers
on every corner, a person would have to be stupid or
crazy to try to take the town back . . .

Luckily, Slash and Pecos are a little of both. They've
been around long enough to see the worst in men—
and they know that the best way to stop
a very bad hombre . . . is to be even badder.

National Bestselling Authors
William W. Johnstone and J.A. Johnstone

BAD HOMBRES
A Slash and Pecos Western

On sale November 2023
wherever Pinnacle Books are sold.

Live Free. Read Hard.
www.williamjohnstone.net

Visit us at www.kensingtonbooks.com

CHAPTER 1

Harlan Benson sat astride his horse in the middle of the road, reached into his coat pocket, and pulled out a fancy notebook bound in soft lambskin. From another pocket he took a short pencil, hardly more than a stub, pursed his lips and touched the lead tip to his tongue. Properly lubricated, the pencil slid smoothly across the first blank page in the notebook recording his initial impression.

He liked what he saw.

Twice he glanced up at the neatly lettered sign by the roadside proclaiming this to be Paradise. He wanted to be certain he copied the name properly. After he entered the name in a precise, small script at the top of the otherwise blank page, he carefully wrote 532 centered beneath it. The declared population of Paradise was 532. A few more observations about the condition of the road and the likelihood of this being a prosperous town because of the well-maintained sign were added.

He took out a pocket watch and noted the time it had taken him to ride here from the crossroads. All the data were entered in exactly the proper form. Nothing less than such precision would do. The colonel expected it, and Benson demanded it of himself.

Harl Benson tucked the notebook back into the inside pocket of his finely tailored, expensive cream-colored coat with beige grosgrain lapels and four colorful campaign ribbons affixed on his left breast. The pencil followed the notebook into the pocket.

"Giddyup," he called to his magnificent coal-black stallion. The horse balked. It knew what lay ahead. He booted it into a canter. He was anxious to see what Paradise had to offer even if his stallion was not.

After climbing a short incline in the road, he halted at the top of the rise. Paradise awaited him. The town lay in a shallow bowl. A river defined the northern boundary and provided water for the citizens. Straight ahead to the east lay open prairie. The next town over was far beyond the horizon. To the south stretched fields brimming with alfalfa and other grain to feed livestock. That told him more about the commerce in this peaceful Colorado settlement. It was prosperous and enjoyed a good standard of living in spite of the railroad bypassing it and running fifteen miles to the north.

Giving his horse its head, they eased down the far side of the incline into town. Into Paradise.

His sharp steel-gray eyes caught movement along the main street. He never missed a detail, especially the pretty young woman who stepped out of the grain store to give him the eye. He touched the brim of his tall center Stetson, appreciating the attention she bestowed on him.

Benson was a handsome man and knew it. Handsome, that is, except for the pink knife scar that started in the middle of his forehead and ran down across his eye to his left cheek. He had survived a nasty knife fight enduring only that single wound. His opponent hadn't survived at all.

Most women thought that thin pink scar gave him a dangerous look. If they only knew.

He was a real Beau Brummell in his dress. The cream coat decorated with the mysteriously colored ribbons caught their eye, but he wore trousers of the purest black with a formal silk ribbon down the outsides. His boots were polished to a mirror finish, the leather a perfect match to his ornate gun belt. The six-shooters holstered there hardly looked to be the precision instruments of death that they were. Silver filigree adorned the sides of both Colt .44s. He wore them low on his snake hips, the butts forward on both sides.

Most of all he was proudest of the intricate gold watch hidden away in a vest pocket lined in clinging velvet to prevent it from accidentally slipping out. A ponderous gold chain swung in an arc across his well-muscled belly. A diamond the size of his little fingernail attached to the chain swung to and fro, catching every ray of light daring to come close.

He was quite the dandy and was proud of the look. It was only natural that all the ladies wanted to be seen with him—wanted to be with him.

Benson slowed and then came to a halt. He turned his stallion toward the young lady openly admiring him.

"Good afternoon, ma'am," he said. "Do you work at the grain store?"

"If you need to purchase some seed, I'll fetch my pa. He owns the store."

"No, dear lady, that's not true." He enjoyed the startled expression.

"Whatever do you mean? Of course he does. He's Neil Paulson and nobody else in these parts runs a store half as fine."

"You misunderstand me, miss. I meant that *you* own everything within your sight. How can such beauty not dominate everyone who chances to cast his gaze on your female loveliness?"

She blinked and pushed back a strand of mousy brown hair. The surprise turned into a broad smile—a smile that promised Benson anything he wanted. Then she looked discomfited. Quick movements brushed dust off her plain brown gingham dress. Her clothing was no match for his finery, and here he had ridden into town off a long, hot, dusty summer road.

"Do I take it you are *Miss* Paulson?"

The wicked smile returned, and she nodded slowly. She carefully licked her ruby lips and tried to look coy. Eyes batting, she gave him a look designed to melt the steeliest heart.

"Clara," she said. "Clara Paulson."

Harl Benson took his notebook from his coat pocket and made a quick notation in it. He looked up from her to the store and made quick estimates of the store's size and its inventory. As enticing as it would be to have the girl give him a tour of the store and detail its contents, in private, of course, he had so much work to do and time pressed in on him.

"That is a mighty neighborly invite for a stranger," he said.

"You want to check the grain bins out back?" She sounded just a tad frantic. A quick look over her shoulder explained it all. A man so large his shoulders brushed the sides of the open door glared at Benson.

Another quick entry into his notebook completed all the details he needed about Paulson's Grain and Feed Store, and its burly owner. Benson caught sight of the shotgun resting against the wall just inside the door. The feed store owner had the look of a man able to tear apart anyone he disliked with his bare hands, but that shotgun? It showed intent.

"I must go, but one parting question, my dear."

"Yes?" Clara Paulson stepped a little closer, leaning on the broom. She looked expectant that he would offer to take her away from this small town and show her a city where all the best people dressed like Harl Benson—and she could show off a fancy ball gown and flashy diamond and gold jewelry like European royalty. "What is it?"

"Do you have any brothers?"

"What? No, there's only Grant and Franklin working here, but they're cousins. I had a brother, but he died when he was only six. He fell into a well. It was two days before Pa found him."

"Good day," Benson said, again pinching the brim of his hat. He glanced in her father's direction and evaluated the man's barrel chest and bulging arms. In a fight, he would be a formidable opponent. But did he have a box of shells nearby to feed the shotgun after the first two barrels were discharged? Benson doubted it.

Benson had faced off with men like Neil Paulson before, men who toiled moving heavy sacks of grain or bales of hay. Their vitality often required more than a single bullet to stop them, even if the first shot was accurately directed to head or heart.

As he made his way down the middle of Paradise's main street, he took note of the buildings and their sizes. How far apart they stood, the construction and position. Quick estimates of the employees in the businesses were probably within one or two of actual employment. He was expert at such evaluations having done it so many times before with great success. Not a single man walking the street or working in the businesses along the main street slung iron at his side. Perhaps this town really was Paradise and men didn't have to strut about carrying iron.

Harl Benson made more notes in his precise script.

The horses tethered outside the stores generally had a rifle thrust into a saddle scabbard. Travelers into town needed such firepower out on the plains and especially when they worked their way into the tall Front Range Mountains to the west. Dangerous creatures, both four-legged and two, prowled those lonely stretches.

He dismounted, checked the horses' brands to find out where the riders had come from, and entered a new notation. All these horses belonged to punchers from a single ranch. Where the Double Circle ran its stock, he didn't know, and it hardly mattered. The hands probably carried sidearms in addition to their rifles and had come to town to hoot and holler. They'd be gone by Monday morning.

Benson entered the saloon. The Fatted Calf Saloon and Drinking Emporium looked exactly like any other to him. Eight cowboys bellied up to the bar, swapping lies and nursing warm beer. That meant they hadn't been paid yet for their month of backbreaking labor. Walking slowly, he counted his paces to determine the size of the saloon.

It stretched more than forty feet deep but was narrow, hardly more than fifteen feet. He settled into a chair with his back to a wall where he had a good view of the traffic outside along the main street.

"Well, mister, you have the look of someone who's been on the trail long enough to build up a real thirst." A hand rested on his shoulder.

Benson turned slightly to dislodge the woman's hand and looked up at one of the pretty waiter girls. She wore a bright red silk dress with a deep scoop neckline. White lace had been sewn along the cleavage since the dress was so old it was coming apart at the seams. If she had let the seams pop just a little more, she would have shown her customers for free what she undoubtedly charged for in private. Benson quickly evaluated everything about her. Her worth matched the cheapness of her dress.

"Rye whiskey," he said. "Don't give me the cheap stuff." He dropped a twenty-dollar gold piece onto the table. The tiny coin spun on its rim and then settled down with a golden ring that brought him unwanted attention from the cowpunchers at the bar.

That gave him a new tidbit to enter into his notebook. Twenty dollars was unusual in Paradise.

"For that, dearie, you can have anything you want," the doxie said. She ran her tongue around her rouged lips in what she thought was a suggestive, lewd manner to inflame his desires. It did the reverse.

"The shot of rye. Then we'll see about something . . . else."

She hurried over to whisper with the bartender. The short, mustached man behind the bar looked more prosperous than the usual barkeep. Benson guessed he owned the Fatted Calf.

He sighed when two of the cowboys sauntered over, thumbs thrust into their gun belts. They stopped a few feet away from him.

"We don't see many strangers in town," the taller of the pair said. The shorter one said something Benson didn't catch. This egged on his taller partner. "You got more of them twenty-dollar pieces?"

"Are you desperate road agents thinking to rob me?" Benson moved a little to flash the twin six-shooters. The dim light caught the silver filigree and made the smoke wagons look even larger than they were.

"Those don't look like they get much use," piped up the short one. "You one of them fellas what brags about how many men you've cut down?"

"I don't brag about it," Benson said. He took the bottle of rye from the floozie and popped the cork with his thumb. He ignored the dirt on the rim of the shot glass she brought with it and drank straight from the bottle. He licked his lips. "That's surprisingly good. Thanks." He pushed the tiny gold coin across the table in the woman's direction. "Why don't you set up a round for everyone at the bar? And keep the rest for yourself."

"Yes, *sir*. And if there's anything more you want, my name's Hannah."

He tipped his head in the direction of the bar in obvious dismissal. Benson looked up at the two cowboys and said, "The drinks are on the bar, not here." He took another pull from the bottle and then placed it carefully on the table with a move so precise there wasn't even a tiny click of glass touching wood.

"You ever killed anybody with them fancy-ass six-guns?" The short one stepped closer. "Or are they just for show?"

Benson didn't answer.

"How many? How many you claim to have gunned down?" The man shoved out his chin belligerently. At the same time he moved his right hand to his holster, as if he was prepared to throw down.

"How many men have I killed? How many men and boys? Well, now, I can't give a good answer about that."

"Why the hell not?" Both men tensed now. Benson had seen his share of gunmen. These two might be good at rounding up cattle, or even rustling them, but they weren't gunslicks. They'd had a beer too many and thought to liven up their visit to town by pestering a tinhorn dude.

"I stopped counting at a hundred."

"A hunnerd? You sayin' you've killed a hunnerd men."

"Only with these guns. The total's considerably greater if you want a count on the total number I've killed." Benson laughed at their stunned expression.

"Hell and damnation, Petey, he's pullin' our leg." The tall one punched his partner in the arm.

Petey's expression was unreadable. The flash of panic mixed with disbelief. A sick grin finally twisted his lips, just a little.

"We got drinks waitin' fer us back at the bar," Petey said.

"Yeah, right, thanks, mister. You're a real friend. You got a good sense of humor, too." The tall one punched Petey in the arm again and herded him away. They got to the bar and the free set-up erased any intention of upbraiding the stranger. In a few seconds, they joked and cussed with their partners from the ranch.

Harl Benson added a new notation in his notebook about the quality of the whiskey at the Fatted Calf. He knocked back another shot of the fine rye and started out the swinging doors. A thin, bony hand grabbed his arm. Again he shifted slightly and pulled away.

"You ready for more fun, mister?" Hannah looked and sounded desperate. "I got a room down the street. It's a real fine place."

"A sporting house?"

"What? Oh, yeah. That's a mighty fancy term. Nobody in these parts calls Madame Jane's that."

He looked over his shoulder toward the rear of the saloon.

"What's in the backroom?"

"You wanna do it there? If you cut Jackson in for a dime or even two bits, well, maybe we kin do it there." Hannah looked hesitantly at the bartender. "Better if we go to my place."

"Madame Jane's?"

Hannah bobbed her head.

"Ain't much in the back room 'cept all the whiskey and other stuff. It's crowded right now. Jackson just got in a new shipment."

"Of the rye? How many cases?"

"Hustle the customers on your own time. Get back to work, you scrawny—" the barkeep bellowed. He fell silent when Benson held up his hand.

"Nuff for a few months. Ten cases, maybe. More?" Hannah looked back at her boss. "Listen, I'll be outta here in another hour. You wait fer me at Madame Jane's. There's a real fine parlor, and she bought a case of that liquor you've taken such a shine to. Fer the payin' customers. Like you."

Benson stepped out onto the boardwalk. A new description in the notebook and he was ready to check on the whorehouse. But first he had one final stop to make.

With Hannah calling after him to enjoy himself until she got to the brothel's parlor, the finest in this part of Colorado she claimed, he walked directly to the bank down the street. Benson counted the paces and made measurements of the street's width and the location of other stores. When he stepped into the bank, his work was almost completed.

Bustling over when he saw his new customer's fancy clothing, the bank officer beamed from ear to ear. A quick twirl of his long mustaches put the greased tips into points equal to a prickly pear spine.

"Welcome, sir. We haven't seen you before in these here parts. What can we do for you?" The plump bank officer pumped Benson's hand like he could draw deep well water. He released the hand when Benson squeezed down. Hard.

"I'd like to make a deposit."

"A new account. Wonderful, wonderful. How much, sir? Ten? Twenty?"

Benson heard the pride in the man's voice. Those were the big depositors in the Bank of Paradise.

"I was thinking more like five."

The banker's face fell, but he hid the disappointment.

"This way, sir. Our head teller will handle your deposit. Excuse me but I have other business to—"

"Thousand," Benson said.

This brought the banker up short.

"You want to deposit five *thousand?* That's almost as much as Mister Rawls out on the Double Circle has in our safe."

"You have other deposits of equal size, I take it? I certainly do not want my money placed in a bank without . . . ample assets."

"Five other ranchers, all quite prosperous. Yes, very prosperous. Come this way, sir, let me handle your account personally." The banker snapped his fingers. The man wearing the green eye shades and sleeve protectors came from the middle cage.

"You," Benson said sharply. "I want you to show me the safe where you'll keep my money. I don't like to deal with underlings."

"I . . . uh . . . underlings? Oh, no, not that. This way." The bank officer ushered Benson to the side of the lobby and through a swinging door set in a low wood railing. "This is our safe. You can see how sturdy it is." The banker slipped his thumbs into the armholes of his vest and reared back, beaming.

"A Mosler with a time lock," Benson said, nodding

slowly. His quick eyes took in the details, the model of the safe and how it had been modified. The safe itself wasn't as heavily constructed as many back East, probably due to the cost of freighting such a heavy load into the foothills of the Front Range.

"You know the product, sir?" The banker's eyes widened in surprise. "Then you recognize how sturdy it is and how, excuse the expression, *safe* your deposit will be. Five thousand, you said?"

"That's correct." Benson walked from one side of the safe to the other. It wasn't any different from a half dozen others of its ilk he had seen.

"Let's get the paperwork started," the banker said, rubbing his hands together. He circled a large cherrywood desk and began dipping his pen in the inkwell and filling out forms.

Ben seated himself in the leather chair opposite and made his own notations in the lambskin notebook. He glanced up occasionally as he sketched the safe. While not an artist of great skill, he captured the details quickly and well from long practice.

"Now, sir, your deposit?" The banker looked expectantly at him. A touch of anticipation was dampened by fear that Benson wasn't going to hand over the princely sum. The banker positively beamed as Benson reached into his inner coat pocket and drew out his soft leather wallet. Making a big show of it for both the banker and his head teller, he counted out a stack of greenbacks onto the desk until he reached the agreed-upon sum.

Benson almost laughed when the banker visually tallied up how much money remained in that wallet. Only through great exercise of willpower did he restrain himself from asking Benson to deposit even more.

"Affix your signature to the bottom of the page. Here's

a receipt for the full amount. And a bank book. See? The full five thousand dollars is indicated right here with the date and my initials to certify it. Should you wish to withdraw any amount at any time, show the pass book. Or," the banker said, winking slyly, "if you want to add to your savings at any time. That will be entered and officially noted, too."

Benson tucked the deposit book and receipt into the same pocket with his wallet. He stood and held out his hand to shake.

"I look forward to doing more business with your bank soon," he said.

The banker hesitantly shook, remembering the bone-crushing grip. This time Benson made no effort to cripple the man. Sealing the deal with the handshake, Benson turned his back on the man who babbled on about what a fine place Paradise was and how Benson would prosper here as long as the bank was part of his financial plans.

Walking slowly, Benson took in every detail of the buildings and how they were constructed. A few more notations graced his notebook by the time he reached a three-story building that might have been a hotel. He saw immediately this wasn't the case. On the second-story balcony several partially clad women lounged about, idly talking until one spotted him down in the street.

"Hey there, handsome, why don't you come on in? I'll show you a real good time." The woman leaned far over the railing and shimmied about to show what she offered. "I'll show you a good time if you're man enough to handle a real woman like me, that is!"

The other Cyprians laughed.

Benson started to make a few more notes but an elegantly dressed blonde stepped into the doorway. She had a come-hither smile that captivated him. Benson had seen his share of beautiful women, but this one ranked easily in the top five. She wore a shiny green metallic flake dress that caught the sunlight and made it look as if she stood in a desert mirage. The shimmering only accentuated her narrow waist and womanly hips. For a woman in a brothel she sported an almost sedate decolletage. Only the barest hint of snowy white breasts poked out.

He couldn't help comparing her with the blatant exhibitionism of the whores on the balcony.

She tossed her head back, sending ripples through the mane of golden hair. Eyes as blue as sapphire judged him as much as his steel-gray ones took her measure. He liked what he saw. A lot. From the tiny upward curl of her lush, full lips, she shared that opinion.

"You're Jane?"

"I hadn't realized my reputation was that big. A complete stranger to town knows me? I'm flattered." She batted her eyes. Long, dark lashes invited him closer.

"It's my job to know things," Benson said, slowly mounting the steps to the front porch. He stopped a pace away. A tiny puff of breeze carried her perfume to him. His nostrils flared, and he sucked in the gentle fragrance. His heart raced.

"It's French perfume," Jane said. "I buy it from an importer in Boston."

"And I thought it was your natural alluring scent that is so captivating. I am crushed. How could I have been so wrong?" He turned to leave, as if in abject defeat.

"Don't go," Jane said. "Come in. Have a drink and let's talk. You might even persuade me to forgive you your . . . mistake."

"I've already sampled the rye whiskey. There's more that I want to sample, and my time is running out."

"You don't look like the sort of man who . . . hurries."

"Not in all things," Benson said. He stepped up and circled her trim waist with his arm. She leaned slightly into him. Their bodies fit together perfectly.

"I'm not cheap," Jane said.

"Inexpensive," he corrected. "And I never doubted it. I'm willing to pay for the best."

"I can tell that you're a gentleman."

Pressed together they went through the parlor into an expensively decorated bedroom.

"My boudoir," Jane said.

"A fitting place for one so lovely," Benson said.

They worked to undress each other and sank to a feather mattress, locked in each other's embrace. Afterward, Benson sat up in bed.

"I wasn't wrong about you, Harl," she said. Jane made no effort at coyness by pulling up the sheet to hide her voluptuous breasts. "You're a real gentleman and about the best I've ever found."

"This town is well named," Benson said, climbing into his clothes. "It might not be Paradise in all respects, but it certainly is when it comes to . . . you." He turned and put his forefinger under her chin. She tilted her head back for him to lightly kiss her on the lips. "You are both lovely and skilled."

"You come on back any time you want. I don't say that to just everyone." Jane's bright blue eyes watched as he completed dressing.

"Thank you for the fine afternoon. I enjoyed your company so much I am going to give you something special."

"More than my usual?" Jane glanced at the stack of ten-dollar gold pieces on the table beside her four-poster bed.

"More than I usually give because you deserve it," Benson said.

He drew his six-gun and shot her between those bright blue eyes.

Harl Benson settled his clothes, smoothed a few wrinkles, retrieved the fee from the bedside table, and tucked it away in a vest pocket, then walked quickly from the brothel. His work in Paradise had just begun, and he wanted to complete it soon.

CHAPTER 2

"Let me drive," James "Slash" Braddock said peevishly. "I swear, you're hitting every last hole in the road. And them holes got even deeper holes at their bottoms. They might just reach all the way to the center of the Earth they're so deep."

Melvin "Pecos River Kid" Baker looked out the corner of his eye, then hawked a gob with admirable accuracy so that it missed—barely—his partner's boot braced against the bottom of the driver's box of their Pittsburgh freight wagon.

"If I let you drive, them mules would balk. And rightly so. They don't much like you 'cuz you don't have a lick of sense when it comes to treatin' the lot of them with dignity."

"Dignity!" Slash roared. "They're *mules*. Mules don't have 'dignity.' They're as dumb as . . . as you."

"I wouldn't have to drive so fast if you kept a better lookout." Pecos reared back and sent his long whip snaking out over the heads of his team. The cracker popped as loud as a gunshot. The mules tucked back their long ears, put their heads down, and pulled a little harder.

"What are you goin' on about?" Slash gripped the side of the box and hung on as the wheel nearest him hit a deep rut. If he hadn't braced when he did, he would have been thrown out of the wagon.

Still minding the team, Pecos swept graying blond hair out of his bright blue eyes and then half turned on the hardwood seat toward his partner. This freed up the Russian .44 settled down in its brown hand-tooled leather holster. He reached down. His fingers drummed angrily against the ornate shell belt. Arguing with Slash passed the time on a long, dusty trip, but calling his ability into question inched toward fisticuffs. Or worse.

After all, there were limits.

"For two cents I'd whup your scrawny ass," Pecos said.

"You don't have that much, not after you lost everything but your long johns to that card sharp last night at the Thousand Delights."

"He cheated. Anybody could see that. Jay should never have let him set down at a table, not the way he dealt seconds."

"If you knew he was cheatin', why in the blue blazes did you stay in the game? Ain't you ever heard the gamblin' advice, 'Look around the table. If you don't see the sucker, you're it.' And you leave my missus out of this argument." Slash glared at Pecos.

"I think she let him play just to humiliate you. Did you and her have a tiff? That'd explain why you're bein' so disagreeable." Pecos thrust out his chin, as if inviting his partner to take a swing.

"Me and Jay are on the best of terms. Every night's like our honeymoon. And don't you go makin' crude comments 'bout that." Slash felt like posing to show off how much younger than Pecos he looked. His thick, dark brown hair poked out around his hat. Streaks of gray shot through it, but nothing like what Pecos sported. His temples and sideburns showed the most. To make his point, he crossed his arms across a broad chest and glared back a his partner. His brown eyes never wavered under Pecos' equally flinty look.

"That's why you've been daydreamin' and not payin' a whit of attention to anything around you. You're rememberin' what it's like to have a woman as fine as Jay snuggled up alongside you in bed." Pecos swerved and hit another deep hole. Both men popped up into the air, putting space between their rear ends and the seat for a long second.

"What's stuck in your craw? You're always a mite cantankerous, but this is goin' way too far, even for you."

"You're not payin' attention, that's what," Pecos said. He drew his lips back in a feral snarl. "We got company and you never mentioned it, not once in the last three miles when they started trailin' us."

Slash swung around and leaned out past the flapping canvas covering the wagon bed. A few seconds passed as he studied the matter, and then he returned to his seat beside his partner.

"Your eyes might be gettin' old, but they're still sharp." Slash touched the stag-horn grips of the twin Colt .44s he carried butt forward on either hip, then fumbled around behind him in the wagon bed and brought out his Winchester Yellowboy. He drew back the rifle's hammer and took a deep breath to settle his nerves.

"There's three of them. Which one do you want me to take out first?" Slash cracked his knuckles to prepare for the sharpshooting.

"You got an itchy trigger finger all of a sudden? What if they're peaceable travelers and just happen to be headin' in the same direction as we are?"

"You're the one what called my attention to them and

awled me out for inattentiveness." Slash leaned out again to get a better idea what they faced. Still only three riders.

Or was that three road agents? In this part of Colorado that was as likely as not.

"It don't change a thing if they're on the road to Portrero the same as us, their business bein' in the town and not bein' road agents."

"You have a time decidin' your mind, don't you?" Slash asked. He gripped the rifle and studied the terrain ahead. "Let me drop off at the bend in the road."

"Those rocks make good cover," Pecos said, seeing his partner's plan. "You can knock two out of the saddle before the third twigs to what's what."

"If they're just pilgrims like us, I can save my bullets."

"If they're like us, they're cutthroats."

"That's former cutthroats," Pecos corrected. "We've given up ridin' the long coulee."

"I gotta wonder why we gave up such an excitin' life," Slash said, jolted so hard his teeth clacked together when the wagon rumbled over a deep pothole. "Haulin' freight shouldn't be this exasperatin'."

He came to his feet, then launched himself when the freight wagon rounded a sharp bend in the road. Slash hit the ground and rolled. He came to a sitting position, moaning from the impact. Such schemes were better for youngsters full of piss and vinegar, not old knees and an aching back like his.

He struggled to his feet and close to fell behind a waist-high boulder alongside the road. It was closer than he liked for an ambush, but he didn't have time to hunt through the rocks for a better vantage point.

Slash knelt, rested his Yellowboy on top of the rock and

took a couple slow breaths to calm himself. Be.
sucked in air for a third, the riders rounded the ben
.

He hadn't decided what to say to them, but it d
matter. They were more observant than he had been.
.
three spotted him right away. The leader held up his han
made a fist and brought his two companions to a halt.

"You have reason to point that rifle at us, mister?"

"I ain't fixin' on robbin' you," Slash said, though the
thought fluttered through his mind. He and Pecos had
given up the owlhoot life and gone straight, as much
through threat as desire. They had run afoul of an ornery
U.S. federal chief marshal by the name of Luther T.
Bledsoe who promised to stretch their necks unless they
did "chores" for him, all of which were outside the law.
Chief Marshal "Bleed-'Em-So" Bledsoe used them to go
after road agents and rustlers and other miscreants in
ways that he could deny, should any other lawman protest
the methods.

In return "Bleed-'Em-So" paid them a decent wage for
carrying out his secret orders and let them run a legitimate
freight company the rest of the time. And bragged he
wouldn't see them doing the midair two-step with nooses
around their neck.

But Slash still felt the pangs of giving up the excitement
of robbing a bank or sticking up a train or stagecoach.
There had always been more than stealing the money.
Nothing matched the anticipation after pulling his ban-
danna up over his nose, drawing his gun, and going after
someone else's money. The uncertainty, the promise of
danger, even the sheer thrill when they stashed the loot in
their saddlebags and raced off seconds ahead of a determined posse made it unlike anything else he'd ever done.

It was always his wits against the world. And he waltzed

ith enough gold and scrip to keep him going for
s until the next robbery. That had been quite the life.

m married now," he said under his breath. That should
e given him all the more reason to close the chapter of
s sordid past and move on.

"What's that? You're married?" The lead rider looked
at his partners. They shrugged.

"Don't pay that no never mind," Slash said. "Tell me
why you're trailin' us. Are you fixin' to hold us up?"

He expected a denial. The leader surprised him.

"That depends on what you're carrying. Gold? Something worth stealing?" The man laughed as if he'd made
a joke.

"Truth is, we don't rightly know what's in the crates
we're haulin'. They're too light to be loaded with gold and
too heavy if they're stuffed with greenbacks."

Slash watched the three cluster together and whisper
amongst themselves. He got a better look at them. If they
were road agents, they were prosperous ones. More prosperous than he and Pecos had been except in the best of
times. The riders wore beige linen dusters. The leader had
his pulled back to show a coat and vest that cost a small
fortune. At his hip rode a smoke wagon big enough to
bring down a buck. And curiously, on his left coat lapel
he wore two colorful ribbons.

A quick look showed the other two also had similar
ribbons, though the rider to the left had only one and the
third horseman two of different patterns.

"You boys Masons or do you belong to one of them
secret societies?" Slash tried to hold down his curiosity
about their decorations and failed. He'd never seen anything
like them except on Army officers' full dress uniforms.

Never had those officers worn their medals or ribbons on civilian clothing.

The question caused the leader to whirl around. His hand went toward his holstered iron, then he caught himself. The Yellowboy aimed at his heart kept things from getting too hot too fast.

"He's asking about our campaign ribbons, Hutchins," the rider with only one decoration said. His tone put Slash on edge. Mentioning those ribbons was worse than accusing them of being thieves.

"What we wear doesn't concern you," the leader—Hutchins—said sharply. His hand moved closer to his six-shooter.

"We got other things on our mind than your fancy duds," came Pecos' drawl from the far side of the road. He had parked the freight wagon and come back to catch the trio in a cross fire.

Hutchins looked from Slash and half turned in the saddle to find where Pecos had taken cover. The huge man saw the rider's move toward his piece and swung around the sawed-off shotgun he slung across his shoulder and neck from a leather strap. The double barrels carried enough firepower to shred the three men and parts of the horses they rode.

"Whoa, hold on now," Hutchins said. "We're peaceable travelers on our way to Portrero. If you happen to be going there, too, that's purely coincidence."

"Why don't you gents just ride on into town," Slash suggested. "We'd feel easier if you stayed in front of us."

"Damned back shooters, that's what they are," grumbled the rider with the single ribbon.

"We don't have time to discuss the matter," Hutchins said. "The Colonel's waiting for us."

"Trot on along," Slash ordered. He motioned with his rifle. "Sorry to have misconvenienced you," he added insincerely.

Hutchins raised his arm as if he were a cavalry officer at the head of a column. He lowered his arm smartly, pointing ahead. The two with him obediently followed.

Slash and Pecos watched them vanish down the road before leaving their cover.

"Now don't that beat all?" Slash said. "You'd think them boys was U.S. Army, only they weren't wearin' blue wool coats and brass buttons."

"You're right about that," Pecos said. He lowered the rabbit-ear hammers on his shotgun and tugged it around so it dangled down his back in its usual position. "No officer I ever saw dressed in such finery out of uniform. And none of them wear their combat ribbons. Now, I ain't an expert in such things but I didn't recognize a single one of them ribbons."

Slash nodded.

"Let's deliver our freight and collect our due. I just hope you don't get any ideas about spendin' the money to buy fancy togs like that just to impress your new wife."

"I'll let Jay get all gussied up," Slash said.

"She'd appreciate you takin' a bath more 'n wearin' a frock coat," Pecos said.

Again Slash agreed, then added, "Even one with fancy, colorful ribbons." Slash pondered why the three riders wore those decorations as he hiked all the way back to their freight wagon. He came up empty about a reason.